CONALL V
RETRIBUTION
DÍOLTAS

DAVID H. MILLAR

TITLES BY DAVID H. MILLAR

Conall V

Retribution

Díoltas

DAVID H. MILLAR

A Wee Publishing Company, LLC
HOUSTON, TX, USA
http://www.aweepublishingco.com/

Paperback ISBN 978-0-9916640-8-5
eBook ISBN 978-0-9916640-9-2
Library of Congress Control Number: 2020919696

A Wee Publishing Company, LLC, Houston, TX

To me! Never thought I would make it this far.

ACKNOWLEDGEMENTS

No author is an island and therefore finished novels are team efforts. Alongside the writer are editors, designers, formatters, and beta-readers. My thanks and appreciation goes to Kahina Necaise (structural/ content editor), Naomi Munts (copy-editor)—both at The History Quill (https://thehistoryquill.com/), Ida Jansson (cover art and interior formatting), Amygdala Design (http://www.amygdaladesign.net/), artist Michael McEvoy (map design), and my beta-readers: Judith Fullerton (Author), Lauren Millar, Jolie A. Reynolds (Author), Susan Robitaille, and Brendan Sullivan.

CONTENTS

PRONUNCIATIONS

Conall V: Retribution—Díoltas is a yarn set in ancient times. It revolves around the Celts, primarily Irish and Scottish Celts. As far as possible, I have attempted to use old Irish and Scots Gaelic words and phrases for personal and place names and the odd curse or two.

Gaelic, in all its forms (Irish, Scottish, Welsh, Manx, Breton, and Cornish), is a difficult, if not impossible, language to comprehend and is made more challenging by regional dialects. I often consider the language to be the result of a warped Celtic sense of humour. Rather than give a complete listing of the Gaelic words and phrases used in the story, I have opted for a compromise.

The following page lists the personal names of the main characters. Also, I recommend *A Beginner's Guide to Old Irish Pronunciation* (at http://www.gaolnaofa.org/articles/a-beginners-guide-to-old-irish-pronunciation/). An excellent site for Irish and Scottish Gaelic names is http://www.namenerds.com/.

However, it is the tale that counts. Feel free to pronounce the Gaelic in the way that gives you the most enjoyment.

One final comment, since the novel is located in Europe, it is written in British English.

IRISH GAELIC

Aodán Mac Conall	AY-awn MAK KON-ul
Aoibheann Ni Fionnséach	AY-veen nee FINN-shay-ah
Báine	BAWN-yuh
Barra Mac Conall	BA-ra MAK KON-ul
Beacán Ó Cathasaigh	B'YAG-awn o KAS-akh
Bláithín Ni Néill	BLAW-heen nee NEE-ul
Bricriu Ó Cathasaigh	BRICK-roo oKAS-akh
Brighid Ni Conall	BREED nee KON-ul
Brion Ó Cathasaigh	BREE-un oKAS-akh
Brocc Ó Cathasaigh	BRUK o KAS-akh
Conall Mac Gabhann	KON-ul MAK GAWN
Craiftine Ó Cuileannáin	KRAFT-in o QUILL-an-awn
Cuán Ó Néill	KOO-awn o NEE-ul
Cúscraid Mac Conchobar	KOO-skRi MAK KRUH-who'r
Danu Ni Conall	DAH-noo neeKON-ul
Deaglán Ó Néill	DEG-lawn o NEE-ul
Deda Mac Sin	DAY-da MAK SHEEN
Fearghal Ruad	FER-ul ROO-uh
Fionnbharr Ó Cuileannáin	FYUN-var o QUILL-an-awn
Íar Mac Dedad	EER MAK DAY-da
Lonán Ó Néill	LUH-nawn o NEE-ul
Medb	MAY-ve
Mongfhionn	MUNN-yung
Mórrígan Ni Cathasaigh	Moe-Rig-gAHn nee KAS-akh
Neamhain Ni Fearghal	NYAV-in nee FER-ul
Onchú Ó an Cháintigh	UN-choo Awn HAWN-tyg
Sárán Mac Craobhach	SAWR-awn MAK CRAY-v-akh
Sorchae Ni Íar	SUR-a-ka nee EER
Tadhg Ó Cuileannáin	TYG o QUILL-an-awn
Toirneach	TOR-nah
Torcán Ó Dubhghaill	TURK-awn o DOO-l

| Uallachán Ó Dubhghaill | OOL-akh-awn o DOO-l |
| Urard | UR-urd |

SCOTS GAELIC

Brandubh Mac Artair	BRAN-doow MAK ASH-ter
Brianag Ni Brion	BREE-uh-nak nee BREE-un
Carmag Mac an t-Sionnaich	KAR-ah-mak MAK an-CHUN-ich
Crum Dubh	CROM doow
Drostan Ruadh	DROST-an Roo-ag
Gràinne Ni Fearghal	GRAN-yuh nee FER-ul
Iasg	EE-ask
Mòrag Ni Artair	MOR-ak nee ASH-ter

Albu
Rinn-Campáil
Mai Dún
Muir Niocht
Cnocán Mórrigan
Andion
Aremorio
Sens
Cenabum
Bibracte
Souconna
Liga
Tourones
Lugudunon
Alpes
Gaul
Rodonos
Massalia
Great Sea
n

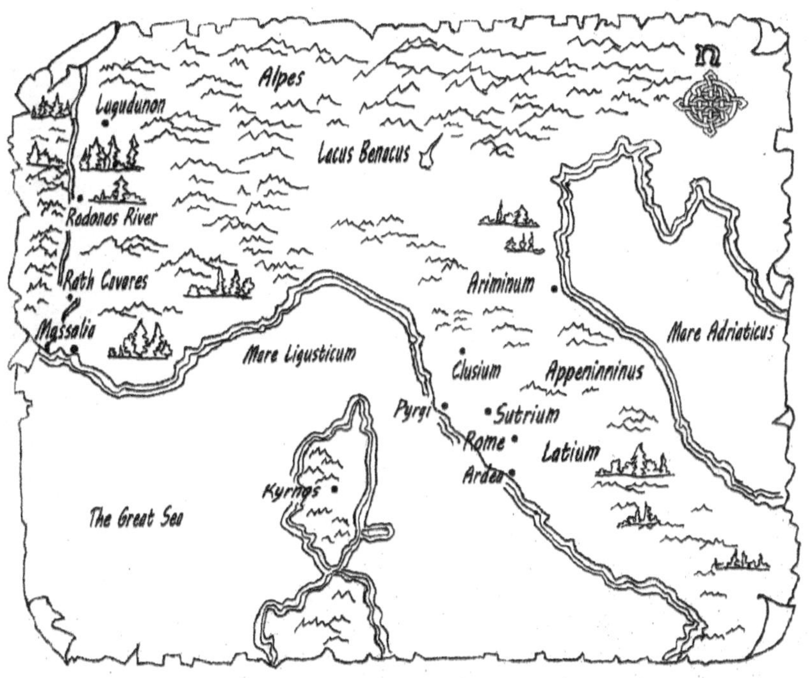

Alpes
n
Lugudunon
Lacus Benacus
Rodonos River
Ariminum
Rath Covares
Mare Adriaticus
Massalia
Mare Ligusticum
Clusium
Appeninninus
Pyrgi
Sutrium
Rome
Latium
Ardea
Kyrnos
The Great Sea

CHAPTER 1

396 B.C.—Lugudunon

"So this is peace."

Conall Mac Gabhann, Rí Ruirech—King Over Kings—of Clann Ui Flaithimh reflected that with age came an increased use of sarcasm. Whether that was good or bad, he let others judge. Fortunately, his words were instantly whipped away by a welcome breeze. The zephyr carried the faint burnt fragrance of a dry landscape in need of rain. The long, hot summer experienced by the Rodonos valley had pushed aside a temperate, if stormy, spring. With the departure of the relentless winds and storms of the Máistir, the river plain and surrounding lands and forests breathed easier. It was a fertile land. Few doubted that rain would come and the earth would once more reclaim its lush appearance.

The king raised an eyebrow as he approached his adversary. It was an action well-known to his friends but likely lost on his opponent. An ornate helmet embellished with gold, silver, and copper concealed Conall's face. He sensed the black plumes, trailing from the golden raven atop the helmet, flare in the passing breeze and flick his neck—perhaps a reminder to focus. Conall wore red plaid triubhas—trousers. A plaited cord, knotted at the waist, prevented the embarrassment of the britches falling down during the rigours of combat. The pants, tucked into soft hide boots, were held in place by criss-crossed leather thongs from the ankle to below the knee.

A loose, long-sleeved, mid-thigh-length léine covered his torso. Like the triubhas, the garment was lightweight and deep red in colour. Conall snorted. Mórrígan was forever cajoling him to diversify his wardrobe. In this respect, her powers of persuasion were wasted. He was comfortable with red and black, and that would never change. The tunic was gathered above the hips by a broad, carved leather crios—a gift from his children. A fist-sized gold and bronze buckle, fashioned as an open-winged raven, a gift from Mórrígan, drew the leather ends together.

On the girdle hung an assortment of weapons—a throwing axe, a short sword, and two daggers. Several knives were hidden in his boots—although "hidden" was an absurd description. It was universally known that all boots concealed blades. The apprentice-blacksmith-turned-warrior-king settled his waisted, oblong shield on his left arm and gripped a battle-axe in his left hand.

With a throwing axe balanced in his right hand, he moved forward. Conall's stride was steady and confident. Yet, it could not disguise the self-assured hubris and boredom he felt. Few in the clann doubted that he was the superior warrior. Conall's demeanour shouted his annoyance at what he considered to be a pointless duel.

Conall's challenger was a head taller than the king. Untamed blond locks fought against an impressive, winged helmet. A sheen of sweat covered a lightly tanned and muscled torso, giving the warrior the glow of oiled skin. Like Conall, axe and shield were his chosen armaments, and like the king, he carried a heavy-headed throwing axe in his right hand. The middle finger of that hand was missing a joint—a sure sign of an axe warrior. Unlike swordsmen, axe-wielders did not have the luxury of a hilt or cross-piece to protect their hands.

The warrior was alert to opportunity. Without breaking his stride and five paces apart, he released the axe and it tumbled through the air. Conall cursed as the weapon embedded itself in the scíath he hastily drew across his body. Conall's hurried response glanced harmlessly off his adversary's shield. He had missed his chance and the gap between the duellists was too close for a killing strike.

The space between the two men was quickly closed, resulting in an inevitable clash of scíatha. Conall felt his left arm throb with pain and then numbness as it bore the brunt of the metal boss of his enemy's shield. Teeth clenched, he followed through with a flurry of axe strokes. Soon wood shavings and ribbons of cowhide littered the flat-topped grassy mound on which they fought.

The opening flourishes over, the combatants settled into a mesmerising dance of feints, dropped shoulders, and misdirection as they circled one another.

In the early days, the tribes surrounding the lands conquered by Clann Ui Flaithimh had thrown thousands of warriors—young and old, male and female, novice and veteran—at the defences of the fortress of Lugudunon. Picked clean by flocks of ravens and scoured by the winds of the Máistir, their sun-bleached, headless skeletons lay scattered around the towering white ramparts.

Originally, the skulls were spiked and displayed on Lugudunon's walls. Now, only those of famed champions adorned the monumental gateways and the tall, wooden trophy posts that lined Lugudunon's main avenues. The rest were crushed underfoot or simply tossed aside. Fame and valour were ephemeral virtues. Often, children, and even some adults and druids, created a macabre form of art or constructed musical instruments from the bones.

Eventually, the attacks became ritualistic. They evolved to become a rite of passage for young warriors and a futile demonstration of Gallic stubbornness. On this morning, the few hundred Souconna warriors who tested the walls of Lugudunon were well aware that they had no hope of success. Over the past five summers, Cúscraid Mac Conchobar, the clann's master of defence, had overseen the renovation and rebuilding of the fort's walls with huge blocks of quarried stone.

The defences were now higher and broader, and the stone so tightly aligned that the fortifications presented an almost smooth face to besiegers. Two-storey, square guard towers jutting from the ramparts loomed over a fertile landscape of planted vineyards and olive groves. Around the city, neat drills of corn and wheat radiated outwards. Innocently pastoral, they disguised a sinister function as the army's killing fields. Beyond this were the wildwoods and dense ancient forests of Gaul.

Lugudunon was built on a south-west to north-east axis. Hence, the eastern entranceway was more accurately the north-eastern gate. Two round guard towers were staggered to slow traffic entering the ráth and enable defenders to rain down a murderous crossfire on enemies. Along the ramparts, heavy ballistae stood silently—tall, foreboding sentinels. Their two-man teams were rarely called upon for minor skirmishes unless tedium provoked a round of target practice. Archers, slingers, and spearmen lined the ramparts. They jostled with as many of the civilian population as could cram into the confined space.

In a festive mood, such was their confidence in Conall's fighting skills, all drank, cheered, and placed wagers. Only a few had the slightest doubt as to the eventual outcome.

***

Gaius Aurelius Atella, maligned and branded an outcast and traitor of Rome, paced the walls. Burnished bronze helmet, cuirass, and greaves glinted in the sun. Given the turning of the seasons, he had forgone his usual heavy red woollen cloak. Gaius pointed to the north and growled at his men, "On your feet. Stay alert. Twenty thousand of the bastards might be hidden in the trees beyond the cornfields."

A few paces from Gaius, Fearghal Ruad, the grizzled battle commander of Clann Ui Flaithimh, snorted loudly. Gaius glanced at him quizzically. There was a time when Gaius was numbered among the clann's enemies. In a whimsy of Fate, they now counted each other as friends. Fearghal directed the Roman's gaze to the duel. "That is no callow youth looking to make his reputation. His goal is not to escape with a few scars to impress and spread the thighs of virgins. *He* covets a throne."

Gaius reluctantly agreed. The duel was a threat, much more than an assault by hordes of unwashed barbarians on Lugudunon. Defeat would be disastrous for the tribe. "Damn your Gallic pride and sense of honour. It will be your downfall." Gaius paused. "Yet, I smell more of Brennus' plotting and mischievousness. His proxies have grown from annoying, impotent flies to wasps with real stings." A grunt from Fearghal signalled his agreement.

***

As if sensing Fearghal and Gaius' trepidation, Conall blinked beads of sweat from his eyes and attacked with a ferocity that wrongfooted his rival. Eschewing blows that required raising his arm above the shoulder or a full arc of the weapon, he reduced his exposure to counterstrikes, forcing his adversary to give ground.

An accomplished swordsman, Conall was more than good enough for the slash and stab of the shield-wall. Under the giant Urard's tuition, he had become a master of the axe, if not yet as good as the man who protected his children. Nevertheless, in a close-quarter fight such as this, he wondered if he should follow the example of Bláithín Ni Neill, a noblewoman of the clann. Her chosen weapon was a short-hafted, double-headed blade. In close combat, she insisted it allowed for more flexibility.

It finally dawned on Conall that his enemy's actions appeared almost nonchalant and the contest manipulated with remarkable skill. With excellent timing, his opponent hooked the edge of Conall's scíath and pulled sharply downwards, wresting it from the king's grip. The shield clattered to the ground, and a booted foot shattered it. Conall grunted in pain as he felt the pressure of an axe blade rake his chest diagonally from nipple to belly. A triumphant sneer ghosted the lips of the Souconna war chieftain. His celebration proved precipitous.

Torn by the axe's cutting edge, Conall's tunic revealed the silver-grey links of chainmail. Conall shook his head as if in mock disappointment at his adversary's surprise. With his left hand, he pulled the second throwing axe from his belt and pressed his attack with renewed vigour.

Before long, his challenger discarded his own weakened shield.

Both men faced each other with battle-axe in one hand and throwing axe in the other. Both watched for the merest signal of intent. A weapon arched through the air. The distance was too close and the throw hurried. Only a glancing blow, still the blade bit into Conall's upper arm, causing him to drop the smaller of the axes. Conall roared, partly in pain but mostly in anger at miscalculating his opponent's skills. Blood trickled down his arm and onto the haft of the remaining weapon, now grasped in two hands. In the fever of battle, the wound did little to hamper the king's movement.

Conall sprang forward. A side-step to the right quickly followed a feint to the left. His reward was the butt-end of an axe in his belly. "Bastard!" he shouted. His opponent laughed. Overconfident, he moved to where he expected Conall to be. It was his first mistake. Rather than scramble away, Conall let go of his axe and, like a log tumbling down a hill, rolled closer, forcing the Souconna chieftain to stumble over Conall's torso.

A shriek of agony muted the cheering from those who accompanied the Souconna chieftain. They watched Conall rise, a bloody dagger in his hand. The challenger attempted to crawl to safety, but Conall severed his hamstring. A calloused hand cupped the warrior's chin and jerked it backwards. Quickly and deeply, Conall drew the sharp blade across the exposed throat. The dying chieftain's last memory was the gurgling of blood as his life ebbed.

"You're not very magnanimous in victory," commented Fearghal as he approached Conall.

"Not so. Alive, he's just another defeated chieftain. Dead, he and his men will be honoured as heroes battling against impossible odds and the merciless Rí Ruirech of Clann Uí Flaithimh. Seanchaithe will immortalise them in epic tales, and they will be remembered in tribal lore forever." Conall turned to his men and pointed to the fleeing Souconna warriors. "Pursue them. Kill all but one. Someone should tell of their battle."

* * *

The lone warrior waited patiently to make his break for the treeline. Scattered around him lay the corpses of former comrades. Grunts and curses told him that the ritual beheading and stripping of the fallen had begun. He inhaled deeply, rose to a crouch, and then ran. A few paces from the dense, verdant cover of the wildwood, relief flooded his body. It was followed by intense pain. The force of the arrow that thudded into his back flung him forward, and he came to rest in a tangle of brambles and ferns. He was alive. The shaft had avoided his heart, but the bleeding was ominous.

Conall removed his helmet, setting it down on a large rock, shook long, lank tresses of auburn hair loose, and looked to his queen. He stretched out his arms with his palms facing the subject of his indignation. "Why?"

Whether to defy or goad, Mórrígan slowly and deliberately took a second black shaft from the quiver that hung from her belt, fitted it to the bowstring, and looked on her partner. The mask of curling symbols on her face caused a shiver to trickle up Conall' spine.

"No!" shouted Conall.

"Not long ago, you let another go likewise and for a similar reason—misplaced mercy. As a result, the blood of many Clann Ui Flaithimh warriors was spilt on these walls." Mórrígan, An Fiagaí Dorcha—the Dark Huntress—made to turn, stopped, and smiled grimly at her partner. "Pity is not for the likes of us, Conall. That is for the Goddess and Fate to apportion." With an unsettling smirk, she shrugged and replaced the second arrow in the quiver. "Besides, I only wounded him. He'll last long enough to reach his tribe and tell his tale."

Conall shook his head. His hand-fast partner and lover since their youth had always been beautiful. She had grown into a woman whose loveliness transcended her physical appearance. The slaughter of their parents had ripped innocence from a young Mórrígan and replaced it with an awful blight on her soul. It was a stain that once had caused

Conall to consider whether his Mórrígan should live. He had withheld his blade and was glad. Yet, he knew she fought a perpetual battle against this darkness and the power that accompanied it.

With increasing frequency, Conall wondered whether Mórrígan's abilities had become more fearsome than those of her mentor, the Sidhe, Mongfhionn. In the dark of the night, the question often troubled the sleep of both Conall and the Sidhe.

CHAPTER 2

396 B.C.—Foothills of the Alpes

The man stood alone on Lugudunon's battlements and revelled in the pleasure of the morning sun. Lustrous, black hair was swept back from his deeply tanned face and styled in a thick braid that hung between broad shoulders. A tightly curled black beard scented with almond and jasmine oil covered cheeks and chin. Scarred hands rested on the smooth stone wall. As the sun rose higher, it bathed his polished bronze cuirass and greaves, and it seemed as if the warrior shimmered. His Corinthian-style helmet, with its long red plumes, rested between two crenellations.

A soft footfall behind him caused Nikandros the Spartan to turn around. He smiled at the approach of Conall's daughters, Brighid and Danu. Yet, their demeanour did not reflect the same pleasure. In their hands, they carried two short swords and carved sheathes. He recognised them. He had crafted and gifted the weapons to the twins at their birth. Danu, marginally the eldest of the two, spoke with disappointment and the tremble of emotion in her voice.

"Assassin. Murderer. Spy. Traitor. These are the names now spoken of you, Nikandros of Sparta."

Danu's formality added a chill to the morning air. The slap across his face expressed her anger. Nikandros flinched. It was common knowledge that neither Danu nor Brighid had much time for rumour or gossip. They must have eavesdropped on higher-level conversations. As

9

if presenting a sacrifice, both girls took a pace backwards, went down on one knee, and placed the small swords at his sandalled feet.

"These are no longer appropriate for us to carry," said Brighid.

There was deep sadness and betrayal in eyes as green as her ma's. For Nikandros' part, he loved the twins as if they were his own. Had they buried the swords in his chest, it would have been more merciful. The Spartan bowed. No words could ever be adequate to salve the pain on either side.

As he watched the twins walk away, Nikandros allowed himself a brief, bitter smile. Brighid and Danu had just warned him that Lugudunon was no longer safe and that he had few friends within the army and the tribe.

✳✳✳

The meeting of Conall and his Chomhairle—his High Council—was convened in the royal fort of Dún-an-Rí, located at the confluence of the Rodonos and Souconna rivers. The gathering was charged with deep emotions. There had never been a good time to explain or justify his tolerance of Nikandros or his knowledge of the crimes committed by the man. By design, Conall had moved the pieces on the fidchell board to achieve his intent and ensure the tribe's well-being. Right or wrong, it was the king's decision.

Given the benefit of hindsight, perhaps there might have been a better path. Did Conall feel remorse for the dead? Yes. Would he take the same decision again? Yes. Still, the game of cat and mouse played since Nikandros' rescue of a young and naive Mórrígan in the forests of Ériu needed to be brought to a conclusion. Whether there was to be justice for the victims and the dead—that was in the Goddess' hand. Yet that resolution provided no salve for Conall's conscience.

To Conall's disappointment, lancing this particular carbuncle appeared to do little more than spread the poison. Celtic passions bubble close to the surface, and in their newly adopted land, the summer heat only exacerbated the fever. The argument at first simmered, then boiled,

10

and then with a few exceptions, subsided into disappointed resignation.

Ancient oak staff in hand, Mongfhionn stared defiantly at her audience, daring them to challenge her—or her chosen king. Few held her eyes. Íar Mac Dedad, the ordinarily ebullient leader of the tribe's horse warriors, shook his head and gave Conall a look that said, "I warned you." In this, he had an unlikely ally in Gaius. Brandubh Mac Artair, Cúscraid, Deaglán Ó Néill, and Lonán Ó Néill were silent. They understood that a king sometimes had to make disagreeable choices.

As for the Ó Cuileannáin brothers, Craiftine, Fionnbharr, and Tadhg, their perspective differed. "How many murders other than Laoise and Cuán Ó Néill can be laid at the feet of the Spartan?" demanded a bitter Tadhg. The bile that rose in Tadhg's gorge burned his gullet, souring his mouth to match his frame of mind.

Craiftine and Fionnbharr's outrage was honest, if selfish. What danger had their brother been put in when asked to investigate crimes that Conall already knew were attributable to Nikandros? All knew that Tadhg was clever, but he was no match for the wiles and weapons of the olive-skinned warrior.

Conall's iron axe head slammed the oak table, startling those present. "Be careful, Tadhg. It was not *I* who put Laoise in the path of an assassin's sword. *You* were warned. *You* chose to ignore the advice."

Stunned, Tadhg stood open-mouthed. "Bastard!" At the insult, Urard rose from behind Conall, the giant axe Breith—Judgment—at the ready. At a sign from Conall, Urard stepped away from the table. All noted the axe remained in his hands.

Nevertheless, Tadhg's protest was muted. Since Laoise's death, he had buried his culpability deep, unwilling to accept even a portion of the blame. Now Conall had ripped the festering wound open and it lay exposed, raw, and weeping for all to see. Among the Council, apart from his brothers, any sympathy for Tadhg's pain had dissipated some time ago. All knew that the price of Tadhg's ambition and his arrogance had been the young whore's blood. Thus, in this gathering, his supporters were few. Tadhg's appeals to the gods brought no satisfaction, no relief, and no absolution. The Goddess judged his offerings as lacking contrition and thus they were not well-regarded.

An ominous silence fell in Dún-an-Rí's Great Hall as Mórrígan stood. Her face, covered in swirling indigo-blue symbols, was grim. "You go too far, friend." The honorific spat from the queen's mouth left few in doubt as to her true feelings.

"None of us is without guilt as to the Spartan, including me. But where were *your* much-vaunted skills of observation and analysis? Did you come to Conall, *your* king, to advise of your doubts, your premonitions, and your unease at Nikandros' activities? The Spartan is most certainly an accomplished assassin and spy, but he is a man—not a god." The Huntress paused and raised a tattooed arm. A long finger pointed at Tadhg.

"I suspect—no, I know—*you did not.*"

An arrow from the queen's bow would have been more merciful. And the quiver of her wrath held more shafts: "How often did you refuse his aid in battle? How many years of life do *you* owe the Spartan?" Those present cringed at Mórrígan's venom.

"*You* sacrificed Laoise to save your skin and your reputation."

Conall's hand touched his partner's arm. "Enough. He's suffered enough."

"No, he hasn't!"

The feral snarl stunned all present. Mórrígan's fierce gaze swept over the speechless occupants of the chamber. "Conall is your king. He is not without fault, but on his shoulders rests the security of Clann Ui Flaithimh. He sacrificed his youth and freedom to the clann, and it will be so until his death. He is the Goddess's chosen Hand." Mórrígan paused and held Tadhg's gaze with eyes so intensely emerald that they seemed black.

"Withdraw. Your presence offends me. The king is forgiving. I am not, and my wrath goes beyond the veil."

Ashen-faced, Tadhg turned on his heels and strode from the hall. With hands raised and sighs of resignation, the remaining Ó Cuileannáin brothers rose from their bench. They bowed their heads in deference to Conall. "He is our brother. Blood is blood. We will not allow him to stand alone," said Fionnbharr. Among those remaining, there was deep sadness as the straw-haired brothers exited in the wake of their sibling.

"Well, that went well," said Fearghal. "We just lost a famed harpist, a seanchaí, and the tribe's best healer.

"Now, what do we do about the Spartan?"

***

Alone or in packs, predators prowled the dense forests that swathed the foothills, bordering the valley of the Rodonos River. They preyed on the young and the weak. Few relished or would risk a head-to-head fight with the healthy. That might cause injury and relegate them to the status of the hunted. Mostly four-legged, recently they had been joined by a band of two-legged hunters.

One hundred men and women comprised the group. All were belligerent, disinterested in communicating with their comrades, and randomly violent. Only their leader and paymaster Tullus Brutus, the former captain of the Pontifex Maximus of Rome's guard, and his two burly lieutenants, kept the band in check. The pack had one simple rule—obey without question. The corpses of the few who had difficulties with this concept bled out on the forest floor. All were Romans, although many in Rome disavowed them.

Only Tullus knew that their services were purchased by Marcus Fabius Ambustus, Pontifex Maximus of Rome. His orders were unwritten but clear. If the opportunity presented, Tullus and his group were to kill the kin and offspring of Conall and Mórrígan. They were to bring strife to a tribe that had become too settled, too accustomed to prosperity and relative peace.

In this, Marcus had an unlikely empathy with the Goddess and the Sidhe. Both had concerns about Conall's diminished zeal to fulfil the geis laid on him as a young man in Ériu. Were shifting priorities and the well-being of the tribe nudging aside the desires and plottings of deities and Romans? Had the Hand of the Goddess become the Hand of Clann Ui Flaithimh? Whether the roles were compatible had yet to be tested.

Tullus' mission was straightforward and should have been well within the brutish capabilities of the band. It was to terrorise the many Clann Ui Flaithimh settlements scattered along the southern bank of the Rodonos. For this, they were paid handsomely in Roman gold. Any plunder they took was a bonus. Staying beyond the reach of enemy hill-forts, they were to burn, pillage, and rape. None, from the newborn to the elderly, were to be left alive. Not because of the threat of witnesses but to demonstrate that they, and by implication their paymaster, were without mercy.

They were, however, under orders not to antagonise the Gallic tribes that populated the slopes of the Alpes. Even the Gaesatae, also known as the Gaiscedach by the Celts, greatly weakened after their defeat by Conall and the death of their queen, Matres, were to be avoided.

The realisation that a good portion of the civilian population of Conall's clann was more than capable of wielding spears and shields in their defence precipitated a rise in the brutishness of the band's activities. No matter the size of the farmholding or settlement, the stubborn Celts, both men and women, refused to give up without a fight or without drawing blood. Defiant shouts of *"Ní ghéillfear, nó cúlú!"*— "No retreat, no surrender!"—rang in Roman ears.

Tullus regarded the latest slaughter and spat on the blood-soaked earth. Two more of his band lay sprawled lifeless in the dirt, and several others were injured. One would not last beyond dusk, either from his wounds or a knife across his throat. The bloody-mindedness of the farming communities had reduced Tullus' group by half in one cycle of the moon. As a consequence, the raiders avoided attacking locations that might have more than thirty people. It was not by choice. The odds were no longer in their favour. The superstitious held that the gods of these lands had put their thumbs on the scales of justice. And not in the thugs' favour.

The latest attack took place on a small farmholding. Its three buildings were home to a score of people of all ages. All were dead, mutilated, and beheaded. The women had been raped while their bodies retained some heat. Nailed to the charred supports of the dwellings or impaled on spears, skulls dripped blood. Far from making crude jokes, pissing on, or laughing at the trophies, his men now gave them a wide berth. All avoided the stares of the dead and the fearsome expressions on faces set by the rictus of death. Yes, they had been victorious, but Tullus detected an unease among the mercenaries that had not been present at the start of the campaign. A growing sense of fear overshadowed the band's early arrogance and condescension.

Many asserted that they were being watched. Tullus agreed. A noose was being tightened around their communal necks. Tullus inhaled, taking in the odour of smoke and charred flesh. He reached into a small pouch and, with a sigh, withdrew a small bronze coin, pushing it into the ruined socket of a child's skull. At the scene of every atrocity, this token had been left—a signature.

It was a command of Marcus', but to Tullus, it was foolish, aiding only those who now hunted them. But then, that was what Marcus wanted—to give Conall undeniable proof of who was the mastermind behind the campaign. Marcus wanted Conall to know that he could reach him, his family, and his people anywhere. That he was in control of the game and Conall was just a piece to be manipulated.

As the sun descended, a flock of ravens rose from the forest canopy and swooped over the massacre site. *A bad omen.* Instinct and the fine hairs on the back of Tullus' neck told him that his enemies drew closer. His thoughts drifted to consider how he and his two enforcers might extricate themselves from a situation that could quickly become deadly.

CHAPTER 3

396 B.C.—Sens

Outside his quarters, rushlights in wooden sconces threw flickering shadows into the spacious chamber. An irritating need to piss frequently did not make for a night of deep sleep but enhanced an instinct for survival. Thus, the soft scuffling on the wooden boards in the sleeping chamber prompted Brennus to action. With a stealth that belied his size, the king rolled noiselessly from his cot and waited in the shadows.

"Gaiscedach whores!"

Alarm momentarily checked the duo of assassins. Instead of drawing a sharp edge across the king's throat and plunging a blade into his heart, the startled killers peered in the direction of the voice. Held in both hands, Brennus' sword cut through the air. It was a weighty weapon made for slashing, and its long edges were honed sharp. The high rafters of the chamber set no constraint on its arc. Guided by a warrior's instinct, the first cut carved a gory path through the bone and gristle of one intruder's neck. Almost cleaved from his shoulders, the man's head tilted absurdly to one side before he collapsed lifelessly to the floor.

The other attacker, splashed by her partner's gushing blood, cursed, and decided that the darkness was insufficient protection. Rather than facing the Senone king with only a dagger, albeit a poisoned one, she chose retreat as the more prudent option. Tumbling over the bed, she paused briefly to gauge her position and started towards the room's entrance. The moment of hesitation killed her. As she rose from a crouch, her head was cleaved in two by the powerful downwards stroke of Brennus' blade. By the time the sword edge crunched through her skull to her upper spine, she was already in Mag Mell.

Brennus coughed harshly as the night air caught his throat. His body was soaked in sweat, acid burned his throat, and he suddenly needed to pee. He reached for the jug of water beside his cot. Several long gulps soothed his throat but only made the compulsion to piss more urgent. The rest of the pitcher he poured over his head.

"Bitseach!"

This time, Brennus was referring not to the assassin but to the Oracle, Rosmerta, who still haunted his dreams although she had crossed the veil. The accuracy of her final prophecies provided a deep well of troubles and increased the terror of his nightmares.

Although not a modest man, Brennus grabbed a light brat to cover his nakedness before stumbling out of the entranceway. He kicked aside the guards who lay with their throats cut. "Useless bastards," muttered Brennus as he stomped down the hall and into the night.

Sens, the capital of the Senones, sat on a high plateau in eastern Gaul. In the deep blackness of night, only the flickering torches and glowing braziers along the settlement's walls broke the darkness. Brennus, King of the Senones, had much to think about, little of which was pleasant. While still capable of fielding the largest army in Gaul, his ambition to become what the Celts called Ard-Righ or High King had crumbled. Persistent rumours of Conall's ambition to be elected Ard-Righ of Ériu, Albu, and Gaul infuriated Brennus.

The strength of Brennus' army remained sufficient to comfortably sustain the Senones' place at the top of a multitude of warring Gaulish tribes. But it proved insufficient to cajole or force them into a unified nation—or even a grand alliance. After his defeats at the hands of Conall, he had witnessed a sharp decline in his influence, and this scarred Brennus deeply.

The Carnutes under Tasgiitios were emboldened with their treaty with Conall and raided Brennus' borderlands to his west. Further west of the Rodonos River, the Arverni made no secret of their ambition to supplant the Senones. In the east, across the Rénos River, incursions by Germani warbands probed for any sign of weakness. To his south, even the Aedui, a relatively minor tribe, openly taunted him with their "brotherly" links with Rome and refused to pay levies to Brennus in full. As for Conall and Clann Ui Flaithimh, Brennus cursed the day Conall had outmanoeuvred him into retreating from the walls of Lugudunon.

And there were always internal troubles. Many now openly challenged Brennus' authority. He grew weary of the increasing frequency of assassination attempts by his enemies and retaliatory slayings by him as well as the public show trials and executions of rivals and their families. Despite his efforts, the number of the rebellious continued to grow. His door frames stank of rotten flesh and groaned with the weight of the latest skulls nailed to them.

Brennus spat into the perimeter ditch as he pissed. His challengers now stooped as low as paying hated Gaiscedach assassins to remove him. The king knew if he did not come up with a path forward for the Senones, eventually and inevitably, his competitors would prevail. Brennus flicked the last few drops of pale-yellow liquid from his manhood, then turned and stormed back to his Great Hall.

"Summon the ambassador from Dionysius," he roared. Then, as an afterthought, he added, "And that bastard druid, Crum Dubh. I may as well get some use of him."

***

Hauled from his bed in the middle of the night and given little chance to prepare, Dionysius' herald's demeanour was infuriatingly calm, pleasant, and controlled. Only the soft swish of the floor-length chiton and padding of tanned, bare feet on the wooden slats broke the silence. *I wonder if he is a eunuch,* mused Brennus as the ambassador approached the carved wooden throne. A boyish smirk rested on the king's lips, and he chuckled. It caused a moment of hesitation from the tall, narrow-shoul-

18

dered diplomat. The action gave Brennus an inordinate amount of pleasure. At last, he had done something to ruffle the man's façade.

The diplomat noted the tall, sallow-faced druid standing to the right of Brennus' throne and took it as a positive omen. *Perhaps we may do business.* The envoy closed the gap, coming to a halt a respectful distance from Brennus' throne. With a flourish, the herald bowed deeply.

"Remind me of your master's offer," growled Brennus.

Sensing victory, the ambassador dipped his head once more and cleared his throat. When he spoke, it was in common Gaul. His voice, although heavily accented, held a rich baritone that was easy on the ears.

"My king, Dionysius of Syrako, is a benevolent lord…"

Brennus broke into laughter. "Your king is a tyrant, a despot whose reputation for cruelty and being extremely vindictive is well broadcast among the nations of the Great Sea."

The ambassador ignored the slight, nodded, and continued, "My king's compassion seeks to bring order to all of Sikelia. In this, he is challenged by the obstinacy of Messene—a small city in the north-east of the island. Reportedly, the ruling body of Messene has close ties with the Pontifex Maximus of Rome. This council seeks to use that relationship to thwart Dionysius' plans to better the life of Sikelia's people. My master considers that Rome's attention would be sufficiently distracted were a friendly ally to settle the lands of the Etrusci and Umbri, to the north and east of Rome."

Brennus chuckled. "Settle the lands. You mean to conquer them. I doubt the Etrusci or Umbri will open their borders and cities to my horde or embrace us as their long-lost prodigal brothers." The Senone king sensed an urgency to pee. *Shite!* His need and frequency were increasing with each season. To avoid embarrassment, he needed to bring the discussion to a quick resolution.

"What is Dionysius' offer? How much gold does he bid for my services?"

"One talent, Greek, of gold. Half to be handed over when you cross the Eridanus. The rest when Dionysius is acknowledged ruler of all Sikelia."

"I do not think so," mocked Brennus. "One talent of gold, Roman. All to be paid before my army crosses the Eridanus. Your master may not be successful. Rulers are notoriously the victims of assassins' daggers, plots, and poisons." The ambassador affected a pained expression, but he knew that his king's need was great and his treasury full. He dipped his head in feigned resignation.

"You strike a hard bargain, but it is within my constraints."

Brennus slapped his hands on his knees and nodded to Crum. "Confirm the details with the druid."

***

The Leader of the Druidic Councils of Ériu, Albu, and Gaul watched as the Greek ambassador made a silky exit. He waited until Brennus returned from satisfying his toilet needs. *I wonder if the king knows how predictable his frequent need to piss has become and how well-known. A gift to assassins.* Brennus appeared surprised at the druid's presence, and a sour look demanded an explanation.

"The Rí Ruirech of Clann Ui Flaithimh and his domain lie between you and the valleys of the Alpes and your destination. You will have to seek accommodation with Conall to traverse his lands. Any attempt to cross without his sanction and the payment of a fair toll will result in war."

Exasperated, Brennus scowled. "Am I never to be rid of that bastard?"

"Perhaps this madness you've agreed to with Dionysius will quench your expansionist desires."

"Be careful, Druid. Keep your counsel impartial, or my blade might take a liking to your neck. My council maintains you already have too many conflicts. The new Oracle in Cenabum is Conall's brother by hand-fasting, and you retain your position on Clann Ui Flaithimh's Chomhairle."

Undeterred, Crum snorted dismissively. "In matters of the Fénechas—the Law—*I* am arbiter and judge. King or freeman, stranger or kin, I make no difference." The druid held Brennus' gaze without shrinking, for he believed his words were the truth. "Beware. *Your* deceit and continued flaunting of the treaty you negotiated with Conall has not gone unnoticed. You use the Allobroges, Arecomici, Arverni, Sequani, Tectosages, and Volcae as proxies to raid his lands, and those to whom his protection extends. Even Conall's patience has limits."

"I will *not* be dictated to where I can journey in Gaul. My army well outnumbers that of Clann Ui Flaithimh."

Crum snorted. "Your army's memory is of being fought to a bloody standstill by a smaller, tired force that had just overthrown the Gaiscedach queen, Matres, at Lugudunon. Although exhausted from their battle wounds, Conall's army prevailed over you. Then he outwitted you—several times, I believe. The difference is that this time Conall will be prepared and has strong allies. Do not underestimate the fortifications at Lugudunon and the new hillforts along the valleys of the Rodonos and Durantia rivers. His shield warriors are the best trained in all of Gaul." Crum paused at the fierce glare from Brennus. "Yes, your Senones are no match for them. And his numbers have increased greatly since last you fought."

The druid allowed himself the semblance of a smile before positioning a final verbal dagger to pierce Brennus' pride. "My information is that several cycles of the moon past, Pytheas, the Greek merchant, brokered a meeting between Dionysius and Conall in Massalia. The king desired that Conall would join him. Conall declined, and Dionysius turned his attention to the Senones—his second choice."

Crum held Brennus' stony stare. "Come to an agreement. Conall is fair-minded." Then the druid added, "Be thankful the gossip that Conall has ambitions to be Ard-Righ of Albu, Ériu, and Gaul are likely from those who have drunk too much wine and beer."

Brennus' hand brushed over the smooth stone that formed the

pommel of his sword. Inwardly, the king was a molten cauldron of emotions that threatened to overpower his usual pragmatic judgment. A bubble of hubris rose to the top and burst.

"You will inform Conall Mac Gabhann that Brennus of the Senones will cross his lands after the feast of Lugnasad. He should step aside or be destroyed."

"As you wish." Crum bowed respectfully, turned, and strode away.

＊

Seated on his throne, Brennus broke his fast with a plain repast of oatmeal, berries, and milk. The drink was warm—straight from the cow and deliciously creamy. Daybreak was his favourite time of the day, and he basked in the morning sun as it flooded through the open, eastern-facing windows. Its rays painted the usually gloomy chamber in golden reds and oranges and were pleasant to his skin. He was thankful for the land of his people. Unlike territories closer to the Great Sea, its climate never became insufferably hot and dry in the summer.

Absentmindedly, Brennus stroked a shaggy, red beard, now splattered with small clumps of oatmeal. As he recalled the conversation with the druid, he mused that the priest was altogether too phlegmatic about the now-inevitable clash between Clann Ui Flaithimh and the Senones. He ruminated on the discussion. It seemed to Brennus that Crum, known for a judicious and sparing use of words, had deliberately prodded Brennus along a specific path. His last impression of Crum was the brief upturn of the ends of his lips as he turned and exited the chamber.

Brennus growled and spat. "A Hag's curse on the meddling of the Aes Sidhe, druids, and oracles." It was with wily restraint that the king did not add gods to his list. After all, no one could afford to burn every bridge. Still, having committed to taking Dionysius' gold, Brennus was faced with a not-inconsiderable challenge. He might prevail upon or twist the arms of the Aedui and the Arverni to join his trek south. Yet, even with these additional warriors, he would have to take the majority of his army with him across the Alpes. This would leave his homeland

22

weakened. The jackals on his borders would be unable to resist attacking. And the Carnutes, the Bituriges, and the cursed Gaiscedach would be at the front of the line to bite off as much they could manage of his lands.

The king swore. A visit to the Oracle in Cenabum was merited, if only as a precaution. As to whether he would get an impartial reading of his sacrifice's entrails, that was down to the gods. Of course, whether he would like or heed what he heard was another matter.

CHAPTER 4

396 B.C.—Cenabum

Bricriu Ó Cathasaigh, brother of Mórrígan and the most powerful oracle in Gaul, lay on his back and inhaled the perfumes of night jasmine delicately imbued with the muskiness of rutting and sweat. *Perhaps being the Oracle is not that bad after all.* In the darkness, no one could see the dimples of his smile. His breathing was shallow, but only to avoid disturbing the soft head of berry-blonde hair that rested on his chest.

The young woman was one of the sanctuary virgins, commonly referred to as the College of the Chaste. In truth, the title was more an honour than a statement of circumstance. There were always nine young women chosen, and they served for at least nine years. An option to serve an additional nine years in three-year tranches was proffered to all.

Candidates were interviewed at thirteen summers. Those selected entered the Oracle's Sanctuary when they turned fourteen—provided their hymens were intact. They came from a diversity of backgrounds, from nobles to paupers, but obviously not slaves. Once accepted into the College, and unless they did something incomprehensibly stupid— which did not include losing their purity to the incumbent Oracle—their status was forever assured.

There was no pressure put on the priestesses to sleep with the current occupier of the Oracle's seat, whether male or female. Some gravitated towards copulation—if there was a male Oracle. Others took a female partner from within the College. A minority remained chaste until the completion of their service. With the passing of Bricriu's predecessor, the ancient Rosmerta, the Sanctuary had, for the first time in several generations, a young Oracle with a healthy libido. Hence, the scales tilted in favour of rutting.

This unwritten arrangement served the Sanctuary well. The Oracle's dalliances were constrained to the members of the College. Thus, the potential for indiscretions that could result in political blackmail was avoided. Having committed themselves to a life of chastity, the girls found to their delight that the rules had more to do with being loyal and dedicated servants of the Sanctuary. Not their sexual appetites or preferences.

One thing, however, was made clear to all beyond the Sanctuary's walls. Should anyone question the maidens' chastity, the guardians—a coterie of one hundred and eighty chosen, veteran warriors akin to a king's caomhnóirí—would ensure the offender's head was promptly pinned to the compound's massive outer gates. His or her remains would be left to rot in Cenabum's perimeter ditches.

For generations, kings, princes, and chieftains, from the far borders of Gaul to the shores of Ériu, vied for the priestesses' favour and companionship upon their retirement. Very few of the College were abused. Only the most ill-advised noble would openly court the wrath of the Oracle. Seers were not shy in wielding their gift of foresight as a weapon. Loss of favour or a doom-laden vision once leaked publicly could quickly become self-fulfilling, ensuring the demise of the foolish. But then, that always assumed that the virgin's well-being had not already been enforced by a guardian's blade.

Above and beyond the considerable prophetic powers of the Oracle and his ability to influence princes and principalities, the priestesses conferred on Bricriu a significantly more dangerous and practical weapon—loyalty. Allegiance to the Sanctuary and the College remained unbroken even after completion of their term of service. Thus, the Sisterhood of the Chaste represented the greatest network of informants in the whole of Gaul, Ériu, and Albu. In more than one sense, Bricriu was the most knowledgeable man among the Celts and Gaels. Even the high druids and Leaders of the Druidic Councils paid close attention to the Oracle of Cenabum's words.

A soft knock on the wooden archway to his chambers drew a sigh from Bricriu and a sleepy half-snort from his companion. The early dawn light shimmered grey-blue on the horizon, slowly mitigating the inky blackness of night. Only his guard, the cooks, or Crum Dubh would be about this early.

"You do realise that if I had been asleep, your knock would not have woken me, Druid."

There was a soft chuckle from the doorway. "Here's me thinking I was diplomatic." The accent held the rolling burr of the people of Northern Albu and was the limit of the druid's informality. "Your day has started early, Oracle. We must talk *now*, for I must be on the road to Ráth Cavares with all haste."

Exhaling at the ominous tone in Crum's voice, Bricriu raised himself from the cot, kissed the priestess, and padded barefoot across the wooden floor to a deep bronze bowl. Crum rolled his eyes at the sound of piss cascading into the vessel. *Nothing wrong with his bladder.*

The Oracle's Sanctuary sat at the heart of Cenabum. It was built of timber and mudbrick and was a permanent, self-contained place of ritual and ceremony, comprising two rectangular structures, one within the other. At the Temple's centre was the waist-high, unhewn cromleac of the Inner Sanctuary and the Eternal Flame.

The great stone altar rested on a gentle slope of dirt. The camber guided the flow of blood, permitting the priest to observe and interpret the rivulets and entrails of the sacrificed, be that animal or human. A single sacrificial dagger lay on its cold, pitted surface. The Inner Sanctuary had an open and simple design. In essence, it was a tent held up by nine tall poles. Long, white linen hangings from ceiling to floor gave the inner room its privacy.

Only the Oracle and the College were permitted to enter the Inner Sanctuary. For the priestesses, ensuring the Eternal Flame remained perpetual was a core duty. Behind the altar chamber were the separate quarters of the Oracle and the College of the Chaste. No doors closed the exterior or interior entrances of the residential buildings, and covered pathways connected the structures to each other and to the Inner Sanctuary. Thirty warriors stood alert on the complex's two-storey-high palisade.

Considered neutral territory, the Sanctuary could, if needed, be defended as well as a small hillfort. A massive double timber palisade with ditches on either side protected the outer square. Along the stockade's sides ran a catwalk and on this stood one hundred and fifty warriors. The single, east-facing entrance was secured by a heavy timber gate and iron locking bar. The gateway, decorated with beautiful carvings celebrating former Oracles, kings, and battle victories, was quite ornate. More ominously, it also sported an array of skulls in various stages of decay nailed to the gateposts. Groves of oak, beech, and cypress softened the austerity of the inner and outer compounds. They also obscured the burial mounds of past oracles, as well as a large heap of bones of the sacrificed—animal and human.

"Brennus intends to cross the land of Clann Ui Flaithimh." Crum paused for effect. "*Without* Conall's permission." It irritated the Leader of the Druidic Councils that this gem of information appeared to be lost on the Oracle—or at least was not news. Even more irritating was the almost dismissive signal that he should offer a fuller explanation. "There will be war. Clann Ui Flaithimh is imperilled. Worship of the Goddess will be endangered." As a final effort at raising the level of emotion of the infuriatingly calm Seer, he added, "Conall, your sister, and their children may die."

"I may be young and not as experienced as Rosmerta, but do not take me for a fool, Druid."

Crum's pallor took on a greyish hue, and his cheeks flushed. Visibly taken aback by the Oracle's scolding tone, he could do little but wait for what followed.

"The Goddess plays a dangerous game and puts in danger the loyalty of Conall, Mórrígan, and the people of the clann. Even those of Conall's neighbours who have chosen to follow. In doing so, she also jeopardises her position." Crum made to protest, but a raised palm stopped him. "I know full well what is going on. My informants have kept me apprised of events." At this, Bricriu paused for effect, much more successfully than the druid. "Brennus came to sacrifice and ask for my foresight. He was wise enough not to ask for my blessing."

The young man allowed himself an inner smirk at the tinge of frustration on Crum's face. "As for your next question as to what I intend to do. The answer is… nothing." A sharp intake of breath hissed through the space in the druid's two front teeth. "*You*, Crum Dubh, for whatever reason, have acted as kindling to this fire. Having had no small part in determining Brennus' state of mind, you are now on your way to inform Conall of impending disaster. Are you not?"

As Crum turned on his heels, the soft voice of Bricriu carried clearly to his ears. "Next time, bring a sacrifice whose entrails I can interpret. That should be an interesting conversation opener."

The druid shivered. He was not overjoyed at the thought of what the Oracle might see in his future. He was also aware that the Oracle was to meet with Tasgiitios, king of the Carnutes, later that day.

"Lying bastard!" exploded the druid as he departed the Sanctuary.

* * *

Tasgiitios, king of the Carnutes, mused that his popularity had recently taken a decided upturn. Brennus had departed, and now a messenger awaited his reply to a request to dine with the Oracle. A single, dark eyebrow lifted as he chuckled to himself. As if there was any doubt that he would refuse the invitation.

Brennus' conversation was predictably brusque, demanding that the Carnutes join his campaign and march to the Eridanus along with the Arverni and the Aedui. When Tasgiitios did not demonstrate a sufficient level of enthusiasm for the crusade, Brennus switched to threatening humiliation and torture, fire and pillage, and rape and slavery. It was a typical, if tiresome, tirade. While acknowledged as a formidable battle commander, few would assert that Brennus' diplomacy was artful. Compromise was an anathema to the blunt warrior. To him, the edge of a sword was the greatest leveller and provider of answers.

Still, Tasgiitios could well imagine the Arverni joining with the Senones. Their king, Celtillos, was greedy for land, power, and wealth. That he saw himself as ruler of a Greater Arverni tribe, which eclipsed the Senones, would undoubtedly make for an interesting dynamic with Brennus during the proposed campaign. The same could not be said for the Aedui. The Aedui were firm friends of Rome and implacable enemies of the Arverni. Ambigatos, their king, would see Celtillos in the Otherworld before clasping his hand in fellowship—no matter how much gold and plunder was on offer.

His discussion with Brennus ended with Tasgiitios informing the king that he would give his proposal consideration. Both men knew that the Carnutes would not fight alongside the Senones. The visit delivered a warning to Tasgiitios: "Don't side with Conall. Don't covet the Senones' land." As Brennus departed, the Senone king was resigned to the necessity of leaving a substantial army behind to discourage any expansionist ideas of the Carnutes. And also to the necessity of the Arverni.

✳✳✳

As he entered the reception hall, Tasgiitios noted the heavy tapestries covering the walls and entrances to the room. In a residence that was typically airy and open, it was a sure sign that the Oracle did not wish to be overheard. The senior priestess of the College, a tall and quite beautiful woman with copper-red hair styled in thick plaits that touched her arse, sat to the right of Bricriu.

The smell of roasted flesh made the king's mouth water and his belly growl. The Oracle smiled and gestured to a table laden with fruit, cheese, bread, and meat and then to the carved seat opposite him. There were also bronze and pottery jugs of wine, beer, and water. Tasgiitios filled a platter, withdrew his dagger, and sat down to eat. He pointed to the joint and smiled wryly.

"The lamb I brought for sacrifice?"

Bricriu chuckled. "Why waste good food? Once the sacrificial knife has done its duty, blood is spilt, and the entrails are read, the carcass would rot if not consumed. What we do not use within the Sanctuary, we distribute to the less fortunate in Cenabum."

The king grunted, wondering if the last remark contained a rebuke. He personally considered his people to mostly be a happy lot who knew their place in a well-defined Celtic society.

Bricriu smiled. "We do not eat the human sacrifices, although from what I gather, some of my predecessors had a penchant for that partic-ular flesh."

Tasgiitios shuddered. Some of the bones he had passed still had strings of pale flesh attached. "Waste not; want not." He paused briefly before carving a bloody slice of lamb and accepting the chalice of beer offered.

"Crum Dubh and my informants tell me that Brennus intends to cross Conall Mac Gabhann's lands—uninvited. The armies of the Senones and the Arverni gather as we speak. I have not heard whether the king of the Carnutes will also join with Brennus."

"And what wisdom do the entrails impart?" asked Tasgiitios.

"They say that you would be a very foolish king to court the wrath of Conall, the Dark Huntress, and the Sidhe." Bricriu appeared to mull over his words before adding, "Or the Goddess." In his private delib-erations, the Oracle had come to wonder on whose side the Goddess sat. "One way or another, Brennus and the bulk of his army will soon depart Gaul. In truth, it is a campaign that holds the promise of great reward for the Senone king and for those who ally with him. Assuming, of course, he survives."

Bricriu chewed on a piece of gristle and grimaced. He hoped that Tasgiitios was not stinting on his choice of sacrificial animals. Finally, he spat the offending meat on the floor, took several gulps of beer, and carved another slice of lamb. "You have a good relationship with Conall and Mórrígan. In my opinion, it would be unwise to make an adversary of either." Left unsaid was that it would also be foolish to make an ene-my of the Oracle. Bricriu paused. "In fact, perhaps you should consider lending more active support to the defence of Lugudunon. The citadel will surely be where the inevitable battle that Brennus wants will take place."

It was a pleasant meal once the two men had discussed the main topic. Bricriu was a good conversationalist who was growing more con-fident and comfortable in the role of Oracle. All knew the responsibility had been thrust upon him and accepted with a high degree of reluc-tance. As Tasgiitios meandered back to his quarters, his mind pleasantly set free by beer, the king stopped to piss. Mid-stream, he reflected that the leader of the College of the Chaste was a striking woman. From her conversation, she was also quite politically astute. However, at twen-ty-nine summers, she was much older than those he would typically choose to rut.

The king laughed in the darkness. At almost forty summers, he was no young buck. A prominent nose dominated his pock-marked face, and a streak of white hair flowed back from his forehead, thus his nickname, the Badger. Of slightly above average height, chestnut hair covered his stocky frame. All this pointed to him not being the most handsome roy-al in Gaul. Yet, Tasgiitios was a brave warrior, fair-minded, and as well-loved as any king could be. He had sired more than a few bastards but had none he chose to acknowledge as an heir to inherit his kingdom.

Tasgiitios thus became increasingly convinced that the Leader of the Chaste would make an excellent queen and was likely still fertile. That the Oracle had probably been between her thighs caused the king no issue. Virgins were hard to come by. That her ultimate loyalty would always be to the Sanctuary was of greater import. Whether he could live with that was the question to be resolved.

As for choosing sides in the upcoming confrontation between Brennus and Conall, that was a much easier decision to make.

CHAPTER 5

396 B.C.—The Road to Ráth Cavares

The band of five hundred warriors walked or rode at a comfortable pace, basking in the heat of a warm yet not oppressive sun. Recent rainfall had refreshed the land and heightened the fragrances from trees, shrubs, and wildflowers. Their route followed the Rodonos south-west towards the marshlands and hillfort that stood sentinel over Massalia. Ráth Cavares guarded the lower reaches of the river and the main road that ran through the marshes to the port's harbour.

After much deliberation, Conall had been persuaded to take up the offer of partnership with the Greek merchant, Pytheas, and Drostan Ruadh, the one-eyed king of the Forest People of Northern Albu. Trade along the Rodonos and the Liga became vital to the economy of Lugudunon and the well-being of Clann Ui Flaithimh. Therefore, it could not be left to the mercy of the tribes and warbands that drank from the river.

Hence, the antecedent of Ráth Cavares was seized from a small local tribe, razed, and then rebuilt as a formidable hillfort under Cúscraid's watchful eye. The site, a leisurely horse-ride from Massalia, perched on a rocky crag that towered over the Rodonos and Durantia waterways and the marshes.

Once built, the hillfort was garrisoned with five hundred warriors, equally divided between foot and horsemen. Conall put the stronghold under the joint command of Mórrígan's brother Brocc Ó Cathasaigh and the bluff Torcán Ó Dubhghaill. Still, both understood that in matters of politics, they should pay close attention to their more astute partners: Bláithín Ni Néill, a tall, elegant Ulaid noble from Ériu, and Mòrag Ni Artair, the voluptuous and somewhat tempestuous princess of the Ravens.

Skirmishes between Clann Ui Flaithimh and the neighbouring tribes were a common occurrence. Still, on this day, Conall chose to think of his party not as a large, heavily-armed warband but as a group of friends, looking forward to celebrating the feast of Lugnasad with comrades at Ráth Cavares.

A timely snort from Toirneach, his black mount, brought Conall back to reality. Mórrígan often chided him for his naivety, although it was also one of the things she loved in him. The king and queen were accompanied by most of the tribe's nobility and the Chomhairle—and, of course, their veteran personal guards. A cloud settled in Conall's blue eyes, and a frown made an appearance on his lips.

"They will be fine, Conall. My brother Beacán is with them." Mórrígan referred to their twin daughters, Brighid and Danu.

Conall's lips pursed. With great reluctance, he had succumbed to the pleadings of his twin daughters and their logic that, at seventeen summers old, it was time they accepted their responsibilities as princesses and warriors. Yet, Conall was uncomfortable with them joining one of the many warbands, hunting the group who committed appalling atrocities on helpless farmers. Conall inhaled, turned to Mórrígan, and mustered up a grin. The look on Mórrígan's face told him she did not believe the smile.

Ever the optimist, however, Conall saw the journey as an excellent opportunity to meet his people and strengthen the bonds between the Rí Ruirech and his clann. It also allowed him to take stock of how the plantation of the land was progressing. Clann Ui Flaithimh's farmers had to cope with a new climate and novel crops and fruits. After the feasting, Conall and a select band would travel on to Massalia. Envoys from

Pytheas suggested that the stocky sailor was concerned about some recent events.

***

Above the thatched farmhouse, sooty, spectral fingers smudged the summer sky. A ribbon of purple and flashes of lightning on the horizon threatened a storm, but that was likely a sunset off. Situated on the northern side of the slow-moving waters of the Rodonos, the tidy smallholding nestled against the gentle foothills of the mountain. The land was no longer wildwood but tamed, with terraced slopes and orchards of well-tended olive trees. To Conall, the trees, bent almost double by the winds of the Máistir, looked like gnarled and crooked old men. Plump clusters of grapes hung from vines planted in rows perpendicular to the home's southern wall. Soon both fruits would be harvested, and the presses worked.

In the distance, a waterfall cascaded over rocks tumbled smooth by the waters. The drone and chirp of insect wings added a peaceful note to the ambience. Farm dwellings and outhouses were laid out with military precision and built with the best available materials. This was unsurprising, given the farmer's background. It appeared an idyllic setting. Yet, where were the sounds of quern stones grinding corn? Or of children laughing as they played, avoiding chores, or of parents scolding them, albeit with a smile as they remembered their childhoods?

Hard hooves pawed at the grass and dirt. It had rained recently, but the earth was still firm. The air was heavy with expectation. Toirneach snorted and dipped his head. The sharp tug on the reins brought Conall out of his musings. He grimaced as he patted the horse's black shoulder. A small puff of dust reminded the king that he needed to brush Toirneach's coat.

"Yes, I agree. It looks too good to be true."

Alongside, Mórrígan stood on her mount's golden back to scan the landscape. Ominously, she had already slipped her favoured bow stave from its sheath and strung the weapon. She smoothed the arrow's red-and-white fletches and nocked a long, black shaft in readiness. In hindsight, the action was pitifully inadequate.

A peace-shattering roar straight from Mórrígan's adolescent nightmares shattered the valley's pastoral harmony. From the roundhouse, the beast charged, bursting through the building's already destroyed entrance and broken farmyard gates. As if to assimilate the threat before it, the bear came to an abrupt halt twenty paces from Conall's party, stood up on its hind legs, and roared its defiance.

Mutterings of "Shite!" and "The Hag's bony arse!" rippled through the two hundred members of Conall's caomhnóirí and the similar number of Mórrígan's band. The soft hiss of weapons withdrawn from sheepskin-lined scabbards and readied for action accompanied the oaths. Rhythmic incantations from the Sidhe and a small grove of druids added a protective spiritual covering.

At almost two javelin-lengths in height and build like a stone broch, this was a giant among bears. It was also a killer with a taste for human flesh. The gore on its black snout and streamers of skin hanging from bloody claws offered little hope that the farmer or his family had survived the intrusion. Conall swore. He knew the family. The father, formerly one of his ceannairí céad—leaders of a hundred—had recently retired.

The farmer, and his partner, had looked forward to a long life tending their farm. Like Conall, he had two daughters, the same age as Brighid and Danu, and a young son. The boy, a friend of Conall's son, Aodán, had almost escaped the tragedy. Prevailed upon to run for help, he reached the gates before the beast's cruel claws shredded the flesh on his back. He died painfully but mercifully quickly before feeling the animal's jaws crush his skull.

Yet no man or beast's passions are clear-cut. Thus Conall might have had some sympathy for the beast had he known its sad story. With its mate and two cubs, the bear's daily routine was to fish in a small river. The stream flowed by the tall standing stones marking the border between Clann Ui Flaithimh's territory and its western neighbours—the Arverni, the Volcae, and the Tectosages. Set upon by Arverni warriors, the beast's partner and young were slaughtered. Wounded, the enraged animal was driven deeper and deliberately into Conall's land. There it proceeded to take bloody revenge on any two-legged animals who crossed its path.

Toirneach's nostrils flared, and its tail raised. A loud splash and pungent smell told Conall his horse had both pissed and shat. Behind, those sanctified by the discharge muttered curses and veiled threats of horsemeat for dinner. The mount took a step forward. Its muscles hardened as it fought its natural fear. A snort thrown at the bear warned that it was prepared to fight. Conall smoothed the velvet shoulder and smiled. "Not today, friend." He sensed the horse's disappointment.

Conall and Mórrígan slipped from their mounts. Javelins raised and ready for battle, Conall's caomhnóirí, lightly armoured due to the heat, stood in two relaxed rows. With Mórrígan was a multi-cultured band consisting of Clann Ui Flaithimh warriors, Cretan bowmen, and Thracian heavy cavalry. They were also accompanied by a few chariots led by Gràinne Ni Fearghal, the reluctant queen of a Cinn Péinteáilte tribe in north-eastern Albu. All but the chariots and Thracians had dismounted. The latter's beasts and Gràinne's vehicles were as much a weapon as their riders.

The bear roared, dropped to all fours, and charged. In that same instant, a huge shadow crossed Conall's path. The animal raised itself up on its back legs and bellowed at the giant who dared stand before it. Beams of sunshine glinted off a massive double-edged axe held in fists the size of bear paws. Mesmerised, the bear tracked the gleaming axehead as Urard raised the shaft, and swung the weapon in circles. Muscles rippled on the familiar, sunburnt torso. "No!" came frantic, shouted pleas from Conall and Mórrígan. But Urard was past hearing anyone's words. Swinging the great axe, Breith, he closed on the beast.

It was marginal which weapon, axe or paw, drew blood first. In no more time than it takes a dribble of water to spill from mouth to beard to chest, Urard's curved axe-head buried itself in the beast's upper torso. In reply, a back-swipe of the bear's paw broke several of Urard's ribs and launched the giant into the air. He fell heavily on his back, and the bones in his lower spine crunched as he hit hard-packed dirt.

Axe buried in its chest and wild with pain, the bear shambled to where Urard lay. Wickedly sharp, curved claws enclosed the warrior's head. The crazed animal, blood gushing from its wound, opened its mouth and bellowed. Its intention was made plain by the rows of large, blood-stained teeth. Blood-infused drool splashed Urard's face.

Amodocus, the leader of the Thracians, and his horsemen reached Urard first. A frenzy of slashing rhomphaiae and the pounding of maces finally subdued the bear. Still breathing, it slumped heavily on top of Urard. The strength of six men was barely enough to haul the beast of the massive warrior.

Iasg, arriving at her partner's body, screamed in horror at the broken, bloody mess before her. It was not immediately apparent to anyone whether or not she was looking at a corpse. A ragged, pain-filled cough from Urard raised hopes. Yet the bloody froth exuding from his mouth and the bluish tint to his lips suggested that the bean-sidhe drew close.

Sarpedon, the leader of the Cretan archers, pushed his way through the circle gathered around Urard. To no one, in particular, he announced, "Give him room. He has many injuries, and his lung has likely collapsed." Iasg wailed once more. Sarpedon tugged on the trim, triangular beard that adorned his chin and then looked to one of his men. The lack of response drew a fierce glare from the Cretan, and a small wooden syrinx was handed over. The owner of the flute winced as Sarpedon snapped off the thinnest reed. Those gathered around the fallen warrior shuddered as he quickly sharpened one end, slit open Urard's flesh, and plunged the tube into the wound. Urard coughed and appeared to breathe less raggedly, eliciting a sigh of relief, and raising the hopes of his friends.

"He remains in great danger," warned Sarpedon. The almost imperceptible shake of Sarpedon's head gave Conall little hope that Urard's sojourn in this life would be long.

With snapped orders, pelts were tossed onto one of the chariots. The great warrior was laid on them and restrained with ropes tied to the cret's iron rings. Lugudunon was too far away. Ráth Cavares was closer—just—but it would be a risky ride. As the small group set off, Iasg was heard to berate her companion.

"Do ye not think yer ugly enough without wrestling a bear?"

As the party moved away, Conall looked at Mórrígan and, with great sadness, shook his head. A tear rolled down the Dark Huntress's cheek. Both knew that even under perfect conditions, it would be a full sunset before Urard reached Ráth Cavares. Whether both body and spirit crossed the fort's entrance was in the hands of the Goddess.

***

The bodies of the farmer and his family had barely been laid on the funeral pyre before a deep *barrr-ewww* of tribal war horns emanated from the forests. The sound was quickly followed by a large group of warriors emerging from the treeline beyond the olive groves.

"Trouble always has company," muttered Conall.

"From the banners, they're Arverni. Maybe with some Tectosage mercenaries. Celtillos, their new verrix sees himself as the High King of Gaul," said Mórrígan.

Conall snorted. "I think Brennus would contest that ambition."

Amodocus and Sarpedon joined the royal pair. The Thracian smiled broadly, flashing impossibly white teeth against a canvas of olive skin that seemed to darken daily under the sun. "It would appear that we didn't do a great job of terrorising our neighbours. I did advise that killing them and burning down their dwellings is much less effective without rape and slavery."

Ignoring the glare from Mórrígan, Amodocus continued, "Oddly, I make our forces evenly matched in numbers. In our favour, half of our force is mounted. Apart from a small group of leaders and shield-men, they are mostly on foot. One-on-one, they will match us for weapons and armour. The Arverni bastards have a well-deserved reputation for the quality of their arms." He nodded at Mórrígan and then Sarpedon. "I doubt they'll have many bowmen—maybe a score for hunting. So that's a clear advantage."

"Oddly?" questioned Conall.

Amodocus smiled. "You, I, and Clann Ui Flaithimh's warriors have a deserved and fearsome reputation." He turned about and gestured at the landscape. "On this ground, tell me, which of our neighbours would choose to fight us without the strength of overwhelming numbers?"

Mórrígan scoured the land and muttered hesitantly, "He's right. Is it a coincidence that we're just beyond mid-way between Lugudunon and Ráth Cavares?"

"You sense a trap?" asked Conall.

"It's at least a sunset's hard ride to either hillfort. We're too distant for signal horns to be heard by either." Mórrígan turned to survey the farm. "We could burn the buildings. Perhaps our forts will see the smoke."

Conall shook his head. "Unlikely. The farm is well built with a solid stone perimeter wall. If necessary, we can use it as our last line of defence." He left unspoken that burning the farm seemed an insult to the memory of the deceased family. Grabbing Toirneach's thick mane, he swung up onto the soft, thick dillat that covered the animal's back. A sweeping hand signalled where he wanted his warband to go.

***

The small group thrashed their path through the profuse wildwood at the foot of the Alpes. Eager to taste blood, brambles and thorns tore strips from brightly-coloured, plaid triubhas to reach and scratch pale flesh. Nettles and thistles stung. Men swore and grabbed fistfuls of dock leaves to rub on blistered skin. By chance, the band came upon a track rutted by heavy logs. Likely, they had been dragged by sweat-flecked oxen and horses. The path led to a circular glade. Stumps of trees were scattered across the clearing—remnants of the labour of the farmer's and his sons' axes. The crofter knew his timber well. His home was likely not far away, and his dwellings and fences would be strong.

Tall, ancient trees, some with trunks wider than three men touching fingers could encircle, guarded the clearing. It was as if they protected a treasure. For here, the dense canopy of the forest was broken. The sun, permitted to shine, bathed the fertile earth with golden shafts of light. Where before the ground had been deeply carpeted with the rusts and browns of decay, now grasses, mosses, and ferns burst from the dirt. Wildflowers added cheerful splashes of colour. The air smelled clean and aromatic. The band's lungs were invigorated by an infusion of fresh air.

The party was one of a score of similar warbands that patrolled the borders of Clann Ui Flaithimh's territory. Many were accomplished horsemen and women, but this was of little advantage and potentially a liability in the wildwoods. In the depths of the forest, progress was swifter and more assured on foot and snares were easier to avoid. For speed of movement, they traded heavy chainmail shirts for boiled leather.

Lightly armed, each carried a small, round shield, three javelins, and a similar number of throwing darts. Hanging from sculpted leather belts and baldrics were an assortment of swords, axes, and daggers. Tucked into soft hide boots were more blades. Many carried bow staves and quivers of the signature black-shafted arrows with their red-and-white fletches. Beacán Ó Cathasaigh, brother of Mórrígan, allowed himself a brief smile. "Lightly armed" was open to wide interpretation. Danu Ni Conall, daughter of Conall and Mórrígan, and a warrior in her own right, spoke, "Something troubling you, Beacán?"

Her uncle, one knee resting on the thick carpet of decayed leaves and pine needles that bordered the clearing, held up his hand for quiet, sniffed the air, and strained his ears. The other hand reached into the dirt as if searching for clues. Fingertips strained to sense vibrations.

To Beacán, the mood of the forest seemed anxious, as if waiting for something to occur. The hairs on the back of his neck refused to stand down. Yet the pack of wolfhounds that accompanied the band gave no warning growls. The rest of the group, spread out before him in a semi-circular skirmish line, raised no alarm.

Brighid Ni Conall, Danu's twin, laid a hand on his shoulder, breaking his musings. She pointed upwards beyond the green canopy. A pair of golden eagles soared high in a cloudless sky. "The Goddess watches," she said.

Beacán smiled. He put more faith in his famed stealth and expertise with knives than in the gods. He chuckled. His brother, Bricriu, now the Oracle in Cenabum, would surely admonish him for his lack of faith. The girls looked at him quizzically. He shook his head and stood up.

"The sun will set soon. This clearing will make a good camp. You know what to do. I'll be back before the dawn." With no more words, Beacán strode off and was quickly lost to the forest.

CHAPTER 6

396 B.C.—Rome

Marcus Fabius Ambustus, Pontifex Maximus of Rome, took comfort in the cool, stone floors of his expansive villa. As expected from a man of his wealth and political stature, the palatial building—it could hardly be termed a home—was located in a select area of the Mons Palatinus. Ornately sculpted arches and open doorways encouraged transitory breezes to flow freely, providing welcome relief to a hot summer. Thus, life was made more tolerable in the month of Quintilus. The elderly patrician hoped that the zephyrs would also make their presence felt in the stifling heat and stink of Sextilis.

Flat-soled sandals slapped the smooth tiles as the Pontifex paced the floor of his chambers. A decadent leer settled on thin, dusky-pink lips, dry and cracked with age. The sound reminded him of the firm smack of a hand on the flesh of his young slaves—both girls and boys. To satisfy his lesser extreme lusts, he used the sons and daughters of patrician colleagues, who sought to ingratiate themselves. Marcus visited his darker perversions, which had increased rapidly with age, on those who were helpless to resist and disposable. Who would care about another missing slave? Who would mourn their passing? His depravities were at odds with Marcus' claim to be Rome's spiritual leader.

Always one for the longer game, Marcus moved men and women like pieces around a latrunculi board. Loath to admit the possibility of failure, he grudgingly conceded that time was not on his side. He was older, his ambitions were frustrated, and his pawns were not behaving. Added to this, his eldest son, Quintus, while passably handsome in a certain light, was plainly stupid. Quintus survived by ignoring his debts and trading heavily on his father's name and influence. Hence, Marcus was perplexed about how he could position his son in a favourable light with the Senate.

In search of a less troublesome topic, the elder statesman's mind drifted to the issue of the barbarian tribes. He cursed the increased number of wandering tribal warbands entering Latium. They filtered through the valleys of the Alpes to settle in the warmer, fertile lands occupied by the Etrusci and Umbri. Some groups had ventured as far south as the land of the Samnites. When anointed Dictator of Rome, Marcus swore that he would cleanse the territories of Rome and its neighbours of these vermin and their religions.

Recently, a disturbing rumour had reached his ears. Marcus' informants in Messene informed him that Dionysius of Syrako had sought to purchase the services of the barbarian army of Conall Mac Gabhann but had to "settle" for Brennus of the Senones. An army of thirty thousand Gallic warriors journeying south over the Alpes was a different scenario to scattered, nomadic warbands.

Still, with unshakable Roman condescension, Marcus could not conceive how such a horde could stand against the might of a unified Roman phalanx. Indeed, perhaps such a scenario could play into his bony hands. It did not cross Marcus' mind to question why Dionysius' preference was Conall, not Brennus. Or whether the cunning king of Syrako was the source of the rumours.

This afternoon the Senate would meet in the Curia Hostilia. Marcus had a score to settle with Marius Furius Camillus, General of Rome, who by all accounts had murdered Marcus' youngest son, Caeso. That Marcus, although not the hand that wielded the dagger, had undoubtedly paid for the enslavement and slaying of Marius' only daughter, Cornelia, he deemed an irrelevance.

Marcus did not like the austere building since it was not a suitably impressive monument for his ambitions. Located in the Forum Romanum, surrounded by temples with imposing stairways and towering columns, the Curia Hostilia was a relatively modest building. Still, the edifice was built on rising ground and so, by default, dominated the Forum. Originally a temple, it was considered sacred as well as functional.

The building's simple façade had been embellished with the addition of two tall columns and an open portico. A semi-circular set of marble stairs led to the Curia's great, sculpted bronze doors. Stone terrazzo-tiled floors, intricately designed and in striking colours, were laid down from the entranceway to the black Shrine of Vulcan located at the far end of the building. Benches of smooth block-stone, enough to seat three hundred senators, were tiered in a semicircle and faced a raised platform for the speaker. Stairways to either side of the doors led to the public viewing gallery.

Senators bedecked in white togas edged with purple sat on the functional stone seats. Like Marcus, many brought a soft cushion to lessen the impact of the harsh surface on aged backsides—some bony, some expansive. Only the swishing of large fans held by an army of slaves ameliorated the oppressive heat.

Loud cheers from the public gallery announced the entrance of Rome's most celebrated general and the commander of Rome's army, Marius Furius Camillus. As the general accepted their adulation, Marcus cursed and ground his teeth. In recognition of his great victories, Marius wore the toga picta. The garment, dyed purple and embellished with gold stripes, certainly set Marius apart from his audience.

Marius' eyes swept the room. He thought it peculiar that less than half the usual number were present. Still, the fragrant scents of summer carried by southerly breezes suggested that perhaps many had already journeyed to their lakeside villas. Designated a special meeting, it was not on the regular calendar. Marius scrutinised the audience more closely.

Disturbingly, of those in attendance, it seemed to the general that very few were friends. More ominously, few held his gaze, preferring to focus on dusty feet and nails manicured by slaves. The more neutral politicians shrugged their shoulders as if in meaningless apology. On reflection, his invite had been open to interpretation. Such was Marius' ego that he had assumed he was to be presented with another honour. It was also the reason for the large public presence. Too late, Marius sensed a snare—and the scheming of his adversary, Marcus. His jaw set, and he swore under his breath.

On the stone plinth, the Princeps Senatus nodded stiffly to Marius and indicated where he should sit. The Princeps was a tall, gaunt man who usually held the air of authority comfortably. It was a valuable trait in an often-unruly body of men. He, too, was reluctant to engage in prolonged eye contact. "Curious," murmured Marius.

The senate leader exhaled, and the forum became silent. The ambience crackled with anticipation. "Marius Furius Camillus, General of Rome, you are accused of treason, murder, embezzlement, and giving aid to Rome's enemies by trading in weapons."

Furious, Marius abruptly stood, and his right hand reached across his body. The Princeps and those close to Marius flinched at the action. Fortunately for those present, weapons were not allowed in the Curia, and Marius was pedantic when it came to obeying rules. There was little doubt that Marius could and would have slaughtered a good number of the members present, and no doubt as to who would have been his first victim. His bellow echoed around the Curia.

"Where are my accusers? Let them stand before me."

The Princeps Senatus coughed nervously, perhaps having considered for the first time the precariousness of his position. Whoever made an enemy of either Marcus or Marius was unlikely to enjoy a long life. Few, if any, would lift a hand in the Princeps's defence. He continued quickly, his jarring words almost incomprehensible as they knocked against each other. "The Senate has taken statements, considered them, and found them satisfactory. Your guilt is clear. All that remains is the sentencing."

Marius snorted, "I doubt whether any of the witnesses still breathe—or will remain alive. They should make peace with their gods."

Fear trickled through the public gallery, followed by the slap of sandals on stone stairways and the scraping of heavy doors on stone. Marius scoffed, "Ah, the rats flee."

Marius turned his ire on the Senators. "*Porcorum!* Your snouts are deep in Marcus Fabius Ambustus' feeding trough. *Irrumatores!* Content to roll around in his shit, you curry favour with this decrepit old man. You sacrifice your sons and daughters, allowing them to be raped, sodomised, and subjected to unspeakable depravities. And for what—political influence and wealth? The stench of your shame assaults my nostrils worse than the sewers of Rome in Sextilis."

Marius' face flushed red in anger as he lifted his right arm from under the folds of the purple toga and pointed to Marcus. "This dog, this traitor, this corruption of the high office given to him will lead Rome into a black pit from whence it may never return. In those days, you will call upon me, Marius Furius Camillus, General of Rome. You will beg me to save you. Pray to your gods that my affection for Rome will overwhelm my desire for retribution." He smiled coldly. "Pray also that I will forget your faces."

In a misguided attempt to regain control, the Princeps pointed to Marius. "You, Marius Furius Camillus, and your household are exiled from Rome. You will be taken in chains from this house, paraded in public disgrace, and confined to your villa in Ardea."

As the Senate guards stepped towards him, Marius raised two thick fingers to his lips. A piercing whistle halted the men's movement and any further foolishness from the senate's leader.

"You take me for a fool?" rasped Marius.

The Princeps blanched. At that moment, he knew he had sealed his fate. A desperate look at Marcus was ignored. The Senate's leader had fulfilled his role, and his removal from the game was of little import.

A hush descended on the forum. It was soon broken by the metallic clack of marching boots on stone. Inside the Curia, consternation settled on the faces of the senators. In the public gallery, an expectation of imminent bloodshed brought gasps of alarm and excitement. Today's spectacle was infinitely more entertaining than the usual boring drone of the entitled.

Through the entranceway stepped a tall, broad-shouldered warrior in burnished bronze armour. A red woollen cloak was draped over his shoulders. On his left arm rested a round bronze shield, and in his right hand he held a spear. Feet planted wide, he passed the spear to his left hand. Slowly and deliberately, he removed his helmet and scratched a closely cropped head. Briefly, he observed the sheen of perspiration transferred from head to hand. Then he smirked at Marius.

"As arranged, your escort is here, General." With a glare to the Princeps Senatus and a barely disguised look of disdain at the Senate guards, he added, "Are we expecting trouble? Should I invite my comrades to join us?"

"For these cowards? By the sudden rise in smell, most of them have pissed and shat themselves. The fullonicae will do a good trade today."

Marius smiled glacially at the Princeps Senatus. "As for you, I recommend a warm bath, a glass of wine, and a sharp blade." With a swirl of his robes, Marius turned and strode from the Curia. Behind, he left a stunned public gallery and a nervous assembly of senators, many of whom now wondered if they had wagered on the right chariot.

Marcus rose from his stone seat with all the dignity he could muster. He smarted from the insult of "old man" thrown at him. Ignoring the hiss from the gallery, Marcus wiped a stream of drool from his chin. Convinced a strategic victory had been won, the sneer on his lips remained fixed.

CHAPTER 7

396 B.C.—The Skies Above Lugudunon

The immense wings of the eagles beat the air several times before the majestic birds gracefully glided into the welcoming canopy of ancient oak trees. They quickly settled into the massive nest of sticks, bones, and mosses. The faint odour of decaying flesh tickled their nostrils. Now at ease, they took in the panorama from their high perch. Yet, one found it irresistible to prod a slumbering fire.

"Your famed Hand and Dark Huntress are not behaving, are they?"

Fate preened his feathers. To his satisfaction, they were far superior to those of the Goddess. But then, in the realm of beasts and fowl, the male is often both more gloriously coloured and has more impressive fur or plumage. The one thing that annoyed Fate was that the Goddess, while reluctantly accepting a dowdier appearance, was much bigger and more powerful than he. Fate smirked, if that was even possible for an eagle, and poked the Goddess once more.

"It seems to me that they have divided loyalties—tribe, family, or the Goddess? And the geis your servant, the Sidhe, laid on Conall appears to be less of a compelling and driving force for vengeance. Conall's home is in this fertile valley with his people. I am not convinced he would return to Ériu, geis or not."

Frustration rippled like a breeze through Fate's feathers. The absence of a speedy retort was an aberration from the Goddess's usual character. He prodded again. "Perhaps you have overplayed your hand.

Too much stick and not enough honey. Humans can be infuriatingly unpredictable."

The hooked yellow bill slashed across Fate's throat. Had he not been alert to a possible strike, his corpse would have provided the Goddess with her next meal. Yet, had the Goddess actually wanted to end his avatar, she would have used her cruel talons. As it was, the smaller, nimbler bird launched into the air, caught an updraught, and soared high.

The Goddess preened her feathers. "Infuriating beast," she muttered. Still, she appreciated being alone. The Goddess of Ériu and the Gaels had much to ponder. Under her guidance, the young apprentice blacksmith, Conall, had become a great warrior king, beloved of his people, with a desire for justice. The latter, however, did not necessarily equate to a need for blood vengeance.

She snorted. Was she worried for nothing? With her guidance, Conall had become a ruthless and shrewd Rí Ruirech in battle, politics, and more recently in amassing lands and wealth.

Furthermore, if Conall was the sword of Clann Ui Flaithimh, Mórrígan was the venom that coated its edge. A core of darkness still resided within the woman. Yet, Mórrígan had wrestled with it, brought it under her control, and now wielded a power that might soon eclipse that of the Sidhe. Perhaps it already did.

The great eagle huffed. She considered the trials set before the pair and pondered whether, as Fate suggested, she had been too harsh. The slaughter of their parents and siblings. The death of Tuathal, their first-born. The kidnapping of the twins. The attempted assassinations and the internal strife and rebellion. The diseases visited upon the tribe.

The Goddess spat. Not all could be laid at her feet. Besides, she was no mother hen, no suckler cow. They lived in terrible times. They had thrived. They had endured. They had overcome and become stronger. But... had they become too independent? The Goddess had little time for sentimentality. Her need was for tools to execute and carry out her will. While loath to admit to a lack of perception or foresight, she had, in Conall and Mórrígan, fostered the creation of two leviathans. Worse, they had minds of their own. Yes, they still gave the Goddess her due sacrifices and worship. But not unquestioningly, and for how long?

As if reading her thoughts, a peal of laughter resounded across the valley. "I am Fate. I will always be Fate. I need no followers or their prayers. You are a god, and all gods have one common bond: the need to be worshipped. Without the adoration of your chosen people, you, Goddess, will fade and be forgotten. People are fickle, and there are many gods. Push them too hard and they will find another to pledge their loyalty. Carefully consider your chosen path."

"Bastard!" the Goddess screeched as she took to the skies, fully intent on ripping the wings from Fate. Yet a worm of doubt wriggled in her brain. Events had already been set in place and could not be changed. Was her destiny in human hands? If so, that was neither wanted nor controllable.

"Enough of this!" she cried. Now was not the time for limitations of the flesh. The lifeless body of the eagle plummeted to the earth.

CHAPTER 8

396 B.C.—Massalia

Nikandros sat in the shade of an awning, the utility of which had greatly diminished with age and wear. Its state of disrepair was a fair reflection of the dilapidated warehouses, brothels, and drinking dens that populated the dockside environs of the port of Massalia. It was also in striking contrast to the majestic temples of Artemis and Apollo that stood as lofty sentinels on the headland above the harbour. The tall, black-haired warrior had no desire to be observed. His distinctive bronze armour and shield resided in a nondescript canvas sack at his feet. Only the xiphos and an elaborate leather baldric testified to his menace. Ironically, the sash was a gift from Conall.

"Better times," he sighed, "better times."

Deemed less prone to outbreaks of violence by the surly denizens of the waterfront, a brothel was Nikandros' preferred choice over an inn. The whorehouse was small and windowless, getting its light from the doorway during the day and torches at night. The main room was open. It smelled of overcooked food, stale liquor, sweat, and sex. Spider lines of mould crept upwards from the slate-grey slabs that constituted the floor, providing a natural mosaic on the whitewashed walls.

Once a pristine white, maintenance was long overdue on the flaking walls. The only furniture was wooden tables with tops smoothed by age and use. Rickety chairs and benches were scattered throughout. All were stained with a diverse variety of fluids—wine, beer, and those of human origin. The bar, a solid bench of aged oak, ran the length of the wall opposite the entrance.

For clients with specific hungers, or those desirous of some semblance of privacy, a mezzanine floor ran around two walls. Most, however, simply slapped a coin on their table, bent the closest whore over the table, lifted her skirt, rutted, and went back to drinking. Depending on the weight of their purses, this ritual was repeated until drunkenness, impotence, or lack of funds triumphed. There was an accessible flat roof. However, few of the whores or their clients favoured the risk of burning their more delicate parts. Also, it could be argued that this location was the least private of all options. News of rooftop copulations spread rapidly, and a gallery of cheering children was assured.

There was a price to be paid for the Spartan's choice of refuge. Wine and beer were not the primary business or the chief source of profit for the establishment's owner. Still, the young girl who knelt before him was very pleasing. Long, dark hair and bright brown eyes sat in a field of honey-almond skin. She released the shoulder pins of her chiton to allow the garment to fall to her waist. Her action was practical. Why risk unnecessary staining? Nikandros appreciated the full and firm breasts. He estimated that she was no more than fifteen summers. In anticipation of the impending act, he sighed softly and watched as she lifted his short, red tunic. Surprisingly, given her youth, she was very adept with both mouth and hands.

As the young whore's head bobbed up and down and her hands worked in tandem to bring him to a climax, the Spartan reflected, sadly, that her life would be short. The clientele of the docks was not known for being gentle or even-tempered. Bruises, broken bones, and knife scars were the girl's future. Likely, she would die in the gutter of some anonymous alley with her throat cut—after being raped.

Nikandros climaxed, exhaled, and thanked the girl. A generous coin was flipped in her direction and caught with the ease of frequent practice. Grabbing a jug of wine, he exited the room and took a seat under the building's stained and mildewed canopy. Disturbed only by the cacophony of noise from the waterfront before him and, behind him, the grunts of rutting interspersed with random slaps of bare arses, Nikandros kept watch.

His lifestyle had taught Nikandros not to burn bridges unnecessarily. Enemy and friend are the two sides of the same coin. One flip of the coin can change everything. Thus, he had told Conall that he wished to visit his home and mother. The reaction from Conall was one of relief. As if a problem had conveniently removed itself.

"Visit my mother, indeed!" The Spartan snorted in derision.

When, many years past, he had returned in disgrace from the Peloponnesian War, the lady, a princess of Sparta, had greeted him with the minimum of emotion. His tears and pleading that he was young and foolish fell on deaf ears. The truth was that full of hubris, he had led a score of men on a fruitless and needless raid. All had died, save himself. Fate can be cruel, and the gods have a twisted sense of humour.

Arriving home naked—his former comrades had stripped him of everything and shorn his head—he had awaited his mother's displeasure. She gave no greeting, no embrace, and little acknowledgement of kinship. New clothes, armour, and weapons were purchased, all of the finest quality and craftsmanship. Then, she led him to Sparta's boundary.

Once there, with deliberation, she stripped, tossing clothing and sandals aside. She turned and, head held high, walked away without so much as a backwards glance. The message was unspoken but clear: "You are no longer my son. Do not come back." Nikandros later reflected that his most enduring image of his mother was the rise and fall of firm buttocks. On occasion, he wondered if she was still alive. Nikandros sighed. He was dead to her, and that would never change.

As he awaited his vessel, Nikandros realised that perhaps for the first time in many years, he was not in control. He put this down to developing an unprofessional fondness for his targets, Conall and Mórrígan. The unexpected return of Íar Mac Dedad to Conall's affections compounded

Nikandros' predicament. There was no love lost between the Spartan and Íar, and now Íar had the ear of Conall.

After he met with the twins, Nikandros detected a rapid chilling of his relationship with the members of Conall's Chomhairle and the army. Their trust in him, like the tide, had ebbed. *Bastards!* And, unlike the surging waves, he doubted it would return. Did Conall not see how many times he had saved his life with timely advice or a sharp blade? True, his motives may have been questionable, but whose are not? He grunted and called for more wine.

✴✴✴

The girl watched Nikandros drain the last of the wine, stand, and walk unsteadily towards the harbour and the waiting ship. Her eyes no longer sparkled. Neither did they hold a smile. That was for paying customers. The mask she now donned was cold and calculating as she nodded to the owner and exited via the rear door. Several streets later, she arrived at an impressive entranceway set in the whitewashed walls of a large compound.

The head servant of Pytheas' household sat in a carved wooden chair to the right of the doorway. His sunburnt, bald head glistened with sweat. Only the occasional swish of a fan signalled that he was not asleep. Sensing a shadow move across his vision, he opened his eyes.

"Welcome, Tisiphone. Do you have news?" The smile was genuine but tinged with sadness.

The girl nodded. "He departed on a bireme. His destination is neither Sparta nor Greece but the port of Agylla. From there, he will likely travel by horse to Rome."

"Your confirmation is welcome. My master will be pleased."

From the depths of his garment, the servant pulled a small pouch and offered it to the girl. She bowed, smiled, and accepted the payment. As she turned to depart, the servant stood and gently clasped her forearm.

"My master has asked me to implore you to accept his offer of employment. Your life is harsh—and dangerous."

"Please give my thanks to my lord Pytheas. His and your concern are much appreciated. Perhaps I will take up your offer… later."

As she walked away, the sorrow in the servant's eyes deepened.

*　*　*

Pytheas sat on a cool, stone bench smoothed with age and countless backsides. The Temple of Apollo was a place of solitude, which he often visited to order his thoughts. Most times, pleasant sea breezes made the temple a treasured sanctuary in the hot summers. This perch also offered a commanding view of the harbour and, beyond it, the Great Sea. The Greek merchant rubbed his forehead as if wrestling with a great problem.

A council of six hundred men called the Timouchoi governed Massalia. All were wealthy aristocrats. However, inevitably the number was demonstrably too cumbersome when prompt action was needed. Thus, an executive committee of fifteen was empowered to oversee the business of government. Even this number proved inefficient, and so a triumvirate was elected and assigned the ultimate power. As was his father before him, and his father before him, Pytheas was a member of the elite trinity.

Today, he looked beyond the harbour and observed Massalia's problem. A fistful of black-sailed penteconters cruised back and forward just beyond the narrow entrance to Massalia's port. They had no distinguishing flags, and most assumed they were pirates or slavers. Yet, pirates were not known for being overly social or patrolling a specific area. They usually travelled alone or perhaps with a second vessel, preying on lonely merchantmen who strayed off course. A disturbing rumour had reached Pytheas' ears. Massalia, like the rich cream in cow's milk, had risen to the top of the list of future acquisitions for one of the Great Sea's powers.

One such party was the tyrant Dionysius of Syrako. Dionysius had well-known ambitions to expand his territory and influence beyond Sikelia. However, Pytheas had frequent dealings with the king and knew that Dionysius was a vain man. Penteconters were old-style vessels. Dionysius' latest project was the construction of a fleet of modern warships—quinqueremes. Besides, the king had his hands full securing the island of Sikelia and discouraging interference from Rome.

That thought brought Pytheas to consider his shortlist of potential aggressors. There were always raids on Massalia's walls by local tribes. The most recent was the Arverni under Celtillos. Conall's hillfort of Ráth Cavares, and the natural barrier of the marshes north-east of the city, had reduced the frequency of land-based attacks on Massalia and the numerous trading caravans that sailed the Rodonos.

The members of Massalia's triumvirate had been well pleased with the additional security and comfort from the garrison at Ráth Cavares—plus, of course, the preferential treatment of traders from Massalia along the Rodonos and Liga rivers. That said, rumblings had begun to surface about the growing influence of the Rí Ruirech of Clann Ui Flaithimh and whether that was in Massalia's best interests.

Pytheas sighed and tugged at his oiled and scented beard. Was Conall a danger to Massalia? Unlikely. A better question to pose might be whether the appearance of the unmarked vessels was connected to the enmity between Conall and Marcus Fabius Ambustus. Marcus had ambitions for Rome and was well-known to mix business with revenge.

That Marcus had recently repossessed a fleet of penteconters to settle debts added weight to Pytheas' hypothesis. The merchant sighed and rose from his seat. He stopped at the stone altar, dropped a generous tribute, and bowed to the bronze statue of the sea god. The figure was a gift from the sailor. Blinking rapidly in the sunshine as he exited the temple, Pytheas was grateful that Conall was already on his way to Massalia. There was much to discuss.

CHAPTER 9

396 B.C.—Road to Ráth Cavares

Carmag Mac an t-Sionnaich, ceannairí na míle—leader of a thousand—and one of Conall's Chomhairle, rubbed calloused palms on the rough tree bark, inhaled the sweet scent of pine into his lungs, and smiled broadly. A long mane of braided, red hair hung from a skull that had borne the brunt of many blades and clubs—and even other heads. His face, pock-marked from his youth and scarred from numerous battles and duels, would not be considered handsome. Yet, the warrior radiated an aura of honesty and determination. As were those who accompanied him, Carmag was as naked as the day he was born. Some said he was just as ugly, too. But they said it out of the reach of his long arms and iron-headed club.

The wild-looking warrior from the forests of Northern Albu lovingly stroked the smooth, sweat- and blood-stained shaft of his massive hammer. It was a treasured gift from Conall, who loved any excuse to practice his blacksmith skills. Broad shoulders and a massively muscled upper torso and arms testified that Carmag was well accustomed to wielding the blunt, ferocious weapon. Coarse, red hair covered most of Carmag's body, but beneath that were the elaborate, dark-blue tattoos that testified to his heritage. Only the profoundly unobservant saw Carmag as a man to be taken lightly.

Commander of Conall's Forest People, Carmag, cherished the woods with a passion that was mirrored by how much he detested the cold, stone walls of Lugudunon. Carmag loved the smell of pine and cedarwood, oak and birch, and the warmth and textures of wood. He smiled. In this, he had empathy with Conall and Mórrígan. Desiring fewer crowds and a more traditional home constructed of wood, stone, and dirt, the king and queen had built Dún-an-Ri at the confluence of the Rodonos and Souconna rivers. The royal residence was protected on three sides by the rivers and on the north approach by a stone wall and ditch that spanned from riverbank to riverbank.

Accompanying Carmag were two hundred and fifty warriors, all young men and women. As recent recruits, they were the least experienced of his force, though the group was salted with a score of veterans to both train and keep them in line. Many of his people had happily rutted and taken partners from the other tribal divisions of Clann Ui Flaithimh. And they did so with Carmag's blessing. However, this batch of trainees was the first of a new crop of pure-bred Forest People who held to the original traditions of the people of Northern Albu.

From the cover of the forest, Carmag rubbed a bearded chin and watched the looming confrontation between Conall and the Arverni warband. He smiled as he recalled the suggestion from Conall that Carmag's trainees should take this route. Whether due to unnatural prescience or simply good informants, it was always wise to heed Conall and Mórrígan's advice. The craggy veteran sensed his band, like a slavering wolf pack, sizing up their next meal.

＊＊＊

Tullus started. Rolling instinctively to his left, he grabbed a sword with his right hand. Rising slowly from his knees, he crouched in the inky blackness. His senses strained to appreciate the situation. Sweat beaded on his forehead, trickling down his face and neck to join several other rivulets that soaked his hairless chest and back.

The dream or vision had been nightmarish. Tullus could still feel the grip of icy, skeletal fingers on his heart, squeezing until he thought it would burst or shatter. The mocking cackle of an inhuman voice as it hissed, "Death is inevitable. How you choose to die is not. Retreat, Tullus. There is no path forward for you." Yet, it was neither the message nor the rapid beat of his heart that drove a spike of fear deep into the mind of Tullus. It was the awful vision of the messenger's perfection.

It was the cusp of dawn. On the horizon, flashes of lightning tempered the darkness of night and backlit the charcoal-grey clouds. The omens pointed to a stormy day. Instincts, sharpened through many battles and assignments, screamed, "Danger!" He shouted, "On your feet! Arm yourselves."

Grumbling and swearing, all eventually stood—save two, and they would never rise again. With a nudge of his foot, the bodies, cold and shrouded in woollen cloaks, rolled over, revealing a pool of shared gore. Both smiled at Tullus through gashes that had almost severed head from neck. *The bastard must have a sharp blade.*

"Where are the guards?" he roared, needing to vent his anger.

Two men were pushed forward. They looked desperately from comrade to comrade, but few met their eyes. Even fewer would own up to friendship with them. None would raise a voice or a hand in their defence. Tullus stood a breath's distance from the men and pointed to the corpses of his aides.

"Where were you when assassins walked into the camp, selected *my* men, and slit their throats?"

The sentries said nothing. Theirs was a brutal occupation, and they expected nothing less than an excruciating death. There was nothing to say, and no plea for mercy would be heard.

"Hold them," barked Tullus.

Two daggers were thrust into the glowing embers of a campfire. After a short time, Tullus drew one from the fire. It smouldered and glowed yellow and white. Fear gripped the men. Bowels loosened, the smell of piss and shit permeated the camp. The stench of burning flesh soon accompanied it. Each man screamed, helpless in the unyielding grasp of former comrades, as Tullus laid the flat of the blade vertically across cheek and eye. The hiss of burst eye fluid sent shivers down the spines of those present.

Released from the grip of their guards, the men collapsed to their knees, clutching at their ruined faces. Each mourned the loss of an eye. Tullus bent close. His voice was cold and devoid of compassion. "If it were not for our dwindling numbers, I would have taken both eyes, gutted you, and left you for the wolves. On your feet. You can still fight with one eye."

Of average height, Tullus was an angular man. There was little fat on his body. That said, his lack of girth belied the strength that rested in his arms and legs. His head and face were shaved. Not from any statement of fashion or intent, but because it was practical. Both showed the shadow of not being recently scraped. His sunburnt face was gaunt without looking emaciated. Dark eyes that had witnessed too many horrors constantly surveyed his surroundings. Warily, the remainder of the miscreant band watched Tullus. They were thugs, not overly bright, and needed direction.

"Arm yourselves. We are going…"

Tullus' order was interrupted by a mocking laugh from the forest. In the still air of dawn, the source could have been standing next to him or far away. That the assassin watched the camp and was unafraid to be heard maddened Tullus. "*Bastardis!* Arrogant bastard!" he bellowed. Then, pointing in the direction of the sound, he shouted, "Hunt the scum down." His band, welcoming the break in tension, yelled in agreement, and charged.

Beacán smiled as he dropped from the tree and set off at a fast lope. He was further away from Tullus' camp than the Roman likely thought and could cover ground at a much quicker pace. Still, it would be a close race to find Brighid and Danu and prepare the band to repulse the attackers.

***

Conall sat on Toirneach. Mounted alongside him were the Sidhe, Mór-rígan, and Íar. Uncomfortable on horseback, Cúscraid, Deaglán, and Fearghal chose to stand. Behind them in a line, bows at the ready, stood Sarpedon's Cretan archers. To their rear were the Thracian heavy cavalry, the remainder of Mórrígan's riders, and Gràinne's chariots.

Bringing up the rear were Conall's two hundred caomhnóirí. The two ranks of veterans were relaxed, allowing space to throw javelins, but would close to form a solid shield-wall as the enemy neared. All gazed with professional eyes and perturbed looks at the army before them. The enemy halted about two hundred paces from the farm's walls—just beyond the limit of an arrow's flight. That at least showed some forethought.

The leader of the Arverni force sat on a tall, chestnut horse. He appeared quite young—no more than sixteen summers, Conall guessed. He had a mop of berry-red hair that framed a milk-pale face covered in a rash of freckles. The gawky youth had yet to come to terms with manhood or his rank as a leader of warriors. Nevertheless, he appeared comfortable on his mount.

His armour, cuirass, and greaves were largely unembellished but clearly were an excellent example of Arverni workmanship. They were also as ill-fitting as the adolescent's demeanour. Conall pointed to him and, speaking to no one in particular, said, "The two burly warriors who flank that young chieftain appear more akin to gaolers than shield-men. Like the bars of a cage designed to ensure there will be no escape."

"I don't like this at all," muttered Fearghal. No one disagreed.

A smiling Conall looked at Mongfhionn and Fearghal. "I think diplo-macy is called for." The look of surprise on the Sidhe's and her partner's faces raised a smirk at the edges of Conall's lips. Conall and Mórrígan were better known for actions that ended in gouts of blood rather than the noble art of negotiation. Íar nodded in approval, Deaglán scratched his head, Cúscraid looked heavenward, and Mórrígan chuckled.

With a soft "Forward" and a nudge of his knees, Conall walked

Toirneach to midway between the forces. In a commanding yet not un-friendly voice, he called out to the leader of the Arverni. "Let us share a meal and discuss our predicament." Conall nodded in the direction of the barn. "There would be a good place for us to determine if there can be a less bloody ending to this day. You have my word that no harm will come to you, and the battle will not commence without you."

A brief scuffle ensued between the young man and his surly shield-men. It ended with him breaking away with a snarl, a shrug of bony shoulders, and a tug on the reins. As he walked his mount towards Conall, the flanking warriors swore and trotted to catch up. The guards protested with renewed vigour, attempting to persuade the Arverni no-ble to fall back. Then, to Conall's anger, they tried to restrain the young chieftain physically.

Close enough to intervene, Conall walked Toirneach forward a few more paces. "Since when have serving dogs had an opinion?" he snapped. "Lay one more finger on your master, and I will have you nailed to the doors of the barn and your guts steaming at your feet."

Head held high and back straight, the youth again moved forward, allowing himself a smirk at his guards' discomfort. In the young man's mind, he did not doubt that the warrior king before him could, and would, carry out the threat. From the alacrity with which the protectors backed their mounts a few paces away, neither did they.

"Why does Celtillos, king of the Arverni, insult me?" asked Conall.

The young man looked puzzled as he chewed on a hunk of bread and cheese and signalled for Conall to continue. "In numbers, we're evenly matched. Given our reputation as fighters, that in itself is a slight. That one Clann Uí Flaithimh warrior is worth ten of any other is not mere gossip."

The young noble took a few deep slurps of cold, creamy milk from a pottery jug and licked his lips. Having no evidence to the contrary, he nodded and resumed his repast.

"Also, even an eejit can see that your army is made up of callow youth and old men and women. I suspect that none have any desire to be here or to fight. Brutes, whose only duty is to cajole them into battle and execute those who hesitate or try to run, guard them."

In the distance, a few short blasts of a Northern Albu hunting horn sang out. Conall smiled. *Carmag must be getting impatient.* The young man frowned.

"I must revise my estimate of numbers. Your force was always out-matched. It is now outnumbered. Leave. There is no disgrace in accept-ing reality. Live. Fight another day when you are older, and the gods fa-vour you." Conall looked with sadness on an adolescent caught on the horns of duty and honour.

Still hoping for a non-violent resolution, with a sweep of his arm Conall indicated the surrounding land and forests. "Walk away. Go with my blessing. My offer is sanctuary in my kingdom, or you can tra-verse the Alpes to the Great Sea. There is plenty of room. Take a part-ner. Have children. Live a long and happy life." Conall gestured to the Arverni horde. "You need not fear this rabble. I will slaughter them to the last man and woman. There will be no witnesses to say that you did not also perish."

The young man shivered at the cold brutality of the statement. A glimmer of freedom, of hope, lighted in the young man's eyes and just as quickly was extinguished. He dropped his head and, with a sigh, replied, "I am the bastard runt of a mighty litter. Likely I am an embarrassment to my father. Why am I here? In truth, I do not know. Celtillos is a cun-ning man who keeps his own counsel. It may be that he simply wishes to eliminate one distant possibility of rebellion." The prince shrugged. "Plus, I'm another thorn to prick you."

The adolescent stood. "Fight you, I must. Die, I probably will. Although the half-son of the king, I will be an outcast and have no place in my tribe if I return with my sword sheathed. I thank you for the offer of sanctuary. Still, I'd rather face a noble enemy and take a spear in the gut than await the ignominy of an assassin's dagger in the back."

Conall stood and grasped the young man's arm. It was a token shared between warriors. "Celtillos is a fool. But so be it. You will die a hero. The rest of the bastards with you I will have staked, alive or dead, along the border between our tribes."

The Arverni prince dipped his head. For a moment, he considered pleading for the lives of his men, but the set of the jaw of the king before him told him that would be futile. With a shake of his head, he took up the reins of his mount and trotted back to his warband. His shield-men snarled at the massed ranks of Conall's warriors as they passed through them. The response was a humiliating round of laughter and mockery.

✴✴✴

"He deserves a king's death." It was Íar who spoke.

"Lend me your sword."

Conall's favoured choice of weapon was an axe, but the long blade of a mounted warrior was much more suitable to the grim task ahead. He gripped the weapon, balancing it in his hand, and urged Toirneach into a fast canter. Mounted on his chestnut mare, the Arverni prince galloped courageously ahead of his band. Not keen to face the Clann Uí Flaithimh warband and perceiving a resolution of their king's unspoken orders, his guards held back. Having no desire to fight, the rest of the Arverni band did likewise.

Prince and king held each other's gaze. It was a brief moment but long enough for the youth to smile and mouth, "Thanks." Conall's sword swept in a high arc parallel to the ground and cleaved the adolescent's head from his shoulders. A bile of rage rose in Conall's gullet, for the Rí Ruirech had come to like the young man, who was not much older than his son, Aodán. Bringing Toirneach to a halt, Conall turned around on his dillat, raised the bloody sword, and roared, "None lives!"

With a great shout of "Ionsaí!" the ranks of Clann Uí Flaithimh charged towards the Arverni. Battles tend to be between evenly matched forces or between an overwhelmingly superior army and a hopeless cause. In the former, the war quickly deteriorates into a prolonged brawl, many injuries, and likely no clear winner. Such was not the circumstance on this day.

The skirmish was bloody, brief, and farcically one-sided. The Arverni guards' plan of deserting the weak and retreating to Arverni lands with their comrades disappeared at the roar from the forest. Caught between Conall's blades and crushing blows from the clubs of Carmag's warband, all but two were slaughtered. With a warped sense of humour or perhaps poetic justice, the Goddess allowed the prince's guards to evade death. Thrown at Conall's feet, they begged for mercy. The lack of compassion in Conall's eyes gave them no hope.

"I made your prince a promise, and I intend to keep it."

A fence was erected long the border between the lands of Clann Ui Flaithimh and the Arverni, a head on each spiked pole. These were the remains of the fortunate. While their demise was not without pain, it had been swift. Now, before the host of dead eyes, two men whimpered pitifully. They screamed themselves hoarse as hard men hammered thick wooden stakes into their arses.

As the posts were dropped into their receiving holes, the juddering thuds prompted the last cry from mouths that seeped blood. In a gush of bone and gore, the sharpened pales exploded from ruined chests. The guards' legs were broken to ensure no respite and no hope. Surprisingly, the method of execution conferred a lingering death. The final end would come from the tearing jaws of predators and the ripping of flesh.

Simmering with rage, Conall turned to Mórrígan. "Have the prince's body and head been found?" The Dark Huntress, her eyes smouldering with the wrath that filled her heart, nodded.

"Make sure he has a funeral pyre fit for a king. Then, take your riders and chariots. Ride to Celtillos' capital, Nemessos. You should be there by meán lae. Show Celtillos that it is not wise to provoke

Clann Ui Flaithimh. When you have delivered our message, meet me at Ráth Cavares."

∗∗∗

Meán lae was not far off when a blood bespattered Beacán, gasping for breath, stumbled into the meadow. Hands on his knees, he fought to control his breathing. Then he glared at what appeared to be the lackadaisical slackness of the camp and the absence of guards. About to roar his anger, he heard a deep, throaty rumble. A pair of wolfhounds stood on either side of him. He looked into their gaping maws. The skin was drawn back, exposing healthy pink gums and rows of sharp teeth. A smell of raw meat came from their throats and drool dripped from their mouths.

Did they really see him as food? He tried to reassure himself. Surely the dogs recognised him, and this was merely a friendly grin. The second growl disabused him of that notion. Holding their eyes, he made to straighten up slowly, but the cold edge of a blade caressed his neck.

"Shame on you, Uncle. You're getting careless. Maybe you're getting too old for this lifestyle. Perhaps you should consider retirement. A small farm with a broad-hipped woman to raise a brood of kids. Maybe tend olive trees and vines and milk docile cows?" There was a smirk in Brighid's voice.

Beacán sensed rather than saw others emerge from cover. The sleeping bodies around the fires remained still. *Dummies stuffed with moss and ferns.* He smiled. He had taught the girls well. "You can remove the knife from my neck, Brighid," Beacán said, standing and turning to face his niece.

Brighid had more of her ma's temperament díont and a wicked sense of humour. The glint in her jade-green eyes held mischief and violence in equal portions. Beacán shivered. The trauma of his and Mórrígan's parents' murders had presaged a very dark period in his sister's life. On the rare occasions that he prayed to the Goddess, his supplication was that Brighid would be spared that path.

Beacán gently swatted the blade aside. "We will have company soon. How are the defences?"

"Just as you instructed. You do realise…" Brighid could not resist adding with a note of disapproval, "that if we had decided to improve on your plan, you likely would have impaled yourself or broken your leg in one of the traps. Dashing into the camp was unwise. Besides, since when do you of all people come crashing into any situation?"

Precluding a retort with a regal sweep of her hand, Brighid continued. "A perimeter of waist-high, sharpened stakes with nettles, thistles, and brambles woven into the fence. In front of that, and for ten paces beyond, calf-high, ankle-breaking holes have been dug. They have, of course, been planted with short, pointed stakes. All are disguised with forest-floor debris. We have a sack of those iron thistles—the ones that Íar detests—but were waiting for instructions as from which direction we can expect trouble before we sow them." Her hands settled on her hips. "Well, old man. How do you want to place your troops?"

Behind the duo, Danu bent double laughing.

✳✳✳

Tullus' men were no athletes. Their profession did not call for the stamina to run long distances. Even less to run and still be able to fight. Their usual mode of action was to ambush defenceless prey in the dark, stab them in the back, and slit their throats. Hence, Tullus was concerned, if not entirely surprised, at the sight of most of his band breathing heavily, retching, and emptying the contents of their stomachs onto the forest floor.

Still, the enforced break gave Tullus time to think. He swore at his unseen enemy and cursed his naivety in blindly accepting the challenge. His temper now under control, the Roman scanned his surroundings. He was reasonably sure the invisible warrior had led them on a merry chase. That goal likely achieved, Tullus deduced that the camp of the Clann Ui Flaithimh warband was close. Tullus' grasp of Beacán's tactics was correct but too late.

Previously hidden by the massive boles of ancient trees, a dozen warriors stepped into view. Before Tullus could bark out orders, three volleys of arrows struck his men. Still heaving and clutching cramped bellies, the lightly armoured band had little time to protect themselves. The iron-tipped, black shafts killed few, however, almost a quarter of his men were injured.

Tullus observed the enemy retreat. It was precise, swift, and orderly and made no attempt to disguise the direction. The warning bells ringing in Tullus' head were interrupted by a piercing whistle. A dozen heavily muscled, rough-haired, grey shapes rose from the forest floor. In less time than it takes to blink, a pack of wolfhounds, many bigger and heavier than a man, were in the midst of Tullus' band. The wounded were the first victims. Forced to the dirt, necks were snapped, faces shredded, and throats torn by strong jaws and razor-sharp incisors.

The speed and brutality of the attack stunned the group. By the time weapons were drawn, the dogs' jaws had claimed more victims. Men shrieked as they were worried by the animals. At the sound of a second whistle from deep in the woods, the beasts snarled as if disappointed, took a few more snaps at exposed flesh, and bounded away. Three hounds lay in the dirt. The number of Tullus' men injured and dead had grown.

Tullus wiped the sweat from his brow and rubbed the stubble on his chin. He had lost half his already depleted fighting force and technically had yet to engage the enemy. By his reckoning, if he counted the hounds, the Clann Uí Flaithimh warband had superior and healthier numbers. Roman pragmatism and self-preservation came to the fore.

"Withdraw!"

The politest response stated into which orifice Tullus should insert his sword. Enraged thugs make poor choices. Suddenly, they had a mission—to avenge their brothers-in-arms, ironically the same comrades whose throats they would have cut for the price of a whore.

With a crescendo of cursing and abuse, the mob stormed the Clann

Ui Flaithimh camp. Tullus shook his head, slowed his pace, and let the band charge past him. He snorted. These were not warriors drilled in battle tactics. True, many were former Roman soldiers, but that was long in their past. Most had been dishonourably discharged from the army, not an easy accomplishment. All they knew was the thuggery of back alleys. Forgotten was how they had struggled against small farm holdings defended by men, women, and children armed with spears, sticks, and stones.

Often in skirmishes, serendipity and unhappy circumstances, rather than battle skills, choose the course. The thug ran towards the picket fence. His only protection a shield of spit sprayed from a mouth of sparsely populated decaying teeth, most of which were loosely connected to black and bleeding gums. The rancid stench of his unwashed body and clothes reached the barrier well before he did. In one hand, he gripped a throwing axe.

If he had a target, it was unclear. His arm rose up and backwards and was about to flip forward when he stepped into a trap. He wailed as he heard and then felt his left leg snap just above the shinbone. The pitch and loudness of his shrieking increased as a fistful of sharpened sticks skewered his foot. Off-balance, and yet with some momentum, the brute released the small axe. Its rotation was the perfect distance for a killing strike.

At the precise moment the axe left the thrower's hand, Danu chose to adjust her grip on the small shield. Her chest was exposed if only for the time it took to sneeze. But that was enough. The axe thudded into her boiled-leather breastplate, brushed it aside, and cut into her chest. Eyes wide, she dropped shield and spear and fell to her knees. In shock, Danu felt little pain. Paradoxically, it was her twin, Brighid, who cried out in sympathetic agony. Both sisters were grabbed under their armpits by muscled arms and unceremoniously dragged from the battle.

Unhurt, Brighid shook off her trauma and her guards and ran to Beacán. He turned around as one of Danu's shield-men stood. He held

up a bloody hand. Beacán howled. Alongside him, the wolfhounds followed his lead, and then the warband. All, man and beast, turned to face
their enemy. Mercy was not found in any of their eyes.

"Shit," muttered Tullus.

It appeared that, by chance, he had accomplished one of Marcus'
tasks—the murder of one of Conall's children. However, surviving
the onslaught of warriors and hounds berserk with rage and looking to
avenge the princess was a tenuous proposition. Furthermore, Tullus had
strong suspicions that there were other Clann Ui Flaithimh warbands in
the forest. Without a doubt, the shrill blasts of hunting horns were to
summon them.

It was a simple and sensible, if ignoble, decision to abandon his
men and run. Sword in hand, Tullus crashed blindly through the forest.
The dense canopy above was of no help in assessing his direction. He
prayed that he was travelling north and east, away from the slaughter. His
intended destination was one of his hidden caches of gold. With that,
he could bribe a local tribe or warband to guide him over the Alpes and
thence to Rome.

It was the simplest of snares. A hemp line hung at chest height between several trees. Perhaps if Tullus had regarded the forest floor less
and the canopy more, he would have spotted the rope. Instead, he ran
slouched, and the taut cord caught him on the chest. The cable whipped
upwards, catching him under the chin. Fortunately, his pace was not such
that he chanced a broken neck or even decapitation. Instead, flipped upwards and backwards, Tullus landed with a thud that knocked the breath
from him. The burning sensation from the abrasions on his neck was
brief, replaced with a sharp blow to his head and blackness.

✳✳✳

In the clearing, the skirmish was short and brutal. Shocked by the attack
on Danu, Beacán's band were left rudderless for a short time. Sensing
an advantage, Tullus' miscreants and mercenaries hurdled the waist-high
fence. This proved to be their undoing. Beacán shouted, "Form up!

Scíatha and spears. Face the bastards. Avenge Danu!" The discipline of the Clann Uí Flaithimh warriors was ingrained by training and by battle, for each one was a shield-wall veteran. Two ranks quickly formed and advanced on the charging mob. Alongside, the great wolfhounds rose and bounded into the affray.

Snapping jaws and spears that stabbed high and low drove the attackers backwards until the palisade halted their retreat. With their backs to the fence, most were slaughtered by an enemy who gave no quarter. Any who succeeded in overcoming the gore-covered stockade were hamstrung by Beacán's knives or fell victim to the numerous traps.

Steeling themselves for the worst and covered in blood, Beacán and Brighid returned to Danu's prone body. Her guards looked up, tears streamed down dirt-ingrained faces for Danu was well-liked. Embedded in her chest, the shaft of the throwing axe trembled, giving a faint ray of hope that the bean-sidhe had not called Danu's name. Beacán knew the axe-head needed to be removed, but doing so could prompt a gush of blood, and that could signal the end of Danu. At a good pace, Ráth Cavares was still a day's journey away. The omens were not good.

"Get me moss, honey, and a wad of woollen cloth. The axe needs to be pulled from the wound and the breastplate removed. Then, the wound should be cleaned and dressed."

"No! You'll kill her!" shouted Brighid. The princess stood, straddled her sister, and hefted a bloody spear and shield.

"Move out of my way," snapped Beacán. "If we don't do anything, the bean-sidhe will take her. Is that what you want?" Brighid shook her head. Beacán looked around. "We have no cart. Fetch brata. Cut long poles. Make a carrying litter."

Beacán knelt beside Danu and inhaled deeply. "Hold her down." He looked at Brighid. "*You* will apply the moss and strapping." Brighid screamed as the axe-head was pulled from her sister, for she felt the pain that unconsciousness mercifully spared her twin.

***

Mongfhionn cried out and gripped Conall's arm with enough strength to make him wince. "Ride hard for Ráth Cavares." The terror in the Sidhe's eyes alarmed Conall and Fearghal. Conall opened his mouth to query the reason, but a milk-pale hand forestalled any discussion. "Ride! You are needed at the fort."

The small group of riders set off, accompanied by a guard of ten from Conall's caomhnóirí. Unmounted, the rest of the band followed at a fast lope.

Before they had settled into a gallop, a hand reached out and grasped Mongfhionn's reins. Fearghal gazed into his partner's obsidian eyes. She looked at him and whispered, "Danu," before looking with anger at the skies.

"Shite!"

Further words were unnecessary. Both knew Conall and Mórrígan trod a very narrow path between darkness and light. The tipping point was never far off. Storm clouds and a darkening sky added weight to the dire omens.

* * *

Midway to the Arverni hillfort at Nemessos, Mórrígan screeched, "No!" and tumbled from her mount. The pale golden mare stood resolutely as her mistress pounded the dirt with blood-stained hands. Amodocus, Gràinne, and Sarpedon quickly dismounted and ran to the Dark Huntress. All were driven back by the look of savagery in the queen's eyes. Such had not been seen for many summers.

The dark, curling sigils on Mórrígan's face throbbed, reflecting her wrath. With a snarl, Mórrígan, queen of Clann Ui Flaithimh, tore off her garments, flung them and her chainmail aside, and leapt back onto her horse. From her body radiated a miasma of dark power. Mórrígan surveyed her company as if they were unknown to her with eyes reflecting only death and wrath. All who she looked upon shivered.

"We show no mercy. We kill every living thing between here and Nemessos. Then we ride hard for Ráth Cavares."

CHAPTER 10

Battle-scarred hands gripped the wooden palisade as Torcán Ó Dubhghaill looked to the north. Typically brash and optimistic, today the veteran warrior wore a rare mask of solemnity. The strawberry mark on his throat burned, pulsating in time to his heartbeat. Bequeathed to him by the Sidhe, the blemish had always been a warning—a portent of unpleasant consequences. The long scar that tracked down his chest to his manhood gave periodic spikes of pain in sympathy. Lugnasad drew near, but the celebrations this season would be marked by tragedy.

Conall was aware of Urard's struggle. Given the severity of the wounds, the king would be saddened but not surprised if the warrior passed beyond the veil. It was, however, improbable that he knew his daughter, attended by a clutch of druid healers, lay still and silent in a cot next to Urard. That the Roman scoundrel responsible was in chains and a dozen of his band bound to stakes in the main square would be scant solace to Conall or Mórrígan. Torcán shivered at the thought of the Dark Huntress. With her powers, he would not wager against her, having sensed Danu's plight.

A trickle of reports had reached Torcán. They told of the slaughter of the Arverni and the pillaging of settlements and farms, even to the gates of Nemessos. In retaliation, Celtillos, the verrix of the Arverni, ordered raids on the trade routes that used the Rodonos. The smoking hulks of biremes and their cargoes littered the banks of the great river.

Beside them lay the mutilated bodies of merchants, sailors, and slaves. Yet, Celtillos could not over-indulge his chieftains' thirst for retribution. The Arverni profited from the trade routes of the Rodonos. Hence, it was not in Celtillos' interest to have a prolonged interruption of trade. Neither was he in a position to provoke a war with Conall.

Mórrígan's riders cut a bloody swathe through Arverni lands as they rode hard for Ráth Cavares. Her anger burned fiercely, and the rural population between Nemessos and the hillfort suffered her wrath. Curling trails of smoke and the cries of the bereaved rose from farms and settlements. They demanded vengeance from Celtillos and the gods to whom they sacrificed. They were disappointed by both.

The Hag help those who cross her path. Another groan escaped Torcán. Where did the Sidhe stand? Why had she allowed this to happen? Did it matter? Were, as many suspected, the powers of Mórrígan and Gràinne now superior to the Sidhe's? From the vantage of the stronghold, Torcán watched Conall and Mórrígan's bands converge as they drew nearer to the ráth. The future Torcán saw was of blood and war.

"The storm clouds are gathering."

Torcán instinctively looked upwards. The blue summer sky was now a dark and threatening purple. He nodded.

"If you want, I can tell him. Family and all that." Sharp features and a wiry build belied the strength within the battle veteran and brother of Mórrígan. The bullish Torcán shook his head.

"Thanks, Brocc. But we should do it together."

Brocc dipped his head and unexpectedly exclaimed, "Shite!" He pointed to a black-sailed bireme, tying off at the jetty that sat at the foot of the cliffs. A small, black-haired man leapt from the boat, turned, and waved to the men. "Pytheas. What next? The poor man will have no idea of the maelstrom he's walking into."

"At least he's alone and not accompanied by the other two members of Massalia's triumvirate. They give me the willies. They wear fancy clothes and speak politely, but at heart, they remain peddlers of flesh.

I've lost count of the number of times they've made an offer for Mòrag. Although, you can understand why."

Torcán smirked and held up his hands as if balancing two heavy weights. Brocc rolled his eyes. Then his face broke out in a huge smile. His friend looked at him strangely as an awful realisation struck. "She's behind me, isn't she?" Torcán, the brawler of Clann Ui Flaithimh, squealed as his arse was pinched bruisingly hard and then slapped by a hand that held the strength of iron.

"And who is to say that your cute, firm arse hasn't a value in gold? The Greeks—and others, I hear—have a penchant for what hangs between your legs. Perhaps I should reconsider the offers *I* have received." Torcán blushed, and the blemish on his throat burned. He offered little resistance as Mòrag took his arm and led him from the walkway. "We will talk more of this later, but first, let us greet Pytheas."

Brocc laughed. The scene was welcome levity. Like Torcán, he foresaw little joy in the near future. The Rí—for indeed he and Torcán had earned the title through battle, wealth, and lands—pushed strands of red-auburn hair from his face. There was always a breeze on the fort's ramparts.

A cough made him turn around, and a stinging slap caused him to swear. His partner Bláithín Ni Néill's lithe shape belied her strength. The weight behind the smack left angry fingerprints on a beardless cheek.

Bláithín mimicked Torcán's hand actions. "What? You had no defence for your partner's tits? No stories of how much gold you have been offered for me. Am I so unattractive—even as a slave? Would no prince or king from the nations around the Great Sea wish to mount and rut me?"

It was one of those occasions when Brocc, unsure as to his handfast partner's mood, decided prudence was the least dangerous option and pulled Bláithín into his arms. Her breath exhaled rapidly. Brocc had a deceptively strong grip and held her in an iron trap.

"I was simply protecting my partner's modesty. The Spartan peplos you like to wear shows quite a lot of flesh, and in a certain light, the linen is almost transparent. Not that I'm objecting," he hastily added. "As you walk the parapet in the sunlight, however, most of the ráth has a better view of my wanton partner's body than I." Brocc's hands slipped down and squeezed Bláithín's buttocks. The inference was obvious.

Bláithín blushed at the questioning of her modesty and then chuckled. The Ériu noble placed a butterfly kiss on Brocc's lips and then took a pace back. "Live with frustration. We have a guest to entertain."

"Later?"

"Maybe."

***

"The Hag's hairy arse!"

Everyone gawked at Gràinne. She looked at the Sidhe, blurted a quick, "Sorry, nothing personal," and pointed to Danu. "The girl's as naked as the day she was birthed! Is nae-one concerned about her modesty?" This from a Cinn Péinteáilte warrior whose only attire was a ribbon of cloth across her hips—and that only in winter—which failed to fully cover her auburn triangle. Then she directed their attention to Urard. "And so is he. Even in his present state, his manhood is impressive—but do we need it to be on show?" She looked around and quickly trapped the druids in her gaze. "Perverts!"

Loud protestations were made of the need for air to circulate and aid the healing of the wounds. "The wound is between the princess' tits, not her thighs." Gràinne turned about and pointed to Bláithín. "Get some of that cloth the Lady Bláithín is wearing. It's so light ye could spit through it. But at least it'll afford some modest cover."

Bláithín, now the focus of many eyes, felt entirely undressed and blushed. Perhaps her liking of Greek fashion had gone too far. Beside her, Brocc chuckled. It was the only relief in a sombre day.

***

The silence was awful, broken only by the sobs of the watchers and the soft splash of tears on the wooden floor. Fists clenched and unclenched;

back teeth ground on each other as jaws set and unset; anger simmered, demanding release. Inevitably, the bubbling and conflicting emotions would unite in rage, and that wrath would insist on the spilling of blood.

Conall's arms surrounded Mórrígan and Brighid. Each drew strength from the others as they knelt beside Danu's cot. The pain in Brighid's chest was a constant throb. Yet, she clung to this as proof that her twin fought for life. The younger of the twins tried to pray but found no love for the Goddess in her heart and no sacrifice she wished to make to gain favour. She looked into her parents' red-rimmed eyes and saw the same emptiness.

Iasg squatted by Urard and rocked back and forward. It seemed that, even in the short time since the battle with the bear, her partner's strength had diminished. His face held a greyish-yellow pallor instead of its usual vibrant ruddiness. She gripped cold, wax-like hands as if trying to impart warmth to them. Iasg prayed but to the old sea gods of her father and his father. Beside her stood Beacán, giving silent comfort, something Conall would ponder later.

There was no one else in the chamber apart from several druid healers, the Sidhe, and Fearghal. The stalwart warrior's shoulder-length hair seemed to have gained a preponderance of steel-grey over red. Steady, scarred hands gripped his partner's, as much to gain strength as to impart it.

Mongfhionn's demeanour gave little away. Yet inside, the Sidhe was stricken and her emotions in turmoil. Why had the Goddess and the Aes Sidhe kept Danu's plight hidden until it was too late for her to intervene? She chose to stand a respectful distance away, unsure if she was wanted. Yet, had she asked, the Sidhe instinctively knew the answer would not have been to her liking. A reckoning was fast approaching.

***

Held only by the delicate gossamers of their loved ones' prayers, the spirits stood alongside their bodies. Each looked with sadness on the broken flesh that was their home. Only the unsteady rise and fall of wounded chests bore witness to the faint flicker of life that remained. A decision had to be made, for, in the shadows, a single bean-sidhe waited. The spirit that was Urard looked at his young ward and smiled.

He growled at death's herald, "I am her protector. My life for hers."

The creature nodded and opened its mouth. Danu's hand rose in protest. The herald paused. In her heart, Danu knew that Urard would not be argued with, and so she whispered a simple, "Thanks, my friend." Urard smiled. The bean-sidhe shrieked, and Urard's life-chain was severed.

Beside his cot, only the strong arms of Beacán kept Iasg from collapsing to the floor. He could not prevent the deluge of hot tears and the long wail of "No!" which tore open the hearts of those who stood watch.

"He is already in Mag Mell. He is whole and well. Free forever of ills and worries." In the half-gloom between consciousness and insensibility, Danu observed the deity she knew only as the Goddess.

The young woman finally snapped. "He is not!" With all the contempt that a spirit could gather, Danu snarled, "What of Iasg, his handfast partner, his sons, and those who loved him? What of those who will die in battle because he is not at his place? What of my father, deprived of Urard's protection?" In a soft but no less bitter voice, Danu spoke again: "Of what use are you, Goddess? He deserved better than this." The Goddess fled from the room, recoiling from the venom that pierced her like an arrow.

Danu coughed, inhaled painfully, and opened her eyes. "Urard," she whispered.

✶✶✶

The funeral pyre of Urard, hero of Clann Ui Flaithimh, roared high into the night sky. That evening, it was the tallest and brightest of the Lugnasad bonfires, scorching the earth black in a wide circle around it. The garrison of Ráth Cavares, arrayed in full armour, stood at attention around the fire. But only those closest to Urard braved the fierce heat radiating from the furnace to stand on the charred ground. Skin blistered and hungry tongues of flame singed hair, but none fled their place. None would break their vigil.

Dawn's light broke on the horizon as the smouldering pyre finally collapsed. Slowly, like the trails of smoke, the crowd around the fire drifted away. Later, at sunset, they would drink copiously to the memory of Urard the Warrior and sing many epic tales of his life. He had departed, but they had to fight another day.

Deep in his own memories, Conall started at the slight figure who appeared before him. He smiled, but it was a sad, weary smile.

"He would have wanted his king to have this." Iasg lifted up the great axe Breith with her tiny hands. Her muscles trembled at the weight of the weapon.

Tears wet a path down Conall's smoke-stained cheek. He shook his head as he took the axe. "No. This is not for me. It will hang in a place of honour behind my throne until one of his sons petitions me for it."

At the mention of her sons, Iasg broke into racking sobs. From the shadows, Beacán stepped forward to add his strength to hers.

"How will I tell my sons that their father has gone? They had no chance to say goodbye."

Conall opened his arms and held her close to him, feeling the wetness of her tears soak his tunic. "You will not tell them alone. I will be with you, as will Mórrigan, Danu, Brighid, Aodán..." He paused briefly. "And Beacán. We are your family. You will live with us in Dún-an-Rí and lack for nothing."

Iasg snuffled and wiped the back of her hand across her face. "Except for Urard... except for Urard," she sighed.

***

Uncharacteristically nervous, the Sidhe paced the long hallway. Inhaling deeply, she straightened slender shoulders. Finally, oak staff in hand, she flung open the double doors. Iron hinges squealed in protest, and splinters of wood flew as the doors slammed against the inner walls.

Framed in the entrance, a halo of dust formed around the grey-cloaked figure. As the force of nature strode to the platform, she gathered more strength with each step.

The members of the Chomhairle looked up from their discussions and then rose to stand behind Conall and Mórrígan. The Dark Huntress stood and scowled at the Sidhe. Mongfhionn flinched under the unrelenting emerald gaze momentarily. She scanned the faces of those present and breathed a sigh of relief. Fearghal was not among the group. At least she did not have to deal with a schism in her own household.

"I apologise for my tardiness. I was not informed of this meeting."

"You were not invited." Conall's tone was curt. While understated, it retained authority. The king's shoulders were hunched as if he bore a great weight. His eyes were sunk in dark circles from a lack of sleep.

"I represent the Goddess and the Aes Sidhe."

"Neither the Goddess nor the Aes Sidhe is part of this conversation. It is debatable whether they may ever be."

Visibly shaken, Mongfhionn gripped her staff for strength and summoned authority to her. "The Goddess raised you from an apprentice blacksmith to Rí Ruirech of Clann Ui Flaithimh. You have sworn a geis to her servants, the Aes Sidhe."

"At what cost, Lady? My parents and sisters foully murdered. My friends and their families massacred. Thousands of dead from war and plague. And all to do what—populate the halls of Tír Tairngire and Mag Mell? The Aes Sidhe, or perhaps just one—*you*—connived with the Goddess to set me on the path of blood. My son, Tuathal, is dead. My daughter, *your* charge, lies stricken. There is a great chasm between your understanding of care and protection and mine. Unlike Urard, you have failed in your duty. Your geis is as dross."

Mongfhionn opened her mouth. Whether to protest, argue, or concede remained unknown as a raised hand from Conall stopped her words. "As for the geis. My honour would never have allowed me to leave it unfulfilled. How dare you question it, Lady? Does the Goddess, do you, reckon me so poorly—and so ill-advisedly?"

Conall briefly sagged in the wooden throne before straightening his spine. His voice took on a chilling tenor. "I will give you rivers of blood. I will give you the dead and the crippled. After that, I never wish to see you again, and Clann Ui Flaithimh will choose a new god to worship."

I did not know, screamed the voice inside Mongfhionn's head. *I did not know.* Only a startled Mórrígan heard the cry.

Yet sadly, much as the predators in the forests, Mongfhionn was a victim of her nature. Admonished before the assembly, anger flared in the Sidhe's cheeks. Her heart pounded in her chest. Obsidian eyes promised death. There could only be one response. Instinctually, she drew herself up, staff at the ready, intending to strike down all before her.

Yet before the Sidhe, An Fiagaí Dorcha stood radiating a power that Mongfhionn knew rivalled her own. "That would not be a prudent path to take, Lady," she said. "It would surely prove fatal to many present and possibly yourself. I heard your pain. Stand down. Passions are inflamed. Blood boils. Emotions run high. Walk from this room. Rest your spirit."

"You."

"Your Goddess betrayed you as she did me, Conall, Danu, and many others. Yet perhaps even she is deceived. I am more than An Fiagaí Dorcha. If not your superior, then certainly I am your equal. Walk away. Even now, in these terrible days, I would not see you harmed or banished."

Mórrígan looked at Conall and smiled. "And, in his heart, neither would Conall."

CHAPTER 11

396 B.C.—Ráth Cavares

Tullus squatted, naked, on the dirt floor. The cell was small, with each wall only about five paces long. It was unfurnished but otherwise dry and reasonably clean. Apart from an open window and cracks around the sturdy door, the room afforded good protection from the elements. Given that it was summer, the breezes flowing through the smaller opening ameliorated the build-up of an uncomfortable level of heat. The chamber smelled of earth and wood with overtones of piss and shite. Regularly, at sunrise, the clay waste pot that sat in one corner was taken away, emptied, and returned. Tullus thought his hosts remarkably considerate.

Nakedness was not an issue for the Roman. The army knocked all sense of personal modesty from its members. Besides, it allowed him to pass the time by examining the myriad, multi-coloured contusions that painted his well-sculpted body. The bruises had been administered systematically and with relish by his captors on the journey to Ráth Cavares. Nevertheless, apart from a few cracked ribs, he thought no major bones were broken. On balance, his condition was no worse, and probably better, than a barbarian prisoner could expect under Roman supervision.

A half-eaten morning meal of porridge, lumps of stale bread, and cheese sat beside him on a grease-stained wooden platter. Clay jugs of milk and water rested nearby. He would consume and drink the rest later. A good soldier never wasted food, and eating helped break the monotony of his confinement. Five sunsets had passed since his capture. During this time, Tullus had considered and dismissed various options for escape. He had no weapons, apart from shards of the pottery jugs if he smashed them. His guards, two tall, burly warriors, occasionally encouraged him to attempt to break out. Apparently, there were wagers on how far he would get and what injuries he would sustain in the meaningless attempt. Tullus gave no thought to the well-being of his band. After all, he was Roman and they mere tools.

The door's unlocking bar squealed as it scraped over iron brackets. Two figures stepped inside the room. Tullus stood, stretched, and squinted in the half-light of early dawn. His movement was not due to any sense of propriety or intimidation. He just wanted a better view of his visitors.

The man wore a thigh-length, crimson tunic gathered at the waist with a tied, woven leather belt. Slightly above average height, he was muscular yet lean. Hair, held in three thick plaits, fell over his shoulders. His arms were covered in the dark, curling tattoos often favoured by Celtic warriors and banded by numerous copper, silver, and gold armlets. On his right temple perched a small, dark sigil that seemed to vibrate in sympathy with those of his partner.

Tullus shivered as his eyes were drawn from the cold, grey-blue eyes of the man to the pitiless depths of the woman's. Taller, though not by much, she was a striking and beautiful woman of about thirty summers. Long tresses of red hair graced her head, hanging free over pale shoulders. A loose, white léine, pinned at the shoulders, briefly paused at firm, ample breasts before cascading to hover over bare feet.

The curling sigils covering the woman's feet swirled upwards like a waterfall defying the laws of nature. Even in the gloomy room, it was evident that the dark, almost black designs swathed body and face. It was equally manifest that they appeared to have a life of their own—a molten river of darkness. It was when he looked into Mórrígan's eyes that Tullus experienced real fear. The Roman felt his will invaded and urged to submit to the woman's dark control. He fought desperately to retain his ability to think clearly and keep his sanity.

"Witch!" Tullus gasped.

"You are not that fortunate, Roman," came the menacing reply.

"No weapons? You take a risk."

"I could kill you with a thought and send your spirit screaming to Tartarus, Roman," the woman said, and in Tullus' head, a spike of pain took his breath away. A compelling demonstration of what should have been a nonsensical claim.

"You slaughtered our people. Worse, you raped and mutilated them, men, women, and children, even when dead." Conall's voice was cold and implacable. He tossed a pouch onto the dirt floor. Small coins burst from the bag. "You even boasted of your deeds. You almost succeeded in killing my… our daughter. Although the bean-sidhe passed her by, she still lies gravely wounded in her cot."

Tullus exhaled. All this and no result. Who protected Conall and his family?

A fist of iron crushing his heart followed the pain in Tullus' head. It reminded him of his earlier nightmares, but the touch was different. He breathed hard. How many witches protected Conall? A bead of sweat rolled slowly down his forehead and travelled the ridge of his aquiline nose. It paused for an agonising moment to navigate the curve of the once-broken nares before splashing to the floor. With perfect timing, another bead formed on his brow.

"It was an accident. The idiot stumbled into one of your traps. You will get no information from me." The latter the Roman spoke with an assuredness not entirely accepted by his senses.

"We do not need anything from you… except for your life, and that will be taken slowly and painfully. There will be no mercy," said Conall.

"The path of retribution is a bloody and tragic one, Conall, King of Clann Uí Flaithimh. Have you considered that you're doing exactly what Marcus wants?"

"Has *he* measured that my vengeance will be bloody and the worst of outcomes for him and Rome?" Tullus shrugged, yet Conall held Tullus' gaze. "Your employer should have left us alone, in peace and the Alpes between us. Instead, he chose once again to stoke the flames of my wrath. He will not be disappointed." Conall turned to Mórrígan. "I have seen enough. We should go."

"Make peace with your gods," Mórrígan counselled.

"I never found them to be much good in the past. Why should I ask the gods favour now?" A dagger of pain stabbed deep into the Roman's heart. He stumbled to his knees, fighting for breath.

"Because you've never tasted *my* vengeance, Roman."

✳✳✳

Sacrifices require attention to ceremony, timing, and an imposing setting. Executions—not so much. Sunrise is too optimistic, sunset too poetic, and meán lae is too hot. Strictly speaking, the Fénechas, the Law of the Gaels, did not favour the death penalty. Its desire was confession, penance, and restitution—the payment of an eiric to the wronged party. However, there were ways around that lofty ideal.

Conall and Mórrígan demanded blood, and none in Ráth Cavares or Clann Ui Flaithimh would object or stand in their way. Thus, the question was not whether the captives' fate was death, but by what method and for how long they would suffer. In the past, Urard's great axe meted out justice swiftly and with unsubtle finality. But that was a warrior's death, and neither Tullus nor his men were deemed worthy of that description.

When the Celts required something more painful and prolonged, they often turned to the staking of their enemies. The method inflicted massive trauma on the recipients but left them with sufficient time to contemplate their crimes. Usually performed in open areas, the final despatch was delivered by the jaws of four-legged predators and the beaks of ravens. Those awaiting death could take some consolation that the Persian method of crucifixion while gaining favour in Rome had not yet crossed the Alpes.

Then there was the Sidhe. When lingering death, unimaginable pain, and gouts of blood were called for, Mongfhionn and her curved sacrificial knives were usually at the head of the queue. However, gossip and rumour circulating Ráth Cavares since Danu's injury and Urard's death suggested that Conall and Mórrígan had broken with the dreaded demi-goddess.

The people of Clann Ui Flaithimh were thankful for the Sidhe's assistance in their many battles and trials. Yet they were never entirely comfortable with the paradox of her ageless beauty and the awful nature and love of blood of her alter ego—the Hag. Thus, if it came to a choice between Conall and the Sidhe, the tribe would be nervous about the inevitability of the Lady's wrath. Still, there would be little doubt whose side the clann would take.

Lightning flashed behind glowering charcoal clouds. Peals of thunder broke the ominous silence. Massive drops of rain sporadically splashed the fort's timbers. It was mid-morning, yet the night was reluctant to accede to the sun. Around the ráth, braziers burned brightly, their flickering flames denying the gloom. Silent or speaking in hushed tones, the people and army of Ráth Cavares gathered on the ramparts' wooden walkways. There were no young children. They had wisely been banned from the proceedings.

Ráth Cavares was built around a central square. In peaceful times, this quadrangle was a bustling marketplace or a place of entertainment. The fort's Great Hall and the only stone building, bordered one side. Its massive oak doors faced east and the rising sun. On this day, thirteen men, stripped of clothing, stood in chains. Behind them were thirteen stakes, driven deep into the dirt, all about a hand's width in diameter. A half-spear's length of each, save the thirteenth, remained above the surface. The final stake was taller by an arm's length, and it stood five paces before the others. Hardened by fire, the exposed sharpened points set a portentous tone. Platforms of rough wood sat behind the stakes. Escape was impossible.

Conall and Mórrígan exited the hall and stood at the head of the broad, tight stone steps that descended to the square. Both were in full armour, though Mórrígan's protection was dark and arcane. She was naked apart from her tattoos. Beside her stood Gràinne, equally naked and painted.

Gràinne Ni Fearghal was clearly ill at ease. The scene unfolding evoked terrifying memories of her heritage and the blood-rites of the Na Daoine Tùrsach priests of Northern Albu. The Tùrsach was a tribe of priest-kings and queens, of which she remained a reluctant ruler. Gràinne had become resigned to an imminent return to her native land. Her daughter Brianag Ni Brion was curious about her heritage and her father, Brion, king of Na Mèadaidh. Brion was a good man, and they deserved to spend time with each other. For her part, Gràinne needed to confront the demons of her past.

Behind this trio stood the Chomhairle—all except the Sidhe and Fearghal. The Council stood grim-faced, but all were in lockstep with the Rí Ruirech. Whatever punishment Conall had settled upon was deserved.

"Murderers, rapists, thieves!" called out Conall. His words echoed off the walls of Ráth Cavares and instantly taken up as a chant by the people. "Your agony will be long, but I will not prolong its start with a long speech." At that, Conall nodded to Amodocus.

Amodocus bowed and snapped an order to his men. Burly warriors ran to each of the prisoners, save Tullus. Chains were unlocked, and the men were dragged, kicking and screaming, to the stakes. With ruthless efficiency, the captives were hauled up the plinth steps, lifted up, and dropped onto the stakes. Shrieks of agony sounded out as the sharpened stakes penetrated anuses.

The first arm's length of wood ripped through soft flesh with relative ease. Blood gushed, pooling in the dirt. As if the gods decided this would be too quick, the momentum through their torsos slowed. Screams turned to hoarse whimpers for mercy. Instead, the Thracians, gripping heavy maces, broke each of the staked's legs. There was no compassion on this day, and the stakes continued their inexorable path of destruction and torment.

Tullus had little sympathy for the men. That said, he was curious about the remaining stake that stood alone at the centre of the square. His death was inevitable. Only the precise manner was uncertain. He turned to face his judges and executioners in time to see Conall nod to his daughter. Brighid stepped forward, slowly descended the steps, and walked to stand before the Roman.

Expecting a knife blade, Tullus braced himself. Instead, the young woman spoke in a voice devoid of pity. "Look into my eyes, Roman. Remember them in Tartarus." Fury and darkness smouldered in the bottomless emerald pools. Tullus shuddered.

"Do not take this path, child. It will leave deep scars and is a difficult one to retrace. Give this responsibility to another."

"*Do mo dheirfiúr*—this is for my sister!" Ignoring Tullus' counsel, Brighid stepped back and nodded to Amodocus.

Tullus shrugged away his guards and walked to the steps of the platform. To resist would have been a futile and painful action. While strength remained, there was hope. It was a laudable thought yet quickly shattered as he was lifted and lowered onto the sharpened wood. He cried out, "*Irrumatores!*" as the wood ploughed a path through his flesh. Yet, amid his agony, he found it impossible to divert his eyes from Brighid's face. Her awful smile portended that his suffering was not complete.

Through a mist of shock and terrible pain, he observed the Thracians bring clay amphorae close. Once more, they mounted steps now splashed crimson with his blood. The sharp smell from the vessels struck a note in his memory.

He gasped, "No!" before being drenched in a viscous liquid. Some flowed into his mouth before he clamped his teeth shut. Pitch, resin, and sand clung to his flesh. He tried to keep his eyelids closed, but the quicklime burned through the fragile membrane. He thrashed and screamed as his eyes burst, feeding the hunger of the chemical. Another smell, that of burning flesh, assaulted his nostrils. There was no escaping the lapping flames that sought to consume him. In his agony, Tullus laughed. It was a peculiarly Roman punishment.

The human torch that was Tullus of Rome burned brightly. His screams ended when the flammable mix took his tongue. His torment continued for much longer. His final memory was of the beautiful eyes and ghoulish smile of Brighid. He thought it a great pity in one so young.

***

Secluded in a corner of the ramparts, Fearghal and the Sidhe watched. Clann Ui Flaithimh's battle commander shook his head and wondered where this would all lead. He winced as sharp nails dug deep into the flesh on his arm. He turned to face his partner as she cried, "No!" and clutched the black ribbon around her throat.

The words of Brighid, "*Do mo dheirfiúr*," rang in the Sidhe's ears. They were the exact words Mongfhionn had spoken when she sacrificed and ripped the heart from Spurius Sulpicia Longus after the battle for Ráth Na Conall. They were the words of her dreams when she envisioned the killing of Marcus and his sons.

"Like her mother, she is in danger, Fearghal. I must speak with her." Mongfhionn's partner nodded.

CHAPTER 12

396 B.C.—Ráth Cavares

Like the wings of a great black crow, Crum Dubh's cloak spread and flapped behind him as he galloped through the entrance of Ráth Cavares. The frantic shouts of the guards to stop and identify himself were ignored.

A strong pair of hands and an authoritative "Whoaaa!" brought the druid's sweat-lathered mount to a stop. Oblivious to Torcán's presence, Crum swept a leg over the blue dillat, planted both feet on the ground, and scratched his arse to relieve the numbness of a bruising ride. When he turned, the sharp point of a dagger pricked his Adam's apple. He flinched, impaling himself on the blade and a drop of blood trickled lazily to disappear under the collar of his ankle-length tunic.

"My guards have a duty to stop and verify all who enter this fort. Your actions will see these men and women flogged for not following orders. That will be on your conscience, Druid. See that you make amends."

Torcán paused and pushed the dagger point deeper, eliciting a gasp of pain. "Next time, instead of the skin off their backs, I will take your head, and the Druidic Councils will need a new leader."

With a snarl, Crum turned about and faced the Great Hall. A vice-like grip on his shoulder halted him. "See to your horse. It has been ridden hard and needs to be walked and watered. And you have made no friends who would share the duty."

***

Finally free of his chores and breathing less harshly, Crum was aware that he smelled of sweat, horse piss, and shite. He was also mindful of the guards who followed him. The doors of the Great Hall were thrown open as he reached them and he was knocked aside by a distraught Sidhe. A scowl, anchored by deep frown lines, settled on his gaunt face.

"What on earth is going on?" Crum muttered as he picked himself up, brushed dirt from his cloak, and crossed the entrance.

Crum coughed to clear his throat and announce his presence. He stood before a long, oak table smoothed with age and stained with use. Facing him were Conall, Mórrígan, and Brighid. The latter looked flushed and distinctly nonplussed. Her parents seemed less angry than concerned. Seated on either side were the members of the Chomhairle present in the fort, excluding Fearghal and the Sidhe. The Council appeared embarrassed as if having intruded in a family meeting. Plainly, things were not well within Ráth Cavares.

A flourish of a hand from Conall indicated a jug on the table. Crum took a welcome sip of the spring water, savouring its coldness after the long ride. After bowing to Conall and having re-established control over his body, Crum's sour façade relaxed. He looked to Torcán. "My apologies for my unwarranted behaviour. If punishment has not been administered, I would plead for mercy for the guards or present myself as an alternative." Torcán smiled and nodded back. His estimation of the druid had risen.

"To say that I am sorry about Danu is true but pitifully inadequate. I will make sacrifices for her speedy and full recovery. With your permission, I will visit with her after this meeting."

Crum inhaled and looked at Iasg. "I can offer nothing that will take away the pain of your loss. Urard was a great man and will be remembered by Clann Ui Flaithimh for as long as one member of the tribe lives. He died as a warrior, defending his king, and I suspect that would be to his liking. He is beyond pain and in Mag Mell, awaiting eventual reunion with you, his sons, and his wider family. Only time and good friends will ease your sorrow." He paused before adding, "I am at your service if you need me." Iasg wiped a tear from her eye and dipped her head.

Addressing those around the table, he said, "I bring no good news and a vision of war. My journey to Ráth Cavares followed hard upon discussions with Brennus of the Senones and the Oracle in Cenabum." At Conall's signal, Crum continued, and the group became more attentive. "Brennus moves to traverse the lands of Clann Ui Flaithimh. Full of hubris and pig-headedness, he refuses to negotiate for permission or the payment of a fair toll. The Arverni will join him. An army of thirty thousand marches on Lugudunon."

"Why?"

Conall's simple question appeared to catch Crum strangely unawares. With a cough and a deeper sip of water, the druid cleared his throat. "Brennus made a pact with Dionysius of Syrako to cause a distraction to the Romans in the lands south of the Eridanus. To do this, Brennus must cross the Alpes and, by default, the lands of Clann Ui Flaithimh."

Mórrígan bent her head to bring her mouth closer to the king's ear. Yet, when she spoke, her voice was loud enough to reach Crum. "The king of the Senones is not our friend, but he never struck me as a foolish leader or prone to making rash decisions. This is an imprudent one." Conall nodded and rubbed his chin, a sure sign that he did not take Crum's words at face value.

"Why on earth did he not approach us first? Better to talk first before spilling the blood of thousands."

Crum Dubh shrugged. "Who can fathom the minds of kings and queens? Perhaps Brennus covets your lands and influence."

Conall snorted. "I could hazard an alternate explanation, but I doubt it would be to your liking, Druid." Under the stern gaze of Conall and the threatening demeanour of Mórrígan, Crum felt cold sweat trickling down his spine.

Unnervingly, Mórrígan posed questions to which she already knew the answers. "Who did you warn at the garrisons of Lugudunon and Dún-an-Rí? Brandubh, Carmag, Gaius, or Lonán?" Mórrígan turned to Conall. "I am sure we have had no riders from Lugudunon."

Crum shuffled uncomfortably. The status of his position meant that he was rarely subject to such a noticeable level of scrutiny or scepticism. He sensed he had made a severe error of judgment, yet he could do nothing but answer truthfully.

"No one. I rode here as fast as possible and by the most direct route."

A gasp of disbelief rose from those around the table. No matter what direction Crum chose, he would have passed within sight of Lugudunon. Irritated, Conall turned to Íar.

"Select twenty of your best riders and mounts. They should ride swiftly for Lugudunon. The fort must be alerted, and the greater army recalled from their farms and homes. Assemble your cavalry. They will depart at first light. Torcán, Brocc, and I will follow after we assess who can be spared from the army of Ráth Cavares." Íar rose and strode for the doors.

Conall looked around the table. Rising, he walked a few paces to stand beside Brighid. Placing a scarred and axe-calloused hand over his daughter's, he softly said, "I would know if I have a battle commander. Fearghal may take the request to talk better from you." Brighid smiled and bowed to her father. As she made to depart the room, her father held her hand.

"Adults become stubborn and cantankerous with age. We rage and then regret our words. Make your peace with the Sidhe. She is not omniscient, but only the foolish disregard her counsel or her power."

* * *

Pytheas shook his head. Had his sacrifices to Apollo been of such poor quality that the god contrived to ensure his arrival at Ráth Cavares coincided with the most inopportune turn of events possible? It had been seven sunsets since Torcán and Brocc had greeted him at the fort's dock. In their eyes, he saw that his timing was inauspicious. Yet, until this day, he had remained diplomatically invisible apart from making known his sympathies for Danu and Iasg and attending Urard's funeral. He shuddered. There were, of course, the executions, an inadequate description of that particular tableau of horrors.

Now, as he awaited his time with Conall, he overheard Crum Dubh's warning of war. The merchant took note of Conall's stream of orders and watched the members of the Chomhairle rush to execute the king's commands. Outside, the cacophony of a garrison called to readiness increased. A nod and a smile from Conall noted his presence. Slowly Pytheas walked the middle of three aisles of the Great Hall towards an almost empty high table. Curiously, he had seen neither the Sidhe nor Fearghal since his arrival.

"Friend, your solemn face and hesitant steps portend a message you do not wish to deliver," said Conall. Mórrígan nodded in agreement. "These recent times have not been served well by joyful news, and I fear that you bring me more ill tidings. Still, you should never be loath to be in our presence. We are family now and far beyond such pettiness. Sit, eat, and drink."

Pytheas smiled at the king and queen as he took a seat. He poured a deservedly generous cup of wine. As this was no time for befuddled minds, he mixed the greenish liquid with water. Pytheas allowed himself a brief chuckle. The scenes painted in red on the vessels and plates before him signified that they were of Greek origin. Probably they were from the merchant's trade stock. Conall matched the swarthy-skinned sailor's laugh with a smile.

"We have come a long way from crude horns and wooden cups, yet I wonder if civilisation is progress," Conall said. Pytheas dipped his head in assent.

It had been some time since he had last visited with the king and queen. A frown crossed his face as he saw the tiredness etched into Conall's weathered features. Unlike many of his tribe, the sun dealt fondly with Conall's skin. Steel-blue eyes, usually vibrant and challenging, held wisps of regret, uncertainty… and disappointment. Visibly, the burden of kingship and the recent events sat heavily on the Rí Ruirech's shoulders.

Conall was in his prime, and yet, Pytheas reflected, few rulers successfully negotiated a graceful path to old age. Those whom the gods loved usually had short lives and a bloody if glorious end. Their last moments were more than likely spent not with loved ones or comrades but the bean-sidhe.

"I regret adding further to your burden, but I must."

Over several cups of wine, Pytheas described the increasingly precarious situation in Massalia. "I believe that Marcus Fabius Ambustus is behind a growing blockade of Massalia. He hopes to take advantage of the economic pain caused to Massalia and the disruption of trading along the Rodonos. It will challenge and diminish the fortunes of Clann Ui Flaithimh as well as our business partnership.

"The issue is the penteconters. Marcus probably picked them up for little cost, if any. They are old-style warships made obsolete certainly by triremes and even by my biremes. Massalia's harbour entrance is no more than the width of three biremes laid bow to stern. Thus, the presence of Marcus' vessels has already discouraged some of the more faint-hearted merchant ships from entering Massalia."

A tug of his beard gave Pytheas time to order his next words. "Rival ports around the Great Sea will be delighted to topple Massalia's position. The leaders of the city have no answer and no expertise in naval encounters, save running away. And the success of the latter is almost solely due to our faster ships. This predicament needs to be nipped in the bud without delay. Massalia's triumvirate, of which I am a member, has authorised me to offer you substantial compensation if you can resolve our problem."

Pytheas was surprised at the break in Conall's sober countenance. A smile crept from the edges of the king's lips, along with boyish dimples. Conall bent his head and whispered to Mórrígan with a soft chuckle. The queen appeared startled and displeased, yet she conceded. The merchant now found himself observed by eyes that sparkled with cunning and mischievousness. The pair were quite unnerving.

"These are difficult times, my friend, but I think we have a solution to your dilemma." The small Greek heaved a sigh of relief as he mopped beads of sweat from his brow. Truthfully, after recent events, he had not held out much hope of success. His joy was tempered when Conall raised his hand and said, "I have a price in mind."

★

Mongfhionn ghosted past the guards posted outside the healing rooms and made her way to Danu's cot. Apart from the girl, the chamber was empty as the druids had inexplicably felt an urge to attend to other matters. When questioned later, they and the guards would be unable to explain their apparent dereliction of duty.

The edges of Danu's garment, strategically parted in the centre to facilitate examination, had drifted to the side, exposing her chest. The ugly wound, red-raw and held together with black stitches, glared accusingly at the Sidhe. On the positive side, Danu's full breasts—unlike Brighid, she took after her ma in that respect—rose and fell with a steady rhythm. On the negative, from the occasional whimper, even the act of breathing caused Danu pain.

Mongfhionn stood at the head of the bed for a moment, touched the black silk ribbon around her neck, and crumpled to her knees. The imperious porcelain façade, carefully nurtured since the murder of her sisters, cracked. Great teardrops splashed the wooden slats as wracking sobs engulfed her. The Sidhe could only remember one other occasion when she had felt such pain and guilt.

Her sisters, after whom the twins were named, had suffered terrible deaths at the hands of Marcus' sons. The strip of cloth around her throat masked a ragged slash from the same dagger that had ended her sisters' lives. Mongfhionn had survived and risen like a phoenix from the ashes. From that time, the Sidhe's driving goal was to wreak terrible vengeance on Marcus and his sons.

But had this myopic focus inured Mongfhionn to the damage she wrought on those she now considered family? Had she been no more than a puppet, a tool for the Goddess's plans? Used by the Goddess, she had spilt the blood of hundreds. All sacrificed to the deity's plan and her hatred of all things Roman.

In turn, Mongfhionn, like a potter, had striven to mould the clay that was a young Mórrígan and Conall into tools of retribution. It was miraculous that along a bloody path, the king and his queen had forged their own destiny. Now, they challenged the Goddess's demand for their obedience. How could Mongfhionn blame them?

Worse, was Brighid, her bond with Danu almost ripped asunder, to become the nightmarish creature her mother narrowly avoided? Her adopted family had placed an unenviable task before the Sidhe: that of choosing sides.

Inhaling deeply, Mongfhionn rose. She placed a delicate hand on Danu's wound.

"I have failed you and your sister, but this I can give you."

The Lady flinched at the sudden drain of power. Where the Sidhe had rested her fingers, no scar remained, and beneath the skin, the wound had knitted together. None in the kingdoms of the Celts could rival the Lady's healing powers. In the place of the hurt lay the delicate pink petals of a feirdhris.

As if sensing the Sidhe's presence and her torment, Danu stirred, and her eyes fluttered open. "Not your fault. None of it is. But our family is only strong when united." Danu's gaze focused on Mongfhionn. "Make your peace with my ma and da and Brighid. They need you— and you, them." With a sigh, Danu drifted back into a deep but, this time, pain-free sleep. The Sidhe padded softly to the doorway, turned, and smiled wistfully. On the floor beside Danu's cot lay the black ribbon.

✳✳✳

In another bed, in another room, Brighid tossed and turned, her sleep marked by dark visions. As morning broke, she sat up in a bed uncomfortably wet with sweat. A strange sensation throbbed in her chest. Unconsciously, she rubbed the spot but felt nothing untoward. Reaching for the polished plate by her cot, she discovered the imprint of a feirdhris.

"Shite!"

Unlike her sister's, the rose's petals were black with pink tips.

CHAPTER 13

395 B.C.—Lugudunon

Eyes closed, chest rising and falling slowly, Fearghal sprawled across the wooden bench outside his quarters. The seat was barely able to contain his bulk and creaked ominously with any movement. To all appearances, the warrior was enjoying the winter sun and ignoring jibes of, "It's well for some!" from good-natured passers-by. Fearghal's demeanour was deceptive. He was deep in thought. The clann's battle commander and former leader of the famed Cróeb Ruad warriors from northern Ériu was both feeling his age and deeply sorry for himself.

"Typical man," he groused.

Fearghal retained a full and thick head of hair, although its vibrant red was now liberally sprinkled with steel. The veteran scratched his winter beard and mused that its removal was long overdue. He never enjoyed the itch of whiskers for much more than a season and had no desire to let it grow rampant. Arms, sculpted with muscle and meshed with the scars of many battles, were covered in fine hair and a rash of ginger freckles. A flat, hard belly belied the veteran's forty-seven summers. The sheathed longsword, testimony to his fighting prowess, lay beside the seat. Sunset or sunrise, it was always within a hand's reach.

The commander of Conall's army knew he was an oddity. He was a warrior and subject to that vocation's mortal perils. By any measure, he should have crossed the veil a long time ago. Each sunrise was a gift, but from whom—the Goddess or the Sidhe? And was his uncommon strength and longevity a blessing or a curse? He reflected with some chagrin that his good fortune was sure to end… painfully.

Perhaps it was time for him to return home, mount his sword above a great carved fireplace, and put his feet up before a roaring fire of wood and peat. He sighed wistfully. The distinctive fragrance of burning peat could never be forgotten. But where was "home"? The Ériu remembered by teary-eyed drunks around campfires was a mirage, shimmering precariously on the horizon of his dreams.

With recent events and harsh words spoken, Fearghal was unsure of his place in Clann Ui Flaithimh or his welcome in Conall's home. The schism saddened and hurt him. He had been a good friend to Conall's parents. He still grieved for them and had nightmares of their butchered bodies. To the aged warrior, Conall was his adopted son and Mórrígan his daughter. He loved their children as much as he loved his own daughter, Neamhain.

As Danu lay wounded in her cot, he knew Conall and Mórrígan felt betrayed by the Goddess, the Sidhe, and perhaps by him. He shivered. The king had promised rivers of blood. What is more, both he and Mórrígan were more than capable of delivering on their oath. If Fearghal was not beside them, who would temper their actions?

Then there was his partner, the Sidhe, Mongfhionn. Following another confrontation with Conall, Mórrígan, and Brighid, a distressed and deeply wounded Sidhe had stormed from the fort and not been seen since. He sensed the prospect of her returning hung in the balance, as did her predictable retribution on those she deemed to have betrayed her. Fearghal exhaled. Retirement to a small farm, hidden among the lush fields, verdant forests, and cascading waterfalls of the gleannta of north-eastern Ériu, seemed more and more attractive.

A shadow crossed his line of vision. Tired, wrinkled eyelids retracted.

"Hello, Brighid." He smiled.

"Grand-da." It took just one small word to allay Fearghal's

misgivings. "My da and ma need you. War is coming, and you're the clann's battle commander. Will you come with me?" Brighid held out a hand that was soon enfolded by the warrior's strong, calloused one.

"Like you need to ask. You are my family. This is my home."

A weight lifted from Fearghal's shoulders. In his heart, he knew his place. Reaffirmation was what he wanted and that Brighid had provided. Complaints of age and bone-weariness dissipated. The commander of the clann's army swung his legs off the bench, grabbed sword and scabbard, and secured the weapon to his back.

Brighid hesitated. Her soft hand touched his arm, and he paused. Prompted by the throbbing rose tattoo over her heart, she said, "I need to talk to the Sidhe."

"We both do, Brighid. We both do."

✳✳✳

Brennus cursed Conall. Yet the true target of his frustration was the straggling caravan of thirty thousand warriors and an even greater number of camp followers that stretched far behind him. He had warned against bringing kin, had threatened them daily, but eventually, exasperated, gave up. Only the armourers, blacksmiths, hunters, and whores provided needed services. Like a plague of locusts, the rest stripped the land of its bounty as they meandered towards the Alpes. At least now the Senones had crossed into Conall's territory, they would plunder that land and not his.

Many anonymous warbands shadowed and raided the largely undefended civilian camps. Brennus snorted. Anonymous! For sure, they were Carnutes, Aedui, and Bituriges. At first, the king sent warriors to dissuade the attacks. Now, he disregarded pleas from the civilians and their warrior kin. Indeed, the king looked sympathetically on or at least chose to ignore the skirmishes. Perhaps a few tragic incidents of mass killing might persuade the hangers-on to turn back. Outbreaks of disease were widespread, especially the "runs". Perversely, Brennus welcomed illnesses as long as they did not touch his army. Unfortunately, that was not possible.

Lugudunon was about seven sunsets distant, or so his scouts informed him. The land the Senones travelled was lush and gently mountainous. Rivers, fields, and forests teemed with game and fish. Brought on by the warm climate and frequent rains, crops grew strong and would yield bountiful harvests. The dirt was firm and in perfect condition for fighting. The king's face flitted between scowling at having allowed himself to be manoeuvred into war and smiling at the opportunities presented.

Dionysius' promise of gold and conquering new fertile lands south of the Eridanus had prompted the Senones' exodus from their traditional territory in Gaul. The opportunity to drive a spear into the heart of Conall's beloved clann was a bonus relished by Brennus. He growled, "Let's see how that bastard deals with his army defeated and his lands ravaged by the surrounding tribes. Even his friend Tasgiitios will turn on him." *Giving Conall a bloody nose, yes, that alone will be well worth the journey. All will see that I, Brennus of the Senones, am the true king of Gaul.*

✴✴✴

Two walls protected Lugudunon. The first, a white, stone block wall, rose from its rock foundations upon which the settlement was built. Young children looked up at the edifice and gaped, awestruck at how the ramparts reached up into the sky. The second was the vaunted shield-wall of Clann Ui Flaithimh. Hard-eyed men and women lined the battlements. Red-and-black scíatha were settled on brawny arms. Spears were gripped in hands, impatient for the fight. Iron tips glinted in the sun. Great red-and-black and gold-and-red banners of king and clann flapped in a light wind. Lugudunon's walls were an open invitation, a challenge to all foes to try their luck.

Brandubh Mac Artair, Carmag, and Gaius stood on the northern ramparts. They peered across fields to the dense forest beyond, squinting to gain a sign. Beside the quartet stood the tall, lanky figure of Sárán Mac Craobhach, the army's quartermaster. As the tribe's Master of

Supplies, and like his father before him, Sárán's expertise in logistics was without equal. He was, however, often the butt of cruel humour because of his choice of dress colour and somewhat quirky nature. Gaius was just about to point out how good a target Sárán made when he realised that with his polished bronze armour, red tunic, and red cloak, he likely stood out just as much—if not more.

Brandubh broke the group's silent contemplations. "When?" he asked them. By nobility, Brandubh, Prince of the Aos an Fhithich—the Ravens—was the one with the highest status and, by default, according to the highly structured society of the Gaels, was in command of Lugudunon. But Brandubh, while a brave warrior and loved by his men, was sage enough to know his limitations. In warfare, his companions' experience of tactics and strategy far surpassed his own. Thus, it was his custom to seek and measure their counsel.

"One, maybe two sunsets," said Carmag, still irritated over Brandubh's tactical decisions. He spat a viscous glob of phlegm over the stone wall. Out of curiosity, his comrades tracked the arc of the projectile. They wondered if the act was a comment on their earlier, heated conversation.

The leader of the Forest People sniffed the fresh morning air. Traces of wood smoke from many Senone campfires filtered through nostrils attuned to the slightest hint of fragrances. He pointed to the cloud of ravens that rose into the air with an annoyed and loud *kraa kraa*. Disturbed from their nesting grounds by Brennus' horde, the birds evidently sided with their silent brothers painted on red shields and flags.

"They come closer," Carmag persisted. "We should take the fight to them, in the trees." It was a final plea for the hit-and-run tactics favoured by Carmag's tribe. He wanted his men and women to do most of their fighting in the forests. Likely they would—eventually.

"No. You will remain in Lugudunon. The city cannot be allowed to fall. Your clubs and spears are needed on the ramparts. I have no intention of throwing one thousand against thirty thousand." Carmag ground his teeth, though he knew that even veterans could not prevail against such odds. Another glob of spittle arced over the walls.

Brandubh ignored it and asked, "What is our strength? When will Conall and the rest of the army reach us?"

Riders, their mounts lathered with sweat, had arrived from Ráth Cavares the previous evening. Belated reports of the Senones campaign were compared with those already provided by Tasgiitios' messengers. The news of Urard's death, Danu's injury, and the rift with the Sidhe was not uplifting. Urard's death, in particular, had been a bitter herb to swallow.

"His presence will be missed," said Gaius. All knew to whom he referred. Brandubh coughed, prompting the Roman to continue. "We are below half strength and outnumbered ten to one. Still, we stand on strong walls. Our need is for discipline and a bit of luck. A miracle is not needed... yet."

Unconvinced, Carmag snorted and scowled. Gaius was not unduly concerned. Carmag's loyalty was never in doubt. He smiled and continued, "The ballistae, archers, and slingers are positioned on the north wall and protected by Carmag's men. Íar, his riders, and Gràinne's chariots should be with us in three sunsets at the most. The rest of the army are expected to trickle in over a half-cycle of the moon. They will assemble south of Lugudunon, in the pastures across the river from Dún-an-Rí."

Brandubh nodded and looked at Sárán. The gangly warrior's response was a terse, "Plenty of food, water, and weapons." This was true, though as an afterthought, he added, "The civilian population has chosen to stay within Lugudunon. However, the children of the Chomhairle nobility and wealthy have been escorted to the safety of Dún-an-Rí."

Left unasked and unanswered were the minds of Conall and Mórrígan. A torrent of gossip and rumour flooded the settlement, adding uncertainty to an already fraught situation.

"The Hag's arse!" muttered Carmag. "No pressure then."

CHAPTER 14

395 B.C.—Battle for Lugudunon

Nature's thistles, thorns, and nettles were the first to engage Brennus in battle. From the tears on his clothing and profusion of scratches on his limbs, he was unable to declare a convincing victory. The sounds of axes, swords, and spears attacking the green entanglement, ably supported by oaths and curses, did nothing to improve the king's humour. "We should have simply sent a messenger announcing our arrival and kept to the road!" he roared, gazing upon Lugudunon from the relative, if prickly, safety of the wildwood.

The sight of the white walls of Lugudunon brought forth a stream of obscenities. To Brennus, the hillfort was an abomination when ruled by Matres of the Gaiscedach and an even greater blemish on the Gaulish landscape under Conall's kingship.

Shivers trickled up his spine. Brennus' last memory of the fort was of Gaiscedach blood leaching into the stone and the charnel house of gore and limbs that witnessed Matres' army's last stand. The stench of rotting corpses, throbbing with fat maggots, and the air thick with black flies had never completely receded from his nostrils or dreams. *Conall Mac Gabhann is a cunning and ruthless enemy. But not this time. Not this time.* He turned to the warrior alongside him.

"Sound the war-horn." The tall horn sounded its deep *barrr ewww,* and hundreds of others took up the refrain.

***

"Our guests have arrived," Brandubh turned to Carmag and Gaius. "Make them bleed."

"It would appear that Brennus has learned from his previous error," said Carmag.

Gaius raised an eyebrow at his comrade's comment. Carmag laughed and pointed at the Senone horde. "Last time we fought, Brennus was arrogant and sent five thousand of his best to chastise us. That looks more like twenty thousand, maybe even thirty."

The Roman grunted and looked at Brandubh. The prince nodded and strode to stand with his warriors. Gaius took up his place at the massive, bolt-throwing ballistae that towered over his men. Smaller, more portable field ballistae were positioned at the eastern entrance.

Only five hundred Romans from Gaius' command had survived the Alpes, his flight from Marcus, and the fight against Matres. As the seasons passed, most came to terms with the likelihood that Marcus had slaughtered their families in Rome as retribution for their disloyalty. Thus, most had taken barbarian partners and fathered pale-skinned, red-haired brats. The ease with which they had assimilated into Clann Ui Flaithimh and severed ties with Rome often troubled Gaius. Yet he understood. Rome had betrayed them.

"Time to dampen Brennus' enthusiasm," Gaius shouted. His men cheered.

***

Brennus watched twenty thousand of his warriors stream past him to cross the fields of green shoots that surrounded Lugudunon. Beside him stood ten thousand of his veterans. His strategy was simple: wear the garrison down with his lesser and inexperienced warriors and then send in the old guard to massacre survivors.

"Where is Celtillos and the Arverni?" Brennus roared at his shield-man. The chieftain shrugged. All knew the Arverni could not be trusted, so he was unsurprised by their absence and a bit mystified at his king's complaint.

***

As it happened, Brennus' shield-man was right. Celtillos of the Arverni had little intention of joining the Senones on what he thought an ill-considered and wasteful assault on Lugudunon. His only goal was to get his portion of Dionysius' gold and pillage the fertile lands beyond the Alpes. He had no interest in a war with Conall and Clann Ui Flaithimh. What was Brennus thinking? This should have been settled with bribery or the payment of a toll.

Better still, they could simply have bypassed Conall's kingdom. Smaller tribes skirted the eastern borders of Clann Ui Flaithimh. Trespass would have caused a delay but been less costly. The only advantage to Celtillos would be if Brennus were killed or crippled or his army weakened, and that thought brought pleasure to the Arverni king. He already had alerted the Gaiscedach in the Alpes of a possible business opportunity.

However, Celtillos' joy was fleeting as his five thousand Arverni warriors fought a war of attrition with the Carnutes. The Arverni had successfully negotiated the land of the Bituriges with little more than skirmishes, minor injuries, and bribes. Honour had been satisfied, and the Arverni had crossed into the territory of the Carnutes.

Here, Celtillos' opinion on Brennus' foolishness was ironic. There was no chance that the Arverni, although a powerful warband, could traverse the Carnutes' domain without conflict. In the longer term, taking into consideration the trade along the Rodonos and maintaining a working business relationship with Conall, Celtillos should have come to an accommodation with Tasgiitios.

Instead, Celtillos faced a well-prepared Carnutes army that matched his own in numbers and whose spearmen knew the terrain much better. He also had suspicions that the bastard king of the Aedui, Ambigatos, had provided Tasgiitios with additional warriors. The Aedui and the

Arverni tribes were long-time enemies. When it came to weaponry and armour, the reputation of the Arverni was undisputed. However, the best armour in Gaul gave little protection against deep holes filled with sharpened stakes—many smeared with shite. Neither did it shield chests crushed by massive logs released from high ground or tall trees.

Celtillos swore. The Carnutes ambushes and traps were a demoralising inconvenience to be endured. The king suspected that once his force was judged suitably weakened, Tasgiitios' army would fight face to face, but on the ground of the Carnutes' choosing. That Tasgiitios was unaware of Celtillos' disinclination to support Brennus in the battle with Conall made him scowl. He should have spoken with the Carnutes king and avoided this fight. However, one thing was clear: Brennus would not be amused at the overlong delay in the arrival of his ally.

* * *

At five hundred paces, one thousand slingers on Lugudunon's northern parapet launched the opening salvos of the battle. The height advantage of the walls favoured Brandubh's Ravens with another four rounds before the slings of the Senones replied. For the Senone stone-throwers, it was a case of hurling the projectiles high into the air in the hope of hitting someone. Brandubh's men and women, on the other hand, could choose their targets.

Stones sunk into soft, unprotected flesh. Men stumbled and fell, clutching cracked skulls and bloody faces. The injured were often trampled on by their comrades. From the ramparts of Lugudunon, stone and lead fell upon the Senones like large hail in winter. Walls and shields protected the besieged, and unlike their attackers, they had an unlimited supply of bullets.

Still, the Senones had far superior numbers. Sensing that many of the defenders of Lugudunon had sought cover, the Senone horde picked up their pace and met the next level of resistance—the ballistae. Here a bloody harvest was reaped, and the momentum of Brennus' attack wavered. Iron-headed bolts, some shaped to slash, others to penetrate, launched from a hundred machines and slammed into the advancing army.

The missiles ploughed bloody furrows deep into the ranks of Brennus' warriors. Limbs were sheared, and torsos gushed blood. Heads disappeared in a mist of pink gore. Adjacent comrades were skewered like rabbits on a spit. Soon, the howling of the wounded rivalled the hoarse, rolling thunder of battle-cries. There was to be no relief from the barrage. Sárán's supply of bolts seemed bottomless. Tightened by well-muscled arms, ballistae skeins first squealed and then were loosed with a cry. The crack of wood against wood was relentless. The air sighed, pushed aside by hundreds of missiles.

The dilemma for Lugudunon's defenders became whether to cheer or watch in awed silence at the carnage. Inured to the terrible wrath meted out by the Sidhe on the tribe's enemies, they found it difficult to accept that they too could be equally creative in the game of slaughter. Their contemplation was abruptly cut short. A shout of "Archers!" resounded from the ramparts, and a cloud of iron was released from two hundred bows. Volley after volley, each spaced by a count of twelve, arced into the spring sky. At the same time, the missiles from slings and ballistae continued to flay the Senone army.

Shrieks of agony vied with curses and promises of bloody retribution. Even so, the Senone horde could do little other than absorb the barrage. Respite finally arrived when the besiegers came to within twenty paces of the walls. The murderous bolts from the heavy ballistae and the bullets of stone and lead from slings ceased. The time for darts, javelins and throwing axes had arrived. At the eastern gateway, smaller field ballistae added their contribution.

Carmag looked over the battlefield and lovingly stroked the smooth haft of his hammer. He bemoaned the increasing detachment from face-to-face fighting and the personal delivery of blunt-force trauma. Beside him, Brandubh shrugged.

"Rocks, slings, throwing spears and axes, arrows, ballistae… who knows what will be next? With each generation, we move further from our enemy's face."

The Ravens' prince laughed. Before moving to take up his position at the eastern entrance, he gestured to the approaching horde and the thuds of scaling ladders smacking against the walls. "I doubt you'll soon have much cause for complaint. Fight well, my friend."

* * *

Brennus was dismayed. To those around him, a confident king roared out orders, directing the attack with his sword, cajoling and threatening chieftains to increase their efforts. Inside, the king was unusually uncertain. It was already meán lae. The battle had commenced at sunrise. Yet, it was only now that scaling ladders crashed against the pristine walls of Lugudunon. Only now that the rams were in place at the eastern gate.

Around the hillfort, the cornfields were strewn with the broken, the wounded, and the dead. "Always looks worse than it is," Brennus muttered. In this, the king was correct. The immediately dead and mortally wounded always formed a small portion of an army's casualties. In contrast, the bean-sidhe's two companions—lingering infection and disease—were patient and only too pleased to wait and claim the biggest tithe of the wounded.

"Shite!" Brennus shouted. "What arseholes built the ladders?" It was noticeable that many of the scaling ladders were an arm's length short of the top of the walls. A bloody day had just become more challenging.

* * *

The young warrior, shield on his back and weapon gripped in his right hand, was moderately relieved to find he was not the first man. No one in their right mind is happy climbing a rickety, unsecured ladder that bellied in the direction of the wall and threatened to break with the weight of each additional warrior. Bad enough to know that he was part of the initial wave because of his inexperience. That strategy never made much sense to him. Surely, sending the veterans first would result in a higher probability of overcoming the wall. It certainly made more sense than relying on frightened desperation.

His relief was short-lived. Any hope that a deity listened to his prayers vanished in a splash of blood and splatter of brains when a large rock dropped onto his would-be protector's skull. He swore at the injustice and the inconvenience. The corpse above him slumped backwards, almost knocking the young man from his precarious perch. The legs still twitching with muscle memory were trapped between the ladder's rungs. The adolescent cursed the body and swore at those below. They had limited patience but an extensive vocabulary of what they would do to him if he did not get moving.

He grabbed the cadaver's belt and tugged hard. Eventually, his effort was rewarded, and the corpse dislodged from the ladder. It dropped to the dirt below, landing with the dull thud of a side of beef. The young man had not known him and did not care. He had to keep going and laboured upwards through a miasma of boiling liquids, cinders, and fire. His senses were assaulted by the smells of boiled and roasted flesh, and the screams of agony as flesh sloughed off bones.

Closing on the top of the wall, he choked on the acrid smoke from numerous braziers and the great iron cauldrons of death. Sweat trickled from his brow into eyes already smarting from salty tears. With a few more battles under his belt, the young warrior would have known not to give in to the euphoria of cresting the ramparts. Still, who could have blamed him for the brief shout of "Yes!" and the raised arms?

His last memory was of a hairy, naked warrior swathed in dark blue tattoos, of muscles rippling, and of the practically effortless swing of a massive club. A heavy lump of iron smashed into his belly, mangling his guts and cracking his spine. A calloused foot kicked him backwards, not with any sense of anger or malice, but simply to retrieve the weapon.

As he fell back and over the wall, the young man felt a sharp tug in his belly. His entrails, entangled with the hammer, were no longer part of his body. The warm meat, for sadly, the warrior was still alive, hit the ground below. His remaining hope was for a sharp blade from a friend.

Alas, his voice was too weak to be heard.

****

There was no end to the clink of metal hooks looking for purchase on the stone walls and no shortage of siege ladders or fools to climb them. At the eastern gate, Brandubh's slingers and archers kept the besiegers at bay. The twin guard towers kept up a deadly avalanche of ballistae bolts, boiling oil and water, and cinders on the Senones. Spearmen waited, anticipating the first Senone heads to peer over the battlements. The path to the gate was deliberately narrow, permitting only the passage of a single wagon and its team of oxen. Soon the alley was littered with the dead and the dying.

And yet, two Senone battering rams carried by teams of men the size of bears edged closer. Covered rams would have afforded some protection, but the tight space and lack of a straight path negated their use. The human oxen's only cover was the shields of the brave, or perhaps foolish, who walked at their side. Leaving the dead in their wake, the boles' transporters slowly and stubbornly gained the solid wooden gates.

Sheaves of straw and bundles of firewood soaked in pitch were tossed from the ramparts and followed by hundreds of torches. To the hugely muscled men, hardened to pain, the flames were an annoyance. The smoke, however, caused them to choke and call for water. It was inevitable that the gates would yield to the rams. The flexibility of the wood from which they were constructed only prolonged the wait for the Senones. A great cheer rose as the barriers were finally breached and the Senones charged forward.

Those attacking the eastern gateway were stunned to discover a second inner entrance and high wall. Their dismay puzzled Brandubh. Brennus had personal knowledge of Lugudunon's defences. Presumably, the king had informed his men of what was in store for them—especially those given the job of battering their way through the eastern gates. Perhaps the frenzy and stink of battle had removed that morsel of information from minds. A lapse in memory was understandable and even forgivable, given the need to avoid the constant storm of iron, fire, and boiling liquids.

A rising wail of fury from the Senones quickly overwhelmed the silence of shock. As the mob crashed over the shattered outer gates, they found themselves in a small courtyard enclosed with high, smooth walls. They looked upwards, following the line of the rampart, and were blinded by the light. The sun had just started its path towards the western horizon and burned in the sky directly above them. Blinking tears from eyes already smarting from the smoke and grime of battle, they shielded their vision with dirt-ingrained hands.

Along the parapet, and well beyond the reach of warriors who had no scaling ladders, they beheld the grim-faced Cinn Péinteáilte of north-eastern Albu. Each carried a single throwing spear, although there was little doubt that more were to hand. A tall, slender warrior with a shaven head stood over the unbroken inner gates. A solitary raven's feather twisted and spun from a thin, gold rope that hung around his neck.

"Go back!" he shouted in the pleasing burr of his homeland. "Ye cannae prevail. Take yer wounded. Live to rut and fight another sunset. There is only death for ye here."

His answer was an angry flurry of throwing axes and knives, which barely reached the top of the wall. With a great shout, the Senones charged the inner gates.

Brandubh shook his head and dropped his hand. The slaughter commenced. Volley after volley of javelins fell on the enemy. Unable to advance or retreat, the mound of the dead rose to become a barrier. Those outside shouted and cursed at their comrades. They had no understanding that the men and women in the yard had already gone to Mag Mell. Or that their deaths prevented their ungrateful comrades from meeting a similar fate.

***

Gaius' men abandoned the ballistae once they were incapable of being depressed further. A few were strategically placed at the junctions of the ramparts and the throwing arms set at chest height. If they were used, it likely would mean the walls were lost, but the Senones would pay dearly for that victory.

The Roman and his men stood shoulder to shoulder with Carmag's warriors. Lugudunon was a relatively small citadel. Hence, even with their depleted garrison, the defenders could form two unbroken ranks along the hillfort's defences.

The apex of the walls was broad enough to allow ten warriors to stand shoulder to shoulder. Therefore, the tasks set before the Senones—attempting to overcome the crenellated barriers and then holding ground until reinforced—were daunting. Two rows of Clann Ui Flaithimh warriors stood parallel to the parapets. The front row's job was to batter and throw the attackers back. The rear rank of the shield wall, waiting with grim faces, locked scíatha and gripped javelins.

Positioned on a large, grassy mound with a rock core, a narrow ledge of dirt ran around the stronghold, but it was barely one or two paces wide. Even if the besiegers had covered rams, there were few places with sufficient room to position and use them. With no gap or cleft to offer purchase, the hillfort's walls remained contemptuous of the tiny creatures crawling towards the crest.

In the Senones' favour, the fort was not surrounded by rocky terrain. Thus, when tossed from the ladders or cut loose when scaling ropes were severed, most fell onto forgiving grass-covered earth. Bruises, dislocations, and sprains were their complaints rather than broken bones, cracked skulls, or death. That the walls would be surmounted was inevitable. Gauls and Celts were crazy warriors capable of overcoming terrible odds. Sheer numbers should tell. The real question was—whose resolve would break first?

The rolling rumble of thousands of throats raw from constant shouting and coated with the detritus of battle grew louder. No longer capable of forming words, the Senone besiegers growled as a great beast. By the time many reached the top of the ramparts, they had insufficient moisture to hack up spit. On an open battlefield, the same warriors could give a good account of themselves. Here, they faced a giant tortoise secure in its stony shell. Strong jaws and iron teeth snapped and rent the attackers' flesh.

Even with superior numbers, it was an uneven contest and favoured the defenders. The two ranks of Clann Ui Flaithimh continually changed positions. Rested warriors faced the tired and breathless. Those who overcame the wall were quickly put down with bloody spears as they struggled to bring shield and sword to bear. The Senones found no break in either stone or flesh to exploit. Gaining no purchase, the will to fight ebbed from Brennus' force. Wiser chieftains recognised the signs. Rather than risk a chaotic flight, the Senone war horns reverberated and the army withdrew.

In the forest, Brennus' rage boiled. His leaders fully expected to pay with their lives.

✳✳✳

She was a willowy fourteen summers, perhaps fifteen. That morning she had sobbed as her ma hacked at her hair. Long blonde tresses, uncut from the day she was born, lay at her feet. Perhaps to make amends, her mother, a progressive woman for the times, dyed random tufts of her daughter's hair red and blue. Then she used a concoction of beeswax, fat, and pine tree resin to mould them into short spikes. The young woman immediately graduated from looking the victim of harsh punishment to the envy of her friends.

The battle over, she lifted her head. Her first sight of the entire panorama of the battlefield prompted heavy sweating and projectile vomiting over the parapet. That gained her no friends among the enemy retreating down flimsy ladders. That it soon progressed to the dry retching of an empty stomach was a relief to them, not her.

Young, deep-blue eyes could barely take in the transformation of the cornfields she had played in and helped harvest. As the sun slowly descended to set in the west, she wondered how the orb could look so glorious and prayed for the darkness of night to hide the battle's gore. She prayed for deafness to stop her hearing the cries of the wounded and the imagined wailing of mothers and partners.

Her hair looked like a sodden tartan cap. Her clothes and what armour still clung to her torso were in shreds. She looked as if she had been submerged in a barrel of blood and gore. Every muscle ached, and every bone throbbed with dull pain. The young woman would have cried, but she had no more tears to give. Her face burned under a mask of dried blood as her nose crinkled, reminding her that she had pissed herself many times—until that well had run dry. She took some solace that she had not shat herself, unlike some who had fought at her side.

Her weapons were gone, captured in the grasping folds of the fat and flesh of her enemy. Ramming the edge of her shield into a slavering, black-gummed mouth was her last memory of its protection before it too disappeared over the wall. The taste of iron in her mouth, a throbbing egg-sized lump on her forehead, and two fists of skinned knuckles testified that she had fought with all that the Goddess had provided.

How she had come to fight in the front line would be a heated, sometimes violent, discussion over beer and food later between the veteran ceannairí céad. The lass flinched at the strong hands now placed on her narrow shoulders. An odour of blood, sweat, and piss accompanied the action. Carmag's gentle voice was at odds with his fearsome presence. He turned her around to face him. His mien was stern.

"Ye shouldn't hae been on this wall." The girl's face became downcast. "Or in this battle. And someone will pay for that." Her chin was lifted up by a rough hand. "Ye fought like a warrior. Ye are a warrior. None will ever take that from ye."

With a sweep of his hand, he gestured to the defenders. "Among these men and women, ye are a hero—a bright light in a day of grief. If ye live, and the Goddess wills it, ye will become a great fighter, a leader of Clann Uí Flaithimh." Carmag released the young woman and stepped back a pace. He smiled as he inspected the lass. "But first, we need to speak with Sárán and the blacksmith. Ye need much better armour and weapons. Then ye should go home, eat, and rest. Oh, and get a bath. Ye smell awful!" Her chin set at Carmag's joke, but she smiled when he added, "Be here at sunrise. Ye'll fight alongside me."

As the young warrior walked away, Carmag shook his head. There was great sorrow in his eyes. "And ye'll likely die alongside me."

CHAPTER 15

395 B.C.—The Forests of Lugudunon

Deep in the forests to the north of Lugudunon, battered and blood-ied men and women slumped against the rough bark of tall pines and gnarled oak trees. Others lay listless, sprawled around thousands of campfires. Many dunked lumps of hard bread in honeyed beer and washed it down with copious volumes of the tepid beverage. They massaged tired muscles and applied salves to wounds.

The atmosphere lacked celebration. No one bragged or jested about new scars or mighty duels. Quiet pleadings from those with mortal or crippling injuries were answered with ostracism. Who wants to be reminded of failure? The lucky ones had a friend with a sharp blade and a simple prayer for a safe journey to Mag Mell.

Belief in themselves and the assurances of their leaders had floundered at the walls of Lugudunon. Vastly greater numbers did not prevail. There had been no quick and decisive victory. There was no plunder or pillage to quench high passions or provide comfort to partners and children. Many had watched comrades fall and die, crushed between the white stone ramparts and the wall of spears.

Arguments sparked into life. Chieftains and warbands accused each other of poor judgment, cowardice, and not fighting hard enough. Only Brennus' brutal enforcers prevented the simmering anger from boiling over and the bitter contagion of defeat spreading. Those of a more pragmatic disposition left their hubris in the blood-sodden dirt at the bottom of Lugudunon's walls and sharpened blades. They counselled that the only certainty was that many more would bleed and die.

Brennus snarled at Celtillos. The Arverni king, younger by nine summers, scowled back, impervious to Brennus' attempted intimidation and desire to ascribe blame for the bloody stalemate. A short time before, Celtillos' battered men had staggered into the chaotic camp. In their battle with the Carnutes, the Arverni had lost five hundred warriors through injury or death. Senone taunts of spinelessness fell on deaf ears. All stood with Celtillos. The siege of Lugudunon was not their fight. In any event, their numbers would not have changed the outcome.

"What's your plan?" asked Celtillos. The king of the Carnutes knew that at most, there were two sunsets before Conall and the remainder of his battle commanders arrived. Even now, two thousand mounted warriors assembled in the fields south of the Souconna. Drawn from all points, the full strength of the shield wall was gathering near Dún-an-Rí. Celtillos' bitter battle with Tasgiitios foretold that Carnutes' blades would hamstring Brennus' rearguard.

"It seems that Tasgiitios fears Conall's return and retribution more than yours," said Celtillos.

"What?" Brennus had only been half-listening. Now, he tossed aside his beer and looked at his ally with troubled eyes. "Conall is not at Dún-an-Rí… or Lugudunon?"

At first incredulous, Celtillos' mood quickly changed to worry and alarm. From there, it transitioned once again to a consideration of the opportunity a weakened Brennus might offer. Perhaps a change of loyalties should be considered. After all, he had no personal animus for Conall. Exasperated, Celtillos stood and ran stubby, thick fingers through lank locks of dark-brown hair.

"What have your scouts, spies, and informants been telling you? Conall and his High Council were at Ráth Cavares for Lugnasad." The leader of the Carnutes pointed in the direction of Lugudunon. "This is not the Arverni's fight. You and I are allies only to fight and plunder the lands south of the Alpes. I have no desire to become embroiled in a war with Conall." In a more sympathetic voice, Celtillos added, "Our people are not made for sieges. Our blood runs hot with passions and quickly cools. We do not have the patience of the Greeks, the Persians, the Egyptians, or even the Romans.

"Concolitanus, king of the Gaiscedach, achieved a miracle in keeping his forces together while he undermined the walls of Lugudunon. Yet he still could not wrench the fort from Matres' grasp. He could not hold his army together for a long siege without weakening his position among the Gaiscedach. You know this. It was *your* assassin who ended Concolitanus' life.

"Conall had the help of walls already shattered by Concolitanus and made worse by the winds and storms of the Máistir and a group of mad, revenge-seeking Romans." The king paused and sighed deeply. "My advice. Seek accommodation with Conall. Accept the bloody nose. Move on. Take your anger out on the Etrusci and Umbri."

Brennus rose from his seat. Drawing himself up to his full height, he looked down on Celtillos and spoke in a voice laden with threat. "A true friend and ally would have informed me of Conall's disposition." He spat on the ground at Celtillos' feet and rubbed the pommel of his sword. "Find a place in the camp far from me, or the Arverni will need a new verrix."

Celtillos stood his ground for a moment. To show weakness would be a grave error. Then he shook his head, shrugged, and slowly stepped away from the fire. His eyes never left Brennus'. The throwing knife, coated with poison and palmed in his right hand, added surety to his calmness until he was embraced by the shadows.

Deep in thought, Brennus tugged on his magnificent beard, then shouted to his shield-man, "Fetch my scouts. I will know why they failed to inform me of Conall's movements or that Tasgiitios had joined the battle." The strapping warrior dipped his head in acknowledgement and turned to leave. Brennus added, "When you have the information—kill them and their kin. Slowly… very slowly." The man once again nodded briefly then hurried away.

The worm of self-doubt wriggled to the surface of Brennus' mind, nudging aside anger. The king berated himself. Why had he not noticed the absence of Conall's famed cavalry? Should he have paid more attention to the Oracle's reading of the entrails? It spoke of great wealth beyond the Alpes, but only if he were to survive Lugudunon. Had pride and jealousy clouded his usually clear thinking?

This day had taught Brennus one bloody lesson, however. A handful of warriors could hold Lugudunon's walls, and he needed another plan to bring Conall to his knees.

✱✱✱

His arse was sore and felt uncomfortably damp. Conall hoped it was from the expanding circle of horse sweat that seeped through the thick, gold-trimmed, red dillat that he sat on rather than having pissed himself. The latter was undoubtedly unkingly. A glance at Mórrígan caught the queen slipping a hand under her bottom. After a satisfying scratch, she sighed and wiped long fingers on the light, woollen léine that covered her armour. She sniffed automatically, snorting in disgust at the unwelcome odour of beast and rider. Feeling eyes upon her, the Huntress looked at her partner and shrugged.

It was midway between meán oíche and sunrise. The moon sat high in a cloudless sky, a sliver of cream deigning to spare only a modicum of light to break the blackness. Two parties had travelled from Ráth Cavares to Dún-an-Rí with few stops. All were tired, hungry, and irritable. Most wanted a beer, hot food, and a space to sleep. They could live with how they stank until sunrise. The Rí Ruirech and his queen, accompanied by Fearghal and Deaglán Ó Néill, led the larger of the warbands. The smaller was under the command of the kings of Ráth Cavares, Brocc and Torcán, and their queens, Bláithín and Mòrag. Íar, Conall hoped, was already at the fort.

Hard, horny hooves clopped on the wooden bridge spanning the confluence of the Rodonos and the Souconna, shattering the night's silence. Since it was almost summer, the river was well past the worst of its strong currents and flooding from the melting snows of the Alpes. Loud cursing rose up from those on foot who took to the river. The day had been hot, but the water retained its chill. The mounted laughed, only to receive a torrent of good-humoured abuse. Now, they all stood at the south-western gates of Dún-an-Rí.

Conall's party was greeted with a gruff, "Unless you want to be pinned to your saddles, come into the light, arseholes."

A round of, "Póg mo thóin, eejit!" was hurled in answer. Conall sat bemused, as the entranceway was in total darkness.

Mórrígan's snapped rejoinder rang out, "I don't need light to put an arrow in each of your eyes." She laughed to herself at not having added "arsehole." The retort elicited a distressed ejaculation. Only newborns were excused from failing to recognise the Dark Huntress's voice.

"Shite! It's the Queen. Open the gates." Torches and braziers flared on the ramparts and gateposts.

"It seems they fear you more than me."

Mórrígan grinned at Conall through a mask of trail dirt and said, "Rightly so."

Once across the entrance, Conall called the captain of the guard to him. "Has Íar arrived?" The warrior nodded enthusiastically, supported by the smell of horse shite wafting in their direction by a night breeze.

"How fares Lugudunon? Can a messenger be sent? I wish to meet with my commanders when the sun rises…" The man dipped his head, hoping he would recall the rapid series of orders. Then he shrugged his shoulders. He would simply ask anyone with a "name" to report to Dún-an-Rí. Conall's most important order came last. "Send an envoy to Brennus of the Senones. Invite him to eat with us on the morrow at sunset."

At quizzical looks from Mórrígan and Fearghal, Conall allowed himself a smirk. "He can't refuse. It would be against all the rules of honour and hospitality. Plus, his ego will demand that he sits down with us." His companions' expressions remained concerned. Conall's grin widened.

"Worst case, it will give us another sunset to prepare."

***

As it climbed above the horizon, the imperious golden orb swept away the waning moon and the purple-greys that painted the dawn. Soon, the morning sky would be flushed red with highlights of orange and yellow. Colours that would seem outrageous to the most creative of artists blended magnificently under the sun's aegis.

The soft padding of naked feet woke Conall from his transient slumbers. He raised himself on one elbow. Aodán stood before him. At twelve summers old, Conall's son was the image of his father. Severe, deep-blue eyes were set in a pale face. Freckles on high cheekbones were a perfect complement to an unruly mop of auburn hair. A brief smile caused the boy's dimples to appear. He always looked forward to seeing his ma and da. Yet, his normal beam was muted.

"I heard sobbing as I passed Iasg's rooms. Where's Urard?"

The stricken look on his parents' faces negated further explanation. No reason would ever be sufficient. Urard had been Aodán's guardian from his birth, and the giant had saved him from the evil Queen Kartimandu. The young man dipped his head and bit his lip to prevent a cascade of tears. He was unsuccessful. Salty jewels spotted the wooden floor as he ran to Conall's open arms. Soon the king's chest was soaked. Moments later, the sobs subsided. Still holding his father's hand, Aodán stood.

"You're the king. You should have saved him, Da." Judgment passed, the boy left the room.

"He will forgive because he loves you." Mórrígan pulled her partner into a warm embrace.

Conall nodded. "He has a big heart." The king kissed his queen's forehead. "But he spoke the truth."

***

Like maggots on dead flesh, the arguments rapidly proliferated, only to transform with equal speed into flies and take wing. "In the field, we're well outnumbered. Why waste good men and women? Let Brennus' horde bleed on the walls of Lugudunon. The fortress is unassailable."

"Matres once thought the stronghold was impregnable. She was wrong."

"Will honour be served by slaughtering the Senones with missiles?"

"Honour be damned. We didn't ask for this. There was no negotiation. We were attacked without reason or warning."

"He cannot be allowed free rein to slaughter our people, to burn and pillage our farms and settlements."

Conall rubbed his forehead. The throbbing behind his eyes intensified. Like a hound trying to bite its tail, most of the opinions were well-intentioned, some were humorous, but all were circular. No phoenix of a strategy rose from the fiery debate. Finally, Conall halted the discussions.

"The king of the Senones is not a fool, but it appears his mind has been swayed by others. If you were Brennus and thinking clearly, where would you strike? Where are we vulnerable?"

Silence fell on the gathering. Some drank from horns of beer or cups of wine while others chewed on cold roasted meat or hunks of bread and cheese. Mórrígan brought their contemplations to a close.

"The future leaders of our tribe sleep in Dún-an-Rí."

✶✶✶

While not a complete shock, Conall's Chomhairle was surprised at the alacrity with which Brennus accepted the invitation to Dún-an-Rí. That he was accompanied by an outwardly self-assured Celtillos produced mutterings of anger and veiled threats of imminent violence. Significantly, the body language and distance between the two kings suggested all was not well with the erstwhile allies. Conall, with a good night's sleep, clung to the hope that Brennus might be open to reason. Still angered by his execution of the young Arverni prince, Conall's thoughts were not so charitable about Celtillos.

Celtillos was a head smaller than Brennus, but then the burly Senone king was taller than most men. To be noticed was a significant challenge when standing alongside the imposing presence of Brennus, but one the verrix of the Arverni accepted and carried off with some aplomb. There was little doubt that the young Arverni prince, Celtillos' bastard son, had taken his looks from his mother. Whereas the prince had been slim and fine-boned, his father had the appearance of a marble statue left unfinished due to the non-payment of the sculptor.

Undoubtedly the king was a fighter. His face was pock-marked, his forehead marked by scars, and his nose crooked from intimate contact with fists, skulls, and helmets. Alert, deep-brown eyes continually assessed his enemies—which Conall noted appeared to include Brennus—and options for retreat. Aggression was natural to the man. Broad shoulders held slightly forward of his waist served to indicate that he was well used to bulling his way through any situation. Bow-legged, Celtillos' rolling gait hinted at a considerable affinity for horses. Final flourishes were provided by the king's armour and weapons: Arverni craftsmanship at its best.

"We meet at last, Conall Mac Gabhann, Rí Ruirech of Clann Uí Flaithimh. And, of course, Queen Mórrígan, or should I call you An Fiagaí Dorcha?" Celtillos dipped his head to each in turn as he stretched out a hand. Both king and queen ignored the gesture.

"I met your son recently. He would have made a fine king of the Arverni."

Celtillos shook his head at Conall's words. "Too slight. Too many thoughts and ideas. Too much care for the people. His mother coddled him."

Conall's voice rasped like a whetstone on steel. "He was honourable and courageous in battle. He refused my offer of sanctuary. He died bravely, like a king. Unlike those who propelled him to challenge me."

The king of the Arverni's mask slipped, if briefly. "His guards were foolish and misinformed of my wishes. You did me a service by their executions. With the deaths of the five hundred who accompanied him and the farms and settlements pillaged by the Dark Huntress, I deem our account settled in full." Unnerved by the slow shake of Conall's head and the look shared with Mórrígan, the Arverni king fell silent.

"*No, it is not!* The sword is not my only weapon. The Arverni have benefited much from the trade on the Rodonos." Celtillos' eyes widened. "The river is in Clann Ui Flaithimh territory. In the past, I have overlooked minor thievery and the taxes you levy illegally. No longer. Learn to live without the wealth from the Rodonos."

Red faced, Celtillos raged. "You can't do this."

"I can, and I will. The garrison at Ráth Cavares will be doubled in strength." Celtillos lifted a hand to protest, but a look from Conall stopped the gesture. "You never asked how *he* died. Or by whose hand." One glance at Conall's blue-grey eyes told the Arverni king all he needed to know. "With one question, I would have taken your hand in friendship."

A chuckle from behind Celtillos told that Brennus had enjoyed the encounter. For his part, Brennus was taken aback at Conall's grim demeanour, which was mirrored in the faces of Mórrígan, the High Council, and commanders. There had always been a vibrancy to Conall's deportment. His eyes had twinkled with sprites of cunning, ruthlessness, and mischievousness.

Now it seemed the king's good nature had departed and a heart colder than the ice on the Alpes lay within that breast. Had the king of Clann Ui Flaithimh taken a step on the dark path of tyranny? Could the attack on his daughter, Danu, have affected Conall that much? Brennus shivered. A Conall with foolish ideals, looking for justice above revenge, was one thing. A marauding despot with the armies of Clann Ui Flaithimh and his allies at his back was a different barrel of fish.

Impatience radiated from Conall as if he cared little what the Senones might say or offer. Indeed, it appeared the king's mind was already made up. Brennus gasped. Conall wanted to fight, and blood was the only acceptable salve for his anger. Any enemy would do, and Brennus had foolishly provided the anvil to be struck by Clann Ui Flaithimh's hammer. Compromise was for another time.

"You, Brennus of the Senones, have disrespected our agreement, crossed my lands without seeking accommodation. You attacked my people. This cannot and will not stand unanswered."

Brennus spat on the dirt floor. "Just words. What's your proposal?"

"A tithe of the gold you agreed with Dionysius." As if answering the question in Brennus' and Celtillos' minds, he added, "You will leave suitable-status nobles as guests of Clann Ui Flaithimh until the debt is paid." Conall looked at Celtillos. Anger smouldered in his eyes. "I am mindful, however, of the low value *you* place on the lives of your kin. We will carefully examine the worth of your representatives."

Unabashed, the Arverni king thought aloud. "As you say. My subjects are mine to use. Perhaps I will leave my more troublesome nobles and their children to be your guests—or slaves."

Mórrígan spoke. "No."

Her voice held a matter-of-fact tone that chilled Celtillos. "Man, woman, or child, I will stake them before the gates of Nemessos. They will bear witness as my army razes that city to the ground. I will turn the land of the Arverni into ashes and sow it with salt. Mag Mell will be populated with your male dead. Your women and children will be delivered into slavery. You, Celtillos, will be remembered among the Gaulish nations as the king who let his tribe be devastated."

Mórrígan's smile sent shivers up the spines of those present. "One way or another, your tithe will be paid."

To Celtillos' alarm, it seemed that the Dark Huntress's preference was for him to decline the offer. Prudence and pragmatism overcame anger. Celtillos hoped that Conall's decision on the Rodonos trade could be favourably renegotiated at a later date.

"I concur. We will agree on hostages with your druid. With your permission, my army will leave for the Alpes in five sunsets. This will allow our injured to rest and be ready to travel. Perhaps we could also purchase supplies for the journey." Conall nodded his assent.

To Brennus, the Arverni king added, "I will meet you on the northern bank of the Eridanus." It was as if Celtillos knew Brennus would refuse to pay the toll.

"So noted," said Crum Dubh. He looked to Brennus. "Is it also agreed by you?" A glimmer of a smile played on the druid's thin lips. It did not go unnoticed by Brennus or by Conall and Mórrígan.

"No!" snarled Brennus. "I'll not be dictated to by any man or woman"—the king stood and strode across the hall, pausing only to stand before Crum Dubh— "or druid," he hissed.

To the dismay of some and the seeming amusement of others, a dagger appeared in Brennus' hand. Crum gasped as he felt the point pierce the loose flesh under his chin. Several drops of blood splashed the floor.

"I don't understand your game, Druid, but know this: You are no longer welcome in the lands of the Senones. Set one foot in any of my territories or the lands of those who pay obeisance to me, and you will forfeit your life. As of now, you are stripped of your leadership of the Druidic Councils in Gaul."

Dagger returned to its sheath, Brennus faced Conall and Mórrígan. He was perplexed at the lack of protest from either king or queen. Whatever Crum had done to annoy them showed that the priest had few friends in the hall. "You'll be needing a new pet druid. This one's power is greatly diminished. I'm sure your Oracle will be able to recommend a replacement." The doors crashed as Brennus left the chamber.

A bemused Fearghal remarked, "Thank the Hag, he didn't kill Crum." Conall's eyebrow lifted in search of an explanation. "I don't think Drostan and his brother, Crum, are close, but one thing is certain. We'd have had an army from Northern Albu at our gates seeking to avenge him." Conall dipped his head to disguise a widening smile. Still, it proved impossible to prevent a soft chuckle escaping from his lips, perhaps the first sign that the Rí Ruirech's bruised spirit was healing.

✱✱✱

Ignored, Crum slipped from the chamber. The loss of power and prestige was crushing. His only hope appeared to be the death of Brennus in the near future. Yet, he observed in Conall and Mórrígan's eyes no hint that even that would restore his fortunes.

Crum sighed. Perhaps he had conjured up too many intrigues. Had he also lost the support of the Goddess? Was he mistaken in his interpretation of her desires? At least he remained the Leader of the Druidic Council of the Gaels and Arbiter of Clann Ui Flaithimh's Laws. Like a good fire on a winter's day, perhaps the fires of ambition needed to be banked.

CHAPTER 16

395 B.C.—Dún-an-Rí

Built on high ground, the stronghold of Lugudunon stood sentinel over an extended loop of the tortuous Souconna River. Except for a strip of land to its east, the hill dropped precipitously to the riverbanks. The small river plain, pleasantly contoured and verdant, was about four hundred paces wide and fifteen hundred in length. Refreshed regularly by flooding waters, the lush parcel of land was used primarily as pasture for the stronghold's herds of cattle.

In the long shadow of the citadel, several wooden bridges, each wide enough to allow two war chariots to cross side by side, spanned the river. The distance between Lugudunon and Dún-an-Rí was not great: a warrior crossing either of the structures would reach one of Dún-an-Rí's entrances without breaking a sweat. Numerous jetties used by merchants and fishers reached out into the Souconna from both banks. However, they were smaller and of flimsier construction than the bridges and in a constant state of repair when the river flooded.

Built on the narrow finger of land at the confluence of the Rodonos and the Souconna, Dún-an-Rí's location was enviable and protected to the east, west, and south by the rivers. Each waterway spanned over two hundred paces. The waters' depth was seasonal, being lower—no more than waist-high—in summer, autumn, and early winter. In the spring, it swelled to flood levels due to the heavy rains that followed the Máistir and the snowmelt flowing off the Alpes.

Constantly shifting sandbanks and tricky currents made navigation challenging for vessels that traded along the waterways. Fortunately, the cedarwood biremes used by Pytheas and many other merchants out of Massalia were light. They could be lifted out of the water and carried by their crews whenever necessary. And, of course, enterprising farmers along the meandering rivers were more than willing to rent out wagons to transport goods over short distances.

Gentle hills to the north gave Dún-an-Rí the advantage of long sightlines. The fort, laid out on a south-west to north-east axis, was positioned midway between the two rivers but closer to where the waters met. Even on the cloudiest and wettest days, Lugudunon and Dún-an-Rí were visible to each other. A bustling community of small farmholdings had sprung up within and around Dún-an-Rí, and at this season, the fields were a patchwork of neat drills of corn.

Scattered thickets of oak, ash, and alder crowned small hills, providing shade for livestock and homes for animals and birds. Seasonal shrubs and wildflowers added splashes of vibrant colour to the vista. These pleasant landscape highlights only existed because Conall and Mórrígan insisted. Had Cúscraid got his way, the scenery would have been denuded of anything over knee height. The only possible exception to this would be thickets of draighean with its profusion of wicked thorns.

The royal stronghold and residence were of traditional wood-based construction and roughly square. Each wall was approximately two hundred paces in length—enough for two hundred shield warriors to stand shoulder to shoulder. Like the Carnutes' settlement at Cenabum, the walls were a series of massive timber boxes filled with earth and stone and tied together with hardwood beams. The stockade was five paces wide and two spear lengths tall. As Conall toured the defences with Brocc, Lonán, Mórrígan, and Torcán, he recalled Lonán's recent advice to add another spear's length to the walls' height. While prescient, it was too late to act on that counsel. A ditch, as deep as two spear lengths, ran parallel to the fence. The dirt excavated was piled up to form a protective berm on the trench's outer edge. Both ditch and berm were liberally planted with sharpened stakes.

Dún-an-Rí had two fortified entrances positioned opposite each other. At the corners and on each side of the gateways, two-storey guard towers jutted from the ramparts. Each tower sported a heavy ballista, a small cohort of archers, and a squad of shield warriors, all positioned to throw down a deadly crossfire on attackers. Conall had put the garrison of Dún-an-Rí under the command of Lonán Ó Néill, a man of few words and seemingly made of granite. Under him were eight hundred foot and two hundred mounted warriors. With family, trades, and artisans, the fort's population had quickly swollen to over five thousand. Over half lived in clutches of smaller dwellings within sight of the walls.

Dogs and feral cats roamed the compound, occasionally scrapping over territory or food. Chickens, ducks, and geese wandered free. They were sporadically forced into frenzied squawking when chased by children seeking a contribution to the evening's cooking pots. Larger livestock were housed outside the fort: horses in corrals and cattle in the lush meadows. On occasion, the population feasted on roast pork, but only when the hunters returned from the forests carrying wild boar. A fierce animal with a tough hide, vicious tusks, and a nasty temper, it had succulent flesh.

At the centre of Dún-an-Rí was a rectangular building—the Great Hall and the adjoining royal family's residence. Traditional timber, rock, and mud roundhouses with grey-brown sloping thatched roofs and floors of stone slabs, wooden planks, or just well-tamped dirt were scattered throughout the inner court. Larger dwellings, able to house twenty or more, were the homes of some of the clann's nobles.

"They will burn quickly," said a blunt Torcán. None in the group disagreed.

Groups of smaller houses accommodated the warriors, artisans, and trades—blacksmiths, armourers, fletchers, bakers, and hunters. Leatherworkers were located on the banks of the Rodonos. Their products were highly sought after, but the stink of the industry was unbearable for the ráth's residents.

Within the fort, the smell of baking and food preparation lent a pleasant homeliness to the community. In the hot summer, this faced stiff competition from the rotting food, animal carcasses, piss, and shite emptied into the perimeter ditches. In most seasons, wide ribbons of blue-grey smoke floated above the fort. Even in the heat of summer, cooking fires and braziers were rarely unlit. Everyone, from the young to the elderly, had their jobs. From the roundhouses came the wet sounds of presses squeezing olives and grapes and the rasp of quern stones grinding corn. The thump and rattle of wooden looms produced the gaily coloured plaids, brata, and léinte.

Dún-an-Rí's strength was its proximity to Lugudunon. Yet its comfortable lifestyle allowed an air of invincibility to slip into the thinking of the ráth's residents. It was an attitude that sorely tempted Fate. Conall looked at Lonán with his unspoken question. The reflection and shake of the head told Conall the ráth would be a nightmare to defend. Dún-an-Rí could never withstand a determined assault by ten thousand, let alone thirty thousand Senones.

Conall eyed the Great Hall. With the advance of Brennus' army on Lugudunon, all the non-combatants had been escorted to Dún-an-Rí for safety. This included the children of Clann Ui Flaithimh's wealthy and nobility. The future leaders of the tribe were now camped in and around the building. *A reasonable decision at the time*, he mused.

Conall chewed on the inside of his cheek and shook his head as if admonishing himself. During his visit, Brennus would have been blind not to observe and hear the children of the tribe at play. Dún-an-Rí was too tempting a target of opportunity and much less of a challenge than the walls of Lugudunon. Mórrígan saw the concern etched deep into her partner's face. She sighed. At one time, Conall's only worry had been fending off the advances of a brash, red-haired lass.

"It was a good decision by Brandubh and the others. No blame can be laid at their feet—or yours." The queen smiled and grasped Conall's hand. "Perhaps it is time to accept progress. Next time we should build with stone but leave plenty of space for trees and gardens." Conall dipped his head in agreement.

"Is the Chomhairle gathered?" Mórrígan nodded.

"Let's plan our response to Brennus."

CHAPTER 17

395 B.C.—The Battle of Dún-an-Ri

"Will our allies fight with us?"

It was Gaius who posed the question, and his eyes were on the Aedui king, Ambigatos. The portly, rosy-cheeked ruler smiled at the Roman. Ambigatos' girth showed that he was fond of food and beer, but all knew he was still a formidable warrior. He also had the uncommon distinction among the Gauls of being loved by his people. His head, swaddled in a mop of shaggy ginger hair and great bushy whiskers, shook in a silent "No." He stood. Beyond his prime, Ambigatos grunted and swore as he felt the creeping pains of age and the stiffness of bones, no longer able to move with the freedom of his youth.

"I had not expected to meet you again, Gaius." The elderly monarch chuckled. "Certainly not in the company of Celts and barbarians." He sighed. "And it would appear that I am to disappoint you once more. The Aedui will return to Bibracte. Our numbers will not be a significant loss in the upcoming battle. Still, they would be missed by my people should Brennus prevail and decide to punish our 'disloyalty'."

Gaius rose and smiled at a man he greatly admired. He knew that in the past, the king had held hopes that Gaius would be joined with one of his daughters. It was a path that, with hindsight, might have caused the Roman to suffer much less pain. He clasped Ambigatos' arm and drew him into his embrace.

"There is no disappointment. You are a good king to the Aedui.

Long may you rule."

The Roman gestured at the commanders, kings, and queen seated around the long table. "I think I can say that all here appreciated your support. And I am sure that, in more peaceful times, the king and queen of Clann Ui Flaithimh will eagerly take up your invitation to visit." Cups and goblets banged on the wooden table in support of Gaius and to respect the king.

As the Great Hall's doors closed behind Ambigatos, Conall rose and looked to Tasgiitios. "And where do the Carnutes stand?"

Tasgiitios laughed. "As if I have any choice. The Oracle made it quite clear the wisdom of aligning myself with Clann Ui Flaithimh. He says that you and his sister would make terrible enemies. More so than Brennus, and I tend to agree. My five thousand will stand with the army of Conall."

***

As darkness fell, all in the Great Hall were in accord. Conall's plan was reasonable, rational, and based on current intelligence. Thus it was doomed. The last dregs of beer from an oaken barrel likely had more value.

At dawn, Brandubh, Carmag, and Gaius walked the walls of Lugudunon, trading insults and jests with their men. Three thousand stood ready. Only the morning birdsong and the random crack from wood expanding and contracting disturbed the silence. The great ballistae stood prepared to rain death on the enemy. Smoke-blackened cauldrons simmered on glowing braziers. Men with hands and arms thickly swathed in wet wool and hide, eyes red and streaming, prayed the battle would start soon.

Brandubh gazed east across the Souconna to where Conall's forces waited. The sight was impressive. Three thousand shield-wall warriors, most wearing boiled-leather armour and others chainmail, sweated in the morning sun. They stood fifty paces back from the riverbank, with multi-coloured horsehair helmet plumes lazily rising and falling in the light morning breezes. The wall had divided into three—one cohort for each bridge plus a reserve. Each comprised two ranks who stood with javelins ready. Signature red shields with a swooping black raven lay on the grass in front of them, all within reach of hands itching to fight.

Conall and Fearghal led the bridge detachments. A self-effacing Deaglán, commander of the reserve, grumbled that Conall and Fearghal would have all the glory. His smirk was mostly hidden behind long red whiskers braided to match his hair. Still, Deaglán knew that if his division were called on to fight, it would not be because Conall was winning.

Behind the shield-walls, Íar's fifteen hundred riders sat astride impatient mounts. Hoofs pawed the dirt. Ears were swept back. Rounds of snorts issued from yellow-toothed mouths. To the side, Gràinne's twenty gaudily coloured chariots rocked back and forward. An early morning sun glinted off tack, and the bronze war scythes. On the other flank, Mórrígan's two hundred cantered up and down the bank, restless to engage the enemy.

In Dún-an-Rí, two thousand men and women under Bláithín, Brocc, Lonán, Mòrag, and Torcán checked armour. Spit-wetted whetstones abraded the edges of wickedly sharp blades. Operating teams of the heavy ballistae housed in the guard towers readied the weapons to throw the first bolts. Archers adjusted leather wristbands, applied bowstrings to staves, and ensured they had a good supply of arrows. Beside them, braziers slumbered. Fire was always an effective way to strike fear into an enemy or to cauterise wounds. The mood was light in the fort. Many groused good-humouredly that they would be unlikely to participate in the battle since all expected Lugudunon and the two bridges over the Souconna to be the main battlegrounds.

The battlefield, set up by Conall like a fidchell board, lacked but one element—Brennus and his Senones. On this pleasant late summer morning, Brennus was not in the mood for games.

***

Concealing the presence of thirty thousand warriors in a forest is not that difficult. On the open ground between the trees and Lugudunon, it was impossible. On this morning, Brennus saw no benefit in concealing his army. The deep *barr-ewww* of the Gaulish war horns reverberated, prompting the Senones to surge forward. Feet, some in boots, others in bróga, and many naked, thudded on the dry dirt. The earth trembled. All on the stronghold's walls braced to repel the onslaught. Ballistae and slings were readied to commence their barrage as soon as the horde came within range.

"The Hag's arse!"

Appalled, the commanders of Lugudunon watched as the Senone army split into two. Five thousand wheeled to the east, heading for the eastern entrance of the citadel. The remaining horde, following a wide curving arc south, stayed well beyond the range of Lugudunon's missiles. As he ran ahead of his warriors, Brennus laughed aloud and imagined the confusion his tactics would cause Lugudunon's leaders.

"Shite!" snapped Carmag. "Did nae one inform that bastard, Brennus, of the plan?"

At Lugudunon's eastern gates, Gaius waited for the attack. The entranceway was lightly defended—after Brennus' last debacle, no one had anticipated a direct assault on the gates. Together with his Roman soldiers, Gaius' primary weapons were the smaller field ballistae and two hundred of Brandubh's slinger-archers. "*Irrumatores!*" cursed the Roman as he watched the five thousand Senone warriors pick up their pace to a fast jog.

Worse, instead of attacking, they veered towards the Souconna riverbank, quickly putting themselves beyond the killing range of Gaius' ballistae's bolts and the Ravens' arrows. That aside, at the speed they had taken up, a mortal strike with any missile would have been mere chance. A hail of stones from the slingers—the only weapon remaining with enough reach—rose high in the air and descended. It was a futile gesture, with the bullets mainly causing bruises and loud swearing.

Gathered at the western ramparts, Lugudunon's commanders watched the main Senone army. Carmag squinted, focusing hazel eyes on the receding horde. "Ma estimation of Brennus as a tactician has risen." The warrior pointed. "If ma guess is right, they're making for the coming together of the Rodonos and Souconna. From there, they will cross and attack Dún-an-Rí. The smaller army on the east is a feint, albeit a sizeable one. That force will assemble on the river plain and threaten the two bridges. I suspect they'll attempt to take the bridges, but their main job will be to keep Conall occupied."

Typically a quiet and thoughtful man, Brandubh was flushed with anger and frustration. "The Hag take the Senone bastard. Ma sister and her children are in Dún-an-Rí." With a deep inhale to control his temper, the Prince of the Ravens barked out orders. "Send a handful of riders to swim the Souconna south of the bridges. Conall must be warned, and so must Tasgiitios. We need his fighters. Send messengers to advise the king we're making for the river junction and would appreciate his support." Brandubh shook his head. Had he any hair, he would have ripped it out in anguish.

"Gaius, you will hold Lugudunon. I have no men to spare, but the walls are strong." Brandubh paused. "Assign half yer men and a score of ballistae to trap those bastards at the river."

To Carmag, he said, "Pick out two hundred of your best fighters to support Gaius."

The burly warrior was disgruntled at his orders. He knew his fighters would prefer to be in the thick of the battle, not on guard duty. Brandubh looked at Carmag, a wry smile on his face. "You have one thousand forest warriors, and I have the same number of Ravens. Even if Tasgiitios joins us, that's not a lot to stop twenty or thirty thousand."

Carmag nodded. "We have no choice but to try." Then he smirked, "I have a plan."

* * *

Lonán slowly and methodically tied boot thongs, tightened buckles and belts, and inspected an impressive array of weapons—swords, axes, javelins, clubs, and daggers. Some were sheathed and secured about his person. Others were placed within easy reach. An oblong, waisted shield that protected from neck to knee rested against the stockade.

The broad-shouldered warrior's long, brown hair was pulled tightly back from his head and tied with a short leather cord. The effect was to make his hazel-amber eyes stand out and the many ridged, white scars more prominent. He tapped an adjacent warrior's shoulder. She turned around, smiled, and then tightened his armour with a zeal that made him exhale sharply.

Like Fearghal, Lonán preferred boiled-leather armour with iron scales affixed between the multiple layers over the trend to chainmail. He had foregone the light woollen tunic customarily worn underneath. Mail gloves, a gift from Torcán, were the one exception to his choice of leather. At heart, both men were brawlers, and the gauntlets were well-suited to their bruising fighting style.

Finally, Lonán checked his bronze-and-iron helmet. As could be expected, it was utilitarian in design and construction. Conical and tapering to a small, flattened oval knub, the helmet had metal flaps covering the ears and a lip to protect the neck. Its only embellishments were a finger-width rope of copper-gold metal that trimmed the headdress and a short, yellow-gold ribbon that fluttered from the crest. The latter raised boyish smirks on the faces of his companions. Lonán's reputation was that of a solitary and private individual not given to public expressions of… well, anything. The ribbon suggested the contrary.

"The Hag's arse!" Torcán bellowed in disbelief as Brennus' army assembled at the meeting of the two rivers and started to wade across. He shook his head at Brocc and Lonán and gestured to the warriors standing on the ramparts of Dún-an-Rí. "We have two thousand fighters in cramped conditions. I can piss higher than these walls. Our poets and seanchaithe tell us that one of our men is worth ten of any Gaul. That will still leave enough of the bastards to behead, desecrate, and strip our bodies of anything of value. How can we stand against so many?"

"That's easy to answer," said Brocc. "We can't." He pursed his lips, and the dimple on his chin deepened. "The real question is: do we stand or retreat?"

Both Lonán and Torcán laughed at the choice. Torcán considered for a moment, and said, "You know what's worse? No Tadhg. There's no seanchaí to immortalise our glorious heroics. Who will remember us?"

Brocc laughed. "I can't see anyone forgetting you, although many might want to." The red-haired warrior exhaled. "They'll likely attack the south-western wall and gateway first. Choose your stand."

Torcán smiled. "The southern wall. If I can throw them back, I'll get all the glory." A loud cheer rose as he turned, raised his shield, and shouted, *"Ní ghéillfear, nó cúlú!"*— "No retreat, no surrender!"

✳✳✳

Conall stood at the northernmost bridge. Like the stopper of an amphora, ten rows of ten shields stood shoulder to shoulder and sealed the deck. Behind him, the rest of his division waited, alert and impatient for battle. The war cries and taunts of the Senones travelled ahead of the horde, but soon the wooden planks vibrated and thudded under the impact of hundreds of feet. A similar scene played out on Fearghal's bridge. It seemed to Conall that the crossing was never meant to withstand such heavy traffic. Hence, the highest likelihood was for the structure to collapse into the waters of the Souconna. *That would be a good result and would spare the lives of many.*

Besides the futility of the current situation, with stalemate being the most probable outcome, an unwelcome sense of foreboding nagged at Conall. The plain on the far side of the bridges was rapidly denuded of warriors as the Senones stepped onto the structures. *Too quickly. Much too quickly.* Perhaps Brennus, anticipating that the garrison would be light, had decided to make his main assault the walls of Lugudunon.

The king spat. Was the occupation of the bridges a diversion to keep his shield-wall occupied and prevent the reinforcement of Lugudunon? Somewhat relieved, Conall exhaled and settled his shield to a more comfortable position. He cursed the moisture already forming on the palm of his weapon hand and adjusted his grasp on the javelin. Brandubh could hold Lugudunon with far less than the three thousand defenders standing on its ramparts and Tasgiitios' force would harass Brennus' rear.

Yet Conall's mind refused to be at ease.

∗∗∗

The situation of the brother and sister, twins of no more than fourteen summers, was not uncommon. Their parents had not forced them to join Brennus' great campaign, but its promise of unimaginable wealth was irresistible. The family was destitute; the father was crippled with bitterness and the burdens of life. The mother had once been comely. Disease, regret, and time took her looks; drudgery drove away youthful dreams. The twins' siblings were hungry. Thus, no one discouraged their choice to fight, and they joined thousands of others with a similar tale.

The need to survive made the pair quick learners. Their story was pitiful but not uncommon. Naïve and helpless in an alien environment, the girl was raped—the boy too. As compensation or perhaps an admission of guilt, their defilers left them shields, swords, and daggers. They were of poor quality, but a borrowed whetstone ground the blades to a fine edge. In the darkness of the night, the two sought out and stalked their despoilers. They watched as the miscreants drank themselves into a stupor. Eventually, when each staggered off to find a place to piss, the young predators closed in.

Exposed and unaware, the heavy streams of piss were deposed by gushing blood. Voice muted by overindulgence and trauma, each stared as his manhood was displayed before his eyes. A slash across each throat was a final act of mercy. The bodies were stripped of anything of value. Armour and weapons were quickly upgraded. The boy clasped his sister's shoulder. She flinched from his touch as the memory of her violation was still fresh. He shrugged and nodded to the final corpse. There was one more task to complete. No one wanted to be pursued by the angry spirits of the dead. And so, the gristle and bone of the neck were sawn until the head rolled free. They did not hide their work. As the men were not nobles, there was no need. This was life in the army of Brennus.

On this new sunrise, surrounded by thousands of screaming, unwashed warriors, many with faces flushed with anger and beer, the two were swept towards the walls of Dún-an-Rí. As she ran with the horde, the girl absorbed its collective rage with no conscious thought. She had never met the enemy. Given spears, they were ordered, under pain of death, to stay on the flanks—a buttress against the Clann Ui Flaithimh cavalry. She thanked her god that they were not at the front. Gossip in the Senone camp made it plain that being assigned that position meant almost certain death. Few expected to survive the stakes of the perimeter ditches or the javelins thrown from the stockade.

A childish giggle slipped from the girl's lips. Amidst the chaos, uppermost in her thoughts was keeping her spear from stabbing or tripping up those surrounding her. She found it a clumsy and unwieldy weapon for a charge. The crack of a ballista interrupted her moment of levity. A zephyr of air brushed her cheek as the bolt carved a bloody path through those who ran beside her. Hot liquid splashed her face and gore stuck to her clothing. She would have thrown up had she time to think.

Heads and limbs were cleaved, only to suffer the further indignity of being kicked aside or stamped on by the mob. The momentum of the assault would not be denied. She trembled and gave her brother, who now loped at her side, a fearful glance. Once more, she offered thanks to her god that he had been spared the missile's devastation. A second tremble trickled up her spine. Instinct told her that she neared the ditch and the walls of Dún-an-Rí.

***

The clamour from thousands of throats, raw from screaming insults and shouting tribal battle cries, reached a deafening crescendo. Under the steady pounding of the dirt by tens of thousands of feet, the wooden stockade trembled. Bereft of even the lightest of breezes, the proud red-and-black flag of Conall and gold-and-red banners and flags of the clann hung limp. To a people uncertain of their standing with the Goddess, it was not a good omen, yet their faith in Conall did not waver.

Torcán's southern-facing walls already faced a brutal attack. Now, the Senone horde swept around to the north-western gateway and ramparts, burning and destroying any home or workshop in their path. Rickety ladders thudded against the fence. Iron hooks and loops of rope sought purchase. Boots and calloused soles gathered splinters as the attackers ascended. Men and women grunted as others stood on their shoulders. Bláithín steadied herself as the walkway shuddered. The Ulaid noble, sporting a prized Cróeb Ruad tattoo—a sword with a red branch entwined around it—on her right shoulder, cut a striking figure on the battlements.

The fine linens and gowns of nobility were gone. Instead, a tightly bound cuirass protected Bláithín's upper body. Made from several layers of boiled leather bonded together, the protection's outer layer was painted and crafted with ornate swirling designs. The breastplate was also imaginatively moulded to emphasise the lady's highly admired figure. After her battles in northern Aremorio, Brocc had suggested one modification. Thus, under the cuirass and resting on Bláithín's hips, was a sleeveless blouse of chainmail. The mail shirt itself lay on a light chemise of soft hide.

It had taken a while for Bláithín to become accustomed to the additional layers and weight. On this day, she sensed that she would need the protection. She groaned. The material was already damp with sweat. Blue plaid triubhas, with patches of chainmail stitched to protect her thighs, were tucked into soft boots laced with thick thongs. A thick strip of sheepskin was wound around each shin. A final piece, the distinctive helmet gifted to her by Brocc, sat atop her head. The covering's short blue plumes were a perfect match for the colour of her eyes.

Bláithín's primary weapons were a pair of short-shafted axes, each with wickedly sharp double blades and vicious spikes that protruded from both ends of the haft. When not in use, they hung in loops tied to a broad, ornately embossed leather belt that rested on the lady's curvaceous hips. A short sword and a selection of daggers sheathed in sheepskin-lined, wooden scabbards dangled on the belt. Several more knives were slipped into her boots. Finally, on her left arm, she carried a small, round, wooden scíath. It was covered in hide, painted blue, and had a boss and rim of iron. In battle, Lady Bláithín Ni Néill was not to be underestimated.

Yet as she stood on the walkway, Bláithín's muscles quivered, and she fought a strong urge to piss. The defenders of Dún-an-Rí were massively outnumbered, and the chances of surviving were low. The embrace of the mná-sidhe and the gates of Mag Mell beckoned. Yet all stood resolute, determined to make the Senones pay a terrible price. She glanced across the parapet to Lonán—her brother by hand-fasting— to Mòrag and Torcán, and lastly to Brocc. Their war faces, with freshly painted dark blue sigils, sought to instil confidence in their men. Beneath the façade, Bláithín saw reflections of her own misgivings.

The thump of feet swiftly dispelled further contemplation. She cursed at being too late to heft one of the javelins resting against the fence. A towering Senone veteran crouched before her. He was naked above the waist with a beefy, hairless chest covered in scars. Pale skin glistened with sweat from the exertions of the ascent. His arms were covered in numerous gold, silver, and copper bands such that it was challenging to see flesh. Several heavy gold torcs enclosed a thickly muscled neck. A wealthy man and a seasoned warrior. Apart from a pair of horns, his helmet was smooth, worn, and free of embellishment—a veteran's helmet. On his back, he carried an oblong shield.

Grasped in hands wrapped in studded leather strips was a heavy sword. Its edges were honed sharp, sweeping down to a rounded tip and it had already begun its arc upwards. As yet, the weapon was free from notches gained in battle. Like those wielded by most of the horde, the sword was a weapon for slashing. The subtlety of swordplay was a luxury in a pitched battle. He looked down at Bláithín and leered. Though perhaps it was an expression of fear. It was difficult to tell underneath the shaggy, blond beard and whiskers that swallowed the man's face.

Nimbleness, and a gore-free walkway, saved Bláithín from the descending blade. Had it been at the end of the battle, she doubted whether she would have had enough strength or room to avoid the stroke. She felt a judder journey up her calves as the sword's tip hit and dug deeply into the planking at her toes. The warrior grunted as he tugged to release the weapon. The moment, no more than a few breaths, was enough for Bláithín to crouch and close on the man.

Bláithín's axe swung parallel to the walkway. She felt the weapon's momentum briefly falter as it met the resistance of dense slabs of thigh muscle. Once breached, the blade continued its path, slicing through layers of flesh, tendons, and arteries. A hand higher and the razor-sharp edge would have taken the warrior's manhood. Shocked, a sharp exhalation of pain and a loud curse escaped the man's lips. Blood gushed from the deep wounds and severed vessels.

She had seen a man bleed out quickly after being gored in the thigh by a boar. His strength waning, the man stumbled forward. Bláithín's rising shield met a face contorted with agony. The iron boss smashed his nose and cheekbone. As he dropped to his knees, the short axe swung once more. Bláithín's arm shuddered as the blade bit through the hinge of the jawbone and continued its path. The man fell forward, his face sundered diagonally from ear to neck. What remained of his life fled.

Breathing heavily from the short burst of action, Bláithín paused. The duel had taken less time than to drink a cup of water. She allowed herself a smile of victory—a moment of celebration. The Senone veteran should have known better than to underrate his opponent. Likewise, Bláithín should have known better than to succumb to battle euphoria. Her skull felt as if a hammer had struck it. She watched her helmet roll along the parapet before her vision blurred and blackness descended.

In the distance, she heard a loud cry of, "No!" Then nothing.

∗

In the confusion of evacuating the fort's children, the wee girl had been overlooked. Her ma made the fateful assumption that she was with her other siblings, of which there were many. At first, she was happy, content in the nook chosen as her hiding place. Unaware that the game of hide-and-seek was long over, tiredness overcame her, and she burrowed into the sweet-smelling stack of fresh straw. The stables were her favourite place. In her dreams, she was the Dark Huntress, bow in hand, and sat atop a magnificent white horse.

Only five summers old, she was a pretty child with milk-white skin, copper-red hair, and eyes that were an intense shade of lapis. She had a loud voice that belied her tiny frame. Yet, as the tears streamed down dirty cheeks and she called out for her ma and da, her voice went unheard in the clamour of battle.

Fear of being alone drove her to the central square of Dún-an-Rí. Round and round, she spun. The Great Hall was little more than a pile of ashes. Terrified, she looked desperately for a friendly face—for someone to see her. But all were intent on killing or staying alive.

The cart's solid, wooden wheels dwarfed the child as it crunched on the dirt and bumped over broken bodies. Hauled by a pair of slow-moving but steady oxen unperturbed by the battle, the quartermaster's wagons forged a path towards the northern gate. Awed by their size, the child's terror ebbed as she watched the beasts and envisaged herself astride one.

"Behind me, child!" A tall man with a shock of red-blond hair and dressed in orange plaid clothes stood before her. "Get behind me!"

Sheltered and clinging to his leg, she felt the judders of his iron-tipped staff as it stung and struck flesh. The cries of injured warriors and the dull crack of breaking bones assaulted her young ears. She peered from behind her hero but only saw angry, bloodied faces who perceived her not as a child but as chaff—an inconvenience to be tossed aside. Four blades, already dripping gore, faced her champion. Their faces were flushed with the heat of battle, their breathing harsh and ragged.

His position made more precarious by her presence, his retreat—their retreat, was less assured. She heard him gasp in pain and felt him flinch under a barrage of sword strikes. Yet, he stood. She gripped the man tightly, hoping that she could add her strength to his. The last blade brought him to his knees. He roared at his attackers and swung the staff in a semi-circle, but his strength had ebbed. His effort was feeble. They laughed at him and moved in. He was all but dead, and they knew it. She felt the wetness of his wounds soak her léine, and in her child's heart, she knew the kind man's time was passing.

"I love you," she whispered and clung to his neck. He smiled, nodded wearily, and slumped forward.

The bloody, muscular arm of Lonán encircled her tiny waist, and she found herself swept upwards and thrown roughly on top of the wagon. She wept for the tall man who remained prone in the dirt—a splash of orange wildflowers in a sea of blood and mud. Around him lay his attackers, slain by the knight who arrived too late. His comrades shook their heads in sorrow, and one hefted the still warm corpse over his shoulder.

The child was glad. It would not have been right to leave him to lie in the mud. His name was unknown to her at that time, but every spring of her life until she too crossed the veil and met him again, the girl would pick a posy of orange orchids in remembrance.

Sárán Mac Craobhach, Master Quartermaster of Clann Ui Flaithimh, crossed the veil and entered the Hall of Heroes and the epic legends of the clann.

✳✳✳

Mòrag gripped shield and spear. More accurately, the weapon was welded to her hand with gore. Dried blood had frozen her face into a fierce rictus. A long plait of copper-red hair swung wildly as she thrust forward with the weapon while simultaneously battering her opponent with her shield. The leather harness she wore on her upper body, mostly as a sop to her brother, had long since disintegrated. Skin-tight triubhas, torn, ripped, and blood-soaked, clung to her lower body with an admirable determination. Exposed, the blood-soaked sigils of tribe and family looked beautifully vibrant among the tableau of horrors.

The battle was lost. *As if it had ever been winnable*, she snorted. The defensive ditches had quickly filled with Senone dead. Like a great wave crashing onto the shore, the attackers had no chance of resisting that fate. Hundreds of tree trunks now spanned the trench. Scores of ladders leaned against the stockade. Many were injured when the unstable steps disintegrated with too much use. Yet, like the attackers, the supply seemed never-ending.

Countless fighters swarmed up thick ropes of hemp and wool. They were unchallenged. Not enough warriors remained to throw them back from the wall. The great cauldrons of boiling oil, glowing embers, and scalding water were long exhausted. The ballistae were silent, their skeins cut, the machines disabled to prevent them from being turned on the defenders.

On the gore-covered walkway, it was impossible to walk without slipping on the veiny entrails of battle. The stench of shite, piss, and blood clogged nostrils. Men and women brawled, slashing with blunt weapons and biting with yellowed teeth stained blood-red. Mòrag gleefully watched as Torcán's headbutt broke an attacker's nose and his hands, covered in chainmail, stripped the flesh from an opponent's face. The victors howled and crowed while the vanquished shouted defiance and died. The rampart was lost. Only a few isolated groups of Clann Ui Flaithimh warriors remained, determined to ensure their enemy would remember the day with fear.

In her youth, Mòrag loved to fight just for the thrill of the battle. To prove herself the equal of or better than any man. It was different now. At just over thirty summers, she fought for her children—for her and

Torcán's sons and daughter. She would show no mercy to any god, man, or beast, who threatened them.

To the twins, bloodied and cut but amazed that they still lived, the tall female warrior was an appalling apparition. Was there a part not enrobed in blood? They watched the gore-bespattered spear cut through the air and then thrust forward. Heard her scream of victory as she kicked another opponent from the parapet. With no dry wood to grip, the press pushed the boy and girl through the slop and closer to the menacing figure.

The flicker in the corner of her right eye drew an instinctual response. Mòrag's spear lunged with the speed of a striking viper. Eyes wide, the young girl felt the cold spearhead plunge deep into her belly and then withdraw with a sharp tug. She stood, staring at Mòrag, her gaze questioning. Her body seemed unsure of what to do. For a moment it stood, a puppeteer's doll, waiting for its strings to be cut. A rough hand pushed her aside, and she tumbled from the walkway. As she hit the dirt, her face held a smile. She had walked through the gates of Tír na nÓg and there was no more pain.

"Shite!" roared Mòrag at the realisation of the young life she had taken.

Yet, there was no time for remorse. A cry of "No!" grabbed Mòrag's attention. The young man was a little older than her son, Barra. Sadly, that was not uncommon. Even a child can kill. She swung her shield at the boy, taking the wind from his lungs and hoping to knock him from the rampart. The mob kept him on the walkway. His spearhead lowered to strike.

Resigned to killing him, Mòrag stepped inside the shaft. Uncharacteristically, she hesitated, recognising the familial link with the girl. Indecision is often fatal, but in time she took a step to the side. The upwards thrust of her spear caught the young man in the soft flesh under his chin. The blade quickly cleaved his brain in two, exiting the top of his skull with a gush of bone and brain matter. By the time his body hit the wooden planking, he had joined his sister.

Exhausted, her limbs refusing to cooperate, Mòrag resigned herself to death. Tears streamed down her cheeks. She thought of never holding her children or hearing their laughter again. In ears plugged with battle grit, she heard the muted sound of horns. She shook her head, thinking she had taken too many blows to the skull. Still, the alarms persisted. A hand grabbed her arm, and Torcán peered into a pair of emerald-green eyes. He pointed over the walkway.

"Retreat!" Mòrag looked at him without comprehension. "Jump!" he shouted.

There must have been some doubt in Torcán's mind as to whether Mòrag would obey. So, he gave her a boyish smirk and pushed. A stream of the choicest of swear words flowed from Mòrag's cracked lips as she tumbled over the edge. Drained of all strength, it seemed to take forever as she floated earthward. Mòrag soon found she was more a lump of rock than a feather.

The Ravens' princess hit the floor of the wagon with a thud and the groan of wood. Fortunately, her landing was mitigated by the straw and tinder used to set alight the ditches, and covered the box's floor. She crashed through the kindling, stabbing herself multiple times. Worse, coming to a halt, she cried out as her ankle twisted in a way that did not bode well. A dull crack of bones accompanied the wrench. She grasped the side of the box to pull herself up, but the leg refused to cooperate, and she fell back, cursing Torcán loudly.

"Do you always have to make it hard for me?" Mòrag growled as Torcán reached into the wagon, grabbed her arms, and hauled his partner across his shoulder. "Bastard!" Yet, there was a smile in her voice.

***

Bloodied, his flesh stinging from innumerable cuts and muscles burning, Torcán held the reins of Mórag's horse. She grimaced at the throbbing pain in her leg. It was clumsily splinted. Most of the druid healers had died in the battle. She and Torcán stood a hundred paces back from the northern gates. Breathing harshly, Torcán leaned against the mount's flank and took a brief moment to look back.

Dún-an-Rí was a butcher's hall. Of the garrison, over half—one thousand men and women—were dead or injured, many with mortal wounds. The deceased had sold their lives dearly. Over five thousand Senones lay broken in the bloody slush. Still, that would be a slim consolation for the defenders' loved ones.

A pall of gritty smoke hung over Dún-an-Rí. Consumed by the frenzy of multiple fires, the supporting beams of many buildings had the strength of a twig of charcoal. Weakened by the flames, most collapsed. Pulled down by hundreds of ropes, vast sections of the stockade spilt rubble into the ditches. The trenches became burial mounds, which was unfortunate for those still clinging to life. The debris provided ramps for the swarming Senone horde, although there was nothing left of the fort to plunder. As Brennus' men were to discover, the ráth held little of value.

The remnant of Dún-an-Rí's garrison was in a fighting retreat. They hoped to link up with Conall's forces, although what use their battered divisions would be was questionable. A frustrated Íar charged past. The ordinarily ebullient warrior's face was flushed in anger. His riders had continuously been challenged by the well-drilled spears of the Senones. The chilling and somewhat maniacal, tuireadh—death song—of Gràinne rang out as, at last, her score of chariots began to take advantage of the increasing number of gaps in the Senone lines.

To Torcán's left was fellow brawler Lonán—as efficient a killing machine as any on the battlefield. Blood streamed from many gashes. The warrior's strength was slowly ebbing. With reluctance, Torcán looked to his right. His friend Brocc's features were normally sharp and gaunt but ameliorated with a broad smile. Now, he fought with a snarl and crazed eyes. The stripe of white that divided auburn-red hair, once a topic of amusement among friends, now brought a feral aspect to an already frightening visage. Something had snapped in Brocc's mind when he watched Bláithín fall. Berserk, Brocc had thrown himself into the fight. The tally of bodies mounted around him. His comrades gave him a wide berth. His enemies, where they could, chose other contests.

Torcán reached out and touched Brocc's shoulder. The reaction was a primal growl, and a sword swung. There was a clash of metal as sword struck chainmail glove. "The Hag! Brocc. It's me." Lonán moved to intervene. Torcán shook his head.

Dim recognition trickled into Brocc's eyes. "Sorry."

"We'll talk about this later. But now, I have a plan." Brocc rolled his eyes. Perhaps it was a glimmer of returning sanity.

CHAPTER 18

395 B.C.—The Plain of Dún-an-Rí

Mórrígan watched the assault on Dún-an-Rí in helpless rage. Her band stood by their mounts, sending volley after volley of black shafts into the flanks of Brennus' horde until their quivers were empty. The effort had less impact than a solitary midge biting her horse's arse. Hands raised, she opened her mouth and howled.

"Howled", however, was an inadequate word for the awful sound that pierced unwilling ears and tore down the veils that protected minds. The morning sun, hitherto confident and majestic, abruptly cowered behind the solitary, dark cloud that smudged the pastel sky. A sudden, wild wind—perhaps a resurrected Máistir—plucked at clothes, pried at shields, and tore helmets from sweat-soaked heads.

It was a performance worthy of the Sidhe. On the far side of the battlefield, strains of Gràinne's tribal death chant made men tremble as it rose up to join Mórrígan's incantations. The effort was laudable, and the angst created was significant. Both women knew it was not enough. Uncertainty made the horde's advance stall, but not for long. The size of the mass was too great. Brennus and strong chieftains cajoled their warriors forward. That the army's sleep would later be filled with panic-stricken nightmares was of little consolation to Mórrígan. Dún-an-Rí needed help now, not at sunset.

Banners flapping and the blare of trumpets announced the arrival of Brandubh, Carmag, and Tasgiitios on the far side of the Souconna.

Mórrígan fumed. Yet, the queen knew it would be foolish for them to ford the waters. The army would leave itself open to attack while traversing the river. All Brandubh could do was bombard the rearguard of the Senones until the enemy was beyond the reach of slings and arrows. Then, they would cross and pray that Conall would drive the Senones back and onto their blades.

Conall pushed his javelin's point into the throat of his opponent and felt the warrior's hot blood splash his hand. His efforts to disengage and take the field against Brennus were thwarted by the stalemate at the bridges. In essence, the battle—a glorious, if inapt, description of the brawl underway at the interface of the two enemies—was deadlocked. Less than a smell apart, ten faced ten. The bridge was not wide enough for more. Both sides had the luxury of rotating fresh combatants into the front rows, thus prolonging the contest.

Although delighted at the sound of pounding hoofs, Conall sensed in the gallop a wave of deep anger transferred from rider to beast. It was matched by his queen's wrathful countenance and the expressions of rage and vexation on her band's visages. He removed his black-plumed helmet, shook long, braided hair, and made his way to greet Mórrígan. Conall's curiosity was piqued at the sight of two warriors who had plainly just exited the river and were sliding from their mounts.

Conall growled. His rumbling held a note of helplessness, of not seeing a way to break the impasse and come to the aid of Dún-an-Rí's beleaguered garrison. The potential loss of his friends and his warriors struck deep in his heart. Íar and his riders had already been dispatched, but without the shield wall, their use was constrained.

"You're not omnipotent."

Conall sighed at Mórrígan's words. She was correct. He was not a god, nor even a demi-god. Yet he was Rí Ruirech, King Over Kings. His was the responsibility to ensure the security of the clann. In his tormented mind, and in the sight of his enemies, he was failing. The bitter taste in his mouth matched that of his roiling stomach. He watched

Fearghal disengage from his position and stride towards him. The warrior's demeanour was as black as his own.

Without warning or apparent reason, Conall's mind drifted back to a battle in Ériu against Ailill Mac Máta, king of the Connachta. It had been fought on a miserable night and on a road of logs built across a bog. Rods of rain lashed both sides. Yet, even in the rain, the roadway had burned. Conall inhaled deeply. Carried on a sudden wind, the scents of pine resin and oil filled his nostrils. A hopeful smile clung to his lips, and then the king laughed aloud. To Conall, it was the best fragrance in the world. He beamed at Mórrígan, who looked curiously at her hand-fast partner.

Then she too smiled. "You've thought of something."

Conall nodded and bellowed out orders. Fearghal roared his approval. And the Goddess smiled at the appreciation of her gift.

* * *

The scent of smoke and burnt flesh assailed the Sidhe's nostrils. Her ears rang with the wailing of the dying and the cries of the mná-sidhe. Was she too late? How was Fearghal? How was Neamhain? Were Conall and Mórrígan alive? Guilt welled up in her mind. Then she heard the howling of Mórrígan and Gràinne's death chant. The Sidhe beamed an awful smile. And then hand and oak staff reached to the sky.

The Sidhe's ululations seemed to reach up into the firmament and pull it down. Like the branches of a great tree, forks of lightning struck the horizon and great sheets of light split the air. Both were made more impressive by the ominous purple-grey darkness that swept across the skies. A wind rose, gentle at first; soon, the waters of the Souconna and Rodonos rippled.

* * *

On the opposite bank, Carmag looked on the confluence of the rivers and blinked his eyes several times—the rivers appeared to be getting lower.

"Shite!"

***

"I think she has returned," said Conall. He looked to the sky and then to Mórrígan. "I've never seen you do that." Mórrígan glared at her partner's cheekiness, but inside she was smiling.

***

Brennus stared northwards from Dún-an-Rí's single remaining guard post. The second floor of the tower had three sides semi-enclosed. The fourth was fully open and led to the walkway. Hair, matted from gore, sweat, and smoke, hung limply around his face. Blood seeped from cuts. His upper body, naked apart from a leather breastplate, bore the scars of battle—old and new. Plaid triubhas, the colour of which could no longer be determined, were ripped in many places, and blood encrusted the material's tattered edges.

A bitter taste overwhelmed his mouth. Concern deepened lines already etched into his forehead, and that was before the Sidhe had decided to flex her powers. It was a Senone victory, of sorts, but did little to diminish Conall's power. Lugudunon still cast a long, contemptuous shadow across the battlefield, and Dún-an-Rí could be rebuilt. Previously buried deep in his mind, the folly of his envy clawed its way ever closer to the surface.

Worse, there was no treasure in the fort. Could Brennus' information have been that wrong—again? No gold. No children. No hostages of value. None captured to be sold to the slavers. The defenders of Dún-an-Rí sold their lives dearly. With their last breath, they died fighting. When the raw emotion of the fight receded, questions would be asked by his nobility, his warband chieftains, and their warriors.

Sweaty, hard men and women were already starting to grumble. The fort's substantial stock of beer and wine kept their griping at a level below rebellion. When the supply was finished, they would be both drunk and belligerent. Brennus huffed and wondered if Conall's bastards had deliberately left the beverages.

To his rear, the Senone rearguard had moved beyond the constant barrage of missiles from Lugudunon's garrison and Tasgiitios' Carnutes. Yet, his foes held their position, refusing to cross the river. It would be as foolish for the Senones to retreat in that direction as for their enemies to traverse the water. Either army would be slaughtered in midstream.

To the east, messengers brought reports of spears and shields lined up along the Rodonos riverbank. The Clann Ui Flaithimh's militia had emerged from the sanctuary of the forest, along with the remaining members of the shield-wall. While his warriors spoke with contempt of the farmers, Brennus knew that men are slow and struggle in the water. It takes little expertise to drive a spearhead down into the soft flesh of those attempting to clamber up muddy riverbanks.

Beyond the gateway, the wounded of Dún-an-Rí slumped in blood-stained wagons, pulled by placid oxen. Unmoved by the turmoil around them, the beasts moved steadily towards the safety of Clann Ui Flaithimh's main force. Behind them, the thousand who remained from Brocc, Lonán, and Torcán's bands faced the enemy with grim faces and dull blades. Brennus cursed and bellowed orders to his chieftains to cut off the retreat. The story of the conquering of Dún-an-Rí already had little flesh on its bones. A tale of an epic fighting retreat would quickly and deservedly supplant his nebulous victory.

The horns of the Senone army swept around the fort, curling in to curtail the flight. Once more, Brennus looked to the darkening skies and swore at the gods, the Oracle, and the Sidhe. The Goddess looked down with disapproval. *Your position is already perilous, Brennus of the Senones. Do not foster another enemy.*

It momentarily occurred to Brennus, too late to be of any good, that his plan of attack had been well executed. He had not, however, considered the possibility of his army being trapped on the narrow stretch of land between the rivers. He looked towards the bridges, and his lips twisted in a snarl. Fanned by the sudden winds, plumes of smoke curled upwards. To the cacophony of battle was added the cries of burning warriors and timbers crashing into the river. The cunning bastard had set the bridges alight.

Brennus gave little thought to the warriors stranded on the far side of the Souconna, and now at the mercy of Lugudunon's garrison. Their blades were of no use to him. Troubles and ill omens mounted for the Senone king. He cursed the black cloud of ravens that swooped and swirled above the battlefield. The birds sensed it would not be long before the vaunted shield-wall took the field. A fully locked shield wall of six hundred men could easily span the narrow spur of land and still allow space on both flanks for cavalry and chariot charges. Conall would have at least five ranks of six hundred shields, and Brennus would have no line of retreat.

Brennus shivered. He was comfortable with hot tempers, chaos, and fury. Yet, his enemy's pace was measured and inexorable—a meat grinder of men. *Where is the glory?* Revenge and retribution were the only thoughts in their battle-hardened minds. But perhaps of most concern for Brennus, the battle would now be fought on open ground and gentle hillocks. Between Gràinne, Íar, and Mórrígan, two thousand mounted warriors and chariots had a perfect terrain.

He cursed at the undulating war cries of Gràinne, Mórrígan, and now the Sidhe that corrupted warriors' minds. "Witches!" Peals of thunder and the increasing volume of Íar's brash-sounding trumpets raised his ire. His men had held their formation against horses surprisingly well—until now. Brennus swore at the fraying of his battle lines. He knew it was an invitation Conall's divisions would not refuse.

***

Two hundred of the clann's finest brawlers, led by Torcán and Brocc, turned from their retreat and, with a cry of *"Ní ghéillfear, nó cúlú!"* attacked. Such was the shock of the Senones at the ferocity of warriors previously counted as dead that many met their end with eyes wide and mouths open. Everything and anything that could be wielded as a weapon, from dirty nails to dulled steel, was used.

Bypassing the tips of the Senone horns, the angry wedge of

red-and-black-shielded warriors quickly crossed open ground and slammed into their foes. Teeth and blood flew as they bit, kicked, and slashed. There was no finesse to the attack. Instead, they gouged a track deep into the enemy's ranks, leaving a harvest of broken bodies in their wake.

"The Almighty Hag! What are those eejits doing?"

Íar was unsure if he should be proud of Torcán and Brocc's bravery or furious at its apparent futility. It brought back memories of Gaius' bloody assault on the walls of Lugudunon—a futile gesture to those watching. Yet, it worked. The tall, strapping warrior spat and raised a bronze horn to dry lips. Shrill, bright notes blasted out. It was accompanied by frantic waving at Mórrígan and Gràinne and gestures towards Brocc and Torcán.

The effect was dramatic. Gràinne and Amodocus were presented with the best gift of their lives. Their frustration at being on the sidelines of the battle ended. Amodocus' horsemen, who carried a virtual armoury on their mounts, charged the flank to Torcán's right. Heavy iron darts, maces, and rhomphaiae battered the Senone flank, diverting attention from the beleaguered but steady stubbornness of Torcán.

Teeth bared in a savage, blood-stained grin, Brocc bellowed defiance as he heard Gràinne's war cries and the harsh squeal of chariot boxes as iron-rimmed wheels bounced over the plain. The war-chariots of Clann Ui Flaithimh at full speed were a frightening sight. Long rotating blades struck terror into the enemy. The protection of the Senone spear hedges dissipated.

"Now comes the hard part," said Torcán.

Brocc slammed his shield into his opponent, breaking yet another nose before stabbing a dagger into the soft flesh of the woman's throat. He squinted and gave his friend an incredulous look. "You think?"

Despite the frenzied storm that swirled around them, Brocc and Torcán miraculously reached the gateway of Dún-an-Rí. Both men knew they owed Amodocus, Gràinne, and Íar a sizeable debt of gratitude. Without their timely intervention, the well-intentioned attack would have foundered, engulfed by loud and angry Senones.

Torcán lifted his eyes, looking around to locate his target. Taking ten men, he dashed across the dirt road that crossed the perimeter ditch. To his right and left were trenches filled with the dead. His nose protested at the stench. As the day approached meán lae, the ripe smell of decay and smoke rose. With one hand on a blood-stained rung, Torcán hauled his protesting body upwards. "Thank the Hag, the Senones didn't think to drop their ladders or cut the scaling ropes," he muttered. He looked around for Brocc but his friend had chosen another path.

***

Brennus cursed the Sidhe. Behind him, the river waters were receding. The bridges across the Souconna were gone, and the once mirage-like red line in the distant haze had solidified. It was possible to discern the black shapes of ravens painted on blood-red shields without squinting. In a short time, the birds' beady eyes would join those of their comrades in the skies above to rebuke the enemy. The fowl would shout their harsh *kraa kraa*, and Conall's warriors would respond with blood-curdling battle-cries.

Constantly harried by Íar's riders, the Senone army's discipline unravelled. Like a multi-tailed whip, Íar's mounted warriors flayed the Senone flanks, first with javelins and then with swords and axes. Spinning scythes on war chariots, led by a wild, painted apparition, and driven by matched teams of shaggy horses, shuddered as they cut into flesh and laid open bone. Blessed by blood, Gràinne's longsword glinted in the lightning flashes. To many, it seemed as if lightning flowed from her sword.

Resupplied from Dún-an-Rí's wagons, Mórrígan's warband taunted the Senones with volleys of the red-and-white-fletched arrows, before re-mounting their horses and riding to attack at another point. The Senones swatted helplessly at the sharp-toothed midges that feasted on them. And still, Conall's shield wall marched closer. Only now, their battle cries for retribution rang out clear and loud.

Behind the fort, there was movement at the water's edge. Driven away by the Sidhe's winds, the waters were no more than knee depth. Assessing that the Senones had reached the point of no return, Brandubh ordered Carmag's Forest Warriors and Tasgiitios' Carnutes into the river. Covered by the slings and bows of the Ravens and anxious to crush skulls with his iron club, Carmag jumped into the stream. Attaining the far bank, they jogged forward to retake Dún-an-Rí, though the fort was little more than a smoking ruin garrisoned by drunks.

"Once more, it is time," Brennus growled at his burly guard, "to take our place at the front of the battle."

There was little to tip the scales of war in his favour. Each army had thousands of warriors. Indeed, more than enough to sustain a long and bloody encounter. More in resignation than enthusiasm, the king exited the guard post, accompanied by his protectors. They stepped onto a gore-splattered parapet that threatened to collapse with each footfall. Weakened by fire, its supporting timbers retained little strength. Brennus signalled to his men that urgency was required.

Brought up sharply by a snarling, badger-like face, made more frightening by the fires around him, it took Brennus a few moments to absorb that a small group of Clann Ui Flaithimh warriors stood before him. The pause was long enough to allow Brocc the first strike. His shield struck Brennus', and a fierce, hacking sword blow shaved a ragged strip of wood from the king's scíath. Both men grunted and recoiled from the blows.

Brennus laughed aloud. This was a fight he could relish, but time was not on his side. His long, double-edged sword swung back and then forward, arching diagonally to strike at his opponent's shoulder. Brought to his knees by the force of the blow, Brocc swore at the rapidly spreading numbness in his upper arm. He was very thankful for the iron scales sewn into his armour.

Two figures stepped forward to either side of Brocc. A scything blade parallel to the wooden planking met one. The blow bit deep into flesh, almost cutting the man in two. His entrails began a slow, inexorable exit from their temple as the bean-sidhe took his spirit. The other warrior fared better. She bore the brunt of Brennus' shield. With a shriek of frustration, she tumbled over the stockade and into the perimeter ditch.

A wild-eyed Brocc, though that seemed an inadequate description of the fury that resided in the man's hazel eyes, challenged Brennus. The king held firm under the blistering assault of sword and shield. Several guards stepped up to give the king a moment to recover his strength, but Brocc dispatched them with contemptuous ease. Brocc's trance-like dance of death drove Brennus and his men back. Fear slipped into the king's eyes, and that seemed only to feed his opponent's madness.

At the thuds of soft-booted feet, Brennus glanced behind. Torcán grinned as he smashed his shield into the chest of a surprised Senone guard. The warrior cried out as Torcán headbutted him and unceremoniously bundled him over the fence.

Torcán took in the scene before him. "Shite!"

His crazed friend was close to opening up a rapidly tiring Brennus' flesh with the axe that had replaced a broken scíath. Torcán grabbed a second shield and strode forward, battering aside Brennus' men. They were taken care of by the revenge-seeking warriors who followed in Torcán's wake. Soon he was alone and behind the retreating Senone leader. With a roar, he lifted one shield and slammed the boss into the back of Brennus' neck. The king dropped like a stone.

Sword and axe descended. Torcán swore as he stood over a prone, senseless Brennus and blocked the blades with his scíatha. The strength of the blows embedded the weapons in the wood. In the brief respite, Torcán let the shields fall loose. Chain gauntlets grabbed Brocc's wrists, forcing them away from his blades. Torcán held his friend's gaze.

"No!" he shouted. "This is not the plan. We need him alive."

There was a moment when Torcán thought the madness in Brocc was beyond a return to sanity. Would he have to kill his friend? Relief surged through the brawler's veins as the fire in Brocc's eyes ebbed and, exhausted, he dropped to his knees. Torcán put a consoling hand on his friend's shoulder. Would he have acted any differently if Mòrag had taken the blow that felled Bláithín? He shook his head.

"Where's Gràinne and her chariots when you need them?"

CHAPTER 19

395 B.C.—The Ruins of Dún-an-Ri

A sullen, bloodied, and bruised Brennus perched on a broad and rough-ly level stump of an oak tree. Wet leather thongs restrained his ankles and wrists. Each time he shifted to relieve the creeping numbness in his arse, the net impact was to expose his buttocks to the attention of more splinters. He swayed and fought to gain control of his thoughts—and stomach. His final humiliation, tied to a pole on Gràinne's chariot and put on display by the whooping Cinn Péinteáilte queen, had left his pride and spirit deeply wounded. His army, dispirited at their king's downfall and caught like a rat in a trap, gave up the fight. To do otherwise would have resulted in an even greater slaughter.

Vanity refused to let him tumble from the stump. "Bastards," he muttered. The king knew the thongs would slowly dry out, and his level of discomfort would increase proportionately. There would be added pain, but that did not bother the Senone ruler. He was already suffering from the battering, and numerous blade strikes taken in the battle. He could feel the scabs of new wounds tighten and his flesh pucker in pro-test. Deep, dull aches and tightness of breath pointed to broken bones.

"Bastards!"

This time, Brennus expressed the sentiment with a fierce intensity. It might have been impressive had it not escaped cracked lips as a mere parched croak. His throat was raw from shouting commands and his vocal cords covered in the grit and slime of battle. It was the ignominy of his capture that caused Brennus grief. Never, even in his younger days as a warband chieftain, had the warrior been seized and bound. Now he sat, a well-trussed piece of meat, his fate in the hands of others.

He inhaled and choked, coughing harshly and painfully. Over and above the stench of blood and gore; the smell of bowels eviscerated or simply evacuated as a final indignity; and the onset of decay hastened by a warm afternoon; another fragrance clung to the air—that of wood smoke. The king chuckled. The stump his bruised and, by now, quite dead arse sat on was at the centre of the still-smoking ruins of Dún-an-Rí.

A shadow fell on the dirt before him. Brennus cocked his head and raised his eyes. Before him stood Conall, Fearghal, Íar, and Mórrígan. A few paces off were Deaglán, Gràinne, Lonán, Mòrag, and Torcán. No one had the triumphant demeanour of the victorious. If anything, all looked as if in mourning. Well, all but a grinning Torcán, who was happily describing his part in the king's downfall to his beautiful partner. That brought some consolation to Brennus.

"A man after my own heart," he muttered.

No one could ever assert that fighting brought anything but joy to the Brennus. His hands were stained with the blood of many hundreds, but his conscience remained untroubled.

"Kill him—and his commanders. Stake them out as an example to the Senones and our neighbours. Cut the head off the beast. Take a body tithe of the rest and sell them into slavery. At least we'll cover some of the cost of this debacle." It troubled Brennus that the conversation took place as if he were not present. Was he that helpless? That impotent and unable to prevent the destruction of his tribe? Without leadership, preferably his and the army, the Senones would be at the mercy of jackals and wolves. The king's head dropped.

"I see you finally got the message." Brennus' head snapped up at Mòrag's words.

"Bitseach!"

"A man of few words. Education is surely lost on this creature."

"Cinn Péinteáilte bitseach!"

"I rest my case," said Mòrag. The others laughed.

"The Hag's arse. Do not bore me with sanctimonious Gael values. Put me out of my misery. Tell me of my fate. Perhaps you would like to see me dance to your pipes and drums. Well, I have never been a good performer. So go rut a goat."

About to expand on this theme, Brennus suddenly found himself on the dirt, gasping for breath and writhing in agony. He would have clutched his chest but for the thongs that tied his wrists. Tears streamed from eyes already red-rimmed from the battle.

"You came for our children," snarled the Dark Huntress.

A mother bear protecting her cubs could have taken lessons from the ferocity of Mórrígan's tone. Laden with murderous intent, the voice held no trace of mercy. She turned to Conall. "Leave the punishment of this pitiful king and his people to me." Contempt dripped from the queen's lips. "I will give the Senones memories that will visit their nightmares for generations. The cries of the mná-sidhe will mirror his torment and that of his people. Your fate, Brennus of the Senones, will be the Otherworld, not the feasting halls of Mag Mell."

"Words. Witches' tricks. You will not cower me. Rosmerta the Oracle could not, and she held real power. I will not beg for mercy. Kill me slowly or quickly. I do not fear death. Or free me. Do not bore the arse off me. It's already numb enough."

Brennus' next words were drowned out as an undulating wail echoed around the ruins, bringing fear to most, a smile to Conall and Mórrígan, and a sigh of relief from Fearghal. A rising howl from deep in the forest rose to harmonise with the chilling phrase. Fearghal shivered. Neamhain Ni Fearghal was only nine summers.

The ominous summer sky regained its blue expanse, and the sun appeared. Twisted branches of lightning danced one final time on the horizon before retiring. The retreating thunder growled, syncopated with the hoofbeats of the midnight-black beast that charged into their midst. The horse's blue eyes, white socks, and white lightning blaze on its forehead were a perfect complement to its grey-cloaked rider.

"Impressive entrance, as usual," said Conall.

In one fluid movement, the Sidhe crossed a leg over the woollen dillat and slipped down from her mount. She unsheathed an ancient oak staff and swept the scene before her with obsidian eyes. "Was the burning of Dún-an-Rí a tactical diversion?"

"Everyone's a smart arse."

The Sidhe turned her attention from Conall to Brennus. Cold, merciless eyes stripped the king of any illusions that he might manoeuvre to a less than fatal outcome. "Witches' tricks, indeed." The Lady snarled. "Fool. Rosmerta had not a fraction of the power An Fiagaí Dorcha holds within her. *I* reside in her shadow. And *you* think you can taunt her with impunity. Fool." Mongfhionn inhaled deeply and lifted Brennus' chin with the tip of her staff. "My daughter, Neamhain, was in Dún-an-Rí."

Her presence drew closer, and for a moment, Brennus looked into the awful face of the Hag. A dark maw opened, showing two rows of overlong and sharply pointed teeth. The breath was foul as if from the Otherworld.

"Pray my daughter has suffered no harm."

Straightening up, the Sidhe looked around and then returned to the Senone king. "And pray to the Goddess that a portion of mercy remains in the hearts of Conall and Mórrígan. There is none in mine." An ashen-faced and somewhat chastened Brennus slumped against the tree stump.

"Where is Neamhain? Is she safe?" asked Mongfhionn of Fearghal.

"She is with the other children in the forests south of the Rodonos." Fearghal resisted the urge to gather Mongfhionn into his embrace, limiting himself to a smile. "They were escorted to safety well before the battle."

Lines of worry faded from the Sidhe's face. A smile spread from the edges of blood-red lips, softening her terrible appearance. "Let's go. I wish to hold my… *our* daughter." Fearghal nodded. In a lower tone, she added, "You shouldn't resist all your urges. After all, we are hand-fast partners, and it has been some time since I had a hug." She coughed. "Or anything else." The final words brought a deep red flush to Fearghal's cheeks and neck and a round of sniggering from those present.

"Do you not wish to stay for the judgment?" asked Conall.

"Do I need to?"

"I suppose not. Go be with your family." Conall smiled as he watched Fearghal and Mongfhionn mount up and ride for the forest.

"I think I prefer her violent and threatening death and destruction. This enlightened Sidhe sends shivers up my spine." The group chuckled at Torcán's words, but behind the levity, there lay a shadow of anxiety.

It was not until he was certain the Sidhe had gone that Brennus found his tongue. "Shite!" he muttered. "All this to no purpose." Brennus looked up at Conall. "I would not have harmed them—the children. Just kept them for a while until you paid their ransom. Well, what is your judgment? Death and dismemberment? My head on the doorpost of a new Great Hall?"

"Why couldn't you have just asked?"

"What?"

"Why couldn't you have just asked to cross my land? What madness made you throw away the lives of thousands? We could have come to terms. Do you love gold so much more than your people?"

Conall looked at Mórrígan and exhaled. It was deep, long, and mea-sured. "A tithe of your warriors, not the injured, will be taken. Half will be sold into slavery to pay for this fiasco. The other half will be taken to the river's edge and beheaded." Those around Conall gasped. Ruthless in battle, he had mostly been magnanimous to the vanquished. Then some remembered his promise to give the Goddess rivers of blood and shivered.

Conall nodded to Lonán. "Cut his bonds." To Brennus, he said, "Go to your army and select the tithe."

Brennus' head slumped to his chest and then lifted up. "No. Kill me and my chieftains, but leave the warriors to lick their wounds and return to their homes. Their guilt was to follow foolish orders." Brennus' eyes held Conall's before his final plea. "Please."

"One promise is required."

"Anything."

"When I call on you, you will fight Rome at my side."

"Agreed."

"Now, get out of my sight. Your injured will be cared for and escorted back to Senone territory. The dead will be stripped of valuables, beheaded, and burned. Collect what's left of your army and people— march for the Alpes. Do not turn around. Never return. If you do, I will follow and slaughter every man, woman, and child."

***

Bláithín Ni Néill sobbed. Although of the Ulaid nobility and its premier clann, she did not consider herself narcissistic. Indeed, she had always frowned upon those who judged others by appearances. Most who knew the lady would have agreed with her self-assessment. Yet, despite the visits of well-meaning family and friends, Bláithín lay on her cot, crying sorely for the loss of her beauty.

On occasion, when her courage was sufficiently strong, she traced a nervous finger along the uneven, raised ridge of tissue and coarse black stitches. It started at her left temple, snaked down and over her cheek, and came to a stop below her jawline. It was then she would rail and shout curses at the Goddess. Yet, the Goddess knew that the lady's angst was because she was afraid. She had almost died. And, like others who have had that experience, she asked herself a selfish but honest question, *Would I have been better to pass beyond the veil?*

"The answer is… don't be a selfish bitseach."

Bláithín's deep-blue eyes sprung wide open at the harsh words.

"You have a partner who loves you and sons and a daughter who would be devastated if you left them."

While her face burned with anger, Bláithín felt more than a tinge of guilt. Slowly, her eyes focused on the tall, grey-cloaked figure who stood at her bedside. "You think I like *this*?" The Sidhe pointed to the ragged scar on her throat. "It is a painful reminder of a time I wish had never happened. Yet, it is also a memory of my sisters' sacrifice."

Mongfhionn paused. Her alabaster face took on a gentler demeanour. Her tone was sympathetic. "I could remove the scar." Bláithín's eyes glistened with hope. It was quickly dashed. "But I won't."

A tear rolled down Bláithín's face. She sniffed. "I understand."

"Ah, but you don't. At least, not at this time. It will forever be a reminder, a harsh reminder, perhaps, that stupidity in battle has consequences. The scar is a trifle. Several of your comrades died protecting what they thought was a corpse. Brocc's mind almost snapped beyond repair, and he threw himself into a furious quest to join you in Mag Mell. Only Torcán drew him back from the brink. You owe that man a huge debt."

"I didn't know."

"Of course you did not, and you did not ask, either. None of your friends wished to cause you more grief by telling you. I, on the other hand, have no such constraints." The Sidhe smiled and knelt beside the bed. Long fingers traced the scar. Bláithín flinched. "Ponder long and learn all the lessons, Lady Bláithín Ni Néill." With a swish of her cloak, Mongfhionn rose and turned to walk away. She paused. "Conall has ordered a feast of remembrance in a few sunsets. You *will* attend."

Bláithín did not know if she felt better or not after the Sidhe's visit. *Her bedside manner's not great.* It was then that a whirlwind named Gràinne made her entrance.

"Sorry, I meant to visit earlier, but there's still a lot of chaos happening." The young woman halted at the foot of the cot and stared at Bláithín as if trying to understand something. "Wow! I love yer tattoo.

Yer one of us now. But where's the scar?"

* * *

Still within earshot of Bláithín's chamber, Fearghal and Mongfhionn paused. The grizzled warrior chuckled. "You're getting soft, old woman."

"And, for that, you're getting nothing—old man."

CHAPTER 20

395 B.C.—Massalia

Banished by Conall. Likely on Mórrígan's "people to suffer a lingering and painful death" list. Bored and without direction. Gold running like sand through restless fingers. Worried about their brother, Tadhg. Such was the temper of Craiftine and Fionnbharr Ó Cuileannáin. Added to this, the persistent furry mouths, sour stomachs, and thumping headaches from increasingly cheaper beer and gut-rotting wine did little to improve their moods. Craiftine plucked a few chords on his harp. It raised a cheer and elicited a few coins from those around him but did little to ameliorate his demeanour. The pleasure of playing had long been dulled by the necessity to earn an income.

For his part, Tadhg sat apart from his brothers. His attention was focused solely on the brothel's lithe serving girl and whore. The girl was named Tisiphone, and there was a name to ponder for those who enjoy puzzling over omens. She was the outcome of the brief coming together of an Etruscan sailor and a Greek whore. Tisiphone never knew her father. Probably, he never knew she existed.

Her mother's care for her was ephemeral. The lady's journey into disease, eventual madness, and a fatal, and perhaps deliberate, fall from Massalia's Temple of Apollo onto the rocks below did little to discourage her daughter's career choice. Youth always considers itself, if not immortal, then immune to the trials of the adults around them.

Tisiphone was little more than fifteen summers but was wiser and more worldly than Tadhg. Silver and gold bought her favour and her body. She danced to please and serve all, yet Tadhg only perceived himself in her eyes. His moods swung like a pendulum from euphoria to despair. Behind her, the ghost of another whore—the tragic Laoise—hovered. Black blood seeped from the gaping wound that pierced her chest. The apparition's face constantly switched between anger, pity, and disappointment at her lover's betrayal. To escape the spectre's judgment, Tadhg closed or averted his eyes. Neither was successful and so guilt crushed him.

"We have to do something."

"Can you be more specific, Fionnbharr?" The tall, blond warrior huffed at his brother.

"Our economic situation is untenable." Fionnbharr scratched at a flea bite that was just beyond his reach. Craiftine chuckled at his brother's discomfort—until he too felt an ominous itch. Like yawning, once initiated, the act perpetuated itself. Curses and glares from the other tables soon followed. "Much as we find the idea distasteful, life as a mercenary would give us gold... and options." Craiftine shook his head in an unspoken "No." Fionnbharr continued, but on the subject that he really wanted to discuss. He nodded to Tadhg and then Tisiphone. "This is unhealthy and can't go on. There is no assassin's blade to drive this vessel onto the rocks."

"She is undoubtedly desirable. She's also highly skilled at her jobs—all of them." Fionnbharr glared at his sibling. Craiftine shrugged. "She needs to work, like anyone." The harpist noted the subject of their contemplation, sashaying around the tables with a large platter of food and drinks. Without causing offence, she expertly avoided groping hands and appeals to rut and suck. It was also obvious that Tisiphone was steadily moving in their direction.

"Did you order?" asked Craiftine.

Fionnbharr shook his head. "I'm not sure we have enough gold for that feast."

Tisiphone quickly laid their table. Unexpectedly, she did not leave but grabbed a nearby stool and placed her firm, round arse on it. Across the room, a sullen Tadhg noted the situation. Disgruntled at the lack of attention, he stomped over and dropped onto a rough, wooden bench. With a broad smile, Tisiphone gestured to the banquet. "Eat. No payment is required. It is a gift from my Master."

Craiftine raised an eyebrow and subtly dipped his head towards the beer and wine stained slab of wood that served as a bar. The girl shook her head, causing her long tresses to flare out, and chuckled. "He is my employer… perhaps. Another is my Master." She inhaled. Her tunic, which in direct sunlight concealed little, strained to contain her bounty. Was the act force of habit or deliberate tactic? "My Master wishes to speak with you. He has a proposition for you to consider." Tisiphone stood. "When you have finished your meal, I will guide you to his home." As she turned, she sniffed the air. "Perhaps a bath would also be in order. It's on the house."

Then another thought occurred to Tisiphone. She turned to Tadhg and smiled. His face lit up in expectation. "To be clear. I can be your friend. If you pay me, I will be your whore for a time. I am not and never will be your lover."

Craiftine looked at a crestfallen Tadhg. "Impressive. I see our benefactor is not one for soft landings."

Fionnbharr nodded, although his eyes were appreciating Tisiphone's departing rump as he ripped a leg off a plump chicken. He pointed the grease-dripping limb at the young woman. "You do realise that she never actually gave us a choice. An extraordinarily talented girl."

✳✳✳

Sat in the armless, wooden chair at the entrance to the residence, the ageing, bald servant laid his fan aside as Tisiphone came into his shadow. He smiled. "It is good to see you. I am glad you are well."

The girl smiled broadly. In the servant's presence, she never had to put on one of her many guises. She gestured to the three men who stood at her back. Tisiphone was pleased. The trio had cleaned up well and looked like seasoned warriors, not beggars. Her Master would also be pleased. "These are the men our Master wishes to speak with."

The servant rose, bowed to the men, and gestured to the gateway. "If you would go this way, I will follow." As the three filed past, the servant reached into a fold of his robe. A small but heavy pouch was placed into the hand of the girl. As always, the man gently held Tisiphone's wrist. "Our Master's offer is always open to you."

Gracefully, the young woman replied, "Perhaps."

* * *

Accustomed as they were to the gloom of inns and brothels, the glare of whitewashed walls caused the trio to shield their eyes. Once used to the intensity of the sun's rays radiating from the walls, they found the court-yard to be a delightful refuge from the stink of Massalia's streets. The air was fresh, likely from the well-tended gardens. The bubbling fountain at its centre added a touch of serenity. Fragrances of jasmine, wild laven-der, and piney shrubs were carried to grateful nostrils on transient late summer zephyrs. A stone bench surrounded the fountain. Fionnbharr indicated it, but the servant smiled, shook his head, and pointed to a doorway that led off the square.

Inside the palatial home, the air remained cool. Mostly, this was due to its open internal design—no doors. On the outer walls, windows were mere slits or absent. The few full-size windows were closed with heavy wooden shutters, which seemed an embellishment and not for practi-cal use. A plethora of servants armed with huge fans to create or pro-pel breezes helped. The rooms were simply furnished, although by no means spartan.

Marble statues, bronze sculptures, and beautiful red pottery tasteful-ly adorned each room. Delicate silk drapes in myriad designs and vibrant colours hung on the walls. The servant basked in the trio's admiration of what he considered to be his home. He signalled that they should proceed through an arched doorway. "My Master will attend you shortly.

Fruit and refreshments have been provided."

"I'm afraid to sit on these chairs and couches," said Craiftine, stroking the gold fringing on a red silk cushion. "They seem much too fine and delicate for rough warriors from Ériu." He looked at Tadhg, whose appearance had thankfully improved since Tisiphone's chastening. "Well, brother. You're the cleverest of us. Crime, hard work, or plunder?" Tadhg considered his brother's question, but a laugh from the doorway pre-empted his answer.

"Oh, I can assure you there were many years of poverty before wealth. As for crime—who among us is as innocent as a lamb?"

"Pytheas!" The shout echoed off the pristine walls as the three brothers bounded across the room to embrace the diminutive merchant.

"I have a proposal. A piece of profit that may tempt you away from the whorehouses of Massalia and provide a task more fitted to warriors than begging in the streets for food and lodgings."

The Ó Cuileannáin brothers looked sheepishly at each other, and their cheeks flushed red at the admonishing tone. With anyone but Pytheas, the implied insult would have culminated in a brawl or drawn swords and blood. Instead, all signalled Pytheas to continue.

The merchant smiled at the reaction to his test. The warriors were affronted but not prickly enough to turn on their heels and storm off. The fish was hooked, and it was time to land it. The swarthy Greek described Massalia's predicament and how he was duty-bound to defend the city and its trade.

"We're not sailors or even pirates, Pytheas. We know little about sailing, save when you tricked us into rowing the galleys in Northern Albu. How do you expect us to confront an enemy who can simply turn and run?"

Pytheas rose from his seat. His broad smile held something that made the brothers wary. "Land or sea, it is a warrior's battlefield. Sadly, my talents lie elsewhere. There is a limit to what bribery can achieve, and I am no warrior, no commander. Therefore, in addition to you, I have retained the services of an experienced master of defence. You may know him."

In the doorway stood a tall man of about forty summers. The broad-shouldered warrior removed his helmet, revealing a closely cropped head of sandy hair, then flicked an imaginary speck of dust off his chain mail and smiled. Green-flecked, hazel eyes seemed to glisten as Cúscraid Mac Conchobar greeted his recruits. "Welcome to the Massalia militia, boys. Glad you volunteered."

"Shite!" exhaled Fionnbharr.

"Bastard reeled us in!" snorted Tadhg and surprisingly, there was more humour than malice in his tone. He appreciated the design that had led them to the current offer.

"But which bastard? Pytheas or Conall?" huffed Fionnbharr.

"Conall, of course. Pytheas just presented the opportunity. And I doubt we've seen the last of his scheming."

"I'm glad I retrieved my harp. Soothing music may be in order this evening," sighed Craiftine.

✻✻✻

Five men, four warriors and a sailor, sat with their backs against the massive, rectangular blocks of stone that formed Massalia's ramparts. Each block was laid on top of or interlocked with the other. The precision did not need filler. Even in the shade, the blocks were hot against light tunics and triubhas, already well stained with sweat.

It was late summer, the sun had reached its zenith, and the heat was bordering on oppressive. Thankfully, cooling breezes fanned the tops of the walls, although they brought with them the fetid smell of decay from the nearby marshlands. Fionnbharr pointed to a group of men patrolling the defences.

"Thank the Goddess you brought an céad warriors from Brocc and Torcán's shield wall. I can see why Pytheas was anxious to get outside help."

Cúscraid dipped his head in agreement and took a long gulp of tepid water from a skin. The guards were the protectors of those in Massalia wealthy enough to afford them. As such, they were rotated to wall duty as both a civic duty and a show of political strength. To the grizzled warrior, they lacked alertness and carried waistlines that wobbled of their own volition.

Worse, the scabbards that held their weapons looked either overly ornate or poorly maintained. Cúscraid suspected the blades would be blunt and pitted with the corrosion enhanced by proximity to the sea. At a distance, and with their height advantage, the sentries might discourage an attack, but only from an unserious enemy. Perhaps in acknowledgement of this, historically, the practice of Massalia's leaders was to negotiate and bribe their path away from invasion and plunder. Cúscraid shook his head. It was a tactic that would fail miserably with the Romans.

Massalia sat on a long, narrow promontory overlooking the large, rectangular harbour that was the source of its wealth. Well-known around the Great Sea as a safe anchorage, the port and its docks, jetties, and warehouses were accessible from the sea only by a narrow channel.

The headland overlooking the waterfront rose to form a central spine that ran approximately east to west and was composed of four elongated crests. A marshy valley protected the bluff's landward border. A road crossed the wetland, terminating at the main gate of the city. From this point, it continued as the city's main avenue, running along the flank of the ridges to the docks.

The city's wall meandered like a drunken snake along its north-eastern border. Cúscraid was dismissive of its construction. "The rampart should be higher, and wider, and have guard posts along its length. But essentially, it is enough to dissuade minor local tribes and warbands from anything more than token attacks. The sea defences?" He snorted. "Well, they just don't exist." A long sigh from Pytheas signalled his agreement.

"You have a solution?" Tadhg queried.

To his brothers' relief, having something else to think about other than Tisiphone's rejection, the warrior's demeanour had improved substantially.

"Have you considered a career as a pirate?"

Like a feather, the question floated teasingly in the air. Pytheas snorted at the tinges of green that replaced the healthy glow of sun-blessed faces.

"Seriously?"

The hoped-for retraction to Fionnbharr's plea never came.

***

It was the easiest gold that Kaeso and the dross of society he had recruited would ever earn. His instructions from Rome, or more precisely from Marcus Fabius Ambustus, were, as all good orders should be, clear and straightforward: disrupt Massalia's trade. This proved a relatively simple task. Traders and their crews were not fighters. Faced with a fleet of five penteconters crewed with fully armed and mostly toothless brutes, few chose to fight. Most fled back to their home or to the nearest alternate port where they could offload or pick up cargo.

Those who chose to fight were outmatched, outnumbered, boarded, and plundered. The hale found themselves on the slave blocks of nearby Kyrnos. The remainder entertained the sadistic wagers and whims of the crews before being thrown into the Great Sea. Their final moments were divided between trying to avoid drowning and providing a buffet for the circling sharks.

Soon, however, this idyllic life lost its lustre. Kaeso's fleet discovered that their actions proved too effective. Fewer and fewer vessels chose to attempt entry to Massalia's harbour. When his fleet attempted to widen their territory and increase the volume of prey, they were quickly disabused of the strategy by the region's "real" pirates.

As a result of the successful blockade, the revenue streams from slavery and looting captured merchant ships drastically declined. Frequent journeys to visit the whorehouses of Kyrnos did little to relieve the growing boredom. Kaeso's crews became increasingly argumentative.

Rumours from Massalia further deepened Kaeso's concern. It was no great surprise that his employer had spies in the port. It struck Kaeso that this was a perilous occupation, as their numbers appeared to diminish almost daily. Initially, he dismissed as fanciful gossip stories of a beautiful young whore with the allure of a Siren and an assassin's skill with a knife.

Today, as he stood at the helm of his ship, enjoying the gentle swell and salt air, he was not so sure. The arrival of heavily armed Celts, presumably to bolster the city's defences, was troubling, but at least they were not sailors. Construction work at the entrance to the harbour served to add to Kaeso's rising angst. What was its purpose?

Yet of more immediate concern to Kaeso was the rapid completion and trials of a new trireme in the harbour. This vessel alone could challenge his older fleet's territorial dominion. Over twice the length and width of his ships, the trireme's deck also sat much higher out of the water. Still, Kaeso consoled himself that he outnumbered the Massalia vessel five to one, albeit with creaking penteconters.

"Mean bastard," muttered the Roman—a reference to Marcus' lack of investment in more seaworthy, better equipped, and faster boats.

A splash of saltwater caught Kaeso's attention. He screwed up his eyes to discern its nature. Although his fleet needed to be reasonably close to the harbour entrance to blockade it efficiently, Kaeso's ageing eyes could not see much more than a shimmering line. "It's a chain!" shouted a sharper-eyed crew member from his perch at the tip of the central mast.

At first, the Roman cursed. Then he inhaled and smiled. Kaeso had no intention of storming the harbour or the city. Thus, he deemed the new defence of no consequence. He exhaled a sigh of relief. Likely, the new two-storey towers on either side of the entrance were manned by a few warriors. Slaves would operate the pulleys and winches that lifted and dropped the heavy chain.

***

Pytheas and Cúscraid were well pleased. Despite their protests, the Ó Cuileannáin brothers had overcome their aversion to deep saltwater. Under the instruction of Pytheas and a contingent of experienced sailors, the Celts became adept at cutting through the waves.

The trireme was new, which caused Pytheas a lot of fretting. Built of cedarwood, fir, and pine, which gave a delightful fragrance to the vessel, and an outer hull of oak, these were expensive ships. Stringent craftsmanship and its design meant that each boat took substantially longer than usual to construct. Pytheas tugged at long, scented whiskers on a weather-beaten face and shrugged. At least he was not financing the building of a fleet of quinqueremes like Dionysus.

In total, the trireme could transport about two hundred men—one hundred and seventy rowers and thirty crew. The latter included the trierarch or captain, several helmsmen, and other officers and sailors with specific responsibilities. While the men from Ériu practised daily on the oars, it became apparent to Cúscraid that, given the proximity of the battlefield to the harbour, this was excellent physical exercise but not strictly necessary. The triremes could be quite adequately rowed by those on the top set of benches—the thranitai. With just one hundred Celts onboard, this also allowed about half of the middle set of rowers—the zygitai— to be used.

Cúscraid looked out to sea and allowed himself a smile. Prows pointing to the harbour, the blockading fleet had drifted closer together. Their oar tips could almost touch each other. Overconfidence or boredom? The Clann Ui Flaithimh commander nodded to the men with him. In the closeness of the tower, the loud crack of a heavy ballista echoed off the block-stone walls, causing him to wince. Only a quick step to the side prevented the loss of his toes as the weapon recoiled and fought against its restraints. In the tower on the other side of the harbour entrance, a second machine flung its missile seawards.

Further back in the harbour, Fionnbharr ran long fingers through shoulder-length, straw-blond hair as he inspected his men. Given that no one wanted to sink like a stone in the clear, warm waters of the Great Sea, all were lightly armed. No chainmail or armour reinforced with iron scales. Helmets and oblong, waisted wooden shields and as many blades as they could carry on leather belts or baldrics were preferred.

An ample supply of javelins was stored on the deck. There were no archers, which according to Tadhg, was a mistake. All sported naked torsos covered in swirling tattoos and wore brightly coloured triubhas. Many had foregone boots or bróga, hoping that calloused soles would give a better grip on a wet wooden deck.

Fionnbharr counted the number of ballistae volleys. Having deemed that Cúscraid had had enough fun, the older brother shouted, "Attack!" The ship's trierarch gave a great laugh and bellowed commands to his two helmsmen and the rowers. Held in place by tholes—wooden fulcrums—forty-five pairs of oars dipped into the water. With sails furled, the trireme leapt forward. By the time the vessel reached the harbour exit, it was a water-borne missile travelling at full ramming speed.

Standing, one hand on the helm in the middle ship of a ragged, flattened chevron formation, Kaeso swore as the first ballista bolt tore through the black sail and dropped into the sea. A second missile splintered the mast of an adjacent penteconter. The bastards were good and already had his range. He screamed orders to turn, to scatter and put some distance between the ships and the harbour. His men, so long indolent, were slow to act. More volleys of thick-shafted, iron-tipped projectiles followed in rapid succession.

Around Kaeso and on the other vessels, the red mist of carnage rose above the deck and splattered the sails. Heads, limbs, and blood-soaked torsos flopped onto wooden planks slippery wet with gore and salt spray. From one ship, a curl of smoke drifted upwards. Its origin an unchained brazier knocked over by a mercenary who dove to avoid a bolt. He was doubly unsuccessful. The shaft effortlessly punched through his belly, impaling him to the mast. Wild with panic, his eyes watched the flames from the overturned brazier creep closer. It was in the gods' hands as to how he would die.

The trireme was longer, loftier, faster, and much more manoeuvrable than the penteconters. In less time than it takes to down a few beers, the great sea-beast was among Kaeso's fleet. Long splinters of shattered oars were flung through the air. Shields raised, on the deck of the trireme, Fionnbharr's men suffered only minor cuts. The mercenary seamen looked as if they had been scythed as a field of corn.

Kaeso felt his ship shudder as the trireme's ram tore through the penteconter's aged timbers. He heard the splash and gurgle of warm seawater, followed by the shrieks of men trapped in the slowly sinking vessel. As the trireme moved between two blockade ships, volleys of javelins were thrown from both sides of its deck. Hurled from a height advantage and at a mostly helpless enemy, the spears penetrated soft flesh. As primary targets, the helmsmen were the first to fall. Rudderless, the penteconters began drifting. Over half of the crews of the two boats were already dead or injured.

"They're definitely not experienced sailors or even good pirates. Another run?"

Tadhg looked at his older brothers, but Craiftine deferred to the eldest sibling. Fionnbharr nodded. The trierarch bellowed, and oars dipped once more into the calm water. The beast turned in a wide semicircle to attack the ships on the opposite flank of the small fleet.

"There's a lot of disappointed men here."

Tadhg indicated the deck. Rows of grim-faced warriors, with weapons and shields ready, waited. Fionnbharr looked quizzically at his brother, prompting an explanation. "No one to fight. Another run or two, and most of this fleet will sink, and the crews will feed the sharks. I don't think they're capable of putting up much of a fight. Whoever is in charge is a terrible commander."

✳✳✳

Kaeso had no good options. His ships were crippled and slowly sinking, and helm control was lost. Volleys of barbarian javelins from the marauding trireme swept anyone with navigation expertise away, as well as over half of the crews. The decks were slippery with blood and entrails and littered with the injured and dead. One of the vessels was firmly alight. Its companion vessels tried with limited success to steer away from the burning wreck. Few relished the thought of death by fire. At this point, the fleet's position was due more to the Great Sea's currents than active intent. With few unbroken oars remaining, propelling the aged penteconters to safety was impossible.

The Roman sighed. Those of his men still able to stand continued to hurl insults at the Celts, but these were met by taunts and javelins. The strength of the pirates' protests quickly diminished, and most chose to cower behind any means of cover. Should the warriors aboard the trireme decide to board the ships, Kaeso and his men knew they were in no state to prevent such action. Kaeso was under no delusion. His fate was death by drowning or sharks or hoping for mercy from his imminent captors. He shivered. The latter held little attraction other than dying on dry land.

***

"Kill the injured. Toss them into the sea along with those already dead. Bind the rest and transfer them to the trireme. Cut any who resist and throw them into the water. The sharks will appreciate our gifts. Set fire to the ships." The commands shouted by the straw-haired brothers were uncompromising and carried out by men frustrated at being denied a good fight.

"And what will be our fate?"

Fionnbharr stared at Kaeso with blue eyes flecked with green. He shrugged. "That's not my decision. Massalia's triumvirate will hear you and pronounce sentence." The Celt snorted. "You're a pirate in all but name. You know the punishment for that profession. Pray to whatever god you worship that your neck snaps cleanly. I suspect that your stay in Massalia will be short. You chose a bad master."

"Needs must," Kaeso retorted.

"He will not lift a finger in your defence. Likely, Marcus would prefer you dead than alive and talking. My men are already wagering on who ends your miserable life first."

* * *

The full, yellow moon sat imperiously in a cloudless sky. It watched over an impoverished and decrepit area of Massalia. Deep shadows shrouded the narrow alleys that snaked off from the docks. Cramped and ill-kept dwellings looked presentable only because of the moonlight. They were inhabited by thieves or those searching for an honest day's wage for a long day's work. Of the two, the thieves were more successful. That said, encroaching civilisation—many of Massalia's wealthy now sought a seafront view—was changing the area. Although, whether for better or worse was debatable.

Instinct informed Tisiphone that she was being watched. At work, sensing danger, the fine hairs on the back of her neck stiffened and tasted the air for threats. Whoever he was, if indeed it was a "he", was good. Her youthful but sharp eyes observed no warning signs. On leaving the brothel, she stopped and watched at the entrance, hoping to uncover the source of her uncertainty. She spat her disgust onto the huge cobbles before sidling off. His expertise was impressive.

On this night, her hair was swept up in plaits and secured on the top of her head by several long, bronze pins. At close quarters, the thin, sharp skewers became deadly weapons. Under a short, sleeveless, linen chiton, Tisiphone was comforted by the pressure of the knife that rested in the sheath strapped to her right thigh.

She smiled and then shook her head. Whoever stalked her was an expert. If attacked, there would be no time for the lifting of even a short tunic. The young whore pulled the blade from the scabbard and gripped the leather-wrapped handle.

Tisiphone padded down the street, enveloped by shadows. She never wore sandals. Keeping to the sides, she avoided the sewage and detritus of life that flowed down the centre of the alley. It was, however, impossible to avoid the stench of piss, shite, and rotting meat. She grimaced and swore— "Lazy bastards!"—as her small, elegant foot stepped into a still-warm turd. Then she cursed herself for being so sensitive. Soap and water would wash away the nasty-smelling sludge.

Momentarily, Tisiphone lost focus. The shadow moved silently and expeditiously. The burning pain in her left side made her gasp, and she felt the warm trickle of blood. Her dagger slipped from her hands and fell, clattering to the cobblestones. She choked as her mouth was covered by a calloused hand, and her neck stretched back.

"Whores should stick to what they're good at—spreading their legs for gold."

The voice was harsh as if spoken through a crushed larynx. The patronising tone made Tisiphone angry. His first strike was good but not perfect. Yet, her soft throat would not resist the edge of his weapon.

He should have known better and finished her without sermonising. Her regard for his expertise diminished. She swooned. It was an old trick. Now a dead weight in his hand, he shifted stance to get a better hold. Feet planted on solid grey stone, she twisted, driving a sharp knee into his genitals. He swore— "Bitch!"—and released her. Bent almost double, she cried out at the spiking pain of her wound. She heard his breath and the shuffle of his feet as he moved to attack again. Her right hand tore a clump of hair from her head as she ripped one of the pins free. With a shriek of agony, she pulled herself straight and plunged the spike into his head.

The effect was not much more than a headbutt to the nose as the pin glanced off the assassin's nasal bone and ploughed through the supporting cartilage. Blood, snot, and tears flowed. It was impressive to see, but Tisiphone knew the wound was not mortal. Gathering her strength, she pulled the second pin from her dark curls. The girl's scream rent the night silence, sending shivers up the spine of any close and awake. The spike plunged into an ear thick and gnarled by many brawls. A sharp twist amplified the damage to the attacker's brain. Speechless, he dropped to his knees. His last thoughts were of not having a coin to pay Charon, the Ferryman.

She stumbled twenty, maybe thirty tortured paces beyond the bloody scene. Back against the wall, Tisiphone gathered her strength, bracing herself against the cool blocks. Her vigour seeped away, and she slid down to sit on the walkway. In the moonlight, the smear of blood looked black on the whitewashed brick. She smiled in resignation. Her head slumped, resting on her breasts. Her breathing slowed.

One word escaped her lips: "Perhaps."

CHAPTER 21

395 B.C.—Lugudunon

It was the dead of night. The two fought to control the harshness of their breathing and the pounding beat of their hearts. Rivulets of sweat ran down glistening bodies and onto the meadowsweet-impregnated bedding. As usual, their lovemaking had been both passionate and violent. Both bore long nail scrapes and bruises. The fiery release of passions provided a welcome escape from recent tribulations and was as fresh, if not as awkward, as the first time in their youth. Conall reached for the jug of cold spring water that sat on the floor by the cot. With a chuckle, he splashed some on Mórrígan's face and breasts before offering her a drink.

As they basked in the flickering light of the log and peat fire, Conall considered that its welcome heat on a cold late autumn night could not compete with that created by their desires. He painted the dark rings around Mórrígan's very prominent nipples with the chilled water and playfully fondled his partner's breasts. The queen shivered and then made a purring sound. Conall laughed. She sounded like one of the better-tempered feral cats.

Long tresses of ginger-red hair stuck to Conall's damp chest as Mórrígan snuggled closer, basking in the warmth of her hand-fast partner's body. He always seemed to generate heat no matter the weather. Her hand brushed his semi-erect manhood, and she giggled as he flinched involuntarily.

"Tickles or did I treat you too roughly, old man?"

"Ha. That will be the day. I'll be good to go again shortly. Or perhaps that would be too much for you. Maybe you'd rather sleep."

Mórrígan snorted, fell silent, and then slowly exhaled. The sound held an anxious tone. With expectation and curiosity, Conall waited. He knew his partner's quirks and how she approached difficult topics. In the aftermath of the battle with Brennus, life had been good, even peaceful, in Lugudunon. The change of weather to cold, wet, and windy dampened the fires of war. And so Conall's interest was piqued. Another long breath was exhaled.

"I'm with child."

"You can't be. I'm good, but even the famed Rí Ruirech of Clann Ui Flaithimh is not that fast." A semi-playful yet stinging slap on his face gained Conall's attention.

"I. Am. With. Child."

Conall propped himself up on one elbow and peered into a face that flickered between delight and frowning. "You can't be. Aodán was a difficult birth. There could be no more." He looked at her, and his anger simmered. "I am content with our sons and daughters." The inference was clear. "Have you been getting potions from the old witches? How could you put yourself in danger? They are charlatans, and dangerous ones at that." In a gentler voice, he said, "I cannot lose you, Mórrígan. That would be too heavy a burden to bear."

Conall's words warmed Mórrígan's heart. After many summers, it thrilled her to hear his declaration of love. He had stood by her side when many would have pitched their tent elsewhere. A trifle exasperated, she now huffed. "I have taken nothing. Consulted no witches. Done nothing different. And yet, I know my body. We are soon to welcome a new addition, or additions, to our family."

"How soon? And what do you mean, 'additions'?"

"Most likely around Bealtaine. I never last the full cycle." Mórrígan smiled. "As for additions, we could have another set of twins."

Conall breathed in deeply as if trying to concentrate his strength. "There can be only one explanation."

Mórrígan nodded. "It's a gift from *her*. Perhaps a peace offering."

"The bitseach!" Conall exclaimed, although there was humour, not venom in his voice. "We're still dancing to the melody of the Goddess's harp." Conall sighed. "I suppose we'll have to resume our sacrifices to her. By the Hag. This will really confuse the people."

Mórrígan chuckled. Then she coughed and traced a finger along Conall's tumescent manhood. "About that state of readiness."

"You're just trying to divert my attention."

"Am I successful?"

"Silly question."

***

The Goddess glanced at Fate and smiled. The look was one of childish contentment. "The family is reforged. It—and I—will be mightier than before."

Fate nodded. "Just as long as you remember, it was my idea—and that they are no longer children. Reason with them. Conall is a noble king and much wiser than you or I had foreseen. He demands loyalty and gives it in return." Fate paused as if to consider his words carefully. "Perhaps you should have your Sidhe withdraw the geis that rests a heavy yoke on Conall's shoulders."

The Goddess growled. "Do not lecture me." Then, mostly to herself, she murmured, "The geis gave Conall a standing stone to mark his path, but there is no certainty that the promise ever bound him."

***

"I'll nae be going with ye to war." Gràinne hastily added, "If there is to be war with the Romans."

Fearghal and Mongfhionn looked up in surprise at the announcement. The veteran commander's face took on a look of hurt and betrayal at the statement blurted out by one he considered his daughter. The Sidhe nodded and smiled. She had been expecting this for some time.

She placed a hand on her partner's thigh to still his passions.

"Hear her out, Fearghal."

Gràinne's Northern Albu brogue was thick with unfiltered emotion. "I'm nae mystic, nae priest, nae Sidhe, nae Dark Huntress. Yet ma sleep is filled with visions and nightmares. I see blood and death. I feel the tears of ma people, the Na Daoine Tùrsach, wet ma skin." Gràinne paused, eyes glistening. "And Brianag asks of her father. It is only right that they should meet."

She was glad and relieved to see Fearghal nod in agreement. "I would like yer blessing. I cannae remember much about me blood ma and da. Both died at the hands of my grandma when I was little." Gràinne shifted uncomfortably from foot to foot.

"These past years, I've come to think of both of ye as being me ma and da. I was hoping ye'd come to think of me as yer daughter and Brianag as kin."

Fearghal rose, eyes smarting with salty tears that would not be held back. A gasp of "Ooofff!" burst from Gràinne as Fearghal embraced her with arms of iron. "Silly child. As if I, or Mongfhionn, would withhold our blessing from you or Brianag. And you're right, a daughter should spend time with her father. Brion was, and likely still is, a good man." Still holding Gràinne by the shoulder, Fearghal took a pace back. A frown landed briefly on his lips, and he turned to the Sidhe.

"But I will not allow my daughter and my granddaughter to walk unprotected into danger." The burly warrior smiled at the looks of alarm on both women. "She will go." He paused at the sighs of relief. "But she will take one hundred shields and a pair of chariots with her. Gràinne is a queen of the Cinn Péinteáilte, and a queen must have a strong guard that has her back." Gràinne opened her mouth to protest but was halted by a raised hand from the Sidhe.

"He is right."

Gràinne exhaled and then smirked like an adolescent. "Aye, Ma. Aye, Da."

"When do you hope to travel?"

"Around Bealtaine when the better weather returns." Gràinne grimaced, and her skin held a pale-green pallor. "I thought that perhaps you could talk with Pytheas. A ship would probably be best and quicker." Fearghal grinned and nodded. Gràinne's aversion to sea journeys was well-known.

"Conall and I will speak with Pytheas. There will be no problems."

"Thanks, Da."

"When will the newborn see the light of day?"

"What?" The word exploded from both Fearghal and Gràinne.

"Come, come. This old man's eyes may have chosen to be blind. Mine have not. I'll wager the swell in your belly is not from overeating."

Blushing furiously, Gràinne stammered, "Early spring. I think."

The Sidhe smiled. "Then Bealtaine would be a good time to plan your travels." She turned to Fearghal. "Do you wish to procure the services of a wet nurse, or should I?" The stunned look on her partner's face raised a loud laugh from Mongfhionn and prompted Gràinne to scurry from the chamber.

Outside of hearing, she exclaimed, "Parents!"

A cough alerted the Sidhe to the inevitability of Fearghal's question. "Who do you think the father is?"

"Are you that unobservant, old man, or do you choose to be when it suits you?" Fearghal tried to glare at his partner and failed. He shrugged heavily, muscled shoulders. "My intuition tells me that the child will likely have a pleasing skin colour and infernally white teeth."

＊＊＊

The weather was favourable, perhaps hoping to influence the outcome of the meeting between Conall and Dionysius. A gallery of covered archways enclosed the cloister. Each was chock-full of warriors—half Conall's and half the Greek king's. At the centre of the atrium and the heart of Pytheas' home stood a large table of pale, grey stone. While the quadrangle's dimensions were impressive, those present wondered how the merchant had managed to place the table. Even on close examination, there appeared to be no joints and no interruptions to its sculpted edges. It was a miracle of artisans and slaves. Around the table, the guests rested weary arses on carved wooden chairs. Noble-blue cushions, fringed in gold, ameliorated travel sores. Scents of lavender, jasmine, and mimosa drifted on zephyrs created by large fans wielded by trusted servants. The effect was pleasant, not cloying. The setting was elegant but functional, as this was a time for business.

Pytheas observed his guests with trepidation. There were enough veteran warriors on both sides to reduce Massalia's population considerably if umbrage was taken by either or both kings. This appraisal of the situation did not show on his face. A merchant's mask of smiles and diplomatic words guided the conversation.

As is often the case, the weather was the opening thrust. "Could you have chosen a more inclement time for this meeting, Pytheas?" Dionysius posed the question, but his tone was good-humoured. "I suppose, however, that Massalia has a pleasing climate and your home an acceptable level of comfort. And a welcome tendency towards Greek art, design, and furnishings. Business must be good."

Conall observed Dionysius and smiled. They were seated at opposite ends of the table. Flanking the king was his ambassador and two tall, burly warriors. All would die before a finger could be laid on their king.

Dionysius was a scorpion waiting his moment to strike. Widely regarded as impulsively cruel and implacably vindictive, Conall also found him hard to dislike. Deep-set brown eyes continuously scrutinised his surroundings, weighing up those in attendance and their level of threat or usefulness. His face was remarkable for the prominent hawknose and dark, brooding eyebrows. The latter contrasted with a head of short, dirty-blond hair layered back in curls and tamed with oils and perfumes. A well-kept beard, which rested on his chest, finished the facial canvas.

"I wish to borrow your fleet of quinqueremes," said Conall. Dionysius laughed. It was brief and stopped when he realised that

Conall was serious. Conall continued, "Only for a few days. Consider it part of their sea trials."

Dionysius combed his beard with long, expressive fingers. He supped a cup of wine and studied Conall. The silence was palpable but surprisingly did not give rise to anxiety. The two were lions—brave, powerful, and cunning. Their strength was evident without the need to preen like peacocks.

For his part, it was the women who most disturbed Dionysius. Seats had been provided, but they chose to stand slightly behind Conall. Each laid one hand on the king's shoulders—Mórrígan on his right, Mongfhionn on his left. It was as if their strength flowed to their king. Unquestionably beautiful, the contours of their bodies were loosely covered by flowing linen chitons, fine enough to be translucent in the light.

The aura of power radiating from the women made Dionysius consider his response carefully. Like two lionesses, they guarded their king. In a fight, he sensed that his bodyguard would be well outmatched. A grizzled warrior sat on Conall's right. His longsword rested at his feet on the terracotta-tiled floor. Dionysius smiled. Fearghal was a man he could understand.

"I made you a proposal before, and you turned me down. I don't usually make an offer twice," said Dionysius.

Conall allowed himself a small smile. Boyish dimples appeared in scraped cheeks. Mórrígan had decided he needed a kinglier style of beard, whiskers, and hair. He sniffed. He was okay with the hairstyle, even if it was a bit more onerous to maintain. The scents and oils he was not overly sure added to his manliness. Yet, other than Mórrígan, who else did he care to please? His only dalliance many summers ago had almost ended in tragedy.

Conall exhaled. "Last time, our goals did not align. This time they do. And you need me." Conall paused. Dionysius nodded, indicating that he should continue.

"Brennus will not be able to give you the army you sought... or bought. By the time he crosses the Alpes and reaches the Eridanus, he will have at best fifteen thousand men, not thirty. The rest of his army…" Conall looked at the tall ambassador and smiled blandly. "as I am sure your envoy and spies have informed you, fertilise the meadows of Dún-an-Rí. My estimate may be optimistic. Brennus will likely have to fight his way through the Gaiscedach in their passes and ravines in the Alpes. Given he had their king and queen murdered, he has few friends among that nest of assassins. Then, of course, there is the toll the gods of the Alpes levy."

Conall reached for a jug of spring water and filled his cup. He relished its coolness as it flowed down his throat. "I can add ten thousand battle-hardened veterans to Brennus' army and the fight against Rome." Conall's eyes hardened, and he held Dionysius' gaze. "Brennus will be an annoyance to the Etrusci and Umbri whose lands he will invade and plunder. He will have little impact on Rome because he will not confront Rome. Why should he? The Etrusci and Umbri will be easier to overcome.

"On the other hand, Marcus Fabius Ambustus, Pontifex of Rome, wants my head on a spear. He will send Rome's army to defeat me and bring me in chains to Rome." Conall scratched his cheek. "Win or lose, Rome will be distracted and weakened. And you will have your diversion."

"Can you trust Brennus?" asked Dionysius.

"He made me a promise and gave his oath."

Dionysius shook his head as if disappointed in Conall's judgment. "Kings make many promises but keep few." He signalled to his ambassador, and the two spoke softly. When finished, Dionysius smiled. "I think Marcus underestimates the beast he has created. Be assured that is one mistake I will never make."

Pytheas' guests relaxed, at last free to enjoy the superb feast provided, and Dionysius gestured again to his ambassador. The two stepped away from the rising babble of conversation.

"Determine what the Rí Ruirech of Clann Ui Flaithimh needs. Draw up the contract." The envoy dipped his head. "Also, prepare for a journey to the Eridanus River. You may have to search for the Senones, but they will probably have made a nuisance of themselves. Gold and the local Etrusci should uncover their location. Be wary. I do not wish word of your visit to reach Roman ears. Brennus will not be pleased with your presence, for you will give him no more than two-thirds of the original price. If you come back with your head, I will reward you. You will, of course, make observations and note anything that would support my longer-term plans." The envoy bowed deeply and smiled.

***

Much to Pytheas' relief, Dionysius and his retinue departed without incident and in good spirits. Cúscraid bowed to the king as he passed him by and then entered the courtyard. The craggy warrior caught Conall's eye. Motioned to sit down, Cúscraid took the empty chair beside Fearghal. As if guarding their partners, Mórrígan and the Sidhe stood behind each.

"There remains one issue to be resolved," said Cúscraid and nodded towards an archway where Craiftine, Fionnbharr, and Tadhg stood.

"I have no quarrel with Craiftine and Fionnbharr." Mórrígan glared pointedly at Tadhg, who seemed to visibly shrink under the queen's inspection. "But *he* disrespected the king and my hand-fast partner. Has he been suitably punished? Is he contrite? Is he loyal?"

"They have been in exile since that day," offered Cúscraid.

Mórrígan snorted. "Is banishment to the whorehouses of Massalia considered a sufficient punishment?"

"We did use them to break the blockade of Massalia, which was likely a scheme of Marcus'," Fearghal said. "By using their services, haven't we tacitly forgiven them? Pytheas is pleased, as are the other members of Massalia's council. Cúscraid has been fulsome in his praise of their skills and bravery."

Mórrígan made a sound of contempt. Conall chuckled and signalled for the three to step forward. Noticeably, Tadhg walked a pace ahead of his brothers. A few paces short of Conall, Tadhg dropped to one knee and bowed deeply. His brothers quickly followed suit.

"Oh, get up!"

Conall regretted his dismissive tone. It was unwarranted. "We're Gaels, not Greeks or Persians. I am Rí Ruirech by the will of the people and not separate from them. I am no tyrant like Dionysius. I need your understanding and loyalty, not your supplication. That is for the Goddess."

The wind taken from his sails, Tadhg rose somewhat uncertainly. A scuffling behind told him that his brothers had risen from their knees. The warrior had a dilemma. He had practised a speech, although not a long one, over and over until he was word perfect. Yet it seemed inappropriate now. Plus, the king had asked for his backing. Even Mórrígan's stern features had softened. Beside her, the Sidhe could barely restrain her mirth at the tableau unfolding before her.

In the end, Tadhg went with a simple, "I'm sorry. I was wrong." Realising that this had excluded his brothers, he added, "Craiftine and Fionnbharr only did what any brother would. They never had any enmity towards or bad words for you. If there is to be retribution, then that should be placed solely on my back."

Fearghal broke the awkward silence. "Oh, for pity's sake, sit down. Pytheas has provided enough food and drink for an army." The veteran commander looked at Mongfhionn as if seeking approval. She smiled and nodded.

"There will be no reprisals, no revenge. Welcome home." Conall's words brought welcome relief and an easing of the tensions.

Fionnbharr coughed. "Does that mean we can come back to Lugudunon?"

"No."

Conall smiled at the crestfallen expressions, but prompted by a dig in the ribs from the queen and a stern glare from the Sidhe, he explained. "Pytheas has requested that Cúscraid, you three, and the hundred shield warriors remain in Massalia. It seems you did your job too well and the good people of the city feel more secure with your presence." Resignation replaced disappointment.

"But that's not the full story," said Tadhg.

"As sharp as ever, although hopefully wiser," chided Conall. "We have made an agreement with Dionysius. You will ensure he delivers according to the contract drawn up."

"How long?"

"The rest of the army will arrive in Massalia after the feast of Bealtaine."

The three brothers exclaimed, "Shite!" in near unison.

Conall laughed. "Surely, Massalia is not an onerous city to remain in. You can learn much from this place. Pytheas has agreed that you can lodge with him in somewhat palatial comfort, or he can recommend some alternative inns, but not whorehouses."

"The rest of the army?" Tadhg gasped and then blurted, "It's Rome, isn't it?"

"I agree with the Rí Ruirech, Tadhg. You are clever but too impetuous at times." It was the Sidhe who spoke. "Perhaps I need to adjust the level of discomfort of the mark I left you with."

CHAPTER 22

394 B.C.—The River Eridanus and Lugudunon

Brennus loved his Gaulish homeland with its tall mountains, ravines with cascading waterfalls, and dense forests—a land constantly renewed by extended periods of rain. However, he had to admit that the beauty of his current surroundings was also magnificent. Set against the backdrop of the towering peaks of the Alpes, Lacus Benacus was a deep expanse of sapphire-blue water marbled with turquoise. The lake was surrounded by pine forests and amply stocked with many species of fish and eels. Pleasant, if sometimes chilling, winds rolled off the mountains, scattering a profusion of scents from the wild flora.

The survivors from Brennus' battle with Conall, and the constant harrying by the Gaiscedach as they traversed the Alpes, recuperated by the lake's shores. However, many became quickly bored with fishing and days of inactivity. Brawls spread throughout the Senone camp while their comrades recovered from injuries. That only ceased when Brennus announced that raids for food, beer, and women in the many villages and farms scattered around the lake's pebbled shores were allowed.

The screams and cries of the despoiled resounded, but the army of Brennus wanted plunder. Soon, larger Arverni and Senone warbands expanded their incursions into the neighbouring lands to the south. The outrage of the local tribes was understandable, if hypocritical since they too were highly active in the very same pursuits. To the southeast were the lands of the Etrusci, to the southwest those of the Umbri—both warlike peoples.

The Etrusci, well-armoured in bronze helmets, cuirasses, and greaves and carrying swords, axes, and shields, preferred to reside behind solid, walled defences. Even the tombs of their dead were fortresses of stone cut into the hillside. Like the Gauls, the Etrusci were prone to raiding each other's lands. Until the arrival of the Senones and Arverni, it did not matter much that they were not unified.

Like those in Southern Albu, the Umbri lived in strategic, well-defended hillforts. As with many Celts, they fought mostly naked, wielding spears and large, round shields. Brennus was happy with the situation. As far as he was concerned, the Etrusci and Umbri could stay in their strongholds while his army took possession of the surrounding lands.

A shout from the substantial wooden stockade protecting his encampment interrupted Brennus' musings. At first, he thought it might have been an Arverni raid. There had been no reconciliation with Celtillos, and the Arverni had chosen to camp further around the lakeside. A lack of the distinctive sound of iron on iron disproved that idea and the king's attention was drawn to the party entering the gateway.

Led by the tall Greek ambassador, whose demeanour acted like a thorn trapped in Brennus' triubhas, the delegation was admittedly impressive. One hundred Greek hoplites in burnished bronze armour accompanied the envoy. All carried long sarissas and bronze shields. A wagon trundled at the centre of the formation, its solid wheels creaking on its axles. It was a gratifying sound, and Brennus envisaged the gold it carried.

Flicking a speck of dust from the embroidered edge of his chiton, the ambassador inspected Brennus' men with undisguised scorn. "I am sure the armies of the Etrusci and Umbri quiver in fear and awe of the mighty Senones." The voice was easy on the ears but laden with sarcasm. "Maybe not the Romans." With a flourish, Dionysius' representative gestured to the chaotic encampment.

Exhausted by the trek through the ravines and passes of the Alpes, the sick and maimed had simply fallen at the first available space and had seen no reason to move. Fingers, toes, and noses were blackened or missing. Disease was rampant. The smell of putrefaction stained the air and many more would cross the veil in this camp of death. The healthy stayed outside, far away from the stockade.

Only the army of Celtillos showed any semblance of discipline and fitness for battle. Truthfully, the Arverni king had been shocked at the poor state of Brennus' forces—and at how few had survived the journey. Afraid of the contagions of disease and defeat and not being on friendly terms with Brennus, he kept the Arverni camp distant from the Senones. He often pondered the foolishness of his alliance with Brennus.

"Dionysius owes me one talent of gold—Roman weight. Hand it over and go."

Brennus' mood was brusque. Though the delegation had tramped through Etruscan land for six or seven sunsets and was undoubtedly weary, Brennus saw little value in welcoming Dionysius' representative with friendship and feasting. He just did not like or trust the ambassador. In this, the feeling was mutual, although the envoy was much more pro-fessional in maintaining a neutral façade.

That said, the ambassador had his limits and a spine of steel. He shook his head. With a flourish of his hand, he indicated Brennus' force. "My king was promised an army. Not a diseased rabble unfit for battle." Brennus' hand gripped the leather-bound hilt of his sword, sliding it a hand's length from the scabbard. "You think to threaten me with death?" The envoy shook his head and laughed. The captain of his guard, a vet-eran of many campaigns, sensing danger, arranged his hoplites around the wagon. "Were I to hand over my king's gold for such a poor return, I would face much greater punishments than losing my head."

Unflinching, the envoy held Brennus' gaze. "Do you want war with Dionysius?" At a signal from the messenger, the guard parted, and the wagon rolled forward, stopping five paces from the king. With a rare smile and some relish, the ambassador spoke again.

"My king knows of your defeat at the hands of Conall. He has therefore come to an accommodation with another to make up for your weakness. Take what is on offer… or nothing."

Brennus bristled, fighting to control his anger. Still, his army wanted their portion, and without gold, the Arverni would desert in an instant. At a sharp nod, several of Brennus' men arrived to drive the wagon away. He needed the cart's cargo. Helpless, his eyes held those of the diplomat. When he finally spoke, it was through clenched teeth.

"You should leave. Now."

As he watched the backs of the Greeks march away from the camp, one word was spat from Brennus' thin lips.

"Conall!"

***

"No!"

The throne tipped over, crashing to the wooden boards. Concurrently, a pottery chalice was flung across the room, shattering into jagged pieces as it smashed against the wall. Its contents stained the cedarwood. A pity, for it was a particularly fine piece of earthenware and the honeyed beer excellent.

However, this was not the anger and indignation of a king. Rather it was the anguish of a father, wishing to protect his family. "Aodán and Barra are too young to come into consideration. Danu was almost murdered and still recovers from her wounds. As for Brighid…" Conall looked to Mórrígan and Mongfhionn. "Well, Brighid has her own issues to resolve."

At the far end of the table, seated with her sister and brothers, Brighid recoiled as if her innermost thoughts had been publicly exposed. Green eyes misted over as she fought to hold back a cascade of tears. She was almost successful.

"Take your da to task later, Brighid. He and your ma are like a pair of wolves, wishing only to protect their pups. Listen to them.

Understand what is behind their anxiety. Later, you and I will continue our discussions."

The younger of the twins started at the sound. The Sidhe's sudden appearance at her side and hand on her arm was unsettling, but she dipped her head in silent consent. Brighid brushed a tear from her cheek. Her jaw set, an action for which her father was well-known, and she glared back at the king.

✳✳✳

The gathering was held in one of the more intimate meeting chambers in Lugudunon's Great Hall. A small and agitated group sat around the age-smoothened oak table that commanded the centre of the room. At the table sat the king, the queen, and their four children. Barra, although the issue of Conall and Mòrag, was treated no differently than his half-sisters and half-brother. Four others sat or stood nearby—Fearghal and Mongfhionn, Íar, and an envoy from Ráth Na Conall in southern Ériu.

In awe of being in the presence of men and women spoken of in epic tales around the fires of Ráth Na Conall, it was to the young messenger's credit that he appeared neither fearful nor discomfited. He related his news with passion and clarity. His delivery was commendable, given that he brought no welcome tidings.

Íar's father, the Rí Curraghatoor, Deda Mac Sin, had passed beyond the veil. While sad, it was not unexpected. Deda had lived a long, full, and colourful life. He had passed away as he had lived—in the arms of two comely maidens. The envoy bowed and then knelt and offered Deda's sword and ring to Íar, now the rightful Rí of Curraghatoor.

The rest of the messenger's news deepened the gloom of the chamber. Even the glowing braziers and wood and peat fires could not banish the shadows. Torcán's brothers, Uallachán and Nuadha Ó Dubhghaill, who had chosen to remain in Ériu, had taken advantage of Deda's death to bring their simmering rebellion to a boil.

Ráth Na Conall was under siege. Roving warbands and miscreants pillaged, plundered, and raped across southern Ériu. Depravities unheard of since the reign of Eochaidh Ruad were visited on the people. Under the command of Onchú Ó an Cháintigh, the garrisons at Ráth Na Conall and Carn Tigherna were stretched to breaking. Onchú was barely capable of protecting his own fort, let alone safeguarding Ráth Na Conall and stamping out an insurrection.

A tearful envoy pleaded on behalf of his people for a return of the Rí Ruirech. His plea was well heard. Mongfhionn bit her tongue until it bled and swore beneath her breath. The geis she had laid on Conall made the messenger's request impossible to satisfy, and the king appear uncaring.

Íar looked at Conall. The king's body language spoke loudly of frustration, helplessness, and deep anger. Regardless of the geis, the army of Clann Ui Flaithimh had just battled the Senones. Once several seasons had passed, there would be a war with Rome. As for Íar, he had long ago chosen Conall over his father and Curraghatoor. His honour would never allow a retreat from that decision.

"There is no choice. Ráth Na Conall must not fall. The rebellion must be stamped out, and the Ó Dubhghaill brothers and their supporters put to the sword or stake. Caher Conri must be razed to the ground and the land around sown with salt. Evil must never rise again from that accursed place."

Conall and Mórrígan looked at the defiant Mongfhionn. Wariness resided in their eyes. This was the old Sidhe. Confident. Arrogant. And likely about to say or demand something unpalatable.

"A new generation must take the field. The princesses of Clann Ui Flaithimh must fight for Ráth Na Conall."

The silence that followed the Sidhe's pronouncement was quickly shattered by an explosive "No!" from Conall and Mórrígan. Conall's hand reached out and gripped his axe. Mórrígan's curling sigils pulsated with power. Yet the Sidhe stood defiant, ancient oak staff in hand.

"You know it must be."

A chair scraped on the wooden boards as Danu stood. Her

movements were slow and full of pain as, even with the Sidhe's help, her recovery was not fully complete. She gripped Brighid's hand for strength, and her sister rose to stand at her side.

"We are princesses. No longer are we children who can leave weighty decisions to others. We are also warriors taught by the best." She smiled at Fearghal and Íar. Ignoring the glares from Mórrígan and Conall, the men nodded and beamed back, proud of their students. "Our responsibility is to the Goddess and the clann. Although they are strangers to us and far away, our tribe includes the people of Ráth Na Conall. With the changing of the seasons, and following the festival of Bealtaine, Brighid and I will sail for Ériu and Ráth Na Conall."

Fearghal walked to the girls and hugged them until they cried surrender. He looked to Conall and Mórrígan, who had taken their seats and whose faces held looks of resignation, apprehension, and pride. Next, he looked at Íar, who nodded as if knowing what his friend was thinking.

"It seems as if we will be prevailing on Pytheas again. Two hundred warriors will accompany Danu and Brighid. One hundred mounted and one hundred shield warriors. Maybe a few chariots, too. Íar will choose riders and horses; Gràinne the chariots; and I will choose the shields." The veteran commander scratched his head, thought for a moment, and spoke to Conall and Mórrígan. "The brave also need wise heads. Perhaps you could prevail upon Beacán and Iasg to accompany the girls."

Finally, Fearghal looked at Mongfhionn. "While her powers are growing, Neamhain is still a child and far too young to accompany Danu and Brighid. Yet, an 'unearthly' presence would be an advantage in the campaign."

Mongfhionn smiled at her partner. "You are the wisest of us all. Devious too. I will seek an audience with the Aes Sidhe. I suspect that my fellow sidhe, while reluctant to meddle, will not be overjoyed at the goings-on at Caher Conri. Hopefully, that will outweigh their issues with me."

In a rush of enthusiasm, the young envoy raised his jug high. "The banners of Conall, Rí Ruirech, and Clann Ui Flaithimh will fly from the ramparts of Ráth Na Conall. The Goddess is good."

***

"I didn't take you for a matchmaker."

Fearghal pulled up and turned to face Mongfhionn as they strolled back to their chambers. His expression was one of puzzlement.

"Beacán and Iasg. Surely even you are not that unobservant?" The Sidhe chuckled. "Or perhaps in some areas, you are."

CHAPTER 23

394 B.C.—Lugudunon—Feast of Imbolg

The Óenach is a rare gathering of the tribe's civic and military elders and leaders. The congregation was called only when momentous decisions, which needed the consent and the sanction of the whole clann, had to be made. Thus, Conall called for an Óenach to approve the war with Rome. The gathering would take place at Lugudunon before the winter feast of Imbolg.

Riders criss-crossed the lands of Clann Ui Flaithimh, requesting the presence of kings, nobles, and civic leaders. Subtle politics would be provided by the presence of the Oracle, the College of the Chaste, and Crum Dubh's druids. More open and aggressive positioning would be the preserve of the clann's warrior chieftains. It was the way of the Gaels. Conall did not seize power through tyranny, bribery, or assassination but was the people's choice. Thus he could not and indeed would not take the army to war in distant lands without the agreement of the Óenach.

That said, few doubted that Conall and Mórrígan would get their way. Even fewer would be so foolish as to oppose their wishes. Conall had led the tribe well and, in harsh times, had ensured the well-being of the people. Still, all remembered well his and Mórrígan's merciless slaughter of the last rebellion's instigators and supporters. Yet, tradition had to be observed, and, according to Fearghal, a lot of boring old farts had to be heard.

"Perhaps there is something to be said for being a tyrant like Dionysius."

It was a position that Conall would only speak aloud in the company of his most trusted advisors. Even then, Íar choked on his beer and had to be soundly thumped on his back by his partner, Aoibheann. A raised eyebrow from the Sidhe suggested that the king should clarify his thoughts and quickly. A few of the more hawkish around the table thought the statement had its merits but diplomatically kept their hopes high and their counsel and expressions neutral.

"Gifts of gold torques for the men and gold rings, bracelets, and jewelled brooches for their partners. Thousands of amphorae of wine and barrels of beer. Is there a cow, sheep, or lamb alive between here and Cenabum or Massalia or the Alpes? The Óenach will put me, and the tribe, in penury. I'll need the Rome campaign just to replenish the treasury." Conall shook his head. "I wish we still had the gold mine in Aremorio."

In a rare exhibition of public affection, Mórrígan ran fingers through her hand-fast partner's dark locks and planted a loud and long kiss on his lips. The action raised a cheer among those present and brought a blush to Conall's cheeks.

✳✳✳

The Rí Ruirech of Clann Uí Flaithimh stood, walked to the doors of the Great Hall, and threw them open. Around the fort and across the river, great bonfires roared, painting the night sky with red, yellow, and orange tinges. Aromatic smells of peat and woodsmoke met him. Later that would be overpowered by the fragrances of stale beer, wine, and puke, as well as the musky scents of rutting.

Cries of jubilation, shrieks, and laughter filled the air from a people—men, women, and children—all determined to have a wonderful time. Even slaves were encouraged to join in the festivities. No matter the cost in sore heads and distended bellies, all agreed that this Imbolg would be a festival remembered for many seasons. Ultimately, the celebration of Samhain would bring loud arguments about who the fathers of the many newborns might be.

Imbolg was a joyful celebration of the people and their leaders. Loyal allies such as Tasgiitios were honoured by their invitations to the festivities. Conall had received the approval of the Óenach. Although he thought it was brought about by the imminent feasting and the need to indulge in some hard drinking and lusty pursuits.

Silence eventually assumed command of the night. In the deepening darkness, the raucous festivities of Imbolg whimpered to a few farts, prolonged snores, and grunts of "Get off!" The soporific effects of beer and wine, an excess of food, and the frenetic pursuits of lust carried the clann into the welcoming arms of sleep and dreams of heroic deeds and infinite libidos.

It was the perfect time for an attack.

* * *

As if on cue, a cloud, previously becalmed, drifted across the moon. Its shadow, and that of another, flowed over the land. Weapons: spears, hand-axes, and daggers, were dulled with dirt, charcoal, and dark weavers' dyes. Naked bodies were covered in the curling tribal sigils of the Gaiscedach. The glaring whiteness of Lugudunon's walls and dwellings would provide adequate camouflage for skins pale from life in the Alpes.

The raiders were the choicest remnant of Matres' army. Defeated, the Gaiscedach were forced to flee the fertile valleys of the Rodonos and Souconna for the forested, high foothills and barren slopes of the Alpes. Their lands and the stronghold of Lugudunon had been invaded and conquered by Conall. Concolitanus, their king, betrayed by his partner, had been murdered by the command of Brennus. Matres, their queen, forced to flee Lugudunon, was later dismembered in an act of bloody revenge by the Roman general Marius. Many of the royal family met their gods when their heads were severed by the mighty axe of Urard.

The plight of the Gaiscedach should have evoked sympathy and support. Yet, that would have ignored a near-universal agreement that the tribe was little more than a gathering of bloodthirsty assassins and murderers for hire. The clann's history was a litany of narcissism and self-pity, taking no account of the terror and killings visited on numerous victims, many of whom were innocents.

Yet, vengeance had moved to within the Gaiscedach's grasp. They had already inflicted many deaths on Brennus' army as it traversed the Alpes. Now, spies—disgruntled malcontents within Clann Ui Flaithimh—informed them that Conall, his hierarchy, and their children lay within reach of their blades. Like a swarm of cockroaches, they scuttled up and over the eastern walls and entrances. Guards were dispatched with ruthless, silent precision. It was hard not to admire their skills. Only the soft crunching of calloused feet on frost-covered stone betrayed their presence.

They crossed the inner gateway with one objective in mind—the Great Hall. Splitting into small groups, they flowed left and right down the dark, unlit streets of Lugudunon. They ghosted along familiar alleys, ignoring drunken revellers who, with full bladders, swayed like corn in the wind as they pissed against walls.

Numbers were not on their side. Hence, they could ill afford to alert the army of Clann Ui Flaithimh or the residents of Lugudunon. Their goal: a surgical strike on the leaders and children of the tribe. Few held any hope of surviving. At some moment during the slaughter, they knew an alarm would sound. The gates of Lugudunon would slam shut, imprisoning them. The stronghold would become their sarcophagus. Hunted down like dogs, they would be subjected to indescribable tortures and eventually death. But they would enter the Otherworld knowing they had retribution. And once again, the name of the Gaiscedach would be feared by all.

As one, undiscovered, they reached the open square before Lugudunon's Great Hall. The building was in darkness. A few allowed themselves a smirk and congratulatory chuckle at the thoughtless absence of security. What hubris gave Conall and his queen such arrogance? It was a fair question and one that many were to ask afterwards.

A solitary wolfhound exposed a flaw in the assassins' design. A lone, prolonged howl rent the night's silence, echoing off the cold slab walls of Lugudunon. From neat rows of cuboid, dwellings came shouts of "Shut the Hag up!" and threats of "Dogmeat for dinner!"

Undeterred, the hound redoubled its chorus. The Gaiscedach exchanged worried looks, and a small group was despatched in the direction of the yowling. A yelp and a whimper made the attackers breathe easier—until another dog took up the refrain… and another… and another.

CHAPTER 24

394 B.C.—Lugudunon—Imbolg

Later, Conall mused that it was the yelp and soft whimper of the wolf-hound's sacrifice that woke him. Impossible—unless the Goddess had taken a hand. Simultaneously, Conall and Mórrígan rolled from their cot, scattering furs, and knocking over jugs of water and pisspots. Pausing only to grab weapons, shields, and helmets, they padded into the hallway. There, they were greeted by a grim body of angry men and women similarly armoured—the nobility along with their personal guards. All were naked, except Crum's small group of druids.

"Do they sleep in those black robes?" muttered Fearghal, eliciting a round of chuckles. Crum and his men stared impassively at the panorama of flesh around them.

Conall looked around. "Brighid, Danu, and Pytheas gather up and protect the young. Arm any old enough to hold a bow, spear, or sword. Crum, take your druids and go with them."

In truth, Danu was relieved to obey her da's command. Nakedness in the clann was not unusual, especially for those of the Cinn Péinteáilte. It was, however, disconcerting to be faced with both her ma and da with skin flushed and enrobed in little more than a thin layer of perspiration. The young woman shook her head, attempting in vain to dislodge the image of what had caused the sweating from her thoughts. Parents just did not do that sort of thing.

Conall turned to face Gràinne and Mórrígan. He was about to

suggest that the noticeably pregnant duo should accompany the young ones. Glares from both women stopped him. Was he that predictable? Prudence overruled his urge to be protective. His troubles were numerous without adding to them.

"The rest of us will defend the wall."

One hundred paces long and ten paces broad, the wall formed the western side of an enclosed square courtyard. Along its length, braziers burned brightly, throwing both light and shadow into the enclosure. At its centre, the entranceway was closed by two massive oak doors, each faced in bronze. The doors bore ornately embossed scenes depicting the history of the tribe. To his constant embarrassment, Conall featured prominently. Beyond the entrance was the king and queen's citadel.

Opposite the entranceway to the royal residence was the rear exit of the Great Hall. Huge torches burned on either side of the gateway. More, set in iron sconces and braziers, flared along the remaining walls. During the deep hours of the night, the smell of burning oil overwhelmed the soothing fragrances of plants and shrubs. Tended by slaves, the fires burned brightly from sunset to sunrise.

It was at this doorway that the Gaiscedach made a second error. They believed informants rather than reconnoitring the battlefield for themselves. Their spies, likely because it was common knowledge among the tribe, neglected to mention one fact. The Great Hall was no longer the royal family's residence as it had been in Matres' days.

With some measure of satisfaction, Cúscraid noted the confusion that momentarily settled on the assassins' faces. On his counsel, Conall had agreed to a new palace built at the rear of the Great Hall. Still, the veteran groaned. At a quizzical look from Deaglán, he pointed to the quadrangle.

"The beautiful flowers and shrubs, the fountains, and the statues that you see will be no more before the dawn's light. Mórrígan will have my head."

✳✳✳

Iasg stamped tiny feet on the frosted parapet. She was perturbed, but not about the cold or the impending battle. As she looked on the statuesque and curvaceous bodies of Mòrag, the Sidhe, and the Leader of the Chaste, she experienced a painful moment of inadequacy. To her eyes, even the lithe forms of Aoibheann and Bláithín were more pleasing than her short, angular frame.

Her eyes dropped to her shrinking breasts and ribs that pushed at flesh. Iasg let out a low growl. She sorely missed her partner and love, Urard, but was that any excuse to neglect and starve herself? He would have been furious at her. A soft tug on her narrow shoulders made her reluctantly turn around to face Beacán. In the light of the brazier, his green eyes flared with tiny tongues of red. His lips curled into a smile that transformed his face and made Iasg's heart beat faster.

"You are as beautiful to me as any of those you so openly admire."

Her head dropped until calloused fingers lifted her chin. The kiss was not long but had the effect of removing any thoughts of imperfection. Flushed, Iasg looked up at Beacán. "If we survive the night, ye'll take me to yer bed, Beacán."

A few steps away, Lonán laughed. "Now there's a promise to fight for."

***

"You Gaels have a strange way of entertaining guests." Standing to Conall's left, Tasgiitios reluctantly dragged his eyes from admiring the naked and highly distracting form of the Leader of the Chaste. The king of the Carnutes glanced downwards, hoping that his admiration was not too evident. In this, he had little to be concerned, for frost is no friend to ardour. A rebalancing of his shield disguised any embarrassment and an adjustment of the spear in his right hand restored his physical balance.

Tasgiitios' focus on the Priestess was understandable. He had asked her during the festival to become his hand-fast partner and queen. In his mind, he already envisaged her sharing his throne and bed—provided both he and she survived the night. Tasgiitios had weighed up the

Leader of the Chaste's loyalty to the Oracle and the Sanctuary against the potential benefits of securing a powerful ally. He had concluded the hand-fasting would be to his advantage and only the Lady's consent was needed. The latter consideration was a seismic change in Tasgiitios' thinking. He was a man much more used to taking what he wanted—especially concerning women.

Conall gave Tasgiitios a grim smile and then looked with concern at the rounded belly of Mórrígan. Given its expanse, he thought his partner's prediction of another set of twins was both highly likely and imminent. The queen smiled at his gaze. She knew his thoughts as well as her own. The bow in her hand tensed and bent as the Dark Huntress nocked an arrow and drew the bowstring back.

The missile had barely left the bow before another black shaft was put to the string and set in flight. Only Sarpedon could match her ability. Conall smiled at his queen's demonstration of strength and roared, "*Ní ghéillfear, nó cúlú!*" The warriors, men and women, the best of Clann Ui Flaithimh, if not Gaul, shouted back, "No surrender! No retreat!" and hefted javelins.

Side by side, fifty faced three hundred.

✳ ✳ ✳

In those times, leaders fought in the front line. Thus, it was fitting, if not surprising, that the first to fall was the leader of the Gaiscedach intruders. His eyes widened in disbelief as the barbs from the Huntress's bow appeared to hang in mid-air before piercing both corneas. Was it the whimsy of the Goddess to pause the passing of time so that he could finally understand his foolishness?

The shafts continued, penetrating his brain, and exiting his skull. Momentum carried him back into the arms of comrades, who promptly tossed his corpse to the dirt. His death was unfortunate for the one who followed in his shadow. The javelin that would have become embedded in the leader's flesh tore through the man's neck, ripping the carotid artery on the left side. The man was doubly ill-fated. Instead of dying quickly, he slowly bled out as his comrades trampled him into the flower beds.

The heavily accented voice of Carmag sounded over the wall, "Kick the braziers over! Burn the bastards. Let them walk on hot embers to fight." Soon the courtyard became an inferno of flame and smoke as hot embers cascaded from overturned braziers. Shrubs and trees, clothed in a thin coating of winter frost, hissed angrily at the fire's hungry tongues. Yet ice proved no defence, and the foliage burst into red and yellow bonfires.

Caught in the unexpected flare of light, the scuttling cockroaches hesitated before resuming the charge for the far wall. They were met with a hail of javelins.

Mórrígan laid down her bow and quiver. A glance to the Sidhe met a nod of approval and brought a cruel smile to Mongfhionn's ruby-red lips. Hands raised to the night sky, ululating invocations flowed from the two women. They were soon joined by a third as Gràinne added her tribal death chant to the awful song. From the palace behind, a fourth voice joined the choir. Neamhain Ni Fearghal may have been little more than a child, but her voice held the strength of her mother, the Sidhe.

The harmonies were beautiful but carried dread in every note. A fog of foreboding hovered above the attackers before descending into their minds. Banished from the skies, the cloud that had cloaked the Gaiscedach's presence was no more. Exposed and their thoughts tormented, they staggered forward and were met with fire and iron.

***

Enrobed in blood and sweat, Brandubh, with grim resolve, cursed as he twisted and wrenched his spear from unyielding flesh. The thrust to the Gaiscedach warrior had been too perfect. The spearhead sliced through soft tissue and muscle, miraculously avoiding major bones, and exited her back in a gush of blood. It was on the return that problems arose. The leaf-shaped blade's tang snagged on the warrior's spine. She screeched and convulsed as her backbone was jerked through flesh. Still, the loathing in her eyes and cruel uplift of the edges of bloody lips into a gloating smile should have alerted the Prince of the Ravens.

The shout of "Behind you!" came too late.

Brandubh was tired. Even in the heat of the frantic battle on the wall, the cold night air was slowly, inexorably sapping his strength. His reactions were dulled. One blade entered his back, piercing his liver and ripping upwards, while another stabbed into the left side of his neck. The pain was excruciating. Both wounds were mortal.

A heartrending cry of "No!" came from a tall, female apparition, and the gods quickly deserted Brandubh's assailant. The iron boss of Mòrag's shield struck the assassin's spine, crippling him, and sending him crashing to the frosted stone with a whimper of agony. He was unfortunate. His injuries were not fatal.

"Bind him. I'll deal with him later." Mòrag's tone was as icy as the frozen lochs of Northern Albu.

The Princess of the Ravens held her brother to her chest. He took comfort from the steady beat of her heart. Cold and shock numbed the pain. For brother and sister, the battle no longer raged around them. Sapped of strength, foes fought with blunted blades and minds, with bodies that begged for rest.

"Don't you die on me."

Great tears flowed down blood-stained cheeks. Brandubh coughed. A mouthful of blood barely cleared his lips, splattering his sister's breasts. In the moonlight, it glistened black. She held him even closer, gently rocking and stroking his bald head.

"Too late, I think, sister."

He fell silent for a few moments. Mòrag wailed, thinking the bean-sidhe had taken him. A squeeze on her hand made the warrior stop. An ember of hope smouldered in her eyes. Brandubh smiled and painfully shook his head.

"It is not to be, Queen of the Ravens." A few weak coughs wracked Brandubh's body. His lips moved, and Mòrag bent her ear to his mouth.

"Wear more suitable clothes, sister. You're a queen now."

"Bastard," mouthed Mòrag.

But this time, Brandubh had passed beyond the veil. A contented smile froze on his bloody lips. For once, his had been the last word.

***

Danu glanced nervously towards the room's entrance. The doors of darkened oak, embellished with tales of men and gods, were solid. But they were not made or meant to take the kicks, the shoulders, or the blades that pounded on them and rattled the locking bar. Iron hinges squealed as if they had no more strength.

She bit her lip until it bled. The taste of iron and salt made her grimace. Her sister, Brighid, glanced back to the young ones behind her. All wore brave faces, and all were terrified. A few babies cried and then stopped as if recognising its futility. Brighid looked at her twin. An almost imperceptible nod of Danu's head blessed her decision, and Brighid padded across the floor.

Her younger brothers, Aodán and Barra, stood resolute, small shields gripped and spears in hand, alongside their childhood friends Brianag, Sorchae, and Neamhain. Neamhain's voice was silent. The strain of matching her mother's incantations had proved too much for one so young. Tears streamed down her porcelain-white cheeks. Of the group, the daughter of the Sidhe was more aware of what Fate might expect of them. Brianag and Sorchae embraced her and whispered soothing words.

"Take the young ones to the far wall. The exit is behind the high table and the heavy tapestries. Should we fall, you will lead them to safety." Brighid paused and smiled sadly at Aodán and Barra. Left unsaid was, "Or die trying." Her brothers nodded. They knew.

Crum Dubh heard the doors groan and witnessed the first and inevitable signs of wood splitting. Dust and splinters floated up, sparkling in the torchlight. He turned to face the small group. "Brighid, Danu, and Pytheas will stand behind my druids and me. Should we fall, then you will judge whether to stand or flee." A rebellious firming of Brighid's jaw brought a flinty look to the Druid's deep-blue eyes. "I will brook no dissent."

Any further argument was curtailed by a loud crash as wood surrendered and iron hinges twisted and crashed to the wooden floor. Crum, flanked on either side by two black-robed druids, turned to face the assassins. Most certainly, the Gaiscedach did not expect to be faced with armed druids or that the priests would wield the swords with a warrior's skill and power.

Black robes swirled as the druids attacked, slashing and battering the enemy. No armour protected the adversaries. Bones shattered, and flesh sundered as blades, honed sharp, bit into soft flesh. Fragments of limbs were sheared, and terrible scars created. Soon, the floor was awash with gore. Yet for all their passion and discipline, the druids' business was not warring. The press pushed them back, and more of the enemy slipped through the doorway to attack the flanks.

Danu, always the tactician, saw the druids' peril. The priests fought well but were tiring. One had already fallen, his lifeblood seeping through the floor's wooden slats. Outnumbered, soon they would be overwhelmed. The pink rose between her breasts flared an angry red. She turned to Pytheas.

"Join our brothers." The portly merchant made to protest but was silenced by a raised palm. "I need someone with experience to take charge of the retreat. You're our hope, Uncle. Guide them well." The Greek trader smiled at the honour of her endearment. Sorrowfully, he dipped his head and obeyed.

"Take the left, sister. I'll take the right. It is time to wet our blades with Gaiscedach blood." The drawing back of Brighid's lips into a nightmarish countenance rivalling the Hag made Danu shudder. The pink tips of Brighid's black rose turned crimson, and trails of blood appeared to trickle from it. Danu had no time to dwell on the omen. For Brighid had given vent to a primaeval war cry straight from the Otherworld and thrown herself into the fight.

Startled by the shout, Crum glanced in its direction. A sharp pain to his lower torso taught him the foolishness of the reflex. The druid felt warm blood trickle down his side. He swore and grasped the spear's shaft with his left hand. He was surprised. An experienced assassin would have let go of the weapon and finished the druid with another blade. Instead, the Gaiscedach attacker gripped the wood with both hands and pulled. A snarl of wicked delight was spat from thin lips when Crum roared out in pain.

The assailant intended to free the metal spearhead and thrust once more, delivering a killing strike. Instead, with both hands holding the pole, he was defenceless as the sword in Crum's right hand rose and viciously chopped downwards. A bloody wedge of blond hair, bone, and brain fell to the floor. His spirit already at the gates of Mag Mell, the Gaiscedach's body tumbled forward. Gushing blood splashed Crum's robe.

The Leader of the Druidic Council dropped to his knees, hoping for a few moments to clear his head from the creeping dizziness. He had only a foggy awareness of his head pulled back and of the blade that opened up his throat.

The leader of the Gaiscedach band took a step backwards, placing a bloody hand on the doorpost. The young woman had started with a score of warriors, many of them kin, but had lost half in the early clashes, first to the druids and then to the fury and blades of Conall's twin daughters. While the wrath of the princesses burned ever hotter, the assassins' motivation flagged. The number of the band able to fight continued to diminish. With the battle on the wall raging, she had expected only a few guards and the simple slaughter of defenceless children. Now, fame and a place in Gaiscedach lore no longer resided in this room.

She exhaled and reluctantly bellowed, "Retreat!"

"Not so fast, bitseach!"

Both twins had heard the Gaiscedach leader's shout. Both hefted and threw their spears. Pinned to the wooden frame, the last memory of the assassin was a face with a nightmarish maw and between pert breasts, a black rose that dripped blood. Her throat was opened by a sharp blade pulled across it agonisingly slowly.

* * *

Alerted by Lugudunon's wolfhounds, Gaius' Romans, a vengeful caomhnóirí, and Mórrígan's warband, the latter two groups in shock at the potential loss of the king and queen, crushed the stalled Gaiscedach attack. Led by Gaius, almost a thousand warriors stormed through the Great Hall. On the far wall, they saw spectral figures, silhouetted against white stone, fight a desperate and grisly battle.

The Romans swept into the smoke-filled courtyard and were instantly assaulted by the smell of charred flesh. The other groups quickly gained the adjacent walls and charged along the parapet to relieve Conall. To the combatants, caught in life-and-death duels, the battle seemed furious and lengthy. Yet, in reality, little time had passed.

Thus, there were a small number of Gaiscedach who had yet to scale the ramparts. They turned to face the new threat. Naked and armed with spears and weapons more suited to stealth and close-quarter fighting, they were no match for the burnished bronze cuirasses and swords of the Romans or the fiery tempers and blades of the Gaels.

* * *

The sun rose over Lugudunon's market square, blushing the white stone a golden pink. In other circumstances, the scene would have been glorious. At this time, it just seemed wrong. Arrayed on the steps of the Great Hall stood the king, queen, and nobility of Clann Uí Flaithimh. Their faces were stained by blood and smoke, and all were attired in furs, heavy woollen cloaks, and soft sheepskin boots. The smaller children had been escorted to safety and to enjoy a hot meal.

Around the sides of the plaza, on the walls and rooftops of neighbouring buildings, the crowds bayed for revenge. The target of their ire was the group of Gaiscedach who, naked and shivering uncontrollably in the dawn frost, huddled together at the centre of the marketplace. Many were injured and rested on the strength of their comrades.

A resounding celebration of victory and relief arose from the throng as Conall and Mórrígan stepped forward. The king looked at Mórrígan and, sensing her accord, turned to Lonán and Amodocus. In a voice laden with cold fury, he spoke.

"Take what men and horses you need. Teach the Gaiscedach the folly of attacking Clann Ui Flaithimh. Burn their farms and settlements to the ground, slaughter the men, enslave the women and the young. Drive them into the high Alpes, where their gods can decide their fate. Show no mercy, for they would have shown us none."

Involuntary gasps of "No!" came from the lips of the prisoners.

"What? You thought I would be compassionate? You thought there would be no consequences for attacking our children? You plainly do not know An Fiagaí Dorcha or me." He nodded to the prisoners' guards. "Punish them as outcasts. Take them to the fields. Bind them to stakes and open up their bellies. Let the ravens and wolves feast on their flesh."

Most of Clann Ui Flaithimh attributed the raid to Marcus and Roman gold, which was easier to acknowledge than the true explanation. The motive of the three hundred assassins was much purer… retribution. Later, in the quietness of their chamber, Conall looked at Mórrígan.

"Are we any better than the Gaiscedach or Brennus? They at least fought with undisguised motives. Ours wears the guise of justice."

Mórrígan shook her head. "Blood for blood. Marcus took our parents, our friends, and our innocence. By his plots and mercenaries, he would take the lives of our children. For that, Conall, I will have retribution. I want him to suffer and his blood to spill by my hands." Mórrígan paused to trace her fingers across her partner's cheek. "And so do you."

CHAPTER 25

394 B.C.—Rome

To say that Nikandros was deeply annoyed, furious even, was an understatement. In expectations of an immediate meeting with Marcus, he had rented luxurious lodgings in the Forum Romanum. But the old man had left his once-favoured assassin and bodyguard kicking his heels over the winter. A dwindling supply of gold meant that his accommodation and the quality of whores to which he was accustomed became too expensive. The constant scratching of his crotch testified to the latter.

The message conveyed by Marcus was unmistakable. The Spartan was of no further use and was perhaps a liability. If Marcus considered him a problem, Nikandros' most likely fate was to be found in one of Rome's sewage-strewn alleyways rather than a pleasant apartment in the Forum.

At last, however, Marcus deigned to give him an audience, and the proud Spartan stood before his employer. To Nikandros, the old man appeared to have put on weight; his belly sagged, and his frame was stooped. A slight tremor in the Roman's left hand was noticeable but may have been an affectation to get sympathy. Dark blemishes spread in clusters over hands and face. There was no denying that age was fast catching up to the Pontifex of Rome. From behind the safety of his father's ornately carved chair, Quintus, the elder son, glared at Nikandros.

Marcus' oldest showed the signs of a dissolute life: a flabby paunch, double chin, broken spider veins on his cheeks, and dark circles visible even under the man's sun-ripened skin. Nikandros sneered at Quintus. The man's palms and fingers were smooth and uncalloused. They had never wielded a weapon in battle unless a dagger for a tough steak was counted.

Quintus and his father paid burly men and assassins to take care of any altercations that might need a physical resolution. Longstanding gossip, which even Marcus' influence could not obliterate, had it that Quintus was not pure Roman nobility. His features were distant from his father. Instead, it seemed more likely that he was the result of one of Marcus' many liaisons with slaves. The slave, of course, had been silenced. Not with gold but a knife drawn across her throat.

As for the middle brother, Numerius, he too was a wastrel, mired in gambling debt and probably lying drunk in a cheap whore's bed. There had been a third and younger brother, Caeso. The best of the litter, in Nikandros' opinion. Many agreed that he had potential. That is until his body was found dismembered and rotting on Rome's garbage pits. His death was retaliation for Marcus' part in the murder of the daughter of the exiled Marius. The Fabii were sad and cursed—although the bane of the family was their lust for power.

Marcus watched the Spartan with eyes filled with cunning. Deciding attack was his best strategy, Nikandros started the conversation. "Let me see if I have this correct. You sent a pack of mercenaries, paid with Roman gold, to foment trouble on Conall's border on the Alpes side. They were instructed to kill, rape, pillage, and, if possible, kill his daughters. They even left clear signs of your culpability." The Spartan paused, "Has age addled your mind?"

"I find your insolent attitude intolerable. You are a servant. Nothing more." Marcus spat his words with much phlegm.

With false bravado, Quintus moved his hand to his dagger. He halted as Nikandros' lips formed the words, "Please try."

"Added to this, many of Clann Ui Flaithimh's leaders, and the tribe itself, hold you responsible for the recent Gaiscedach attack on

Lugudunon."

"That was neither my doing nor funded by my gold," spat Marcus. Quintus walked to a table and refilled his cup of wine. The offer of a drink was contemptuously dismissed by his father and not made to Nikandros.

"Oh, I know that, and so does Conall. But, thanks to you, his iron grip on the tribe has never been stronger."

At a signal from his father, Quintus flung a pouch in Nikandros' direction. It tumbled a few times on the smooth, stone floor before sliding to rest at Nikandros' feet. The Spartan slowly bent down, one hand resting on the pommel of his xiphos and eyes on both Romans. The pouch was lifted and transferred to a pocket in the fold of his robe. It was a reasonable weight. Parsimony was one of the few things of which Marcus could not be accused. Nikandros shook his head and smiled. How far would he get beyond the villa's entrance before feeling a blade or arrow in his back?

He spat his next words. "I am no servant and no employee, Marcus. And not to be purchased or silenced by a *small* bag of gold. Although, I will keep this as a token of my new position. My role has ascended to one of protector, counsellor, and keeper of secrets. I know of your plottings and succour to the enemies of Rome. And of your grand scheme to bring barbarian disaster to the gates of Rome. To graciously accept the title of Dictator of Rome and use your army to be its saviour. Yet, you are blind to the flaw in your strategy."

"What?" snapped Marcus.

"You… no, *we* have been duped by a barbarian. I sought to direct Conall's path, but he chose other counsellors: his Chomhairle, the Sidhe, and Mórrígan. I kept him from the assassin's blade but, in truth, I now suspect he was playing with me. I fomented internal rebellion, but the idiot Cuán tried to assert leadership. He died by my hand. That insurgence was put down, to a man and woman, by Conall. Despite Conall's noble thoughts of being a just king, he shows no mercy and will slaughter any who threaten his family or his clann."

"Is this leading to a point? I have other duties to attend to."

"Yes. *I* decided that the best for Conall and Rome was for the tribe to settle in the lands of the Rodonos valley and Lugudunon. For the past five summers, Conall's people have been content to plant crops, fish, trap, and mine. His wealth from his partnership with Pytheas the Greek likely surpasses quite a few kings' and definitely yours. His army would remain in their stone and wood strongholds or on their farms, only fighting when their borders are breached."

"Yes, yes, yes. You are Rome's protector, not I. Perhaps the disgraced prince of Sparta wishes for a place on the Senate." Quintus chuckled at his father's words.

"Fools!" snarled Nikandros. Marcus and his son blanched at the venom in the Spartan's tone. "You have no idea what your creation, the 'tool' to be used to make Rome kneel at your feet, has become. When his family is attacked, Conall and his partner, Mórrígan, are implacable and without mercy. He pursued Kartimandu, Queen of the Aos Na h-Àirde, killed her and all but wiped out the tribe. The Queen's sin was to kidnap his daughters. Even she, unlike Matres of the Gaiscedach or you, was not foolish enough to try to murder them."

Marcus yawned imperiously, and Quintus feigned boredom. Unruffled, Nikandros continued, "The Celts have always been vaunted warriors and are employed as mercenaries by many nations. Conall commands an army that is the best of the Gauls and Gaels. Far superior to any under Rome's or your authority."

"Nonsense!" snapped Marcus. "You have lived with these barbarians and their beer-induced dreams of domination for too long. Take your gold. Disappear. Drink yourself to death."

The smile that settled on Nikandros' lips chilled both Romans. "But I have not told you the best, Marcus. Many witnesses—hundreds in fact—remain alive to testify to your sedition. Conall, courtesy of your selling weapons to the barbarians, has ballistae. *And* he has Gaius

Aurelius Atella and his men." The tremor that made the contents of Marcus' now refilled cup of wine slop over its lip gave the Spartan an inordinate sense of satisfaction. "Yes, Gaius lives and instructs the barbarians on the weapons' use. As we speak, Romans guard the walls of Lugudunon."

"No. No Roman would side with the barbarians. You are mistaken," said Marcus.

"You did," snarled the Spartan.

"Think also on this, Marcus. Matres may have wielded the blade that slit her throat, but the blame for the events that led to Gaius' wife Cornelia's enslavement and death rests on your head."

Nikandros watched as Marcus regained his patrician composure. "And…" he added, "Marius and Gaius, who remains a son to the general, know it and have the proof."

"Anything else? Any more barbarian wisdom you wish to confer?" growled Marcus. The conversation was brutally honest and not to his liking.

"Just one thing. As you know, Dionysius of Syrako paid Brennus of the Senones to cause trouble for Rome. After a battle where he lost almost half his army, Brennus negotiated Conall's lands and crossed the Eridanus around the festival of Lupercalia. At the moment, Brennus' focus is the Etrusci and Umbri. But Conall's price for letting Brennus go was an oath to fight by his side against Rome. *Your* creation has always been a practical man."

"Get out!" screamed Marcus.

"I'll lodge in one of your apartments. Our futures are linked, and I should protect my investment." The Romans watched as Nikandros, back straight and head held high, turned and walked confidently from the room.

✱✱✱

"The Spartan cannot be allowed to live, Father."

"Are you going to challenge him?" snapped Marcus. Quintus'

mouth gaped open at the suggestion, and his shoulders slumped. "I thought not. Get out!"

Marcus' ire, though, was not totally for Nikandros or even Conall but for having sons bereft of anything resembling brain or brawn. Cold, disappointed eyes tracked the back of Quintus as he exited the chamber. In his mind, Marcus pondered the use of adoption to provide him with a suitable heir. Perhaps the Spartan. After all, the man had proven to be as cunning and ruthless as Marcus himself.

Nikandros would have little problem, and no regret, in disposing of Marcus' sons. A thin smile alighted on the Patrician's pale lips. Perhaps all was not lost. He called for more wine and the pretty young slave he had recently acquired but had yet to defile. Drool dribbled from his lips in anticipation.

* * *

Quintus was understandably furious as he left his father's presence. The Spartan's condescension was as intolerable as his father's contempt. Yet the Roman knew that neither he nor his brother was a match for Nikandros. Even if they hired someone to take care of this problem, there was no guarantee of success and every probability of revenge.

Nikandros was a formidable warrior. A sigh of resignation perched on Quintus' lips. A few moments later, it was replaced by a smile. The same could not be said of his father. He was old, and the elderly often have fatal accidents. Few would mourn his passing. Quintus inhaled. "I must speak with my brother."

CHAPTER 26

394 B.C.—Ariminum

"It never got this hot in Sens," grumbled Brennus to his shield-bearer, who grunted in agreement.

Another droplet of sweat formed on Brennus' shoulder and soon joined dozens of salty rivulets. A massive hand shielded his eyes from the glaring sun, hovering over the city of Ariminum. *Perhaps I need a slave to keep me in the shade.* The port's location on the shores of the Mare Adriaticum was idyllic. Long, white, sandy beaches touched azure waters. On its land side, the town was surrounded by lush meadows and fertile plains. In the distance, the purple heights of the Appenninus Mountains reached skyward.

It had taken several cycles of the moon to conquer the lands between the Eridanus and Ariminus rivers. That was slower than Brennus had hoped, but the battles with the Etrusci and Umbri were skirmishes with swarms of fleet-footed warbands rather than decisive confrontations. As such, they delivered neither a complete surrender nor grudging obeisance.

In the end, Brennus left the local tribes to their hillforts and walled cities and took control of the land. The forts would be starved or beaten into submission at his leisure. Still, he had no option but to leave sizeable Senone warbands to discourage local uprisings. This brought its own unintended consequences. Many of his men, seeing a better way of life for them and the kin who accompanied them, chose to settle and work the land. Indeed, it seemed that he had lost more of his men to farming than to fighting.

The Senone army set up camp on the northern bank of the Ariminus River. Brennus hoped that the sight would frighten the shite out of the leaders of Ariminum. He looked on Ariminum and saw not a city to be razed to the ground and plundered, but a possible home. He was no sailor or merchant, yet even he could recognise the value of the port and the possibilities for adventure beyond it. Furthermore, high mountains protected the territory from the Eridanus to the Ariminus.

With his throne established in Ariminum, Brennus did not doubt that he could hold and rule this new Senone kingdom. Now, he waited impatiently for his envoys to return from the city. They carried a simple message to its leaders. Bend the knee or watch Ariminum destroyed and its citizens slaughtered and sold into slavery. No matter how much Brennus admired Ariminum, he would have no hesitation in destroying it. After all, he could always rebuild.

* * *

South of the Eridanus, and unlike the level plains of the east coast, the western side of the Appenninus range was a landscape of forested mountains, deep valleys, and cliffs that sprang from the rocky coastline. The Umbri hillfort, now little more than a burning ruin, perched on a rocky promontory—a long finger stretching out into the clear waters of the Mare Ligusticum. In the distance, triremes' oars splashed into the waters as avaricious merchants, and predatory slavers plied their trades to and from the coastline's many ports.

Celtillos of the Arverni savoured the smell of smoke and burnt flesh. The king perched on a mossy boulder and relished the wanton destruction of the settlement. Celtillos had basic, some said base, pleasures. And these were enhanced by the wailing of the raped and those who mourned the slaughter of their kin. The Umbri warriors had been slain to a man.

Those surviving and of no value—the old, the sick, and the very young—were killed or used for sport, which usually had the same conclusion. After being used to satiate his army's lusts, the men and women remaining were sold to the slave ships. The peddlers of flesh, appreciating the increased and constant source of product, followed the Arverni horde as it travelled south.

Once again, the Umbri warriors proved no match for Celtillos' armoured Arverni. Only the Etrusci's walled cities were a challenge. And much as it pained the king to admit it, Etruscan armour was as good as any his Arverni could produce. Hence, unless Celtillos wanted a good fight or was bored, he left the Etrusci to Brennus. There was much to plunder among the local Umbri population centres, and, so far, his men and women were happy with their accumulated riches.

Unlike Brennus, the Arverni marauders brought with them very few followers and kin. Thus, significantly fewer of his army "deserted" to settle down in what was undoubtedly a pleasant land, not too dissimilar to their homeland. Still, the Arverni king was down to about four thousand men, and that could not be allowed to diminish further. A recent conclave with his chieftains ended with the king stressing that further losses would not be tolerated and their heads would be the first to roll.

Celtillos frowned at his passing consideration of Brennus. The two had not departed on friendly terms. Indeed, it surprised Celtillos that he did not have to fight Brennus to get his portion of Dionysius' gold. That said, it was many sunsets before he stopped looking over his shoulder.

The Arverni king was unsure whether he would meet the Senone king again and under what circumstances. The towering spine of mountains between the two tribes was a blessing from the gods. Celtillos knew that he would be no match for a Senone army fully fit and seeking retribution.

He shrugged. What was the profit in worrying about a future he had little control over and battles that had not happened? He stood and smiled. Now was the time to enjoy the trio of young Umbri captives set aside for his personal pleasure. He would use them and then pass them to his guards. Eventually, they would be sold as slaves, but not before their lives were irretrievably ruined. As for Celtillos, having suffered no consequences, he would move on to the next settlement and the next victims.

"I'm a king. I deserve my rewards," chucked Celtillos to no one in particular.

CHAPTER 27

394 B.C.—Lugudunon and Massalia

Like the dying embers of bonfires, so the festival of Bealtaine smouldered and finally drew to a begrudged close. Spectral, smoky fingers expended the remains of their substance, grasping at the pink-and-orange glow of the dawn sky. In the background, lungs that belied their age sucked in air and expelled it as loud demands for instant nourishment. The wailing was soon replaced by the not-so-gentle sucking noises of mouths determined to exhaust the supply from Mórrígan's breasts.

At the sight and sound of the voracious feeding, Conall chuckled. He raised his eyes and allowed himself a brief snort at the Goddess. Was it from uncertainty that she had chosen to bless them with twins—one boy and one girl? Or perhaps it was a desire for balance. He now had three sons and three daughters.

Conall stood, sighed, and walked to the throne room. Decisions had to be made. Some of his friends would be disappointed, but he was the Rí Ruirech. The burden of choice rested on his shoulders like a heavy yoke on oxen. Sometimes he envied those beasts. Their lives seemed so calm, but perhaps they had great problems that he could not discern. As he entered the room, a score sat around the solid table. Conall felt deep pain at the absence of the fallen and wondered who was next to walk the feasting halls of Mag Mell. Conall met the smiles on the expectant faces of those present with eyes that gave nothing away. Each was considering the same questions: Who would be chosen? Who would survive? Yet, none would shrink from their duty.

"How many do we take? Five thousand? Ten thousand?" called out Deaglán.

"Do we think this is necessary?" Silence dropped like a stone.

"Retribution has a blood price. Many will die, and likely some in this room. How many mourners will the tribe need? How many orphans will be made?" A frisson of anger charged the room as the contrary voice continued. "Marcus is an old man. He will be dead soon. Do you want to hasten that? Then send assassins to remove him and his family from the face of the earth. Let them be tortured and die in agony if it is revenge that is required. I believe the Persian is available."

That it was the Sidhe who spoke increased the enormity of the questions and the lack of retort. Some wondered if she meant the words or was just being perverse. The marble face gave no clue to her true thoughts. Beside her, Mórrígan sat immobile, and yet the swirling designs that covered her body lay at rest. It appeared that the two powers were in agreement and that in itself was an omen—but of what?

"Revenge, retribution, or justice?" posed the Sidhe.

"Natural justice."

It was Íar, perhaps the most honourable of the leaders, who spoke. "Many summers past, a peaceful settlement was slaughtered under the orders of, and paid by the gold of, Marcus. I lost no family, as many here did. Your pain will always be sharper and deeper than mine." The tall warrior exhaled. "Yet, there has been no remorse. No eiric or compensation has been offered by either this man or Rome. We are less than nothing to these people. This cannot go unanswered, or it will happen again and again. Rome needs a reminder that a price has to be paid. At this time, we are in a position to deliver the message."

"Good. That is settled. Personally, I want the bastards who murdered my sisters to suffer a long and agonising death. But I'll go with honour and natural justice." The ghoulish grin that perched on Mongfhionn's ruby-red lips sent shivers up the spines of those present.

All, that is, except Mórrígan. If anything, her visage was more terrible. In her mind, she visualised the image of her slaughtered parents.

After the question of "Should we fight?" had been answered, the conversation turned to the practicalities. Conall stood. Five thousand shields, and needed support, but not family or followers, would travel to Massalia. The army would also include one thousand of Íar's cavalry and one thousand Cinn Péinteáilte led by Carmag and Mòrag. That Mórrígan's warband would join the company was never in doubt. Terror is always a sharp weapon. No chariots were to be part of the horde.

✳✳✳

Informed by Conall that he was not to travel with the army to Rome, Cúscraid was especially displeased. Instead, his charge was to command those who remained. To defend Lugudunon, the tribe's homeland and wealth, and those who would become Clann Ui Flaithimh's leaders. It was a good decision. It was a king's decision. To Cúscraid, his elevation to Rí of Lugudunon could not flush a taste as bitter as a stalk of caisearbhán from his mouth.

"The last time you were this mad, you punched me in the jaw."

Fearghal rubbed his chin at the recollection of the painful memory. Yet, he fully understood his friend's chagrin as well as Conall's command. Cúscraid took another gulp of the tribe's strongest beer. He had been drinking since Conall had given him the news.

"The Hag, Fearghal. He wants me to miss the battle of a lifetime. Tales will be told and sung of this as long as the tribe lives."

"He made a good decision, Cúscraid. And we both know it. Who better to inherit the king's mantle if we don't come back?"

Cúscraid's brows knitted. The idea of Conall not surviving the battle had not entered his mind. He doubted whether anyone in the clann had given it any consideration. To the people, Conall was invulnerable, if not immortal. Yet, the gods were capricious. Who knew their thoughts or reasoning? Also, if Gaius and his men were a measure of quality, the Romans would be a challenging enemy. Who could know what might

237

happen?

Cúscraid rubbed the stubble on his chin and shook his head in weary resignation. Then he smirked. "I wonder if I'll get the citadel. I'll be Rí after all."

Fearghal laid a strong arm across Cúscraid's muscular shoulders and chuckled. "I very much doubt that. While alive, Conall will remain Rí Ruirech. But Matres had a suite of well-maintained rooms in the Great Hall. If I were you, I'd move into that accommodation. It's better than any you've ever had." More sombrely, Fearghal added, "If you ever take ownership of Conall and Mórrígan's fort, then it means we're all dead. And that is something neither of us desires."

✳✳✳

After the attack by the Gaiscedach, the clann's artisans restored the courtyard between the palace and the Great Hall to its former glory. The debris had been cleared, new gardens and trees planted, and fountains and statues replaced or restored. Yet, the square had not quite recovered its former tranquillity. Even scents of jasmine, lavender, and pine could not entirely vanquish those of smoke and charred flesh.

As Cúscraid and Fearghal entered the square, it seemed as if another war had broken out. Fearghal tapped his friend's shoulder. "Maybe we should retrace our steps and find another way." Cúscraid nodded. Neither wanted to be drawn into the battle that raged before them.

Two fiery temperaments, roused to full heat, flayed each other with words laced with venom and strong accents. Gràinne and Amodocus roared at each other in widely differing languages—Cinn Péinteáilte and Thracian. Still, that did not seem to detract from either combatant's understanding. To an impartial observer, the scene could be perceived as either lethal or quite humorous. As the maelstrom abated, a plainly disappointed Amodocus shook his head.

"Why were you going to leave without a word? Do I not deserve to hold my daughter one last time?"

The issue was Gràinne's imminent departure for Northern Albu.

The decision and timing had been withheld from Amodocus. Now, as she stood before the glum father, she reflected that this might not have been the fairest or most prudent choice she had ever made.

After many long and sleepless nights, she had made up her mind to visit Brianag's father, Brion, Rí Na Mèadaidh, and her homeland. The former she looked forward to, but the latter she considered with a high degree of dread. Yet, until recently, she had only considered the issue from her perspective, which was without question selfish. Still, in her defence, this had been her strategy for most of her life and had helped her survive awful times.

True, she had informed Fearghal and Mongfhionn, but she considered them her parents and wanted their blessing. That she had not given the same consideration to Amodocus suddenly felt wrong. But Gràinne was a proud Cinn Péinteáilte queen, not given to backing down and reluctant to acknowledge her many flaws. The sound of water trickling over smooth stones in the courtyard's ornamental gardens became a salve for the heat of the lovers' argument. It all became too much for Gràinne, and her tears joined the waters' flow.

Strong arms surrounded her, and as Amodocus pulled her close to his chest, the familiar smell of musk, citrus, and sweat soothed her. "I have no issue with Brianag or you travelling to your ancient home. It is a good decision. But you and I have a daughter, and it was not right that I was ignored." Gràinne nodded and snuffled.

"I will go to Rome with Conall's army. I may or may not return."

Startled, Gràinne pulled back from the embrace. She had not considered that her Thracian might die. Her head dropped to her chest. Amodocus smiled and, with a gentleness at odds with the wild warrior's usual character, lifted up her chin and kissed her.

"But..." Amodocus began. Gràinne's eyes widened. What could he be about to say? "But should I return, *I* will travel to Northern Albu, and *I* will find you. And *you* will have a choice to make."

"Shite!"

CHAPTER 28

394 B.C.—Rome

Tadhg was unsure whether Conall's command to scout out Rome and the surrounding lands and cities was an expression of confidence in Tadhg's abilities or a cunning punishment conceived by Mórrígan. His brothers were doubly unhappy at being excluded from the choice of his companions. And even if Tadhg did not return, the army of Clann Ui Flaithimh would still set sail for the western coastline of Latium. In the steaming heat of summer, Tadhg drew closer to the enemy and swore he would prove his worth.

Rome sat on the eastern bank of the Tiberis. For most of its length, the Tiberis was a wide, swift-flowing river. The water was deep and spanned over one hundred paces, making walking across a hopeless task. Swimming was possible, but only for the strongest of athletes. Fortunately, to the west of Rome's main entrance was a large island, the Insula Tiberina, and below this was an expanse of slack water. At this point stood an ancient wooden bridge that traced its history back to the city's first days. The structure was known locally as the Pons Sublicius because of the enormous piles that formed its foundation.

Conall's spy felt an inordinate pleasure at cheating on the toll levied. Due to its historical significance, upkeep of the bridge was the responsibility of Rome's priests—the pontifices, and ultimately the Pontifex Maximus, Marcus. The Pons Sublicius was Rome's only bridge. From it, a broad avenue—an earthed road with a gravelled surface and partially paved—led to the main gateway in the city's walls.

To Tadhg, "walls" was an exaggeration and frankly, he was disappointed. Plainly, Nikandros had embellished his stories of the majesty of Rome. The ramparts of Lugudunon and even Massalia were more impressive than the rambling, mostly wooden, and not terribly well-maintained stockade that enclosed Rome. Signs of construction pointed to the replacement of the timber defences by walls constructed with blocks of lava rock. Even with a plentiful supply of slave labour that would take more than a few seasons to complete. Therefore, Tadhg could not conceive how the current defences would prove an obstacle to the combined armies of Brennus, Celtillos, and Conall. And this perturbed the warrior. What was he missing?

A series of ridges dominated Rome's skyline. The Mons Capitolinus, while not the tallest, was undoubtedly the steepest. It was also the most magnificent by virtue of being the location of the Temple of Jupiter Optimus Maximus Capitolinus. The Roman aristocracy resided predominantly in substantial homes in the Mons Palatinus, close to the Forum Romanum.

The main population lived in crowded apartments in the Mons Aventinus area. Lack of suitable building space, as much of the vicinity was swampy, meant that these rickety buildings had begun to expand upwards. Those on the top floor had the cheapest dwellings and best views. However, the actual price they paid was death, for they had no escape from the frequent fires.

The broad road from the bridge passed the cattle market, the Forum Boarium. Tadhg's nose wrinkled at the strong smell of cow shite borne to his nostrils on a breeze. Such winds would become more welcome but rarer as summer became established and stifling heat sapped the city's energy. After a short walk, he took a sharp right onto a street of levelled earth. Soon, the odour of cattle was replaced by that of man and the crowded districts of the Mons Aventinus. A surprising abundance of gardens, flower beds, and ornamental trees scattered throughout the city mitigated its malodours. Rome's main arteries and the paths in the more affluent districts were being upgraded, but most of the thoroughfares remained little more than well-kept farm tracks.

Tadhg's destination as he joined the throng was the Circus Maximus and a rendezvous with the four who had accompanied him. The Circus was constructed in the valley between the two main population centres. Tadhg swore as he swatted yet another fat fly from his face. Their presence was unsurprising since the structure was built on land reclaimed from wetlands. According to the locals, the area often flooded when the Tiberis overflowed its banks.

The Circus was Rome's racetrack—specifically chariot racing—and all strata of society enjoyed the sport. However, the quality of seating and prime viewing locations were firmly dictated by wealth. The building was constructed totally from wood. The sand-covered, oval track was about one thousand paces long and wide enough for twelve chariots. In this, Tadhg was impressed.

Pleased at the result of the day's closing race, the crowds roared their approval and stamped feet on the building's wooden boards. "Gràinne would have done well here," murmured Tadhg. Then he swore and scratched at a flea bite. Clann Ui Flaithimh's premier investigator, and now it would appear spy, found his disguise discomfiting. No weapons, no chainmail, and no scíath. Only the dagger strapped to his thigh provided any solace. Togas were worn only by the free citizens of Rome. Hence, Tadhg's clothing was a knee-length, sleeveless linen tunic of uncertain colour, quality, and origin. It was an inferior version of a Greek chiton cinched at the waist by a length of twine.

Slaves comprised almost one-third of the population of Rome, so Tadhg fitted in with little difficulty. People either treated him as if he were not present or brusquely shoved him out of the way. Adopting the gait of a slave, he shuffled towards one of the exits. Eyes, when not staring at the ground, continuously scanned for threats. The young and those in their prime were frequently chosen to satisfy the darker desires of Rome's citizens. And not only the patrician class were guilty of abuse. For a moment, Tadhg felt a twinge of guilt for his treatment of the clann's slaves. The remorse was short-lived. There always had been and always would be slaves.

Like a forest of pines when a strong wind died, the fine hairs on the back of Tadhg's neck stood up. A shiver of unease trickled down his spine. Some premonition caused him to glance across the track. A jolt of fear, swiftly followed by rage, threatened to overwhelm and propel him to rash action. In the flickering light of thousands of torches, for dusk was approaching, he stared into black eyes.

Rationality called on Tadhg to dismiss the probability of correctly identifying one person in a crowd and across the racetrack. Yet the burning crimson, heart-shaped imprint on his chest said otherwise. "Shite!" The exclamation caused curious glances from those nearby, but he was less than nothing in most of their eyes, and they had their own troubles.

***

"Zeus' arse!"

Nikandros shook his head at the impossibility of what his eyes reported. He peered harder, but the crowd had consumed the figure. "Shit!"

***

From dawn to dusk, the sun's rising always brought the peril of discovery. That Tadhg's band had survived with few misadventures was a salute to Conall and his choice, their skills, and the use of Rome's garbage trenches to dispose of bodies. It seemed to Tadhg that almost half the population of Rome was either slave or foreigner. Therefore, the entry of another small group was neither news nor newsworthy.

The night, however, brought real danger. Rome's streets after dark were not for the unwary or defenceless. Frequent shrieks of agony echoed off walls as the wealthy were relieved of their gold and jewellery by the many roving bands of thieves. In this, the definition of "wealth" appeared to have a very flexible meaning. Tadhg had witnessed men and woman with their throats cut for nothing more than a ring or a few coins. Invariably the women, and sometimes the men had been raped before they were slain.

Standing at the foot of Mons Capitolinus as dusk drew near, Tadhg looked up and whistled long and low. Not since Ráth Na Lairig Éadain or perhaps the bluffs of Aremorio would Conall's army need to scale such a sheer ascent. During an attack, the normal path that allowed the flow of goods and people to the Temple and other buildings on the hill's plateau would likely be blocked. Still, while it would be a challenge, it was not unsurmountable.

It was Tadhg's opinion that a surprise strike could scale and overcome the cliff. The warrior mulled over the information obtained by him and his group. He had a good sense of the locations of key buildings, including both of Marcus' homes. As expected, one, and a palatial one at that, was in the Mons Palatinus district. The other sat in the shadow of the Temple of Jupiter. It was a smaller villa but impressive because of its location.

By the light of several torches, Tadhg used sticks of charcoal to commit his map of Rome to several thin leaves of wood. He smiled. As a seanchaí, he was more used to memorising long tales and recounting them over and over to many audiences. It was a surprisingly efficient process and not as prone to error as many would think. Perhaps writing would eventually overcome the Gaels' oral tradition. Yet, that was no guarantee of truth or accuracy. So, where was the advantage?

The hairs on his neck suddenly stiffened. A scuffle drew his attention away from his scratchings. His hand reached to his dagger.

"Too late for that, Tadhg. You were always clever but also foolish."

Nikandros' words were emphasised by a sharp prod to Tadhg's lower back. Conall's spy felt blood trickle slowly down. The young warrior turned slowly and deliberately and looked into dark eyes. In a fluid movement, the Spartan placed the dagger under Tadhg's chin. One jerk upwards and his brain would be carved in two. The bile of rage at facing

Laoise's murderer burned his throat and soured his mouth. Yet Tadhg felt no panic, and the mark on his chest, so often the progenitor of trouble, was calm. His demeanour raised Nikandros' alertness.

"Rome will fall. You will fall. With retribution, balance will be restored. Laoise will be avenged. You're not stupid, Spartan. Surely you see this?"

"No longer Spartan, barbarian. I am now a son of Rome." The Spartan's blade pressed against soft flesh. "No more words." Tadhg felt the pressure increase. Soon it would slice through his throat. Yet he was strangely untroubled as, without flinching, he held the assassin's gaze.

"You boast and preen too much when you should be listening... or acting."

The smile on Tadhg's face should have alerted Nikandros. Yet the blow when it came was a total surprise. Tadhg looked on the prone body and nodded to his companions. Their expressions were easy to read. Gut him. Avenge Laoise. Tadhg shook his head. "He will die. Just not this night. He serves Conall's plans better alive—for the moment."

As he turned to walk away, Tadhg muttered, "Shite!" and then delivered several kicks to Nikandros' face and ribs. The act was petty but thoroughly enjoyable. He was sure he heard ribs crack.

Rumours—and there was a thriving trade in gossip in Rome—pointed to a sizeable barbarian invasion on the eastern coast and a lesser army on the west. There were also growing signs of an attack by Dionysius on the southern tip of the peninsula. All added to the atmosphere of unease and fear that permeated the city. Tadhg and his companions had little hesitation in adding to the rumour mill whenever possible. Still, after three sunsets, it was time to go. Nikandros would be unlikely to fail if given another opportunity. Besides, Tadhg had orders to complete, and finding Brennus was next on the list.

According to reports, Brennus and the Senones appeared to be a five- or six-sunset ride away. Fortunately, Tadhg had found a small farm between the port of Pyrgi, where Pytheas' bireme had deposited him, and Rome. The owners were old and poor. Therefore, they raised no objections nor asked questions about the strangers who corralled their mounts and left armour and weapons in their safekeeping. Gold was gold, and their guests were generous.

✱✱✱

Nikandros paced up and down the smooth, flat stone floor. His ribs ached, and his sun-tanned face was swollen and bruised purple and red. Sprawled on couches several paces away, Quintus and Numerius did not conceal their joy at the condition of their new "brother." It was some solace for their father's betrayal and the ruination of the plans for their father's demise and their enrichment. Neither of the two stood a chance if they chose to challenge Nikandros directly. Their faint hope was that he would lose their father's trust and a knife in the back would carry him to Hades or Tartarus.

"What can a few barbarians do?"

Marcus studied Nikandros and pondered whether his judgment had been flawed. Then he looked at his blood sons and shrugged. What choice did he have?

Incredulous, Nikandros held the old man's gaze and wondered if he should snap the scrawny neck. The sons would prove no challenge to his sword. The guards, hovering outside the chamber, would rationalise the action as necessary to maintain the continuity of their wages.

"For a start, Conall, Mórrígan, and the Sidhe know where *you* live. And do not for one moment think that the heights of Mons Capitolinus will protect you. Another king once thought that, and he is long dead."

The change in Marcus' skin tone to a greyish pallor and the projectile expulsion of wine from Quintus and Numerius ameliorated the Spartan's mood. Perhaps he should kill them all and retire to their lakeside villa south of Rome until the barbarian threat disappeared. He shook his head and smirked at the questioning looks the action elicited from all three.

"It means that Conall has decided to join his forces with Brennus and if my sources are true, a third—the king of the Arverni. Add in a few Etrusci and Umbri warlords unhappy with Roman expansion and Rome could have thirty thousand warriors at its gates."

With some relish, Nikandros added, "It is time to alert the Senate that they may soon have unwelcome guests."

Marcus still could not conceive of a barbarian victory over a well-armed Roman army. Yet he stalled as he was about to wave his bony hand with patrician disdain and dismissal. Something in the way the Spartan tugged at the tight curls of his oiled and perfumed beard bothered him.

"What?" snapped Marcus.

"Even with Brennus' sworn oath to Conall, I do not think he will battle Rome without justification. So what possible reasoning could unite them against Rome?"

"You overthink. The barbarians have taken up residence in your head."

"And you're getting old. You assume too much and question too little."

CHAPTER 29

394 B.C.—Lugudunon, Massalia, and Ariminum

As Conall's army departed Lugudunon, crowds stood on the citadel's ramparts and lined the dirt road that trailed from the ráth. Raucous cheering filled the air. The celebrations would last until the army was well out of sight and voices too hoarse for anything more than a croak. Hundreds of bodhráns beat out a steady rhythm. Yet, there was sadness in many of the young drummers' eyes. This time they would not accompany the army into battle. Brightly coloured banners of both clann and king were hoisted high and swung wildly. Over-enthusiastic youths were given a swift cuff on the head by more senior members whenever a flag came too close for comfort.

As the army tramped out of the main gateway, men in burnished armour and red cloaks formed an honour guard on either side of the roadway. Gaius' men saluted former enemies but now friends for whom they would gladly die. Leaning over the broad, black shoulders of Toirneach, Conall grasped Gaius' forearm and smiled. Between them, there passed a silent moment of sadness, of acknowledgement, and of a promise to be fulfilled. Only with the ending of Marcus would the death of Cornelia, Gaius' wife, be finally avenged.

Solitary watchmen, Lugudunon's great ballistae, cracked in unison. In the army's ranks, men and women flinched as if with a collective memory as the volley of bolts, with long, multicoloured ribbons attached, arced high into the air. A huge sigh of relief rose as, instead of bringing death and dismemberment, the missiles fluttered harmlessly to the ground.

It took a half-cycle of the moon for Conall's army to traverse the terrain of forested hills, olive groves, and golden river plains between the fortress of Lugudunon and the port of Massalia. All were lightly armoured. The advent of summer meant the days were increasingly hotter. Men, women, and animals were soon covered in a sheen of sweat. By the time they reached their destination, man and beast would vie for who drank and stank the most. Trouble was not expected, for although the Gauls and Celts were renowned for being hot-headed, they were not stupid. Besides, the most likely challengers—the best Arverni warbands—were with Celtillos in the land of the Etrusci.

That said, Conall's army was prepared to fight if necessary. After several days marching and riding and a growing accumulation of blistered feet and bruised arses, many began to hope for skirmishes to break the monotony. The great warhorses of Íar's cavalry snorted their frustration at the slow pace. At a fast canter, they could easily cover the distance in three or four sunsets. However, the army strode forward at the speed of its slowest members: the massively muscled oxen who carried precious cargoes of weapons, armour, and gold and the herds of cattle who were more interested in grazing on lush grasses.

***

Salt-imbued sea breezes kept the warm summer's day in Massalia from being oppressive. It could have been one of the port's many festivals, as crowds lined the main thoroughfare and maze of side streets. Flat, whitewashed roofs groaned ominously under the weight of spectators. The nearby hillside, and any high vantage points, were packed, with many holding onto precarious positions. No one wanted to miss the spectacle. The crowd cheered as the city's gates were flung open in welcome. Young men and women imagined themselves in the ranks of the hard-bodied veterans. Those past their prime sighed wistfully in regret of opportunities missed.

Closer to the harbour, a city of tents waited to receive the bulk of Conall's army. Conall and Mórrígan, as well as Fearghal and the Sidhe, would stay at Pytheas' home. The remaining members of the Chomhairle and ceannairí na míle were housed with trusted families of Massalia's council. Temporary corrals had been erected for the horses and the cattle that had not been butchered.

In the markets, traders rubbed their hands in anticipation of a rich windfall sent by the gods. In narrow alleyways, paved with hexagonal blue-grey cobbles, and in the brothels of the less salubrious denizens of the docks, whores preened themselves. Some dreamed of finding a long-term partner. Others simply wanted to earn enough gold to leave the lifestyle while healthy and still having a choice.

Not all, however, were as unequivocal in their welcome. Many of Massalia's council, the wealthy and wielders of power, chewed on the bitter fruit of impotence. In reality, they could do little to stop Conall's army, or that of any despot, from marching through Massalia's gates. The recent blockade of the port by a handful of ancient ships underscored their feebleness and fed their paranoia. That there was a fleet of black-sailed quinqueremes anchored beyond the sea wall gave them little succour.

Rumours and gossip circulated—some deliberately—that Pytheas had kingly ambitions. Many, jealous of Pytheas' friendship with the Rí Ruirech of Clann Ui Flaithimh, gnashed yellowed teeth. That with this relationship came the favour of Conall's army did nothing to assuage their distress. Yet, both men were innocent of the allegations.

It was true that Conall had Pytheas' back, but neither he nor Pytheas had any ambitions for the dominance of Massalia. Indeed, the weather-beaten merchant simply wanted to increase his wealth and explore far seas and lands in the process. For his part, Conall had a kingdom to rule and a people to protect. He needed no further burdens. Yet, uprisings and revolutions have begun on shakier foundations.

✳✳✳

Seven sunsets later, Pytheas embraced Conall and Mórrígan and pleaded for them to "Take care and return hale." Later, from the sanctuary of the Temple of Apollo, he watched the vast fleet set its course for the port of Pyrgi on the Etruscan coast and made offerings to Apollo for their safe return.

Cheering crowds lined the harbour, and the council of Massalia heaved a great sigh of relief at unfounded fears. In the markets and brothels, merchants and whores shared a mutual regret. Their consolation was the weight of gold in the folds of their clothing.

***

It was meán lae when Tadhg arrived at the gates of Ariminum. Stiff muscles and a bruised arse brought a grimace to his face as he brought his mount to a halt and dismounted. Removing his helmet, he shook long, sweat-soaked, straw-blond braids and smiled as he surveyed the entranceway. *Excellent accommodation—an improvement on Sens.* He took a distasteful gulp of lukewarm water from a worn waterskin, cleared his throat, and called out to the guard towers flanking the entrance: "I am Tadhg Ó Cuileannáin, ceannairí na míle of the army of Clann Ui Flaithimh. I am an ambassador of Conall Mac Gabhann, Rí Ruirech and Hand of the Goddess. I have an important message from my king and seek an audience with Brennus, King of the Senones."

Of all the receptions that Tadhg could have imagined, being set upon by a gang of brawny Senones and then dragged, stripped, and thrown into a foul-smelling cell was not at the top of the list. "It seems that Brennus has unresolved issues with Conall," he muttered as he chewed on a chunk of mouldy bread and sipped more lukewarm water. He grimaced. The water's taste suggested the guards had augmented it with piss. In the gloom of the chamber, it was impossible to tell if its colour would confirm his suspicions. Sitting naked on the dirt floor, he awaited his fate and hoped that the messengers he had sent to Celtillos would fare better.

Several sunsets later, Brennus observed a slight Tadhg, hands tied, and flanked on either side by two burly guards, stride down the rectangular hall towards him. His only clothing was a dirty, threadbare, knee-length tunic that hung loosely from narrow shoulders. The warrior's head was held high and, despite his dress, a hint of arrogance accompanied the envoy as he walked barefoot and silently on the paved floor. Indeed, his guards were continually adjusting their pace to keep up with Tadhg. *Give him a sword or spear, and I would not wager against him besting his "protectors".*

There were no tremors of fear in the captive's demeanour, which was unusual in itself. Apart from a few bruises and both body and clothing being unwashed, Tadhg seemed strangely comfortable in his surroundings. One eye blackened and recovering from a meeting with a guard's fist added a rakish look to a face that had its share of scars. Apart from the fact that they were a deep blue, the eyes reminded Brennus of an eagle's: sharp, always watchful, and assimilating all around him. Brennus' wariness heightened. What was he missing?

Tadhg allowed himself a momentary smirk before diplomatic neutrality resumed control of his face. The king was visibly discomfited, whereas he was just hungry, a mite angry, and wishing he had salve for the many flea bites. As for his bruises, he received harsher treatment in weapons practice with his brothers. Still, he was Conall's ambassador and should act as such.

Therefore, Tadhg came to a halt a respectful distance from Brennus' throne chair, bowed deeply, and waited. For his part, Brennus glowered at the envoy. What was it about this breed that gave him an itch that demanded painful scratching? That Tadhg's composure reminded him of Dionysius' negotiator only served to raise his ire.

Brennus chastised himself. It was just that anything to do with Conall and Clann Ui Flaithimh seemed to bring out the worst in him. He was king and should know better than to get so irritated. After snapping, "Unbind him," at the guards, he inhaled deeply, forced a smile to his face, and with a flourish gestured to the table and chair to his left. The table was laden with fruit, meats, cheeses, and a selection of drinks.

"My apologies, Tadhg Ó Cuileannáin, ambassador of Conall, Rí Ruirech and, if my memory serves me well, the famed seanchaí of Clann Uí Flaithimh." Tadhg smiled and dipped his head in acknowledgement of the compliment. "It would appear that my men were over-zealous in protecting me. I was only just informed of your presence and the uncomfortable accommodation you experienced. Eat and drink, and then we shall talk." The king paused, sniffed, and glared at his men. "A bath and new clothing *before* bringing him to me would have been appropriate."

Simple needs often control men. For his part, Tadhg was having difficulty in controlling the loud rumbling in his belly and just wanted to eat. He bowed and smiled before taking the proffered seat. Both men knew that Brennus was lying, but after all, what is diplomacy if not the exchange of untruths and honeyed words of deceit? Stomach satisfied, Tadhg took a last gulp of cold, creamy milk. He needed a clear head and thus had resisted both wine and beer. After dipping greasy hands—the duck was excellent—in a small bowl of warm water pleasantly scented with wildflowers, he nodded to Brennus. Time for business and hopefully not a return to his former accommodation.

At odds with convention, Tadhg spoke bluntly. "By my reckoning, Conall and an army of ten thousand veterans has arrived at Pyrgi." The number was only a slight exaggeration. "He intends to attack Rome and bring retribution to his long-time enemy—the Pontifex Maximus of Rome. Marcus is the murderer of his, his queen's..." Tadhg paused as emotions long quelled rose in his chest "...and my families."

Tadhg was impressed at the silence that followed his announcement and the stunned looks on many faces. Only then did he fully observe the sleek, satisfied demeanour of those in the chamber and the wealth that adorned their bodies. The king and nobility of the Senones were content with their lives, and he was about to ask them, if not to give that up, then certainly to put it at risk. The likelihood of a return to his cell seemed inevitable. *Shite!*

"No!"

Brennus was not stupid. The abrupt answer to a question not yet posed caused Tadhg to wonder if it was Brennus' final word. Was there room for manoeuvre? Tadhg once more scanned the hall in the hope of discerning a more favourable response. Many had lost kin and friends in the battles with Conall, and Celts had quick tempers and long memories. The only "friends" in this room were those who calculated the potential opportunity for gain, and they were pitifully few.

"You swore an oath at Dún-an-Rí," said Tadhg.

"I swear many oaths. This one I do not recall."

"Then the glory will be ours." Tadhg smiled. "And, of course, the Arverni's."

"What?"

"Envoys have been sent to Celtillos with a similar offer."

"He'll not accept."

"Oh, I think you and I know that he will. Celtillos' ambition and avarice are well-known. The king of the Arverni covets access to trade and taxes from the Rodonos, and that is within Conall's purview." The look on Brennus' face was enough to confirm that Tadhg's bluff had proven correct.

"Perhaps I should gather my army and confront Conall. He is greatly outnumbered and on foreign soil."

Tadhg groaned. He had no wish to raise the ire of Brennus by reminding him of his defeats at Conall's hands—the last of which had proved especially humiliating. Another tack was needed, although that had its perils. "Perhaps, and yet the outcome of two armies meeting in battle is never guaranteed. What is sure is that *both* sides will likely suffer loss, especially if both Celtillos and Conall confronted the Senones. That would be a much closer contest. It would certainly jeopardise your rule over this quite pleasant land. Conquerors have many enemies."

"I have no quarrel with the Romans. They remain south of the

Tiberis. We do not wish to rouse them or their army. They are too mighty."

"I'm sure that Dionysius would be pleased with that philosophy," Tadhg muttered reflexively and then instantly regretted his words. The black look on Brennus' face did not bode well for his future. Aloud, he said, "I have been to Rome and counted their army. Their might is great, but their walls are weak."

A flurry of activity and raised voices at the room's doors drew Brennus' attention from the discussion. He gestured to several men and, with a fair amount of obeisance, they bowed and walked towards Brennus. Diplomatically, Tadhg took several steps away from the king's throne. Still, within hearing range, he caught one word from the heated discussion—Clusium.

***

During the summer season, the Great Sea was mostly untroubled, and the voyage had only taken two sunsets. That said, Conall was glad once more to step onto solid land. Around him, man and beast were in accord with his sense of relief. Not wanting to overwhelm the port or cause mass panic among its residents, the quinqueremes disgorged their cargoes on pebbled beaches north of Pyrgi. The Etruscan seaport was located a hard sunrise-to-sunset march northwest of Rome.

The grass on the hilltop smelled dry. It tasted dry also, and so a disappointed Conall spat the yellowish blade from his mouth. Mórrígan raised an eyebrow. Conall shrugged broad, tanned shoulders. Unlike many of the tribe, he was one of the more fortunate Gaels whose skin only burned slightly before bronzing. Mórrígan's skin remained as milk-white as the day she was born, and the sun never appeared to bother her. Perhaps because it too feared An Fiagaí Dorcha. Conall preferred to attribute her immunity to the curling sigils that covered most of her body.

Conall and Mórrígan gazed down on Pyrgi. It was not a substantial settlement. Its defensive walls, constructed of limestone and sandstone blocks, were little more than three hundred paces in length on each of its four sides. The most prominent feature of the harbour was an impressive temple dedicated to the sea goddess Leucothea. Conall smiled and pointed to a small group exiting the town.

"I think we will be entertaining visitors shortly."

"Do you think they will believe us when we inform them that we mean no harm? And that we will pay for anything we need?"

"Probably not. However, we have Pytheas' seal. Likely, the city elders will pay more heed to our partnership with our friend and the need to keep on good trading terms with Massalia."

CHAPTER 30

394 B.C.—Clusium and Rome

As the sun approached its zenith, the hall became ridiculously hot. Most of those present wore a sheen of perspiration on heat-flushed cheeks and foreheads. Under the loose, knee-length tunics worn by many, rivulets of sweat streamed down hard-muscled torsos to stain the stone floor.

Much to his surprise, Tadhg's circumstances had improved considerably since his earlier audience with Brennus. Conall's ambassador wore clean garments and a fragrant aura of scented oils rather than horse shite. That said, a quick sampling of the air confirmed that many of those present had not bathed in several sunsets. Fortunately for the assembly, the king had arranged a steady flow of cool drinks. "A few slaves with giant fans would have been appreciated," huffed Tadhg. He stood a respectable distance from, but still within earshot of, the small group surrounding Brennus' throne.

The envoy before Brennus, a man called Arruns, was a wealthy and high-status member of the Etruscan city of Clusium's ruling council. And there, clarity ended. Depending on who you believed—and many were willing to offer their perspective—there appeared to be two competing versions of why the city's representative petitioned Brennus.

Those of a more romantic disposition asserted that Brennus had been asked to intercede in a domestic dispute—an affair between Arruns' wife and the leader of Clusium's council. The lady was a beauty and, like the fabled Connachta queen, Medb na Pluide Cairdiúil—Medb of the Friendly Thighs—was both politically astute and free with her favours. However, why Brennus would wish to insert himself into that threesome's activities was unclear to Tadhg. Unless the king also had his eye on the woman.

The other explanation was more believable, if not as fascinating. This described a political fight for control of the ancient Etruscan city. The council was divided on who they owed their loyalty to and who would be their protector—Rome or Brennus. Arruns had made it well-known that he was firmly of the opinion that an accommodation could and should be reached with Brennus. His rivals, led by Clusium's council leader, looked to Rome. His political adversaries accused Arruns of royal, even dictatorial ambitions. Given his lineage—Arruns' bloodline could be traced back to the first Etruscan king, Lars Porsena—it was a credible argument.

The opposing sides were locked in a stalemate, and the chasm between them seemed unlikely to be bridged. Thus, Arruns concluded that a show of force was needed to convince Clusium that he was right. That Brennus had not told Arruns to go back to his city and leave him out of its petty squabbles intrigued Tadhg. Conall had thwarted Brennus' ambitions to be king of Gaul. Perhaps he saw the lands between the Alpes and the Tiberis as a more realistic empire. In which case, control of Clusium would make sense. Tadhg chuckled. The most likely losers would be Arruns and the council, for Brennus ruled alone.

***

For perhaps the first time, Nikandros considered that he had lost control of the game. Indeed, whether he had ever had command plagued his recent thoughts and dreams. While the sighting of Tadhg in Rome had surprised him, the sudden arrival of Conall's army at Pyrgi truly shocked the Spartan. It was one thing to argue that Conall could confront Rome and another to see the event unfold before his eyes. Undoubtedly, they were the best of Clann Uí Flaithimh, and that was problematic.

Nikandros considered Rome's four legions, twenty-four thousand men, impressive but untried in major battles. That Conall's forces had disembarked from a fleet of quinqueremes owned by Dionysius of Syrako added to the Spartan's concern. Had the tyrant Dionysius and Conall joined forces to destroy Rome?

Apart from the guards, three others were in the chamber with Nikandros—Marcus, Quintus, and Numerius. As usual, Marcus summarily dismissed Nikandros' concerns. Patrician condescension made light of the storm clouds divined by the fledgeling Roman. How could any barbarian—and in this Marcus encompassed Dionysius—challenge Rome? The argument that the Senate should be recalled immediately was disregarded. While Marcus looked with disdain upon Nikandros' anxiety, his "brothers" sniggered like children at the Spartan's open frustration.

"An old man with dreams of power and two fat imbeciles," he roared.

Even the usually taciturn guards were startled at the outburst. As Nikandros' hand caressed the pommel of his xiphos with obviously malign intent, the soldiers' thoughts were of whom they would support. Hence, they were relieved when the Spartan stormed from the room. The choice could wait for another time.

***

Several sunsets later and seated astride his reclaimed horse, Tadhg sweated like a pig. The reason? The knee-length burnished chainmail that he wore over a light linen tunic. Fortunately, it was sleeveless, and, as a sop to the heat, he had foregone the usual over-tunic that kept dust and trail dirt from permeating the mail's tight rings. Brennus had laughed at the sight of Tadhg in full armour. "We're not going to war… at least, not yet." Still, the straw-haired warrior was prepared to suffer a period of uncomfortable sweating if it afforded him some advantage over his newfound "friends". Experience had taught him that trust was a precious commodity and only given with extreme caution.

In his mind, Tadhg had become convinced that Brennus, despite his sworn oath, had no interest in joining Conall's quest against the Romans. Too much enmity roiled the waters between the men. Hence, the warrior and envoy was not altogether sure why he was included in Brennus' delegation to Clusium. His mount's timely snort punctuated his thoughts. *Delegation indeed.* Tadhg rode with the king and his chieftains at the head of an army of ten thousand Senones.

Tadhg gazed upon the walled city of Clusium as he sipped the last few mouthfuls from a depleted waterskin. He was impressed. This was how he had envisaged Rome. Clusium was a major Etruscan conurbation and, according to Arruns, one of the original members of the Etruscan League of twelve cities. As with other Etruscan cities, cemeteries, and tombs—the most notable being the mausoleum of its famed king, Lars Porsena—surrounded Clusium. The double-walled defences were solid and strengthened further by the city's location on a hill, overlooking the valley of the Clanis River. Being navigable by boat, the Clanis conferred on Clusium both strategic and economic value. The river was a vital tributary of the Tiberis and provided a direct route to Rome.

Yet even the name of the city reflected the deep political divisions roiling its citizens. The "progressives" who favoured closer relations with Rome preferred Clusium. Those who wanted to retain traditional Etruscan values and who basked in the glory of Porsena preferred the name Clevsin. It was not surprising that Arruns chose to side with the traditionalists since he was named after the son of Porsena.

✳✳✳

"Why am I here?"

"Conall sent you to treat with me. We are continuing that discussion."

Tadhg shook his head. "On that issue, you made up your mind at our first meeting. The Senones will not join Conall in the fight against Rome. You made it plain that your oath to Conall was meaningless."

Tadhg frowned. Was his reply overly blunt for a diplomat? Fortunately, chewing on a particularly stringy piece of meat of uncertain origin mitigated his facial expression. Failing to digest the morsel, he spat the glutinous lump onto the tent's dirt floor, took a long gulp of beer, and hoped the next slice of meat would be more digestible.

"Am I a hostage?"

Brennus laughed loudly. It was echoed by the group of chieftains seated around the makeshift table. The bout of sympathetic comradeship made Tadhg distinctly uneasy. "Are you worth ransoming?" Tadhg smiled and shook his head. Conall and Mórrígan would likely seek bloody retribution should anything happen to their envoy but would not pay gold for his return.

As if reading his thoughts, the king spoke. "No. Likely I would just have a few hours' entertainment, a headless body, and another war on my hands." The king paused. "And An Fiagaí Dorcha's band terrorising my people."

Gesturing to the men around the table, Brennus added, "Like you, none of these would expect me to pay for their return. Even those who are kin." The king stood and stretched. Then, setting both hands, palm down, on the wood, he looked into Tadhg's eyes. "No. By reputation, you are a clever man, and Conall places trust in your judgment. What I want is your untainted eyes and counsel when I meet with the council of Clusium."

＊

Inside Clusium, a storm raged. Paradoxically, Arruns had achieved the impossible. He had united both sides against what was perceived to be a common enemy. However, in doing so, he had isolated himself. Alone, he surveyed the mass of tents, torches, and campfires that encircled Clusium. In reality, Arruns had brought a siege to the city.

His thoughts fought with each other. Was he genuinely acting in the city's best interests? Had the lust for power made him foolish? How far could he trust Brennus? Would he be no more than a puppet? The blood of his renowned ancestor boiled at that image. More to the point, in what state would Clusium be should Brennus decide to attack? Arruns sighed. Only one thing was evident. His safety was no longer assured within these walls. He inhaled, sampling Clusium's ambience one last time, and moved towards one of the city's minor exits and thence to Brennus' camp.

Dawn brightened as the sun rose in the eastern sky, bathing the land in golden tones. This far inland, the few scattered clouds scampering across the firmament would soon be consumed and leave an expanse of unblemished blue. Arruns' steps were heavy as he trod the path to Brennus' tent. He had no good tidings for the barbarian king. Still, his unthinking use of the word "barbarian" gave him pause to consider his motives.

Were the Etruscan aristocrats and he no better than Rome's patricians or its citizenry? They contemptuously considered all the Gaulish tribes to be mere savages and tools to be used. In the interests of acquiring political power and wealth, they were to be crushed in battle, their lands seized, and their people enslaved. That did not sit well with Arruns, who perceived himself as a fair-minded man.

"The council will not meet with you in the city."

Brennus was not surprised. He was rarely made welcome by people he intended to subjugate. Death and suffering were his constant companions. In any event, his night with Arruns' wife, a woman with remarkable talents, appetites, and ambitions, had provided him with all the information he needed. It would have been less traumatic and less bloody for the citizens of Clusium if their leaders had negotiated with him, as had those of Ariminum. Still, he had brought an army with him, and they had expectations of plunder and sating the desires of the victor. Both of which Brennus had no intention of denying.

He smiled at his dupe. It would be best for Arruns to die bravely in the inevitable battle for Clusium rather than from a slashed throat by agents of either side after the event. But on which side would he fight? Either way, the Etruscan was, to all intents and purposes, dead. No matter the merit of his motives, once a traitor, always a traitor.

"How many fighters has Clusium within its walls? One thousand, two thousand, maybe three thousand?"

Arruns was taken aback at the question, but more because he sensed Brennus precisely knew the state of Clusium's defences. Had he gravely underestimated this barbarian king?

"No need to answer. My army well outnumbers them. You will return to the city and prevail upon the council to meet and eat with me here to discuss *my* terms. Assure them that their safety is guaranteed. No Gaul would transgress the rules of hospitality." *Unless the treacherous bastards try to assassinate me, and it will be me who judges that.* "I am sure we can reach an agreement of mutual benefit."

Tadhg chuckled. Only Conall was a better tactician than Brennus.

* * *

The small delegation of elders was taken aback at the generosity of the Senone king. An impressive pavilion had been erected with tables laden with food and drinks. A bevvy of comely and half-naked slaves ensured that no cup or platter remained empty, despite protests of being satiated. There was a benign tolerance of any who wished to fondle or rut the servants. Each "guest" received a thick torc of gold. It was Brennus at his most engaging. Yet Tadhg noted the steely glint in the king's hazel eyes and the paucity of beer and wine imbibed by the Senones. *The Etrusci are fools.*

The hammer dropped as dusk fell. Replete with food and drowsy with wine, the eyes of the representatives from Clusium struggled to keep sleep at bay. Their minds drifted from what they considered a dreary conversation with the barbarian king. Brennus stood, cup in hand. "Friends, the night draws close, and you should retire to your homes, your wives, and your children." The benign command elicited a rumble of agreement.

"After dawn and once you have broken your fast, you will freely open the gates of Clusium to me. Or"—Brennus paused for effect—"you will have no homes, no wives, and no children. The choice is yours."

The group that crossed Clusium's gates were very sober and very afraid.

"They'll not surrender, and they have strong walls and a good position."

"I agree, Tadhg. I have no intention of attacking that stronghold. I would lose thousands of men." In a less pleasant tone and with lips curled into a snarl, Brennus continued, "I well remember Lugudunon." The king shook his mane of shaggy red hair as if to marshal his thoughts. "My army surrounds the hill and the city. There is no way in or out except through me. Either they allow me in, or I will starve them into surrender. Either way, the city is mine. Yes, there will always be the warriors—the strong and the heroes—who will fight, but their number is few. For the many, the ordinary citizens, despair will descend quickly and spread like a plague."

As he took his leave, Tadhg shook his head and questioned Brennus' comfort in his unassailable position. "The gods are capricious. There is always a thorn that finds a way to pierce defences and draw blood."

In this instance, the barb was a small boat that, in the dead of night, drifted past the Senone camp and let the current take it to the gates of Rome.

***

The public gallery of the Curia Hostilia was in an uproar, but that did not trouble Marcus. Cracked skulls and chains would soon bring order. Of more concern was the rising reticence of those senators who owed him favours to rally to his side. It also appeared their numbers were depleted as more moved into the "undecided" camp, if not to those who outright opposed him. His political enemies were gaining ground, and the shouts of "Shame!", "Recall the general!" and "Incompetent!" had risen well above the usual muffled murmurs. He would have Nikandros prune the senatorial ranks when the present turmoil was resolved.

The Senate was in open revolt, and Marcus had little time to force a decision in his favour. Rome was already aflame with tales, no longer unverified rumours, of the barbarian horde's successful invasion of the lands of the Etrusci and the Umbri. The sighting of a fleet of quin-queremes in the waters beyond the port of Pyrgi and subsequent landing of more barbarians added grist to the gossip. Finally, there were ominous accounts of an incursion by Dionysius, albeit well to the south of the peninsula. The final straw that inflamed the population to fever pitch was the arrival of two messengers from Clusium who brought tales of a great siege.

Clusium's precarious position gave Marcus the most concern. He had eyes on that prize as the next expansion of Rome's influence and territory. Even with his contempt for the barbarians, he could not allow them to gain a city that had a direct route to Rome. A diplomatic resolution of the siege would bring Clusium's council into the grasp of his bony fingers and shore up his political power in Rome.

The clamour in the chamber brought Marcus' thoughts back to the day's main agenda item. He dipped his head in the direction of the new Princeps Senatus of the Curia, the former having passed away suddenly.

Marcus smiled. The Princeps had a predilection for young boys, which the Pontifex was more than willing to encourage and supply. The price was the man's submission. On cue, the Princeps took his place on the stone plinth, coughed to clear his throat, and somewhat nervously spoke.

"I propose that the sons of Marcus Fabius Ambustus, Nikandros, Numerius, and Quintus, are appointed ambassadors. With the authority of the Senate, they will travel immediately to Clusium and assist the city to negotiate an accommodation with the barbarians."

It was unclear whether the stunned silence that descended upon the Senate floor was due to the sheer effrontery of the proposal or the lack of a viable counterproposal. None had thought that far ahead and thus, with a slim margin, the motion was passed.

CHAPTER 31

394 B.C.—Pyrgi and Clusium

Celtillos allowed himself a smile as he entered the stockade that secured Conall's camp. The Arverni were camped a respectable distance away. It was a reasonable precaution given that the two armies held little affection for each other and there was no sense in offering an opportunity for confrontation. With hopes of a reconciliation with Conall and at some personal risk, Celtillos limited his bodyguard to just ten mountain-sized veterans.

In the event of an unsuccessful meeting, which would most certainly be marked by weapons unsheathed and blood spilt, his protectors' job was to die while allowing the king to escape. Thus, Celtillos was relieved to observe that the large tent to which he was escorted was a short walk from the perimeter entrance. Still, it would appear to be much longer if he had to run for his life. That Conall had requested his presence augured well for some sort of deal. Celtillos inhaled deeply, donned a smile, and entered the tent.

Conall chaffed at being close to Rome and his enemy, yet unable to take the next step in the campaign. He had questioned Tadhg's spies at length about Rome on their return from their mission. Still, he needed better insights and intelligence on the city, and that would only come from Tadhg. Conall scratched at the stubble on his chin. It bothered him that Tadhg had not returned from Brennus. He prayed that the Goddess was keeping his ambassador safe and that he did not have to start another war with Brennus.

A sharp squeeze on his forearm made him wince—apparently, long nails were now judged fashionable. Alerted to Celtillos' entrance, he stood with Mórrígan beside him. The queen scowled as she rose but, with effort, adopted a diplomatic smile. The action was not lost on Celtillos. In return, the Arverni king dipped his head respectfully to both Conall and the Dark Huntress and then to those members of the Rí's Chomhairle present.

On its face, it should be a simple negotiation. Conall needed Celtillos' warriors if his campaign were to become anything more than a barbarian raiding party. More than that, and as much as he disliked their leader, the king of Clann Ui Flaithimh considered the Arverni to be strong and resourceful fighters. Added to this, Conall had long admired the quality of their armour and weapons.

As for Celtillos, he needed gold—and lots of it. His fight with the Umbri had been successful and added to his men's wealth. But so far, it had not delivered Brennus' flowery promises of bountiful riches. In short, Celtillos' treasury was almost empty, and therefore the future of his reign was uncertain. He could not take the conquered lands back to his homeland and had no intention of ruling a territory distant from his capital. Thus, Celtillos' goals were simple: a trade agreement for the Rodonos River and a slice of the victors' spoils in the upcoming battle with Rome.

But how far could Conall and Mórrígan be pushed before retaliating with steel and fire? Celtillos shuddered. In a simple battle of warriors, he was optimistic that the Arverni would prevail against the meat grinder that was the Clann Ui Flaithimh shield wall and the tribe's vaunted cavalry. But, as he looked on the tattooed faces of the women who flanked Conall, Celtillos shivered. He sensed the subdued aura of dark power purring like a feral cat within Mórrígan and the Sidhe. Its hunger for an excuse to pounce was palpable, and the diplomatic smiles on their faces did nothing to disguise the threat. No, with Conall, it would never be—it could never be—a simple, honest battle. He glanced once more at the ladies before dragging his focus back to Conall.

Perhaps now was not the time for bluff and bravado.

***

"What about Brennus? The spoils would be divided further, but his men would add more certainty to the outcome."

Conall nodded and took a long sip of honeyed beer. In the heat of the tent, the beverage was no longer chilled but was not unpalatable. The two sides had come to an accommodation that satisfied each other's needs with remarkable speed. The conversation over food and drink would almost have been considered amiable by an outsider. "We will await news from Tadhg about Rome's defences and Brennus' intentions."

"But not for too long. Our warriors will become restless for battle. And it would be a bloody mess if they turned on each other."

Conall nodded. "Agreed."

***

"The council wish to meet to discuss the siege and its lifting."

Brennus scrutinised Arruns' demeanour. The loneliness of the noble's duplicity sat heavily on his shoulders. The man was uncomfortable, and not just with being in Brennus' presence. A surge of anger and irritation prompted Arruns to continue. Exhaling sharply, he added, "Not in the city but here, in your camp." Arruns swallowed and scorn for his fellow Etrusci thinned his lips. "Three Roman envoys will accompany the delegation—members of the Fabii family, I believe."

"Shite!"

Brennus raised an eyebrow at Tadhg's outburst. The envoy, standing in the shadows of the tent, lifted his hands in apology. "Perhaps later." The look from the king in response assured Tadhg that there would be no "perhaps".

The Senone king gestured for the captain of his guard to come forward. "Firstly, find out who let messengers from Clusium evade our guards and, secondly, who compounded the error by permitting Roman envoys to enter the city without my knowledge." The man turned but was halted by a firm hand on his forearm. "The damage is done. Execute the men—slowly and publicly. Remember their names. Their kin should have the same fate."

Brennus turned to Arruns and was pleased with the man's ashen-faced demeanour. Another lesson communicated. More pleasantly, the king smiled. "Advise the delegation from Clusium—and Rome— that I will welcome them on the next sunrise."

* * *

Much had been spoken of them, yet this was the first time Tadhg had set eyes on Marcus' sons, and he was unimpressed. Etched into their faces and postures were the signs of a life of privilege and debauchery. Certainly, these were no warriors but men who paid others to fight on their behalf. It proved impossible for Tadhg not to sneer at the duo. Yet his respect for Gaius and his men urged caution, if not for these envoys, then for Rome's armies. That, and the tall, dark figure who preceded them.

After paying his respects to Brennus, the Spartan smiled mockingly at Tadhg. Yet, behind Nikandros' smile, there was an edge of wariness. Like Tadhg, his hand reflexively reached for his sword, but since weapons were not allowed in the tent, both men exhaled frustrated growls. *What on earth was Conall's man doing in Brennus' camp and at the Senone king's side?* Nikandros did not care anything for the fate of Clusium or its people. Brennus could slaughter and sell them into slavery for all the Spartan cared. But Nikandros had a premonition that Tadhg's presence did not bode well for Rome.

For his part, the interplay and body language between the two piqued Brennus' curiosity. Blood had been shed for less.

Drawing his brothers aside, Nikandros hissed with as much venom as he could muster without arousing the attention of the others in the tent: "Do *not* take sides. Remain neutral. Provide prudent counsel or be silent. It is not worth sacrificing Rome's security for an Etruscan city."

It was no surprise to the Spartan that the advice fell on ears plugged with years of patrician wax. Distance from Rome had increased the swagger of Quintus and Numerius. With supercilious condescension, the elder brother retorted. "We need no guidance from an assassin and thug who, himself, is little more than a barbarian."

Nikandros sighed. In his life, he had paid little heed to the gods, their oracles, or the temple priests and Vestal Virgins. Still, even he sensed that the omens were inauspicious. *I should have cut the throats of my "brothers" before this mission.* The shake of his head and lack of demurring should have alerted Quintus and Numerius. It did not. In their arrogance, they chose instead to celebrate a rare victory over the usurper. Yet, at that moment, they sealed their fates. The only question to be answered was, which hand would hold the blade?

In the end, all arguments were brought to a head by Brennus. The king stood and bowed somewhat mockingly to the Etruscan and Roman representatives. "*You* may keep Clusium." Any celebration of victory was caught in Etruscan and Roman throats by the next pronouncement: "*I* will keep all the lands that surround it—and the crops and fruits produced. You will pay taxes to me if you wish to travel beyond Clusium, including use of the Clanis River. If you wish to eat, you will purchase crops from *my* farmers at a price that I will set."

Brennus smiled cruelly. "Now, you may leave."

CHAPTER 32

394 B.C.—Clusium and Rome

Wine flowed like a river in Clusium's banqueting hall. Inspired by it, a rebellion was fomented. Weasel words, promises of bribes and trade and great Roman phalanxes to vanquish their enemies puffed up the egos of the city elders. For once, Nikandros was impressed by how ably Quintus and Numerius worked the chamber crowded with the city's fawning wealthy and nobility. *Both sides are suited to each other.*

Honed by decades of nefarious activities, the Spartan's senses alerted him to danger. Above the conversation rose a strident call for the Etruscans to fight back, but not just with words. *Fools!* The Senones outnumbered Clusium's militia by more than five times. It would be battle-hardened barbarians against the untested and those who imagined themselves warriors. The Etrusci were safe and strong within their walls, and that was where they should remain. Yet, over and over, he heard the condescension of the Roman envoys overwhelm prudence. How could civilised men and their armies not be victorious over a rabble that was no better than animals? Quintus' argument was foolish and deceptive, but it served to inflame passions and flatter Etruscan pride.

Shades of purple and grey gave the sunrise a glorious if apocalyptic outlook. Only the sun itself appeared to be missing, preferring to cower behind dense clouds and avoid the persistent scarring of the sky by lightning. Peals of thunder hid the preparations for war and the assembly of Clusium's army in its streets. Dressed in rust-free armour that likely had never seen battle, a small number of those claiming ancient lineage awaited the arrival of their mounts. These knights would lead the city's bid to break the siege. "Bloody amateur warriors!" Nikandros raged, not at the Etruscans but at the sight of his brothers riding at the head of the siege-breakers. Less loudly, he muttered, "You forget your role." Their father's parting counsel, to do nothing stupid, was long forgotten.

The blare of horns alerted the Senone guards that something was amiss. With disbelief, they watched the Etruscan army descend the hill on which Clusium sat. Soon the great Senone war horns sent a deep *barrr-ewww* in reply and called the Gauls to battle. Tadhg was impressed at the calm with which Brennus assimilated and acted on the unexpected news. The speed with which his chieftains received their battle orders and marshalled the men under their command was admirable. Brennus' tent sat on the crest of a small hill—indeed, it was more like a mound of dirt. Yet, the height was sufficient to give the king—and, alongside him, Tadhg—clear sightlines of the immediate position.

✳✳✳

Tadhg watched a large band of Senone warriors quickly insert themselves between the Etruscans and the camp perimeter. Armed with shields and spears, they bore the brunt of the initial attack, blunting and slowing it down. It was they who bought time for the rest of Brennus' strategy to be implemented. Mouth open, Tadhg observed the Senone army create a wide channel to the king's mound and then enclose it. On either side of the avenue was a thick and impenetrable hedge of lances. In effect, Brennus had created his version of Rome's Circus Maximus with the Etrusci as entertainment.

The king chuckled at Tadhg's open admiration. "I don't think I was ever at my best in the battles with Conall. The Etrusci are well outnumbered. Most of them will escape with cuts and bruises, but a few will die. Why waste my men in a pointless battle? This will be good sport." Brennus grinned through his bushy beard and long moustache and pointed to a group of his chieftains. "They are taking wagers on the outcome. Perhaps you would like to take part?" Brennus sighed, "Besides, I'll take my revenge on these idiots when I sack Clusium at a time of *my* choosing."

Tadhg coughed and, with apologies to his royal status, tapped Brennus' shoulder and pointed. "It seems that ambassadors of Rome hold to a different ethic than other nations."

"Bastards!" Both watched the two Romans ride with the Etruscan cavalry. It was evident from the angry gesticulations that the nobles of both Clusium and Rome were highly frustrated with the Senone stratagem. Their annoyance was exacerbated by the mounting shouts of insult and mockery at their helplessness. Some Senone warriors with a sense of humour started calling out wagers as to who would complete the "course".

Still, many of the Etruscan rank and file came to appreciate the Senone strategy. Perhaps, this was not the day on which they would die needlessly. The same could not be said of the elite with their fragile, puffed-up egos. More than willing to risk a massacre to assuage their tarnished honour, they flailed at the hedge of spears and railed at their men.

* * *

The Goddess huffed. She was bored. Comedy was a poor substitute for violence and bloodshed. Lately, the effete Roman gods had become infuriating. They mocked her perceived weakness for Clann Ui Flaithimh's royal duo and implied she could no longer control her subjects. She snorted at that assertion. Had she ever been able to control Conall and Mórrígan?

Not one for philosophising, she returned to the core issue—her boredom. With a flick of a godly wrist, the spear, previously flailing in Quintus' soft hand, left his grasp and flew into the chest of a Senone chieftain. That he was also kin to Brennus added meadowsweet to the beer. It was a challenge to discern who was more shocked: Brennus, Quintus, or the Senone noble with the spear shaft protruding from his chest.

***

Brennus was enraged. Like Íar, Conall's larger-than-life cavalry commander, the Senone king had a code of honour. Although the Senone king's principles were more flexible than Íar's, an integral part held that ambassadors should not take sides in a conflict. That the dead man was kin was the lesser of the king's issues. Once more, hundreds of Senone battle horns reverberated within the camp and around Clusium. The Etrusci glanced about nervously. The hard-faced Senones before them no longer bore any semblance of humour. Sensing disaster, the Etruscan and Roman nobles quickly retreated to hide behind Clusium's walls.

As darkness fell, loud celebrations of a faux victory gushed through Clusium's relieved inhabitants. Indeed, after the ominous, deep blaring of the Senone war horns, the residents had fully expected an assault and bloody slaughter. Now, the population looked down upon a dark and empty valley. There were no campfires, for the Senone army had disappeared. Only Nikandros did not join the celebrations. Instead, he grated his teeth at the self-congratulatory backslapping. *This will bring no good outcome for Rome.*

Further south, in a newly erected Senone encampment, a brooding Brennus conferred with his advisors. In reality, Brennus had a council of one—himself. He knew this was not a time to show any weakness. Therefore, his primary consideration was who should be the subject of his wrath.

Summoned to the king's tent, Tadhg thought there was a high probability that his neck would be stretched or his head removed... or both. He was the perfect sacrifice, and hence he waited in silence for Brennus to speak.

"At sunrise, you will take as many horses as you need to make the fastest time to Conall's camp. You will prevail upon the Rí Ruirech of Clann Ui Flaithimh, his queen, and the Lady Sidhe to meet me on the plain between Sutrium and Nepet. He should bring his army and that of Celtillos. My Senones will leave for the valley at dawn."

A relieved Tadhg dipped his head and exited the king's pavilion. There was a broad smile on his face.

***

In the Curia Hostilia, the public gallery was hushed and the leaders of Rome curiously subdued. Previously feted for their diplomatic victory, Quintus and Numerius, standing alongside their father and Nikandros, now faced rows of stormy glares and frustrated fury. Murmurs of "Shame!" floated like feathers from the balcony to alight on patrician ears.

Roman honour and justice, long held up as a lofty example to imitate, had been sullied. Outside the former temple building, crowds—residents, merchants, slaves, even a smattering of the patricians, who usually avoided closeness with the lower classes—gathered on its steps and in the streets.

The senators, even Marcus' supporters, were extremely resentful at having been so blatantly backed into a corner. They had listened, in silence, as two envoys of Brennus presented a watertight case that Quintus and Numerius should be handed over for judgment, sentencing, and, most likely, execution. Everyone knew the brothers had contravened the rules governing the functioning of ambassadors. Indeed, the arseholes, and Quintus in particular, had openly and drunkenly bragged about killing a Senone chieftain. With each telling, the story became more and more embellished. Now, the gossip in Rome's drinking dens and brothels resounded to tales of a hero single-handedly vanquishing the barbarians and rescuing Clusium.

Marcus stood. To the Senone envoys, he brazenly asserted that his sons were not only ambassadors but also tribunes with full military and consular authority. Their actions, by implication, were sanctioned by Rome and could not be contested—certainly not by mere barbarians. The Pontifex Maximus stood resolute in defence of his sons, daring the assembled members to defy his will.

Caught between Scylla and Charybdis, the senators faltered. How could Roman citizens take the side of a barbarian king? Those present in the Curia Hostilia had an opportunity to uphold the integrity of Roman justice and the ambassadorial position. Much to Marcus' glee, they failed miserably.

"There will be war."

The four words were the last spoken by Brennus' envoys before they bowed, turned about, and exited the chamber. The phrase spread like wildfire through a city already on the edge of panic.

"Bluster and words. The army of Rome, led by my sons, Quintus and Numerius, will not be defeated by a band of barbarians who are no better than slaves." Marcus turned to Nikandros. In a much softer tone, he whispered, "Select five hundred from the best of my legions. They will be my guard, and you will command them to ensure my safety. We will relocate immediately to my residence on the Mons Capitolinus."

The Spartan dipped his head, and then, with a mocking smile, he looked at the pale faces of his brothers. He sniffed the air, sampling fragrances of fear, urine, and shit. It had dawned, albeit slowly, on Quintus and Numerius that soon they would participate in a real battle.

***

Considered by many in Rome as the gateway to the Etruscan lands, the old town of Sutrium perched on a rocky crag, surrounded by crevices and ravines. Sutrium overlooked a vast and mostly flat plain, which was now occupied by the combined force of the Senones, Clann Ui Flaithimh, and the Arverni. The host also included a score of Etrusci, Samnite, and Umbri warlords who had accounts to settle with Rome. The Gaul and Gael army were no more than a two-sunset march from Rome.

The city elders of Sutrium received assurances from Brennus that there would be no raping of their women—young or old. And no pillaging of the wealth of its citizens or those of the outlying farms. Furthermore, he pledged gold for all supplies. Surprisingly, the massed armies were well disciplined and mostly kept to Brennus' pledge. Despite this, the population was not convinced, and the majority chose to remain within Sutrium's environs. To no one's surprise, Sutrium's merchants and whores set aside their fears and cultural differences in the pursuit of gold.

"Like a bowl, the city is protected, enclosed by, and built upon a series of ridges. The Romans call them hills," said Tadhg. "The key areas are the Mons Palatinus where the wealthy reside, the Mons Aventinus where most of the working population, the poor, and the slaves live, and the Mons Capitolinus. On this fortified crag stands the Temple of Jupiter. Many of the more influential senators, including Marcus, have a second home on the Mons Capitolinus. Rome's walls are weak, constructed mostly of wood and broken in many areas. The city's main protection is the Tiberis River. It is wide and deep, although less so at this time of the year, and its currents are strong and treacherous. There is only one bridge across the water."

"Army?" asked Celtillos. Tadhg had already briefed Conall more fully on the city's defences.

Tadhg scratched his straw-coloured mop of hair. "Certainly four well-equipped legions, each with about six thousand men—all paid professionals. They will probably be supported by another five or six thousand civilian levies. So, around thirty thousand fighters. The legions are heavily armoured and fight in a Greek phalanx formation."

"I am a bit disappointed. Where is the glory in matched numbers? I was hoping for a much larger army to defeat." Brennus looked at Conall and laughed as he quenched his thirst with a large horn of beer. Streams of the liquid poured down his beard and long, plaited moustache to soak his linen tunic. The Rí Ruirech of Clann Uí Flaithimh stood and stretched.

"I propose we draw them out of the city. Tadhg's men have surveyed the land between here and Rome. There is a small stream, the Allia, which flows into the Tiberis. The surrounding land would be a good battleground. We could reach it in one sunset and dig in."

Brennus stood. "Well, I have to piss. Let the men enjoy the night. We march tomorrow when the sun rises."

* * *

It was long after sunset, but thoughts were furiously racing through Conall's mind. Good or bad, the resolution of his enmity with Marcus and Rome would soon come to pass. Did he seek vengeance, justice, or retribution, and did it matter? Perhaps the designations were arbitrary and dependent on his mood. The one unalterable fact was that the dark and bloody memories that haunted his dreams would always be with him. But at least he would ensure Marcus and his sons would suffer before sending them to Tartarus.

Conall murmured into Mórrígan's fiery red tresses, "You always smell of spring flowers." His lover's head lay on a muscled chest sparsely covered in auburn hair. Often, he considered scraping away the paltry offering but deemed the effort required as not worth it. In the still, stifling heat, he could feel beads of sweat gather on his brow and trickle from his armpits. Likely, perspiration covered his body. Conall found it strangely comforting that he had no control over this function of his body. He made to move, seeking to minimise the dampness for his partner.

"Don't. I enjoy your smell—sweaty or not—and the dampness doesn't bother me." Mórrígan snorted, "And no, I don't always smell of flowers. More often, I smell of stale sweat and horse piss and shite."

Mórrígan's hand travelled down her belly and paused mid-way. The twins were born around Bealtaine, and a short time past, they had celebrated Lugnasad. In the intervening time, the queen was pleased that laborious exercising had rendered her stomach almost flat. Conall insisted that she was beautiful to him no matter what. But then, men always say that, and few mean it. It pleased her that her hand-fast partner was one of the few. She touched the additional silvery stretch lines that adorned her skin. They seemed to meld pleasingly with her dark, swirling designs. She exhaled. When would she see her children again?

"Soon," said Conall with a broad smile.

Startled, Mórrígan propped herself up on an elbow. A flick of her head extracted her partner's face from the thick mane that threatened to suffocate him. Had she spoken her thought aloud or was he reading her mind? There were times when she considered that she might not be the only one with "powers" in the relationship. After all, Conall had been the Hand of the Goddess since his youth. She smiled. Was he not still young? In Mórrígan's eyes, he would always be the easily embarrassed apprentice blacksmith. Still, the Goddess was whimsical enough to gift him special abilities, and he was infuriatingly good at circumspection.

"I have listened to Brennus' plan for battle, and the king of the Senones was wise enough to agree, with a few embellishments, to what you were proposing. Now, Conall Mac Gabhann, Rí Ruirech of Clann Ui Flaithimh, Hand of the Goddess, and father to our children—what is *your* plan? How are the pieces on *your* fidchell board to be played?"

In the flickering light of rushlights, she watched the smile spread over Conall's lips, exposing his teeth. While not in the same category as Amodocus' gleaming whiteness, against the canvas of a well-sunburned face, they came close. It lent him an almost feral look.

"I will tell you, but only after I enjoy your company much more intimately."

Mórrígan laughed. "Are you not sweaty enough?"

CHAPTER 33

394 B.C.—Rome and the Banks of the Allia

The riders dismounted from horses on the brink of collapse. Their mounts were well lathered, but it was impossible to say whose breathing was the more laboured. Perhaps the horses. The messengers would recover, but the beasts had given all, and the reward for their service would be death and the dinner plate. Still, stains of blood on torn tunics and open cuts to their skin testified that the riders had not escaped their ordeal unscathed.

Nikandros needed good information, so he had despatched a score of scouts. Only two had returned to Rome, and that in itself was ominous. If these men were alive, was it because Conall allowed it? The Spartan shook his head. Perhaps, as Marcus thought, he was paranoid and saw barbarian conspiracies everywhere. He snarled, but not because Marcus could be right. Nikandros had no time to interrogate the men and rehearse a more appropriate version of their news before they were ushered into the Curia Hostilia and the waiting assembly. The story would be told as Conall wanted it.

"Thirty thousand well-armed Gauls, mostly on foot but with a sizeable contingent of cavalry, march towards Rome. Unless stopped, they will reach the Tiberis and gates of Rome around Kalendis Sextilis."

Nikandros nodded in approval at the terse delivery. Perhaps he had misjudged the men. The message was short and blunt, prompting a ripple of fear through the public gallery. Kalendis Sextilis was less than a quarter cycle of the moon away. The sift and whisper of sandals on the stone stairs indicated that it would not be long before the city's population was alerted.

A stunned silence descended on Rome's senators, but only for a moment. Loud and strident calls for the immediate recall of General Marius Furius Camillus from his exile in Ardea erupted in the chamber. Howls of laughter met the angry ripostes from Marcus that, under his sons' command, the Roman phalanxes would vanquish the barbarian mob. The idiocy of the statement was apparent even to the Pontifex's most ardent supporters. Fortunately, four legions meant four tribunes in command, so perhaps there was still hope. Nikandros' sensible plea to stay within the city's walls and let the Tiberis be Rome's bulwark was ignored.

"Granted, Marius is a veteran commander," the dry, rasping voice of Marcus cut through the clash of quarrels. "He is, however, well-known to be a vengeful man with a long memory. Who will argue with me that the first to fall by his sword will be from this assembly, not the barbarians?" The desperate yet cunning intervention by Marcus sparked off an intense bout of whispering, but inevitably the gist of the murmuring coalesced to one issue—self-preservation.

Patrician teeth ground and stomachs roiled at the ruling they were about to adopt. But how could they help Rome if they were dead? Quintus and Numerius were to retain command of their father's two legions, and Rome's army would be mobilised. Marcus smiled. After a few bumps in the road, his plan was back on track.

As Rome's army marched towards the Allia River, to Marcus' disgust, the city's residents gathered up their families and belongings and fled, east and west, to the safety of the walled cities of the Etruscans. That many of the city's priests, and the Vestal Virgins, joined the exodus suggested the gods were not as convinced of the outcome as Marcus.

***

The following sunrise brought what the Romans called the Kalendis Sextilis. Seeking refuge from the clamour of the main encampment, Conall and Fearghal stood on a hill overlooking the meeting of the Allia and Tiberis rivers. It was mid-afternoon as the two looked on the Roman army.

Conall muttered, "Why?" A raised eyebrow from his battle commander encouraged further explanation.

"They allowed us to choose our position and will fight with the sun in their eyes. There are not even basic stockades or defensive ramparts. Half do not have tents in which to shelter." Conall scratched his head in disbelief. "Do they hold us in so much contempt?"

Fearghal chewed on a blade of grass, smiled, spat, and pointed out that since the Celtic armies had reached the battleground first, the Romans had little choice in the siting of their force. Additionally, they did have a strategic hill on their right flank, which could cause problems. Conall disagreed.

"Not so. They could have camped to our east. That ground is good and is further from the Tiberis." Fearghal shrugged. It was what it was. On the next sunrise, they would fight. Perhaps they would die.

"How is Mongfhionn?"

The question startled the grizzled commander, mainly because it concerned the one topic that he and the Sidhe avoided discussing— the death of her sisters. Or more pertinently, avenging their murder at the hands of Quintus and Numerius. More brusquely than he meant, Fearghal snapped, "She trusts the Goddess to deliver Marcus' sons into her hands." Then he sighed in apology and raised his hands. "For my part, I pray that the Goddess doesn't. Vengeance has a bitter and long-lasting taste."

CHAPTER 34

394 B.C.—Banks of the Allia

It was the evening before the battle. The black battle horse snickered and pawed at the dirt. Instinctively, the warrior leaned forward to stroke and pat its black velvet neck. "Patience, Toirneach. Soon… very soon."

From his vantage point on the high ground where the tents of the kings and nobles were pitched, Conall contemplated the Celtic army assembled at the confluence of the Allia and Tiberis rivers. That said, "river" was a grand name for the trickle of water that flowed into the Tiberis.

About thirty thousand warriors gathered under Arverni, Clann Ui Flaithimh, and Senone banners—even some Etrusci, Samnite, and Umbri. Many had crossed the Alpes and then Northern Latium from their homeland beyond the Rodonos in Gaul. Now they camped a short march from Rome and an even shorter distance from the Roman army.

They were tall, powerful, and proud warriors distinguished by tribal paint, hair colour and style, and weaponry. Apart from their nobles, most wore little by way of clothes. The hot climate of a Latium summer exacerbated the Celts' natural fondness for nudity. Many chose not to wear armour. They assembled in families and clanns but fought fiercely as individuals for glory and plunder, whether man or woman. Indeed, the women of the Celts fought as fiercely as any man and demanded their share of the rewards.

Conall looked to the centre and smiled as he studied his army. The

"Warriors of the Wall", as they had become known, had been forged and battle-hardened for over twenty years. Except for the cohorts of Carmag and Mòrag's Cinn Péinteáilte, most wore leather body armour inlaid with iron scales, although an increasing number wore chainmail. Their helmets, although functional, had grown more ornate and fantastically decorated over time. He had permitted this since it had proved one way to identify particular warriors in battle.

Familiar, oblong, curved scíatha emblazoned with a black raven on a field of red rested at their sides. Sheathed in beautifully designed and crafted leather, scabbards and baldrics were double-edged short swords sharpened to a vicious cutting edge. When in formation, each man or woman carried four javelins—three for throwing, one for stabbing. Most retained a preferred weapon—their favourite axe, club, or long-sword—for when they were allowed to fight with no constraints. Most owned several daggers and knives of various shapes and sizes for throwing, stabbing—or just carving food.

Distinctive in their armour and weaponry, Conall's warriors, most from the lands of Ériu and Northern Albu, contrasted starkly with their Gaul comrades. His army, seemingly at ease, stood alert compared to their allies and retained a well-ordered formation. Behind the front two rows, each containing a thousand men, another three thousand formed up in two columns, each with two rows of seven hundred and fifty warriors.

Marked by the red-and-black foxtail crests of their helmets, a thousand cavalry guarded the flanks of his men. They carried smaller oval shields, javelins for throwing, and longer swords or long-handled axes for slashing. All these were safely secured on either side of their mounts— for now. Conall had conceded long ago to Mórrígan's wisdom on archers, especially since his travels through Albu, Ériu, and Gaul. Her warband of two hundred carried composite bow staves of wood and bone slung across their backs and quivers full of the signature black-shafted arrows with their red-and-white fletchings.

His men shared good-natured craic, laughing at the constant flow of insults and the bare arses and genitals flaunted by the main army of Gauls. Conall still considered them Gauls, not Gaels. For their part, Brennus' Gauls looked disdainfully on their heavily armoured allies. Yet, both sides remembered the bitter battles fought between these former adversaries, now united against a common enemy—Rome. The insults masked a high level of respect for each other.

Brennus, a winged helmet crowning his shoulder-length mass of red hair, tugged on a great beard and moustache. The king looked grim, his honour had been deeply offended by the behaviour of Rome's ambassadors, the Fabii brothers, at Clusium. Foul-tempered and arrogant, the men had negotiated in bad faith. Adding insult to injury, Rome had covered up the brothers' sins by appointing them military tribunes. For Brennus, it was one insult too many.

The tall Gaul nodded to Conall and then pointed in the direction of the Roman camp. "Likely, Celtillos and I could have done without your men. There are not that many Romans to fight."

Conall nodded warily, somewhat in agreement. The Roman army numbered around thirty thousand men. However, a sizeable element of that appeared to be a civilian militia. The Gauls and Celts had roughly the same numbers, but many kings and kingdoms acknowledged them as superior warriors. That said, Conall wanted his men in the front. He needed to be the first to cross the Tiberis and the first to enter Rome. After a score of years, he had business to bring to a close: one final vow, one geis to complete. Retribution for Rome was at hand.

Conall grinned wolfishly. *That is always a bad sign*, thought Brennus. "Of course you could, but how many do you want to lose against the Roman phalanxes? If my men are killed, there will be more spoils for the Senones and the Arverni. And if I pass beyond the veil, then you can rest easier at night."

Brennus had witnessed too many times what Conall's army could do against elite warriors even when well outnumbered. He had lost too many warriors and too much territory to Conall and his commanders, the feared ceannairí na míle. Brennus grudgingly respected the Rí Ruirech of Clann Ui Flaithimh, but he did not trust him or his ever-present companions—Mórrígan and the Sidhe.

He had no love for Conall or his men, and in his gut, Brennus remained convinced he was dancing to Conall's harp. No doubt the bastard had his own plan for the dawn. Still, he would be more than happy to see Clann Ui Flaithimh's army culled and even more delighted to mouth platitudes over Conall's funeral pyre.

He smiled. "Would death rid me of you? Let us see if the Romans can teach you some humility, Conall Mac Gabhann. Make sure your men are ready to march at first light."

***

Mórrígan observed the shadow emerge and glide, although that was a poor description for an action that held so much intent and purpose, towards the camp's northern exit. She smiled as the figure, with an economic wave of a pale hand, circumvented the guards and moved deeper into the darkness. No earthly creature could track or would dare to challenge the apparition. But then, the Dark Huntress was not totally of this world. Mórrígan followed the shadow until the lights of Gaul and Gael campfires became no more than the flash of lonely fireflies. With a smile, she moved closer. It was time to confront the mystery.

"Going somewhere, old woman?"

The creature stopped and turned. The folds of the dark cloak swirled; white teeth shone behind ruby lips that looked black in the silver moonlight. "Took you long enough."

"You knew?"

"I've been around a lot longer than you. In the dark, sharp ears and experience often transcend power."

"I know what you're thinking of doing."

"Not 'thinking of', just doing. I made a promise, and I intend to keep it."

"To the dead?"

"I would have thought that you, of all people, would understand that death is not everything."

"I do. I'm coming with you."

"I doubt that I could stop you. But what of your friends?"

It was Mórrígan's turn to grin. "They're back-up—just in case. Amodocus may be infuriating, but there's no doubting his expertise, and Sarpedon, day or night, is the best with a bow in the army." The Huntress sensed a raised eyebrow and smiled. "Yes, he may even be better than me, although not as dark in purpose."

Silent as the wind yet without causing its usual impacts on beast, man, or shrubbery, the small group slithered, snake-like, towards the Roman encampment. Though, the description of the Romans implied a depth of organisation and defence that was absent. *Foolish hubris.*

Amodocus tapped Mórrígan on the shoulder. He was not stupid enough to try such an action with the Sidhe. He pointed to a garish eyesore of a tent. It was isolated as if wishing not to be soiled by contact with common soldiers and surrounded by torches whose light had begun to wane. This was no warrior's tent. A true commander's pavilion would have shown a more discriminating palate and respect for those about to do battle.

Unlike the Celts, the only women in the Roman camp were whores and slaves, not warriors. Quintus and Numerius' male guards took their masters as role models, mimicking the brothers' vices and lassitude. In the faltering torchlight, burnished cuirasses, greaves, and helmets made them stand out like gaily plumaged peacocks. Their postures, with slumped shoulders and loosely held weapons, were at odds with their duties. The smell of wine was carried on sour breaths. Crude jokes were exchanged, slurred with over-indulgence. In itself, this was not unusual. Always on the cusp of death, warriors often had a taste for brutal humour. The sentries' words stopped only after a wine-sodden exchange with the tent's occupants.

Mórrígan swept the bow stave from the sheath on her back, strung it, and nocked a black-shaft. Amodocus and Sarpedon mirrored the action. Arrows make surprisingly little sound as they enter fragile flesh. Taken from the side, the guards died without falling backwards and thus avoided crashing into the tent. Red-and-white fletches fluttered in a transient night breeze as the men bled into the rich soil. It was as if the feathers mirrored their final breaths. No sounds disturbed the night. With the ruin of their throats, the men had no voices to cry out or broadcast their demise.

The small group swept into the tent. Too much wine, impotent rutting with whores paid to moan in faux ecstasy, and too little sleep robbed the brothers of the capacity to resist. Feeble attempts to rise from their cots resulted in them collapsing to the dirt. With snorts of disgust at the lack of fight, Amodocus and Sarpedon rammed wads of cloth into the men's mouths. Wrists and ankles were quickly tied before the Romans were bundled over brawny shoulders.

***

"You should leave. This will not be pleasant to watch… or hear."

The party stopped on a small grassy rise mid-way between the two armies. Ironically, here grew two tall stone pines with straight boles and lush canopies. Ravens, disturbed from their sleep, croaked *kraa kraa* in protest. Quintus and Numerius, stripped and secured to the thick trunks, stared at each other wide-eyed. As the stupor of wine drifted away, their hearts thudded in their chests. Drool-soaked gags siphoned moisture from their parched mouths, allowing only muffled protests. In their eyes resided the surprise of the privileged called to account for their misdeeds.

Mórrígan hesitated. The queen was reluctant to leave her friend. She smiled. For the first time, she acknowledged that the fierce Sidhe was perhaps her closest friend. Mongfhionn returned the smile as if accepting the compliment. Then she shook her head.

"Go. It is time to honour my geis."

The departure of the night brought a glorious dawn and flame-red horizon. The brothers slumped against their restraints. The darkness of night should have given them time to reflect on their iniquities. Sadly, it was not long enough. The Sidhe wrenched the sodden wads of cloth from dry mouths. At first, the men croaked and then shouted curses and obscenities at the naked beauty that stood before them. In their rage and lust, they did not consider the awfulness of the Sidhe's perfection. Then her cruel, curved sacrificial blades flashed red in the dawn sun.

"Shout all you want. None will rescue you. None will hear you—at least not until I begin."

Mongfhionn stood before the elder of the brothers, grabbed a fistful of lank hair, lifted up his head, and then tilted her head back. The scar on her throat throbbed red, raw, and livid. "This, *you* did to me before burning my sisters—and then me." For a brief moment, Quintus' eyes filled with horror, but that was quickly consumed by lust for the body before him. The Sidhe looked down and laughed. Quintus flinched as the razor-sharp tip of a blade was drawn along his semi-erect manhood. He felt the skin part and blood trickle and inhaled in expectation of a more significant loss. A spiteful chuckle sent shivers up his spine. "Oh, no. That I will keep for later, for now, it is your brother's turn. Watch.

"Look upon my face, Roman."

Numerius fervently desired to avoid the obsidian eyes, but his resolve was no match for the Sidhe's will. With no choice, he looked straight into the awful visage of the Hag. A whimper escaped cracked lips. "This vision you will take with you to Tartarus." Numerius screamed as slim fingers plucked his eyes from their sockets. Tossed aside, the soft orbs landed at Quintus' feet. The older brother averted his own eyes from their accusing stare.

In one sense, the loss of his sight was the least of Numerius' concerns. Mongfhionn proceeded to chant while peeling long strips of skin from his body.

"Bitch!" spat Quintus.

While he could turn his face to avoid the horror, his ears could not ignore the sound of his brother's shrieking and the Sidhe's sinister incantations. Selfishly, he wished the apparition would rip out Numerius' tongue and save him from the ghastly sounds. Her only response was a malicious cackle, along with more screaming from his younger brother. Numerius' manhood, sliced at its root, joined a growing collection of skin and body parts at Quintus' feet. Sickened yet enthralled, Quintus watched as Mongfhionn drew the sacrificial blade across his brother's already blood-stained belly. A long rope of intestines slopped at Numerius' feet. Suddenly, there was a sickening crack and the worst screech of all before there was silence.

"*Do mo dheirfiúracha*—for my sisters," was all the Sidhe spoke before she turned her attention to Quintus.

Without a trace of shame, Quintus thanked Apollo for the quiet. His brother's life ebbed, and yet the older brother's thoughts were of the firm, round arse of his torturer. As she turned and took several paces towards him, it was not his sibling's blood, which splashed the Lady's porcelain, milk-white skin that drew his attention. Thin lips curled into a lecherous smirk as he imagined the ample breasts bruised by his fingers and the lush, red triangle between her thighs penetrated by his manhood. The Sidhe shook her head. Quintus was a man beyond redemption.

Indeed, the Roman's mind never understood his fate until his brother's still warm, bloody heart was pressed against his forehead and then his lips. Thick heart-blood siphoned into his mouth. Quintus gagged, puked, and continued to retch until only bile dribbled from his mouth. It was perhaps the first time Quintus considered the awful pain he was about to endure. In the haze of pain and suffering that followed, Quintus came to an unpleasant realisation—the Sidhe had let his brother off lightly. He prayed to Apollo for deafness, but this time it was to stop hearing his own screams. He begged the apparition for mercy, but his prayers went unanswered. The Sidhe had no forgiveness, and the gods had long ago washed their hands of Quintus.

*"Do mo dheirfiúracha—*for my sisters."

* * *

Conall watched the campfires doused as the dawn brightened to a crimson sunrise. He breathed in the comforting scent of woodsmoke. It rankled Conall that Mórrígan had put herself at risk by aiding in the abduction, if not the demise, of the Romans. Yet would he have done anything differently for a friend? As for Fearghal, the veteran was simply disappointed that his partner had not included him in her plans and had slipped away without him by her side. He had no qualms that justice, or at least the version that the Aes Sidhe held to, had been served.

"Shite!"

Brennus spoke, but the sentiment was heartily echoed by the Arverni and Senones gathered in the king's pavilion that morning. The screaming and dark incantations across the plain had begun just before dawn and had continued until the sun climbed midway to its zenith. From those who were of Clann Ui Flaithimh, there was a dispassionate detachment. Conall looked to Fearghal and then to Mórrígan. Both shrugged.

Had anyone expected anything different?

The eyes of those gathered in the tent were drawn to the intense shaft of light as the Sidhe pulled the entrance's flap back and stepped inside. Head held high and framed in a corona of sunlight that shimmered with the myriad dust particles caught in the beam, the tall Sidhe dipped her head and smiled. Not a speck of blood or a hair out of place gave any clue to her recent activities. Conall thought that her face, still fearsomely beautiful, held a measure of peace that he had not hitherto witnessed.

In a rare act of impetuosity, he embraced Mongfhionn in an iron grip. A soft "Ooof!" escaped her lips. "I'm glad you're back... safely, my Lady." For the first time, Conall noticed that her skin held the scent of feirdhris. Had he never been this close to her? Or had the resolution of her pain gifted it to her?

A murmured "Thank you", and a single tear escaped before the porcelain façade recovered. "Well, my business is completed. When does the battle commence?"

"I'm glad that you haven't lost your touch for dramatic entrances," Fearghal quipped. Conall grinned like a small boy before erupting into laughter. The others quickly joined him and the tension in the tent dissolved.

✶✶✶

"*Irrumatores!* Thank the gods, it has stopped!"

In truth, the sentiment was not about the loss of the tribunes, Quintus and Numerius. Few had any respect or love for the Fabii brothers, and the two remaining tribunes had forbidden their subordinates to attempt a rescue. The rationale that the barbarians were trying to lure them into a trap was accepted without argument. Thus, there were no volunteers to liberate the siblings—even among Marcus' legions. Indeed, few appeared keen to prompt the start of the battle. Having witnessed the size of the barbarian army, most in the legions and all in the civilian levies hoped the barbarians would see the folly of their position and go away.

Whether or not they divined it, the battle had already begun with the Sidhe's chanting. As the sun climbed in the morning sky, the sense of dread that infiltrated the simple minds of the rank and file would not abate. The tribunes, trained to be military commanders from birth, were political appointees, as had been the Fabii brothers. Both men had served, but in minor conflicts with massively outnumbered foes. Neither could be considered veterans, which was unsurprising. Many with experience chose to follow Marius into exile rather than remain in Rome. The risk to them and their families of being impoverished, held on spurious charges, or killed by a knife in the back brought forward their retirement.

And so, on the morning of the Kalendis Sextilis, the Roman legions formed a phalanx between the Allia and the Tiberis—twenty-four thousand men in four divisions, each ten men deep. Civilian militias and levies—another six thousand men—were positioned on the hills south of the Allia on the legions' right flank.

∗∗∗

"I don't like this."

The speaker, a retired centurion, surveyed the battleground from the hill where the civilian levies were positioned. He was no one of consequence, yet his pronouncement raised a few eyebrows.

"No one consulted the oracles. No priest made sacrifices to the gods. No Vestal Virgins flashed their tits." The last irreverent comment drew chuckles from those close by. Yet, the sentiments caused those gathered to consider whether the Romans had made another mistake: the gods dislike being ignored.

CHAPTER 35

394 B.C.—Allia River

"They look pretty."

Conall's words were to no one in particular and undoubtedly under-stated the panorama. Formed up on the river plain, the Roman phalanx stood to attention. Bronze armour, helmets, and shields glittered. With barely a whisper of wind, cloaks and tunics of red and blue were still, adding emphasis to the orderliness. To the Celts, it appeared the legions were ready for a parade, not a battle. Still, Conall's experience of Rome's soldiers cautioned against dismissing their battle skills.

In contrast, the riot of colours of the Gaels and Gauls arrayed along the grassy droimnín—a low ridge of high ground between the Allia and the Tiberis—was more appropriate to a festival. Most had bare torsos, and many wore little more than a broad belt or baldric whose only function was to carry weapons.

The air resonated with the blare of battle horns, the pounding beat of bodhráns, and shouts of insults and curses. Men and women alike flaunted bare arses. Pale manhoods were grasped and waved like flags at the opposing army with shouted promises of their use on Roman women. Only the preponderance of reds and blacks worn by Conall's force conferred any semblance of uniformity. Yet even that tapestry was embellished with splashes of green, orange, and yellow. It was left to the wolfhounds, with their furs of muted grey and brown and lolling pink tongues, to appreciate the solemnity of the occasion.

A stifling hot midsummer's day was assured as the sun climbed higher, showering its largesse on those beneath its throne. Yet, on the horizon, angry tones of grey and purple had begun to invade the blue expanse. The air crackled with the threat of thunderstorms. It was a day-light often witnessed following a storm. Rainbows appear in still-threatening skies, hues are made more vivid, and the air throbs with the sharp smell of freshness. Mongfhionn gripped her ancient oak staff, tapped the hard dirt, and smiled at Mórrígan.

"We can work with this."

✳✳✳

"Will they accomplish what you desire?"

Fate waved a spectral hand towards Conall and Mórrígan, clad in sleeveless chainmail that held not a speck of rust and with matching crimson-red over-tunics. The duo could never be mistaken. On their heads were the ornate helmets gifted to them by the people of Ráth Na Conall. Great black plumes of horsehair trailed from the golden ravens that crested each covering. Both sat astride their horses, scrutinising the enemy from the loftier perch. Tall, black Toirneach pawed impatiently at the ground as if knowing that soon his master would dismount and join the shield wall. The beast snorted in frustration while his companion, the pale golden mare that Mórrígan sat astride, waited patiently. She knew that soon gore would splash her coat as she carried her mistress into battle.

The Goddess sighed, aware her guidance of her chosen had been flawed and knowing that today would only postpone the inevitable. Yet, she derived a measure of amusement and satisfaction from the disgruntled pantheon of Roman gods. She turned to Fate, pointed in the gods' direction, and smiled. "Spoilt children!" While the Gauls and Gaels, to a man or woman, had dutifully dropped their sacrifices of armour and gold into the Tiberis, the Romans had not.

"I believe so, but will it be enough?"

✳✳✳

Fearghal pointed to the Roman formation. "I would have chosen the other side of the Tiberis and forced us to attack across the river. Instead, the waters have become a trap instead of a defence." The battle commander shook his head. "What sort of leaders do they have?"

Conall nodded. He, too, was surprised and perturbed at how the Romans had formed up. Stretched across the plain between the Allia and the Tiberis, their ranks were not as deep as he had expected.

He recalled Nikandros' stories of magnificent formations sixteen men deep or more. Was the Spartan present? Why had the Romans given up strength in numbers in favour of territory? He began to suspect a trap. Was there more to those positioned on the hills to his left? Perhaps they were the veterans and the long phalanx line a lure. He made up his mind and turned to Brennus and Celtillos.

"My warriors will attack the Roman right flank and the hill. You take the middle and left flanks."

Both men dipped their heads for both considered that Conall had bitten off more than he could chew. Yet, a weakened right flank would suit both kings. If Conall's force suffered high casualties or, better still, was defeated, Brennus and Celtillos would shed no tears. They were confident that their men and women would overwhelm whatever remained of the enemy.

Before the combined army, the kings affected a comradely grasp of forearms and enthusiastically shouted their wishes for each other's success. Few took the act seriously. Each king and his warriors would delight in the death of the others. With a final dip of heads, the Arverni and Senone kings wheeled their mounts around and cantered back to their armies.

Conall turned to Mórrígan and the Sidhe. His demeanour was grim, his jaw set, and a steely-eyed resolve locked in place.

"Break their minds. The army will break their bodies."

Arms stretched to the sky, the incantations began in low, almost reverent tones. To the Celts, the song was poignant and tragic, like the ballads often sung by the seanchaithe. Eyes smarted with a salty infusion of sweat and tears. At some point, the hymn seamlessly departed the realm of life and crossed to the darkness of death. Sensing, but not adversely impacted by the change in mood, the Gauls and Gaels shuffled their feet restlessly. They were war dogs awaiting release, held on a leash and protected from the rising crescendo of dark horrors.

To the Romans, it was not that the wailing was terrible, which it undoubtedly was. Against a background of lightning flashes, growling thunder, and sporadic splashes of large raindrops, rose the ululations of the cursed witches. The seeds of horror, planted in the previous night's visions as their ears witnessed the torture of the Fabii brothers, were nourished. Across the plain between the Allia and the Tiberis, Rome's military consuls and centurions fought against their terrors and attempted to calm their legions.

On the hill, the veteran centurion uttered one word—"Shit!"—and appealed to his gods. His supplications, like those of Rome's army who had suddenly rediscovered their faith, went unheard. The gods' egos were bruised and their ears shut.

***

They had not carried the field ballistae with them. Conall and Fearghal judged that the battle would be fought brutally and supported by swiftness of thought and fleetness of foot. The war machines would only slow them down. That said, both men were surprised but delighted that the Roman army also had foregone the use of the long-range weapons. Whether that was due to stupidity or arrogance was of little consequence to the Rí Ruirech and his battle commander. Still, Conall thanked the Goddess that the bloody carnage wrought by such weapons would be avoided. Instead, the earth would gorge itself on blood spilt from flesh slashed by iron and bronze blades.

As if to signal the start of the battle, or perhaps to add their blessing to their brethren painted on the red Clann Uí Flaithimh shields, conspiracies of ravens left nests to soar and swoop above the arena. The first of

Conall's army to strike were Mòrag's slingers. Although much mocked and maligned for their crude simplicity, few relished being on the receiving end of stones and slugs whipped into the air by long, braided cords. On the right flank, the Roman phalanx trembled under the storm. Men were very thankful for their bronze armour and shields, now dimpled with dents and scrapes. Ears rang painfully from the assault, but that was a good sign—at least they still lived. It was a short hailstorm, for the pouches of missiles soon emptied. Shaken and bruised, the Roman formation held firm and replied with shouted insults that very few of the Celts could understand.

Good tactics or stupidity? Conall shook his head in disbelief. The Roman phalanx, preferring to hold the formation, did not attempt to engage. Sensing the Romans' relief at the cessation of the slings, he gave a dark chuckle and signalled Mòrag. The Ravens' queen ordered the switch to bows and loosed a cloud of black-shafted arrows. Red-and-white fletches fluttered as the missiles arced upwards as if seeking to join with the circling ravens before descending on the enemy. On this day, each archer carried a light quiver of only twenty shafts. At one arrow per count of ten, the volleys were released and reached their targets almost before the first struck home. By the time the last arrow pierced flesh, Mòrag's people had already settled shields on their arms and picked up spears.

***

From his patch of dirt and brittle grass, the veteran centurion observed the start of the engagement with rising trepidation. He watched the barbarian shield wall divide, with surprising speed and order, into two halves. One section advanced on the rightmost cohort of the phalanx until the red shields were a javelin's throw from the legion. The other swung around until parallel to the Romans massed on the hill, and there it halted. Both contingents relaxed their tight wall. Their intent was obvious to the veteran. Still, he wondered if the tribune in command understood the threat.

Led by a full-bearded, giant warrior whose horned helmet failed to constrain a mane of red hair, the barbarian cavalry partitioned into two. One platoon cantered forward to stand behind the shield wall, facing the phalanx; the other walked slowly and came to a halt at the foot of the grassy mound. The Celts' supply of stones and arrows exhausted, the Roman noted, with rising anxiety, the former slingers and archers joining with a similar-sized group. Dark-blue tattoos covered their almost naked bodies.

A pace in front of the barbarians stood two women—one a statuesque beauty, the other a tall, slender lady. The latter was notable for the short, blue plumes trailing from her helmet and a tattoo that curled like a snake from temple to neck. A short distance from them stood a hirsute warrior with a massive club. All were noticeably impatient for battle. As bare feet stamped the dirt, they were joined by those behind, raising a reddish stoor around ankles. To the Romans on the mound, it appeared the barbarians floated above the ground.

Ripples of alarm spread throughout the muster. In loose formation, the civilian reserves milled around, uncertain about their role or if there was a plan for them. Many had assumed that their presence was simply to make up the numbers—to make the Roman army look more impressive. Perhaps, like onlookers at the Circus Maximus, their actual part was to spread the word of a glorious victory and the many deeds of valour of the legions.

In contrast to the well-drilled phalanxes on the plain, those on the hillside tugged at poorly fitting armour that chaffed skin and raised angry welts in the growing heat. Few had or could afford a complete set of cuirass, greaves, and helmet. Those with battle experience quietly and unobtrusively read the omens. They settled battle-bruised shields on tanned arms, tightened leather chin straps, and gripped whatever weapon, sword or spear, gave them the most comfort. In the absence of a defensive perimeter, these wiser heads shuffled backwards, pushing their inexperienced and over-eager comrades to the fore.

The centurion's head snapped around as one of his mates shouted a warning. On the right, a band of two hundred riders swept to within an arrow's range and dismounted. Around the horsemen, there seemed to hover a low mist of grey and brown. Shafts are not that substantial, and horses are accustomed to carrying heavy burdens. Each of Mórrígan's band bore four quivers, each containing thirty arrows. While Mórrígan's and Sarpedon's men were masters of the bow, the Thracians under Amodocus were not inexperienced. At this distance, the target was hard to miss.

At a sharp command from Mórrígan, a black cloud arced high in a sky that ominously continued to darken before descending. The poorly armoured on the hill cowered under the missiles' onslaught and prayed for its ending. Yet, this was only the beginning of their suffering. As the arrow storm ceased, the barbarian riders remounted and cantered towards their enemy's right flank. A favourite weapon of the Thracians was their heavy darts. Soon, showers of the wickedly tipped missiles savaged an increasingly ragged Roman perimeter.

Mórrígan's Clann Ui Flaithimh contingent preferred javelins, and each horse carried six in leather sheaths lashed to their flanks. Screams of agony filled the stifling summer air as bodies were torn and limbs sheared. It was then that the focus of the attack on the mound broadened. Led by Íar's hand-fast partner, Aoibheann, five hundred horses cantered quickly up the hill.

In truth, the incline of the slope gave little challenge to mounts who appeared as eager to enter the affray as their riders. Thrown from lofty horsebacks, volleys of javelins shredded the Roman perimeter. And yet, the barbarians did not close on their opponent. A chill trickled up the centurion's spine. This was not the hot-headed onslaught expected of barbarians. These Celts approached the battlefield with cold deliberation.

Mórrígan nodded to the warrior beside her. He lifted a bronze horn to his lips. Underneath the blare, there came a low whistle pitched to the grey-and-brown cloud surrounding her band. In the chaos and space provoked by the volleys of missiles, it was the perfect time for the tribe's wolfhounds to enter the battle. Conall's strong affection for the dogs denied their use against the long sarissas and shields of the phalanxes. However, the theatre on the hill was one they could enjoy. Several hundred heavy, hard-muscled hounds quickly rose and bounded towards the Romans. In the blink of an eye, the beasts were among the enemy. Gore and blood soaked grey and brown muzzles. Shrieks of pain and panic spread throughout the Romans.

As the wolfhounds terrorised those on the hill, Bláithín, Carmag, and Mòrag led their warriors at a fast pace up the gentle incline. Ahead of them, Mórrígan's band and Aoibheann's riders breeched the now torn and blood-soaked outer perimeter. The slaughter was terrible. The outer shield of the Roman levies peeled away, giving no more resistance than the skin of a grape. Slashing blades of swords, spears, and axes, clubs draped with ribbons of skin and pitted with shards of bone, and the teeth of man and beast ripped a bloody path through the core of the Romans on the mound. A stench of gore and loosened bowels pervaded the air. The cries of the dying sought mercy but found none. The waters of the Allia ran blood-red.

＊

The older centurion wanted to turn and run. Many already had and were streaming off the hill. In the hope that they could outrun those behind, they abandoned weapons and armour. They prayed that their enemy would be sated with the blood already spilt. Over two thousand lay dead or dying on the mound, and many more would enter the Elysian Fields before any found safety behind the walls of Rome.

A fearsome apparition, covered in gore, stood before the centurion. In massive hands, it held a huge hammer bloody from the bodies it had broken and the skulls it had smashed. Its chest heaved with each breath inhaled and expelled but gave no sense that it was tired.

Deep hazel eyes held those of the centurion. The Roman flinched but settled his stance at the raised club. The thick-set Celt shook his head and pointed away from the battleground. The meaning was clear and the offer tempting. But the former soldier's honour would not permit its acceptance. He smiled, shook his head, and settled a battered shield on his forearm. The heavily tattooed warrior dipped his head. He understood. Yet, there was sadness in Carmag's eyes as he stepped forward, swept the Roman's blade aside, and crushed the man's head. He hoped the soldier had someone to mourn his passing. Sadly, the veteran did not.

At the foot of the mound, Torcán and Brocc's shields watched the rout impassively and then turned about to face the right flank of the phalanx.

✳✳✳

"Shit! *Irrumatores!*"

Wild-eyed, the younger of the remaining tribunes looked at his leader and the senior centurions. The howls of the hill's defenders reached a crescendo and then ominously fell to whimpers and cries for mercy from those too injured to run. There was no wind or sounds from nature to distract from the slaughter on the hillside. The skies continued to darken, but the patter of rain remained intermittent without sufficient force or volume to disturb the sun-hardened ground.

The more senior of the tribunes cursed. An exhibition of panic and inexperience was not a productive way to instil confidence in the ranks. Taking the younger man aside, he snarled, "You embarrass yourself and Rome." The object of his ire glared sullenly at the commander and then shot an angry look at the small group of centurions. As veterans, it was a look they knew well and had seen before. *Speak of this, and I will take revenge on your families.*

The higher-ranking tribune swore again. Firstly, he had been gifted the Fabii brothers instead of battle-experienced generals. And secondly, his fellow tribune, while well-educated in military history and tactics, was for all practical purposes a novice. That said, he hoped neither was as stupid as the deceased siblings. He raised an eyebrow at the centurions, hoping that one would step forward and offer sage advice. To a man, they looked away, some with a knowing smirk at his floundering.

Indeed, in their minds, the centurions had fallen into the same trap as the patricians in the Senate. They could not conceive how a barbarian mob, no matter how large, could triumph. To these men, those on the hill were not "real" soldiers, so their defeat was expected. Yes, the tribunes were temporarily embarrassed, but the rank and file inevitably would come to the rescue. The men would get gold, plunder, and whores, and the tribunes would be honoured with the toga picta and parades. The barbarians, taught a bloody lesson, would crawl back to their tents. All would assume their rightful place. Once again, Rome would be victorious and prosper.

By this time—and in reality, the meeting had been short—the senior tribune had remembered his father's advice: *Do not hesitate. Do something. Take a decision.* With a deep inhalation, and in a tone the tribune hoped projected confidence, he spoke: "Take the two rear ranks. Reinforce the right flank. Stand firm. They're just barbarians." It seemed an excellent strategy to the other consul. The centurions shrugged. What could go wrong?

***

Brennus watched the battle, savouring the bloody chaos that had descended on the grassy hillock to his left. That said, rout and slaughter were more apt words for the confrontation. He sighed. So far, the king was deeply disappointed in the Romans' performance. Still, it was hard not to admire Conall, his commanders, and his warriors. There was no doubting that Conall was a ruthless bastard and his army were efficient killers—possibly the best in Gaul. Yet, where were the fiery passions of the Celts?

Far from placing their best men on the hill—a sensible and more defensible plan—it appeared that these Romans were little more than civilians with swords and spears. Brennus grumbled that Conall might have outfoxed the Senone king—once again. Did the bastard know the make-up of the mound's defenders? Was the Rí Ruirech's choice of battleground based on better information?

"Bastard!"

The king's visage, however, cracked into a smile as he watched the Roman phalanxes shed their rearmost rows to reinforce their right flank. Perhaps, here was justice for Conall and an advantage for his men. The king of the Senones signalled his horn-blower. A great war horn sounded its deep *barr ewww*, reverberating across the plain. Hundreds of others quickly took up its refrain. With a roar and weapons held high, the Arverni and Senone hordes charged the Roman centre and left flanks. Brennus laughed as he rushed forward. He would show the Rí Ruirech of Clann Ui Flaithimh how Gauls fought with passion and fire.

In the central phalanx, a battle-scarred Primus Pilus muttered, "Shit!" as over twenty thousand barbarians charged. Aloud, he roared, "Spears down. Stand firm. Hold the formation."

The veteran's gut told him that this was not going to be a good day. And so he muttered a quick prayer to his gods or the ones whose names he could remember. It had been a long time since he had last sacrificed in a temple. The slashing Arverni sword that cleaved his head in two confirmed the futility of his supplication. Worse, he entered the Elysian Fields with the curses of his neighbours ringing in his ears. For, blinded by blood spurting from his torn arteries, they were defenceless against barbarian blades.

CHAPTER 36

394 B.C.—Banks of the Allia

Mongfhionn paced back and forward until it finally dawned on her—she was fretting about something. It was a feeling of which the Lady had little experience. Thus, an uncharacteristic indecision as to how to deal with the emotion raised the Sidhe's level of frustration. Her brow furrowed, although she did manage to assert some control and banish the frown that threatened to settle on her lips.

The Sidhe's part in the battle was over unless she wanted to get her knives wet. That did not appeal to her. Yes, she was more than capable of and many times had demonstrated a proficiency in slaughter. Yet, she preferred the ritual of sacrifice, which required time, preparation, and, of course, pain. She sighed. Sadly, the sacrificed rarely understood the greater picture, even if it was something relatively simple such as revenge.

Her gaze travelled along the glittering line of the Roman phalanx. Lips pursed, she barely restrained a snarl of contempt. The execution of the Fabii brothers had not expunged the Lady's hatred of all things, Roman. Once again, she sighed. At least she had fulfilled the promise to her sisters. Perhaps her dreams would cease to be haunted by the disapproving faces of the Aes Sidhe. The demi-goddesses favoured quick, bloody, and deadly actions and had little use for or understanding of long-range planning.

Mongfhionn's descent into more morbid ruminations suddenly

halted, and her face broke into a radiant smile. Her salvation came as her dark eyes fell upon her long-time and longsuffering partner, Fearghal. Eyes that rarely allowed tears misted up. She blinked several times to sharpen her vision.

As all in Clann Ui Flaithimh well knew, she and Fearghal had a volcanic relationship built on short tempers, fire, and passion. That said, none would dare to suggest that the well of their devotion was shallow. Theirs was a love until death… and quite possibly beyond that door. The Sidhe watched as Fearghal and Conall readied the shield wall. She observed the looks on the men's and women's faces. If asked by either man, they would march unquestioningly into the maw of the Otherworld. She blinked once more.

There was something different in Fearghal's demeanour. Something at odds with the grizzled veteran's usual bearing. There was a spring in the warrior's step that belied his almost fifty summers. Most heroes never attained such a venerable age. Those who did, retired to their hillforts, the company of young whores, and the spite of progeny who coveted their wealth and power. Many more fell in battle and now dwelled with friends and enemies in the feasting halls of Mag Mell.

What was it that bothered her so much?

"Shite! The bastard!"

A scream rent the air as the Sidhe ran for her black horse. She had to get to the battle.

✳✳✳

Standing a pace in front of the shield wall, Conall looked up and down the ranks. On his right was Fearghal. Ordinarily taciturn, the battle commander appeared quite cheerful as he swapped jests and insults with the men behind him. As if seeking reassurance that his favoured longsword would slip smoothly from the wool-lined sheath strapped to his back, he reached over his shoulder to grasp its hilt. Conall smiled. Fearghal was accomplished with a javelin or short sword, and within the shield wall, there was none better. Yet, his real love was that blade. There was little doubt that his general's desire was for the Roman phalanx's swift demise so that he could fully enjoy the fight on a more personal level.

To Conall's left stood the tall, flame-red-haired Deaglán Ó Néill, a veteran of many battles, large and small, and perhaps the most accomplished swordsman of the tribe. Conall smiled. It was ironic that the two men who flanked him in this, the most important of battles, were Ulaid warriors from northern Ériu. In their homeland, they likely would have faced each other as enemies.

The Rí Ruirech glanced to his far left. He could imagine the frustration of Íar and his riders. Thousands of bony hooves stomped the dirt as if in sympathy with those they carried. But Conall refused to throw away the lives of good men and horses needlessly. Íar's orders were to hold back until the shield wall had engaged and breached the Roman phalanx before entering the affray. Conall knew that the giant would obey his commands and also that Íar would stretch the definition of what constituted a breach to its limits.

Finally, Conall looked to the far side of the Allia. The stream—for in midsummer it was little more than a trickle of water—ran red with the blood of those slaughtered on the hillside. Pleas for mercy still resounded as the injured faced the Celts while their comrades fled the mound. On this day, the Romans knew that compassion was not high on the minds of their enemy. Flight was an inexact description of the Romans' dilemma. How were men, many wounded, to outrun powerful wolfhounds or the riders of Mórrígan's warband and Aoibheann's cavalry? Even the Cinn Péinteáilte, led by their gore-enrobed leaders, Carmag and Mòrag, appeared to give chase with unnatural strength.

At the foot of the hill, the now-indistinct bank of the Allia ran almost perpendicular to Conall's column. Here, on ground made soft by blood, stood the other half of Conall's shield wall. It was commanded by two of the clann's most famous brawlers, Lonán Ó Néill and Torcán Ó Dubhghaill, as well as Mórrígan's brother, Brocc. The choice was both unsurprising and tactically astute. Their task was to break the vulnerable points of the Roman phalanx—its right flank and rear.

In the shimmering heat, and as meán lae approached, there was a brief moment of eerie silence. Within chests slabbed in muscle, hearts thudded steadily at first but with increasing rapidity. Under armour that sought to burn and brand frail skin, sweat trickled down as-yet-unbroken bodies. A final gush of piss flowed down thighs, pooling briefly at the feet of thousands and tainting the air with its pungent odour before disappearing into the earth. From their lofty thrones, the gods watched the bloody spectacle.

A triumvirate of sounds shattered the calm. Clann Ui Flaithimh trumpets blasted shrill notes into the air. A black cloud of ravens took to the skies, adding their harsh *kraa kraa* to the horns' strident calls. Yet above this, one cry transcended all—the anguish of the Sidhe.

"Oh, shite!" muttered Fearghal.

Conall cast a glance at his friend. He briefly wondered why Fearghal had traded his usual distinctive helmet for one that, while perfectly functional, had no embellishments. For a moment, the Rí Ruirech of Clann Ui Flaithimh frowned, but there could be no hesitation.

Javelin raised high, he shouted, "Forward! *Ní ghéillfear, nó cúlú!*"

Thousands took up the battle cry, and the ground trembled as they marched resolutely forward to close the gap with their enemy.

***

The Primus Pilus of the rightmost phalanx was a veteran of many campaigns. Like many of his rank, he was a pragmatic man not given to heeding signs and portents. Yet he sensed on this day, in the withering heat of Kalendis Sextilis, that change was inevitable. Not a religious man, even he could divine that the slaughter of the civilian levies on the hill was an ill omen. Still, this was not what truly bothered him. Surely even the pampered tribunes could see that this battle would be different from the clash of phalanxes and sieges of walled cities he had known during a long career. The Roman's recall of previous skirmishes with barbarians was that they were more akin to sport. The Celts were game to be hunted and killed, their skulls spiked on the walls of Rome, and their families enslaved.

He snorted loudly through a broken, fleshy, aquiline nose and then chuckled at the querying looks of those beside him. Ironically, the gods had provided the centurion with an alternative. He owned a farm by a lake in the south of Latium to which he could retire. The holding had been purchased a long time ago with plundered gold. It was a property he had never visited. Slaves kept it productive.

He had served long enough to retire with honour, but instead, he did the only thing he had known since his youth: he re-enlisted. He snorted again. Why in Hades had he bought the place? He had no family save a few bastard offspring from whores. Likely they would all, mothers and children, fight over the property when he was dead. The slaves probably had more right to the land, but that would never be allowed. He tried to scratch the stubble on his shaven head only to grunt in annoyance at the bronze helmet that blocked the action.

The veteran was torn abruptly from his reveries by a shout. It came from a barbarian in an ornate helmet with long, black horsehair plumes trailing from a golden raven. Men would fight and die over ownership of that helmet—it was probably worth several years of wages.

"That bastard's better armoured than us," he muttered.

Those close to him laughed, but the sound was hollow. They, too, sensed that something was just not right. The Primus Pilus scrutinised the barbarian formation before him, the other to his right, and the cavalry that waited impatiently. Something scratched annoyingly at his mind but refused to declare itself. He swore in frustration and roared at his men to tighten the phalanx and hold their long sarissas steady. The Roman watched the warrior lift a spear high in the air and then point it, seemingly aimed at the centurion's heart.

Well-spaced apart, the barbarian shield walls advanced, halting a spear's throw from the Roman formation. Commands roared out, shoulders tensed, and fifteen thousand javelins, in three volleys, were lifted and hurled by hard-muscled men and women. The storm was over quickly since each man only carried three spears for throwing. Conall's division threw their missiles high. The targets were not those at the front, protected by great round shields of bronze, but those standing in the ranks behind. In contrast, Torcán's cohort kept their spears low and parallel to the dirt. Their focus was the right flank and rear, both unprotected by shields. Once more, the air rang with loud commands. The shield walls tightened, and the Gaels marched forward.

Awareness struck the Primus Pilus like a thunderbolt from Apollo. He struggled for breath and gagged as if drowning. His nails cracked and bled as they tore at the bronze cuirass. Yet, it was not a bolt thrown from the heavens but a wooden shaft tipped with an arm's-length spike of iron. He was submerged, not in cool waters but his own blood. There was none to help pull him to safety because those beside and behind were gone. At the moment before death, the centurion gained understanding. This was not a barbarian mob to be hunted for sport. It was an organised army, and they knew the phalanx's weaknesses. The Roman soldier died, and was glad he would not witness the battle.

＊

The tribune unclenched his jaw and swore at what he perceived as the unfairness of the battle. Did these barbarians not understand their role? The Celtic beast had ceased its snapping at the phalanx. Now, its maw locked firmly onto his armoured ranks. Like the great wolfhounds that accompanied them into battle, the shield-wall began to bite deeply, ripping and worrying. He was shocked to find himself admiring the barbarians' tactics.

He suspected that the primary purpose of the storm of spears thrown into his ranks was not to kill and maim. It was to disrupt the formation and allow the cursed shield-wall to close. Grudgingly, the tribune acknowledged it had achieved that goal. Now, the barbarians' waisted, neck-to-knee, wooden shields proved to be a better design than the traditional circular ones his men carried. Without a covering of bronze, they were much lighter too—always a factor in a prolonged fight.

As for the cavalry, the huge, red-haired bastard who rode a massive chestnut bay directed his riders with a precision many Roman generals would envy. Volleys of javelins, hurled from horseback, penetrated deep into his ranks. Their supply of missiles exhausted, the barbarian horsemen switched to slashing his vulnerable rear with long-handled axes and swords with lengthened blades. Any who broke from the phalanx quickly became isolated, hunted down, and dispatched. The tribune was grateful for the additional reinforcements. Still, they had little time to settle and proved unable to cope with the fury. Added to this, the men faced the wrong direction. If not for their cuirasses' backplates, theirs would have been a senseless and bloody sacrifice. As it was, many fell not to blades but to bony hooves that crushed their armour.

A scream to his left ripped the tribune's attention from musings about strategy and barbarians not knowing their place. Men fell as the barbarians pierced the Roman phalanx. Along the lines, many more Celtic blades drove deeper and bloodily into the formation. The shape, and its strength, was slowly sundered. Deep fissures appeared in the protective shell, exposing the vulnerable. As always, the veterans—the tried and tested—stood in the front and right flanks. Those enclosed by them rarely anticipated that the fight would reach them. They were its reserve and used to plug gaps. Like a fortress, the phalanx was impregnable, immovable. All put their faith in its strength—until now.

Since its utility was gone, the tribune viciously thrust his long sarissa forward one final time. He snarled as the spear glanced off a barbarian shield. Still, a shriek of pain gave the Roman some satisfaction that the leaf-shaped tip had found flesh. Just in time, he wrenched his sword from the ornate scabbard hanging from an equally embellished leather belt. Both were gifts from his mother. Instinctively, he raised the weapon to stop a slashing blade wielded by a wild-eyed Celt. It was a young woman, her face painted in dark blue and white swirling sigils. Her presence stunned him momentarily—there were no women in the legions, and this one looked no older than his daughter.

The slamming of her shield against his, numbed his left arm and saved his life by jolting him to action. How could she be so strong? He roared. It was a primal shout and brought a grin to the girl's face. At that moment, she had reduced him to her level, challenging him to fight like a barbarian. The tribune pushed back hard, unsettling her stance. In the confined space, several economic but powerful blows with her sword tested his shield as well as his resolve.

As her sword thrust over, under, and to the side of her shield, probing for flesh, there was little doubt she was well-acquainted with close-quarter fighting. In the tight melee, where room for manoeuvre was limited, all the tribune could do was to parry and wait. He feigned a stumble, and she committed to the attack. Her blade lifted to shoulder height and slashed diagonally downwards. It should have cleaved neck and shoulder. Instead, the Roman's sword drove into an open mouth about to claim victory. Emerald-green eyes flashed a smile at him. Why was she not angry? The tribune was not aware that the bean-sidhe had already guided her to Mag Mell.

"Try me, Tribune."

That the Celt before him knew his title irrationally annoyed the Roman. The warrior was of average height. Auburn hair tumbled from an iron helmet embossed with bronze and copper and capped with a golden raven whose black plumage trailed behind. If judged by the sculpted arms ringed with many bands of gold and silver, his body was likely well-muscled. An outer tunic of red linen, already torn in several places, revealed the chainmail that glinted underneath. The Roman cursed at the unfairness. Surely, barbarians fought naked.

The red scíath balanced effortlessly on the fighter's left arm was decorated by a black raven whose eyes stared malevolently at the tribune. In his right hand, he gripped a war-axe whose blade was already stained red. But the warrior's most unnerving feature was the blue-grey eyes that smouldered with hate. *What did I do to deserve such loathing?* The tribune shook his head. *Perhaps I can end it all here.* In the tribune's mind, there was no doubt that he faced Conall, the king of the barbarians.

Only admiration for his friend, Gaius Aurelius Atella, prevented Conall from dismissing the threat from the Roman. Still, he could not avoid his lips curling into a sneer at the colour of the tunics of those behind the tribune. It was blue and marked them as Marcus' men, adding a sweet irony to Conall's attack on the phalanx. With little pause, he took a step closer to the tribune, slammed his scíath's iron boss into the Roman's shield, and swung his axe at his enemy's unarmoured upper arm. Conall reluctantly conceded that the man had sharp reflexes, saving him from losing a limb, if not a long, shallow laceration.

Stung by the speed and force of the attack and the weeping cut on his arm, the Roman stepped backwards. Constrained by the tight press of the phalanx, the tribune had little room for manoeuvre. Barely able to steady himself and with no space for retreat, the tribune took the only option open to him and attacked. Over his round shield and to its right side, the Roman's sword snipped, snapped, and slashed at his foe's head and torso, seeking any weakness, any advantage. His sword arm burned with the sustained effort needed to maintain the attack and the knowledge that he could not afford to let up. By his measure, the heavy bronze-faced shield had doubled in weight.

It was a headbutt of which Torcán would have been proud, and was made possible by the more open helmet worn by the tribune. A clash of heads ended the duellists' flurry of shield bashing and blade strokes. The Clann Ui Flaithimh king's shorter stature afforded him an advantage and his armoured forehead connected with the nosepiece of the Roman's covering. A gush of snot and blood was followed by a loud curse. It brought a smile to Conall's lips, and he took a short step back to admire his work. The arrogance in the move angered the tribune. It severely bruised his patrician ego, and he inhaled deeply in preparation for another attack.

A sharp stab of pain took his breath away and blurred the tribune's vision. Blood flowed from his mouth. He would have fallen to his knees, but the spear driven under one armpit to emerge from the other had spitted him like a roasting chicken and cleaved his heart in two. No doubt he would have died quickly, but the blow from a second sword removed his head, ensuring his suffering was brief.

"Kill him. Don't play with him. He fought well and deserved better."

The judgment of the brawny leader of his caomhnóirí stung Conall, but he nodded in agreement. The final look in the tribune's eyes had accused him of dishonour.

Like a stone thrown into a pond, the brutal death of the tribune sent ripples of fear spreading across the lake of Romans and shattered whatever order remained within the rightmost phalanx. The slaughter was terrible as Conall's army took bloody revenge for the wrongs visited upon their king and queen and their friend's families. The butchery of the peaceful community of Ráth Na Conall—men, women, and children, at the whim of a Roman—was replied to many times over.

***

Phalanxes are vast, tight formations bristling with spears and defended by bronze-faced shields—but only to the front and on the left. Historically, battles were much more akin to pushing contests between two ponderous beasts. No one told the Celts the rules. Thus, to their dismay, the Romans discovered that their much-vaunted tactical superiority proved obsolete against the momentum of a horde of slavering barbarians. The weakening of the phalanx's ranks by the removal of its two rearmost rows proved an unexpected bonus for the swarming Celts. The Gauls suffered high casualties as they flung themselves at the hedge of spears. But, in the sweltering heat, fiery passions began to tell. Long spears were snapped through attrition, trapped by flesh, or sundered by slashing iron blades.

Without the strength of the rear ranks to dig in and shore up the front rows, the formation slowly but inevitably gave ground. The remaining tribune and his centurions shouted themselves hoarse—cursing, cajoling, and encouraging. Yet soon, dust and blood made their words indistinct. The phalanx's integrity began a rapid surrender. Bearing the brunt of the attack, the centre sagged and bellied towards the Tiberis.

Brennus' barbarians were far from being simple-minded fools who would demonstrate the might of Rome. They soon discovered they could charge through the open channels between each of the phalanx's divisions and attack the formation from the rear. The Romans' resistance, stretched to its limit, finally broke as the centre shattered. At that moment, the legions found that long sarissas were clumsy weapons in hand-to-hand brawls.

Reeling from the ferocity of the barbarian onslaught, the brief moment needed to switch from spears to swords was time those in the legions could ill afford. With the phalanx sundered, a great tide of Gauls rolled over the Romans. Blades dripped blood as the slaughter—it was never a battle between equals—raged from the Tiberis to the Allia. The barbarians, caught in a frenzy of bloodlust, showed no mercy as they drove their enemies back and into the deep waters of the river. Many Romans threw shields and weapons aside, frantically tearing at their heavy armour. Many more jumped into the deep water, only to find a watery tomb as they sank under the weight of the armour in which they had put their faith. In turn, the Celts cursed as they watched wealth disappear into the bloody waters.

* * *

In Fearghal's experience, few men, whether brave or cowardly, give up their lives without a fight. At the moment of possible death, many discover reserves of strength and resolve that, if uncovered earlier, might have propelled them to outstanding accomplishments. In the knowledge that the phalanx was shattered and the battle lost, the Romans surrounding the famed battle commander chose not to run. Instead, they showed every intention of making at least one barbarian pay. Shield long since discarded, his longsword gripped in gore-soaked hands raised high and glinting blood red in an unforgiving sun, Fearghal gave a great roar and charged.

It started furiously, and Fearghal's famed sword cut through flesh like a knife through cheese curds. Severed arteries gushed blood. A head clung by strings of gristle and muscle to the body it used to rule. Body parts, from dirt-encrusted fingers to arms and legs, were cleaved without a thought for the foe. In battle, to be merciful is to die.

Irritated by the constant ringing in his ears from many strikes, Fearghal tore off his helmet and flung it at his opponent. The act caught the man by surprise. Open-mouthed, he stared at Fearghal. The emotion was ephemeral as steel filled the Roman's mouth. Fearghal sneezed explosively, and a wad of bloody snot splattered another challenger. His airway unblocked, Conall's battle commander inhaled deeply, then ended the man's disgust.

Time, although not long, passed, and the edge of the blade dulled. The longsword became a club held by two cramped and weary hands and wielded by muscles that screamed for rest. His boiled-leather armour, slashed beyond recognition and its iron scales exposed, maintained only a semblance of integrity. The cuts were many, and the bright blood flowing from them streamed down exposed flesh. Individually, most were not life-threatening. Together, they sapped Fearghal's strength.

The pack around him smelled weakness and moved closer. Unlike those he faced, the veteran was neither young nor in his prime. He relied on experience and cunning more than power and sword skills. But wielding the longsword had drained more and more of his vigour. His mind, usually sharp and thinking many moves ahead, seemed wrapped in curls of wool. He began to yearn for a final attack, for a single thrust to his heart that would end his life swiftly.

For the first time in his life, Fearghal embraced the concept of defeat and dropped to his knees. He could barely raise his head, and enfeebled arms swept the blade in tortured, trembling circles. Eyes stung by sweat and blood streamed salty tears. Even the random strikes landed on his enemies' legs caused him more pain than joy. With dulled ears, he heard a great cry of, "No!" His torment finally came to a close, but the Goddess denied his plea for a quick end.

Conall dropped to his knees, took his friend's bloody body in his arms, and wept. He felt the weak beat of Fearghal's ancient heart fluttering as it struggled for life. It tormented Conall that he had arrived too late. Bubbles of blood seeped from the veteran's lips as if Fearghal had something to say. It was as if he held back, as if Conall was not the right audience. Conall gently caressed his friend's head. He smiled at the stark contrast of pale skin against a mask of dried blood. More tears splashed the veteran's face, carving deep canyons in the gore. A hand rested on his shoulder, and he looked up at Deaglán.

There was pride and sorrow in the warrior's eyes. "The Hag's arse, Conall. Look around. How many did he kill?" A berm of the dead and dying encircled the small group.

Words stuck in Conall's throat. Helpless, he looked skyward as if to ask, "Why?" His rescue came as a dark shadow enveloped the men. Mongfhionn dropped to her knees and stretched out her arms to claim Fearghal's body. Conall gave it up, albeit reluctantly. The Sidhe nodded, understanding the pain of the king. Since the butchery of Conall's parents and sisters, Fearghal had been a father to him and Mórrígan. Standing back, Conall was heartbroken at the scene as Mongfhionn held her partner.

If Conall's tears were a river, the Sidhe's were a great waterfall, washing away the red, encrusted mask of battle. Conall marvelled at the widening crimson that stained the Lady's cloak. Since he had known Mongfhionn, never had one drop of blood ever blemished her garments or skin. In sympathy for a hero, the sky lost its last vestiges of blue and the storm that had patiently waited broke. Thunder growled, lightning flashed, and heavy rain swept across the battlefield.

✶✶✶

"Sorry." The single word that escaped from Fearghal's bloody lips was a painful effort.

"You will be. That is not in doubt."

"It was time."

"That decision was not yours to make… alone. *Táimid ar cheann.*"

The song began low, rising slowly as the incantation gathered power. Never had a melody held such pain or weaved such a spell. The battlefield fell silent with respect and fear. To interrupt would be blasphemy. Always passionate, the Celts on the field bowed their heads and quietly wept for the warrior. As one, all turned their eyes away from the couple as if not wishing to intrude. The Sidhe's ululations rose higher, but the refrain began to change. Subtly at first, it soon became a tale of triumph and glory. The Celts joined in the chorus, finding words that were not theirs, yet felt appropriate.

And then, once more, there was only the soft patter of rainfall. Conall exhaled, steeling himself to look upon his friend one final time. He turned and smiled. The pair were gone. Fearghal's torn armour lay in the blood-soaked dirt—although not his longsword. To the astonishment of those around him, the Rí Ruirech laughed aloud. Conall imagined the argument that now resounded in the underground halls of the Aes Sidhe.

Raising his axe high, he shouted, "To Rome! For Fearghal!" The battle cry thundered across the plain.

***

On a grassy hill closer to Rome, Mórrígan brought her golden mount to a halt and turned towards the battlefield. Tears flowed down her cheeks at the loss of her friends. In that brief time, the Dark Huntress encapsulated a lifetime's mourning. Then she smiled.

To Conall, she whispered, "They will be well."

***

Covered in gore, Brennus and Celtillos rested tired bodies on their shields and took a moment to survey the sodden battlefield. While the king of the Arverni relished the victory and bloodshed, Brennus shook his head. He could not comprehend the enormity of the carnage.

For sure, the Gauls had lost a few thousand warriors, with many more injured. Yet, by Brennus' reckoning, the Roman army had suffered the loss of two-thirds of its men—twenty thousand soldiers. The waters of the Tiberis swirled red as blood continued to leach into the river. On the far side of the river, a remnant of the Roman legions fled west, hoping to reach safety in the walled city of Veii. Maybe they would regroup, but it did not matter. They would give no succour to the population of Rome.

Celtillos pointed to the Clann Ui Flaithimh army as it left the battlefield, obviously marching in the direction of Rome. "We should follow."

Brennus removed his helmet, shook his wet, shaggy hair, and surveyed the arena. "Our armies must work together to behead the corpses and gather up the wealth of the dead. We should tend to the injured and honour those who have passed beyond the veil."

The Arverni king grunted in frustration. "Even working with all speed, it will take until sunrise just to collect the plunder."

"Agreed," said Brennus, "But, I'll not leave the wealth of Rome to the mercy of Conall. Prepare to march at dawn. If needed, we will leave part of the army behind to finish the work." Celtillos nodded, for once in agreement with Brennus. As the Senone king stared in the direction of Rome, the words of the Oracle of Cenabum came back to him:

Never stand in the path of a man bent on retribution.

✶✶✶

Near the golden fields of corn that surrounded Lugudunon, two horses grazed on the lush grass that grew by the banks of the Rodonos. Sorchae Ni Íar gazed open-mouthed at the red dillat on the white mount. Moments ago, her friend, Neamhain Ni Fearghal, had been seated on the thick blanket astride her mare. Now, only the horse remained, and the beast seemed unconcerned about her rider's sudden absence.

Yet, Sorchae had an understanding that belied her young age. With a loud chuckle and the broadest of smiles, she shouted, "*Go dté tú slán*— safe journey, Neamhain!" Then, in a moment of sadness, she prayed to the Goddess, "I hope we meet again."

The Goddess smiled. "You will." Sorchae and Neamhain were favourites of hers, and she had plans for both girls.

CHAPTER 37

394 B.C.—Rome

A steady stream of bodies, pale, corrugated, and bloated from the murky waters of the Tiberis, floated under the Pons Sublicius and slowly past the gates of Rome. Some became stuck on the timbers of the bridge, entangled in roots, or stranded on sandbanks. Some paused for a moment as if to remonstrate with the city's residents before continuing their journey to rot and oblivion. Fortunately, it was not the season for floods, or else the dead would have delivered their message inside the walls of Rome.

It is understandable, to make defeat more palatable, that the vanquished exaggerate the ferocity of the enemy and attribute dark designs to their actions. Hence, rumours of cannibalism and severed heads hanging from belts surged through Rome as survivors from the Battle of Allia stumbled across the old timber bridge. The tales of human flesh-eating were overstated. Those of bloody skulls, not so much.

From slave to patrician, a stunned Rome attempted to comprehend the enormity of the rout of its celebrated army. Few families were left untouched by the slaughter. Defenceless, many feared what would transpire when the barbarian horde inevitably arrived at the city's gates. Ordinary citizens cursed the hubris and neglect of Rome's patricians and its senators who had prevaricated and not invested in solid defences.

Political factions sensed an opportunity and railed at those in power. They shouted from street corners and the forums about how they would have done much better—if only their grievances had priority. In normal times, the agitators' reward would have been bruises, cracked heads, and quite likely death. Now, their audiences listened and wondered.

Rome's numerous slaves donned neutral miens or feigned shock and sadness. Inflamed passions, fear, and street justice dictated it was death to do otherwise. Many had lost owners and were even more uncertain of a future over which they already exercised no control. Beneath the façade of neutrality, however, only the wholly subjugated grieved. The rest contented themselves with an inner smirk that said, "Serves the bastards right." In private, many prayed to numerous barbarian gods for greater horrors to be visited on Rome and dreamed of escape and freedom.

On the smooth steps of the Curia Hostilia, purple-red blood swirled and seeped into the white stone. The Princeps Senatus was the first casualty within Rome. The poor man was an easy target. Dragged, kicking and screaming, from his perch, he was stripped of his toga, beaten to a pulp by angry citizens, and left to bleed on the steps of the edifice. The Senate's guard, sensing that a sacrifice was needed to assuage the crowd's rage, and with a nod of approval from Marcus, did nothing to rescue the senator. All that was missing from this tragedy was the man stretched and gutted on the black marble altar of Vulcan. That said, the guards' instinct proved correct. Order was restored following the unfortunate man's demise.

Nikandros fingered the smooth pommel of his xiphos. Strictly speaking, weapons were not allowed in the building, but the Spartan had brushed aside protestations from guards and senators. His dark and threatening demeanour quashed all objections. As he stood beside Marcus, he sensed danger and was not about to relinquish his weapons—more blades were hidden within his robe.

Casting a downwards glance at the seated Marcus, it was hard not to sympathise with the elderly man. Tales of the terrible deaths of his sons and the retribution taken by the Sidhe sat heavily on Marcus' frail shoulders. It was, after all, on his orders that the Sidhe and her sisters had been executed. That said, in the case of Mongfhionn, that remedy did not appear to have had any permanence.

Marcus' adopted son, and now his sole heir, watched the man's gnarled hands tremble as they were grasped continuously and then released. What was going through his father's mind? Was he considering the loss of his sons or the legions he owned? It appeared, from several soldiers interrogated by Nikandros, that the most significant damage fell upon the cohorts loyal to, and paid by, Marcus. The irony that it was Conall's army who delivered the slaughter was not lost on the Spartan.

The other option—and in Nikandros' mind the more likely one— was that the depraved senator was reliving his latest perversion and corruption of prepubescent youth. A movement from Marcus diverted Nikandros' attention. The Spartan observed with contempt the older man's hand slip under the folds of his toga. Apparently, memories of despoiling young slaves took priority over the death of his sons, his men, and quite possibly Rome.

A low rumbling of discontent and argument pervaded the chamber as senators clustered to negotiate new political alliances. Assurances of protection and immunity from retaliation were sought from those who were previously political enemies. That Marcus sat with a few loyal friends on the periphery of the discussion made it noticeably clear that the elderly senator was not considered even a minor player in the proceedings. Suddenly, silence fell on the assembly as one man, a longtime opponent of Marcus, rose. His face mirrored his contempt for the Pontifex, although he did manage to avoid a smile of satisfaction. He pointed accusingly and spoke.

"You, Marcus Fabius Ambustus, are the cause of the maelstrom that surrounds Rome. You are stripped of your position as Pontifex Maximus and Senator of Rome. Be thankful that the Senate does not wish to pursue justified charges of treason. When Rome has negotiated these troubled waters, you will depart and never return to the city—upon penalty of death.

"Finally, General Marius Furius Camillus is to be recalled to Rome and, if he is willing, appointed Dictator."

"No! Never!"

It was to Nikandros' surprise that the old man could both stand erect and summon enough strength and venom to cower a good number of those present. Even the public gallery seemed shocked. Uncertainty and fear gripped the assembly. Had they chosen wisely? An old viper, after all, is still a viper until its death.

Still, Nikandros knew this would not last and might provide the only opportunity to escape the chamber with a minimum of bloodshed. He prayed that Marcus' personal guard of five hundred were close. The disgraced Pontifex grunted in pain as the Spartan's vice-like fingers gripped his elbow and propelled him roughly towards the Curia Hostilia's great bronze-faced doors.

"Open the doors!" roared Nikandros.

The guards looked hesitantly towards the senators. But the Spartan's reputation, his proximity, and the sword gripped in his hand won their acquiescence. Nikandros and Marcus exited the former temple in time to hear those assembled regain their courage and shout, "Stop them!" The lack of nailed boots ringing on stone made Nikandros breathe easier. He spat at the Senators' ineffectual bleating. *Cowards!* Yet it was the sight of his personally chosen five hundred that made him laugh aloud. Pushing Marcus to the centre of the formation, the Spartan spoke: "We go to the Mons Capitolinus. Kill any who try to stop us."

In the Curia Hostilia, the senators had to be content with the blood of the few still loyal to Marcus.

***

She was a pretty child, but then at her age—no more than six or seven summers—all children are delightful. The daughter of slaves, her clothes were of poor quality and her feet unshod. Long copper-red hair framed a freckled face, which was smudged with mud, as were her knees, arms, and legs. The dirt was more due to personal choice and ignoring her mother's gentle chidings. Yet none of this diminished her beauty and was roundly trounced by a glorious smile. As dusk drew near, her belly rumbled, a reminder that she should return home to eat. Yet, the child was reluctant to desert her post on the ancient bridge that spanned the Tiberis. She loved the feel of wood on her bare feet and the sound of the water as it splashed against the pilings.

The child understood little of the world of the grown-ups. Yet, it upset her to see people hurt. The bodies that continued to float under and past the bridge saddened her. She did not think she knew any of them, although their identity would have been difficult to determine. The little girl cried. She did not understand the concept of mourning, and yet, for those who drifted past, she was the only one to grieve their passing.

A sound of shouts and cries startled her, and she looked back towards the city walls. Crowds lined the wooden parapets, gesticulating frantically. Surely, she was not that late for her evening meal. For a moment, she felt fear, but she was unsure of what she should be afraid.

It was then she felt the timbers of the bridge tremble. At first, she thought it was just one of the earth tremors that sometimes visited the city. Suddenly she heard the sound of horses snorting and hooves clip-clopping on the wood. Slowly, she turned around. Her eyes widened, and her mouth fell open. Along the far bank of Tiberis was a vast army of men, women, and horses—a sea of black and red. In the skies above, a raucous flock of ravens swooped and swirled. The girl blinked. Did these people bring the birds with them? A shadow fell across her, and she looked up to see a warrior on a giant black horse. It snorted at her, but not, she thought, with any animosity. Alongside the black mount was a smaller, although not by much, golden-yellow beast. On the green dillat sat a woman, although that seemed an inadequate description. Were they gods?

The woman reached down, and the child felt herself swept up and onto the horse. She heard wailing from the city and was quite sure it was her mother. With one hand holding her firm, the lady turned the girl around to face her. With the other, she removed a helmet that looked as if it was made of gold. Several of the long, black plumes tickled the child's nose, and she sneezed. A shake of the lady's head loosed long, red tresses much like her own. Eyes of the deepest green smiled at the child, and it was then that the girl realised she was not afraid. With increasing curiosity, she examined the swirling sigils on the woman's face and saw they were not constrained to that area. She sighed. The woman was beautiful… and strong.

"It seems you have made a friend in Rome, Mórrígan. Maybe the only one."

The voice was strong, deep, and friendly. The man removed his helmet and smiled at her. His eyes were an intense blue-grey, and over one, there was a small, dark-blue tattoo. *They really like their skin painted.* The child wondered what pattern she would choose—if allowed. The child shook her head. Her mother upbraided her for a speck of mud. Thus, it was doubtful whether she would permit even a tiny design. The queen looked at Conall and then at the girl.

"What is your name, child?"

"Fainche."

The startled expression on Mórrígan's face reminded the child of the look her mother often adopted when she had done or said something wrong. Her lip trembled. The embrace of arms that were both soft and strong soothed her fear. "You're a long way from home, child." Fainche was puzzled. Her home was across the bridge in Rome.

A cough from the man brought all back to an unpleasant reality. Conall twisted on his red dillat and beckoned Tadhg Ó Cuileannáin to his side.

"You were right. The walls of Rome are very disappointing. No challenge at all. Can you speak their language?"

Tadhg nodded. "Enough."

"Accompany me. If they do not understand my words, then you will make my meaning clear." Conall then nodded to Íar. "Bring one hundred." To Mórrígan, he said, "We should also bring Sarpedon's archers... just in case." The Huntress smiled and dipped her head.

Conall turned to Fainche and smiled. The girl thought he should smile more often. "Let us find your mother and father. These are much too dangerous times for you to be left alone."

At the gates, a hush descended on the crowd as Conall cantered to within calling range. "I am Conall Mac Gabhann, Rí Ruirech of Clann Ui Flaithimh, Hand of the Goddess, and Destroyer of Rome's army. Is there anyone of stature in this gathering?" It was a moment before several men, each dressed in a white toga with purple stripes, reluctantly appeared on the stockade. Conall nodded to them. "We will talk presently. But first..." Pointing to a beaming Fainche, who seemed to enjoy being at the centre of attention, Conall asked, "Where is the mother of this child?"

A round of intense discussion rose and fell. Few showed any enthusiasm for opening the main gate even a fraction and not for the child of a slave. The argument ended when a man's voice roared, "Arseholes! Do you think this gate will stop them from entering? Open the bloody gates! That's my daughter."

Moments later, and amid rumblings of anger and threats of harm, the gate opened wide enough to let a man and woman squeeze through. The two ran and fell on their knees before Conall and Mórrígan. The woman held up her arms and whispered, "Please."

"She is a beautiful child and was never in danger... at least from us." With a sweep of her arms, Mórrígan dropped Fainche into the arms of her mother.

In a low voice, Conall spoke to the man. "Your brogue tells me that this is not your true home. Do you have other children or family in the city?" The man shook his head. "In that case, my offer is that you walk, not back to Rome, but across the bridge. My army will ensure your safety. I doubt you will receive a friendly welcome if you return to the city." In a darker tone, Conall added, "And I very much doubt that Rome's tribulations are over." The father of Fainche bowed and guided his family to the far side of the bridge. As they walked across the timbers, Fainche looked back and gave the king and queen a big smile. In her heart, she sensed her future had taken a different path.

"Now for diplomacy," said Conall with a grin. Yet the tenor of his voice suggested that mediation was far from his thoughts. In a severe tone, he addressed the senators present. "Your army is defeated. I have ten thousand men. By morning, Brennus of the Senones will be here with twenty thousand more. My quarrel is with Marcus Fabius Ambustus, not the citizens of Rome. You will open the gates, or my army will tear them and your pitiful walls down, and I will raze Rome to the ground and slaughter all within."

Conall tasted the fear of the crowd and savoured it. "You have my word that I will not attack the people of Rome, whether civilian or slave. *But* if any strike at my men, I will take your lives without mercy. If any of what remains of your army assaults us, I will crush them." Conall smiled ghoulishly. "Take my charity and be thankful. Your leaders dishonoured Brennus, and he will not be as courteous as me."

As the army of Conall entered Rome, he turned to Íar. "The shield-wall and Cinn Péinteáilte will go with Mórrígan and me to the Mons Capitolinus and a reckoning with Marcus. Take your riders to the Mons Palatinus. Relieve the wealthy of their burdens. We should get some payment for our troubles." Íar smiled and nodded.

CHAPTER 38

394 B.C.—Mons Capitolinus, Rome

"Shit!"

Dusk and with it the cloak of darkness would arrive shortly, but would it come soon enough? The object of Nikandros' ire was the cordon of Conall's army, surrounding the Mons Capitolinus. He had witnessed Conall's men scale the sheer heights of Ráth na Lairig Éadain in full armour and defeat an entrenched army. Hence, there was no doubt in his mind that the force could climb Mons Capitolinus. But where would the attack focus? Logically, it should be the wall that looked upon the Tiberis and also protected Marcus' villa. But then, Conall had a knack for doing the unexpected.

With his back to the rough stone wall that enclosed the hill, the Spartan looked around. He snorted. At least the summit of the Mons Capitolinus had a solid wall, unlike the city. Besides the five hundred of Marcus' private guard, another two thousand armed soldiers gathered on the hill's summit. The description of "soldiers" was a flexible interpretation of the word. They were a remnant of the militia slaughtered at the Allia plus a sizeable contingent of the Roman phalanx who most certainly had deserted early in the fight. How else could they be here and not lying as corpses on the battlefield? Lacking leadership since most of the centurions were dead, they milled around looking for direction. If the rumours of ten thousand barbarians were true, then those on the Mons Capitolinus were outnumbered and outmatched.

Nikandros huffed. If Conall chose to attack, the defenders would be overwhelmed. None were equal to the shield wall or the savage Cinn Péinteáilte, who were certainly among those present below. There was only one path off the hill, but undoubtedly it was well-guarded by the Gaels. He knew of no escape tunnels, which was both good and bad news. Bad, because alternate paths to retreat were non-existent. Good, because at least Conall's forces could not breach the Mons Capitolinus' defences by that route.

"They're attacking the east side!"

The Spartan was puzzled at the shouts, but at least it appeared events were coming to a resolution. As one of the few with authority—Marcus' adoption gave him considerable power—he commanded the Romans to defend the east wall. To his men, however, Nikandros' order was unequivocal.

"Defend the villa… and me. Gold will be your reward."

***

Sunset approached, and the shadows in the cavernous room began to lengthen, accentuated by torches lit by nervous slaves. Two silk pouches slapped heavily on the smooth stone floor, skidding to a halt before the disgraced Pontifex's sandalled feet. A faint trail of red on the pristine tiles gave a clue as to the contents. Seated on an ornately carved and deeply cushioned curule, Marcus looked up and scowled with patrician disdain.

"The Sidhe sends her regards. Quintus and Numerius died cowards, begging for mercy, screaming in agony, and missing quite a few body parts. I suspect the Sidhe would have preferred to prolong their experience, but there was a battle to win."

Conall nodded at the small bags. "Their spirits, but not their hearts, travel to Tartarus."

Marcus flinched, almost imperceptibly, at the confirmation of the termination of his line. Then a cold sneer spread over the aged man's gaunt face. The hairs on Conall's neck stood up as an armoured

Nikandros stepped from the shadows.

"You should have kept running, assassin," spat Conall.

The Spartan smiled as he gripped his polished bronze shield and unsheathed his xiphos. "Why?" He pointed to Marcus with the tip of his sword. "His sons are dead, and I am the sole heir to the old man's wealth." Marcus blanched at the affront and scowled as his son continued. "Even with recent events, he is still of considerable value. As men of power do, he used other people's gold while salting his own away." Nikandros smiled, white teeth gleaming in his tanned face. "I couldn't have planned it better."

Nikandros settled into a crouched stance, preparing to attack. His knees bent as his arms rose to give balance. A perplexed look crossed his face. "You would be wise to defend yourself. At least put up some fight." Yet the merciless smile on Conall's face spoke not of fear but of vengeance delivered. What was he missing? Where were the guards? And why was there no sound of fighting? Illumination, when it came, made his heart thud faster in his chest. The bastard—the attack was a feint, a ruse.

An almost imperceptible nod from Conall was the Spartan's only clue. Nikandros' eyes widened in alarm. A fraction too late, he made to turn around. The arrow took him under the arm. At the short distance, the black shaft buried itself deep into his chest, piercing his lung and scarring his heart. The red-and-white fletches fluttered in an evening zephyr.

"You're not the only one whom the shadows befriend," said Mórrígan as she emerged from behind a wide column. She nocked a second arrow as she spoke.

Livid, Nikandros spat foam-flecked blood onto the white stone floor. "Cowards!" He turned painfully to meet Conall's gaze. "Where is your vaunted honour?"

"An assassin, a murderer, and a deceiver deserves no respect. Your fate will be that of a rabid dog. Your corpse will be thrown into a ditch to be ripped apart by beasts. You will rot in the shite of these Romans you love so much. You will have no hero's death, Spartan. No old age to enjoy Marcus' gold. Your mother foretold your fate when she turned her back on you."

Nikandros' face flushed red with rage at the insult. A hint of desperation found its way into his voice as he faced Mórrígan. "I saved your life once."

"You would have slit my throat had it better served your purpose." The second arrow entered his throat, tearing the Spartan's vocal cords and emerging in a gush of blood and bone. His shield clattered to the floor as he dropped to his knees. Conall crossed the floor, unsheathing his sword as he walked. In a fluid, backhand motion, Nikandros' head was cleaved from his neck. Still in his helmet, the skull clattered to a stop alongside the bloody pouches at Marcus' feet.

The soft slap of sandals on the stone floor brought grim smiles to Conall and Mórrígan's lips. His life imperilled, for one old and supposedly frail, Marcus summoned enough strength to move with remarkable speed. But he was not faster than Conall, who blocked his escape. Furious, Marcus reached under his toga, pulled out a dagger, and stabbed at Conall. A flash of steel followed, and then a scream. Slowly, painfully, Marcus retraced his steps to his chair and slumped into it, gripping a bloody hand. His fingers lay scattered on the stone floor.

Like vultures eyeing their prey, Conall and Mórrígan set their implacable gaze on Marcus. "You have caused our families, our friends, and my people much pain. It is time for justice." Conall nodded to Mórrígan.

Marcus laughed. "Without me, you would be no one. I nurtured your hate and thirst for blood. You are my children and my legacy."

Silence fell on the room as Conall and Mórrígan pondered Marcus' words. Conall shook his head. "No. Without you, our parents and friends would be alive, and I would be a blacksmith." Conall looked at Mórrígan. "And we would have been happy." Once more, Conall spoke to An Fiagaí Dorcha. "Show him the error of his ways."

Marcus was old and his body unable to withstand prolonged physical violence. But his mind remained strong and lasted considerably longer. And so did his screams for mercy.

As Conall walked past the guards, he said, "When the queen has finished with him, throw him over the wall. The dogs in the street need feeding."

EPILOGUE

394 B.C.—Massalia—Autumn

Conall, Drostan Ruadh, and Pytheas lounged on Massalia's harbour wall. Only the presence of heavily armed guards suggested it was anything other than the meeting of three wealthy business partners. That said, even the most unobservant could not but see that the three enjoyed each other's company. It was a meeting of kings, for Pytheas was king of Massalia in all but name. Ripping the leg off a plump chicken, the one-eyed Drostan used it to point out the vista. With a wry smile, he asked, "How can ye love this land, the blue seas, and the awful hot, sunny weather? I know ye cannae return to Ériu, but there's always Albu. Come back with me. Come home."

Conall smiled and wondered whether his friend had developed a talent for sarcasm. Pytheas roared with laughter, his belly trembling as he fought to control his merriment. In a Greek accent made much thicker by wine, he said, "Yes, I am sure Conall misses the constant rain and dampness that rots feet, the freezing winters, and skin as pale as milk. There are also those unruly, naked Gaels in their pine forests." Drostan laughed and gulped back another jug of beer. The king of Northern Albu's Forest People had yet to develop a fondness for wine.

In a more sombre tone, Drostan added, "The Na Daoine Tùrsach are rising. There is a new prophecy gaining traction. Damn all seers and oracles. It speaks of the return of a young queen who will lead the tribe to victory in battle and re-establish the priesthood through the blood of their enemies."

"The Hag's arse! I thought we had uprooted that cancerous weed with the death of Diadhaidh and her son."

"It only takes a few miscreants and a pouch of gold to start an uprising. There's always those who crave power and fools who will follow."

"Shite!"

Drostan looked curiously at Conall. A raised eyebrow asked for more detail.

"Gràinne and her daughter, Brianag, have departed for Albu. Gràinne thought it time that Brion Ó Cathasaigh, king of Na Mèadaidh and my brother through hand-fasting, met his daughter."

"Bollocks! Never mind the potential for trouble from the Na Daoine Tùrsach, Brion has enough problems with his worthless son, Cassán. There are well-founded rumours that Brion once asked Gràinne to be his queen. If she accepts, their daughter, Brianag, is likely a more worthy heir to the throne of Na Mèadaidh. Cassán's misplaced sense of worth or his penchant for causing trouble will only worsen with Gràinne's arrival."

Drostan stood and stretched. "I must be going." He looked at Pytheas, "Can ye arrange a ship?" The merchant nodded and pointed to several masts in the harbour.

✳✳✳

The tall ambassador crossed the tiled floor of Pytheas' courtyard, stopped, bowed low to Conall and Mórrígan, and then to Pytheas. All were seated around the fountains, enjoying the fragrances of jasmine and lilac that permeated the air in autumn and the soothing burbling waters. A raised eyebrow from Conall was all the envoy needed.

"My king, Dionysius of Sikelia…" Conall smiled at the new title. The ambassador nodded in appreciation. "My king, Dionysius of Sikelia, sends his congratulations on the success of the Roman campaign." Conall nodded, and the envoy resumed, "In this, he has asked me to present a small token of his gratitude." At a quick signal from the messenger, four men entered the enclosure. Between them, they carried a large casket, and by the strained muscles and sweat, the box was weighty. At another signal, the men lowered the chest to the tiles. The envoy opened the lid, revealing a considerable fortune in gold. Another raised eyebrow from Conall signalled that he expected more explanation.

"My king is well pleased with the welcome, if unexpected, destruction of Rome. It will take many years for the inevitable recovery, and that is to my king's advantage."

"And?" This time it was Mórrígan who spoke. The envoy bowed gracefully to the queen of Clann Ui Flaithimh.

"My king also wants to convey with this token of friendship his wish that the future of the tribe of Clann Ui Flaithimh is one of prosperity and security." The ambassador smiled, "And that its army remains on the northern side of the Alpes."

* * *

Two eagles soared and swooped along the valley of the Rodonos. "Are you satisfied with the outcome?" Fate asked.

"How can I be? You and I know that this was but a temporary remedy, a delay of the inevitable. The age of my unruly and passionate Celts will draw to a close, likely stamped underfoot by a vengeful Rome."

Fate sighed. "You are cunning, but in this, your tactics were wrong. No Gaul or Gael king could ever hope to unite the many tribes of the Celts. With Conall, you had a chance. He could have been the Ard-Righ, High King, of the Celts and Gaels. Instead, you set him on a path of vengeance." The Goddess huffed, and Fate smiled. It was as much of an admission of agreement as he could hope to receive.

"When—or what—are you going to tell *her*?" The eagle's golden eye spotted a red-haired woman galloping along the river plain. "Or will you just take over? She is the Mórrígan. Always has been."

The Goddess shrieked and wheeled in a wide circle. "That one is too wilful, too clever for me to 'take over'. Who knows where her path will lead?"

***

As the evening sun descended, a wash of reds, pinks, and oranges painted the walls of Lugudunon. Raucous celebrations for the return of the king and queen of Clann Uí Flaithimh continued and would endure for several more sunsets until all were exhausted. The smell of woodsmoke from hundreds of massive bonfires lit in remembrance of the fallen consumed the air—and the forest. Yet, there was relief among thousands of partners, sons, and daughters that their loved ones had returned. Two figures wrapped in each other's arms stood on the stone parapet. It was a glorious evening and a fitting panorama for the return to their home.

"What next?"

"The Senones are weak. Brennus and his army will likely stay on the far side of the Alpes. Celtillos and the Arverni will return to their lands and once more become a thorn in our side." Conall chuckled. "Dionysius has already enquired how much five thousand of our warriors would cost. His ambition knows few limits—as I hear, does the Persians'." The Rí grinned. "The Greeks are always fighting among themselves. Perhaps, in memory of our dear and recently departed friend, Nikandros, we could lend assistance to Sparta."

"Sarcasm was never your strong point."

Conall pulled Mórrígan closer to him and shook his head. "Surely we deserve some peace—a rest from war. Time to watch and enjoy as our children grow strong. The clann needs time to heal, to build, and to enjoy this land." A squeeze from iron-muscled arms took Mórrígan by surprise, and she gasped. "Since the Goddess has blessed your womb, perhaps we should, as a duty, explore expanding our family."

Mórrígan sighed. "But will *she* allow us to have peace?" The Huntress sensed her partner's raised eyebrow.

"Now, that's the real question."

"I think a visit to my brother, the Oracle, is in our near future."

After a moment, a girlish giggle broke the duo's sober musings. It was a sound from Mórrígan unheard since their journey had started. Memories of their early years flooded back. "We've done our duty here. Let's go rut!" Mórrígan's quick squeeze of Conall's manhood showed her that he had no objections.

* * *

Aoife loved the sheltered cove and spent as much time as she could walking barefoot in the white sand or splashing in the cold waters that lapped the beach. Whether summer or winter, she did not mind the temperature of the sea, considering it a small price to pay for the pleasure it gave. She loved the feeling of the wind messing up her long, black hair and laughed with every gust. Unlike her brothers and sisters, Aoife had few chores, which left her lots of time for adventure and exploration. After all, she was only six summers old.

A cheerful child, only the thought of growing older and not being able to visit the bay as often made her sad. In her prayers, she asked the Goddess to forestall that future and dropped sacrifices, that were precious to her, into the stream that ran past her family's farm. While the Goddess sympathised and valued Aoife's gifts, she knew that only death would give Aoife her desire. And so, she restrained Fate and the bean-sidhe. Today, as compensation, the Goddess gave Aoife a memory she would never forget.

Brighid Ni Conall, Princess of Clann Ui Flaithimh, leaned forward with both hands on the ship's bow rail. With mixed emotions, she gazed in the direction of the hillfort that was her clann's ancestral home. The screeching seabirds and the gentle crash of waves on the shore soothed her ears. Not so much, the ring of iron striking iron, shouts of warriors, and cries of distressed citizens. With a loud gulder, she alerted her sister, Danu, who held her place at the prow of the second trireme. By the alert posture of Danu's body, she was well aware that all was not well. "Trouble, sister. Disembark your warriors and form up on the beach," she called out.

Three triremes swept into the sheltered, sandy cove. Black sails tumbled to the decks as the vessels cut through the final hundred feet of calm water. Two ships came to a halt on either side of the sole wooden jetty. Brighid pointed to the sandy coastline, "When we've disembarked, beach and secure the ships. Pytheas will not be amused if we let his precious children drown." The helmsman, his face a dark mahogany from the climate of the Great Sea and having the texture of boiled leather, cracked a rare smile at Brighid's concern. Triremes were very efficient and powerful vessels, but the woods used in their building became waterlogged if left in the sea overlong.

With practised efficiency, one hundred fully armoured men and women rested their oars, grabbed their weapons and armour, and jumped from Danu's ship into the shallows. Many uttered curses as the cold water soaked through plaid triubhas and boots. These were not the warm waters of the Great Sea. Neither was the air, even in midsummer, filled with the warm breezes of the Rodonos River valley or its skies blue and cloudless. The warriors splashed forward, coming to a halt on the packed, damp sand at the shore end of the dock. Iron trims of oak scíatha, each painted red and emblazoned with a black raven, clashed as the shield wall formed. With javelins at the ready, they waited for orders.

Brighid's trireme docked but only as long as it took for a hundred men and women to disembark. These were mounted warriors and chariot teams. Their horses, two for each rider and four for each chariot, were in the third ship. Space was limited on the vessels, and therefore a third was needed to carry mounts, stores, and equipment. Emptied of its warriors, the ship slipped back into the waters of the cove to allow the final trireme to moor at the jetty.

Teams of men and women carried the crets, wheels, and fittings of three chariots down the gangway. Once on firm sand, they began their assembly under the glare of the chariots' commander, Báine. Next, clip-clopping down wooden ramps that flexed unnervingly with each step taken, and guided by their riders, came the horses. Soon the midsummer sea churned as the mounts grasped that they were no longer captive and stretched cramped muscles. Yet the beasts sensed that all was not as it should be and put up little resistance as their riders guided them into two ranks beside the shield wall.

The princesses' caomhnóirí had been chosen by their da, Conall Mac Gabhann, and ma, Mórrígan. The protectors consisted of two hundred battle-hardened veterans and the chariots and were a microcosm of Clann Ui Flaithimh's army. Led by two wily ceannairí céad—leaders of one hundred—the foot and mounted warriors were as expert with slings and bows as they were with axes, maces, spears, and swords.

Unsurprisingly, the horses were selected by the clann's best horseman and breeder, Íar Mac Dedad, whose ancestral home of Curraghatoor was a day's ride north of the hillfort of Ráth Na Conall. The charioteers and drivers were picked by Gràinne Ni Fearghal, the fearsome Cinn Péinteáilte queen from Northern Albu. However, unlike the cavalry mounts, the chariots' teams of horses were bred from the smaller, shaggy horses of north-western Albu.

At a signal from Danu, the ranks tramped north-west towards Ráth Na Conall, which was silhouetted against the mountains to its west. Fortunately, the land before them was one of gentle slopes and verdant farmland, and they made good progress. Brighid and Danu walked their horses forward of the warband but, hearing a second pair of horses come alongside, stopped. "Iasg and I should scout ahead." Beacán Ó Cathasaigh, the twins' uncle, looked in the direction of his slender companion, Iasg, who dipped her head in agreement. "None of us know what we're walking into or whose side we should take."

"Agreed, uncle. But from the clamour, the ráth does appear to be under attack," replied Brighid. With an impish smile, she added, "Technically, that is our property. So either we support the residents repel the attackers or expel them as unwelcome squatters." Beacán sighed. The stubborn set of his nieces' jaws reminded him of their father. They had already made up their minds.

The End

TECHNICAL NOTES

The Battle of Allia set back Rome's ambitions for about one hundred years. It demonstrated that Rome was vulnerable and opened the way for other nations and cities to go on the offensive. On a positive note, it also prompted an urgent review of Roman battle tactics and the abandoning of the Greek phalanx formation. That said, perhaps if Brennus had not given a fledgling Rome such a brutal kick in the arse, then it would never have changed its ways and would have disappeared. But perhaps that is another novel!

A word about Rome: I had gone into this series knowing that it would end in Rome. Still, I had assumed a city not that different from what is seen in historical movies or popular TV series. My wife, Lauren, and I had the opportunity to visit Rome in the summer of 2019. Like millions of tourists, we marvelled at the stunning architecture of the Coliseum, the Forums, the magnificent arches, the baths, and the under-floor heating! Temples, many in ruins, still retained a breathtaking quality. Indeed, today, Rome remains one massive archaeological dig site.

Yet, one thing perturbed me. Where were the famed Mons Capitolinus (Capitoline Hill) and the cliff-like sides that rose from the ground? This was to be the closing scene of Conall V. Hours of frustrated tramping the streets of Rome seemed to provide no answers. When we discovered the Capitoline Museums on the Piazza del Campidoglio, I realised the famed Hill was no more. It was little more than a "bump" in the landscape buried under countless layers of civilisation. Today's layout dates back to the sixteenth century

when Michelangelo created the Piazza del Campidoglio at the top
of the hill. It is reached by an imposing staircase, the Cordonata,
which admittedly is exhausting to surmount after a hard day's sight-
seeing. However, the climb is not quite as challenging or as impressive as the sheer walls of the original hill.

All that remains of the summit is a museum, which is well
worth visiting. The splendid Temple of Jupiter is gone. Yet I still
held to my belief in a magnificent Rome until, in one far corner of
the museum, I spied several illustrations of the Hill around Conall's
time. There, indeed, were the Temple and several buildings on a
towering hill that ascended from the earth. But majestic Rome was
nowhere to be seen.

On returning home, I did some more research and found that
Rome in Conall's time had undoubtedly improved from the iron-age
hut village of 753 B.C. but remained not much more than a well-de-
veloped agrarian city. Its defences were quite weak, and marble
was several centuries off. A few streets were paved, but the majority were still little more than dirt farm tracks. The Circus Maximus
was, as in the story, a building of wood. If you would like to see
some views of Conall's Rome, then please visit my Facebook page
(https://www.facebook.com/aweepublishingco/).

What pebble started the avalanche that resulted in the first Sack
of Rome? The popular explanation is that Brennus of the Senones
was called to the Etruscan town of Clusium by an influential young
man named Arruns. The Senone king had been asked to settle a
domestic dispute. According to Arruns, a city elder, Lucomo, had
"debauched his wife". Things went swiftly downhill and ended with
Brennus besieging Clusium. The Romans were asked for help to
negotiate a truce. The story is believable, if only because human
history is replete with disasters sparked off by petty actions. An alternative, if less "romantic", rationale was that Brennus was hired
by one of two political factions at loggerheads. The Etrusci were

politically divided and, with no help coming from other Etruscan cities, appealed to Rome.

There is wide disagreement as to what happened at the Allia, apart from the fact that it ended in a great slaughter of the Roman army. Less than a third of the Roman legions survived the battle, while losses for the Gauls were minimal. How many fought? Ancient writers, such as Plutarch, Dionysius, Diodorus, and Livy, number the Roman army between 24,000 and 40,000. Others claim either that the Gauls were outnumbered (12,000) or that they heavily outnumbered the Romans. One thing is clear. The Roman commanders got their tactics terribly wrong and were overwhelmed by the brute power of the Gauls.

An example of unanticipated consequences, or serendipity, was the sacking of Rome. From the historical accounts, it appears that the Gauls were not that interested in harming the civilian population—they wanted gold. In the city, the plebeian (working-class) community barricaded themselves in their homes. With stereotypical disdain, the patricians put on their best clothes and sat in their curules at the entrances to their homes. All was going well until one elderly senator took offence at something and hit a Gaul on the head with his ceremonial ivory staff. The senator was killed, which sparked the slaughter, first of the patricians and then the general population. The city was also set on fire.

What happened after the Battle of Allia? Again, there are a variety of opinions. This is unsurprising. The accounts of the battle and the sack of Rome were written centuries after the event—and mostly by Romans. Hence their provenance and motivation are questionable. In one account, General Marius Furius Camillus, now Dictator, reached Rome before Brennus had left and ordered the ransom deal torn up. He then fought and defeated Brennus in several clashes. Modern historians, however, suspect that this is more akin to face-saving Roman propaganda.

The ending was likely a combination of several factors. The survivors who were besieged and starving on the Capitoline Hill acceded to Brennus' demand for gold. As for Brennus, his army succumbed to disease, and likely his negotiation was mostly bluff before his army disintegrated and he was forced to leave empty-handed. After departing Rome with his ransom, Brennus does appear to have fought the Etruscan army on the Trausian Plain and at Caere. Given the gold Brennus was carrying, it would not be much of a shock to find that he was an extremely attractive target for outlaws, armies, and cities.

That said, my personal favourite ending is provided in the *Historia Regum Britanniae*—a medieval (A.D. 1136) work by Geoffrey of Monmouth. This tome states that Brennus was king of both the Gauls and the Britons. He besieged Rome for three days until his brother, Belinus, came to his aid. According to Geoffrey's history, Brennus remained in Rome and ruled ruthlessly for the rest of his days.

Sadly for the Gauls and Celts, after the Battle of Allia and once Rome got its act together, it was all downhill. Hot tempers, a propensity for bribes, and tribalism overwhelmed their fighting prowess and artistry. Always vulnerable to a strategy of "divide and conquer", the Celts declined, and Rome prospered. In the end, only the Cinn Péinteáilte—the 'Painted Ones' or Picts—in the far north of Scotland survived, and there is an argument that these people were not actually Celts. The Gaels in Ireland also did not fall to Rome but may have traded with the Romans.

Perhaps, as Fate remarked in the story, the Goddess should have focused on raising a leader—a High King—like Conall to unite the Celts. In which case, the history of the Celts and Europe might have had a different ending.

***

So ends the story of Conall Mac Gabhann and Mórrígan—or does it? I suspect that it is a challenge for any author to cut the ties to their characters, especially the first ones. The Celts were well-known mercenaries in the ancient world, and the shield-wall and cavalry of Conall would receive a welcome in many a king or pretender's court. So, as Tisiphone was wont to say, "Perhaps."

That said, I think Conall and Mórrígan will be taking a well-earned rest. As for "What's next?", the only sure thing is that it will have a Celtic theme or foundation and will be in the past, although possibly not as far back as 400 B.C.

Thank you for reading the Conall series. Don't be a stranger!

DRAMATIS PERSONNÆ

CLANN UI FLAITHIMH

Conall Mac Gabhann

Mórrígan Ni Cathasaigh (joined with Conall Mac Gabhann)

Brion Ó Cathasaigh (brother of Mórrígan, king of Na Mèadaidh)

Brocc Ó Cathasaigh (brother of Mórrígan and Brion)

Bricriu Ó Cathasaigh (brother of Mórrígan and Brion)

Beacán Ó Cathasaigh (brother of Mórrígan and Brion)

Barra Mac Conall (son of Conall and Mòrag Ni Artair)

Brighid Ni Conall (daughter of Conall and Mórrígan, twin of Danu)

Danu Ni Conall (daughter of Conall and Mórrígan, twin of Brighid)

Aodán Mac Conall (son of Conall and Mórrígan)

Fearghal Ruad (Battle Commander of Clann Ui Flaithimh)

Mongfhionn (the Sidhe)

Neamhain Ni Fearghal (daughter of Fearghal and Mongfhionn)

Craiftine Ó Cuileannáin (famed harpist)

Fionnbharr Ó Cuileannáin (a healer)

Tadhg Ó Cuileannáin (ceannairí na mile and famed storyteller)

Cuán Ó Néill (Ériu noble—deceased)

Bláithín Ni Néill (wife of Cuán)

Lonán Ó Néill (brother of Cuán)

Cúscraid Mac Conchobar (Master of Defences)

Deaglán Ó Néill (ceannairí na míle)

Íar Mac Dedad (son of Deda mac Sin, king of Curraghatoor)

Sorchae Ni Íar (adopted daughter of Íar)

Aoibheann Ni Fionnséach (wet nurse of Sorchae)

Nikandros (the Spartan and former assassin)
Sárán Mac Craobhach (quartermaster)
Torcán Ó Dubhghaill
Mòrag Ni Artair (sister of Brandubh)
Urard (protector of the twins)
Iasg (partner of Urard)

CLANN UI FLAITHIMH—CINN PÉINTEÁILTE

Brandubh Mac Artair (son of Artair)
Carmag Mac an t-Sionnaich (ceannairí na míle)
Crum Dubh (the Druid)
Gràinne Ni Fearghal (adopted daughter of Fearghal Ruad)
Brianag Ni Brion (daughter of Brion Ó Cathasaigh and Gràinne)

AOS NA COILLE—PEOPLE OF THE FOREST

Drostan Ruad (king)

SICILY

Dionysius I of Syracuse (king and tyrant)

THE CRETANS

Sarpedon (leader of Cretan mercenaries)

THE GAISCEDACH

Matres (queen)

THE GREEKS

Pytheas (merchant and sailor)
Tisiphone (whore and spy)

THE ROMANS

Gaius Aurelius Atella (former centurion in Marcus' army)

Marcus Fabius Ambustus (Pontifex of Rome)

Quintus Fabius Ambustus (son of Marcus)

Numerius Fabius Ambustus (son of Marcus)

Marius Furius Camillus (General of Rome)

Tullus Brutus (mercenary, former captain of Marcus' guard)

Kaeso (pirate)

THE GAULS

Ambigatos (king of the Aedui)

Brennus (king of the Senones)

Celtillos (king of the Arverni)

Tasgiitios (king of the Carnutes)

THE THRACIANS

Amodocus (leader of Thracian mercenaries)

LOCATIONS MENTIONED

Albu (Britain)

Aremorio (North-west France)

Ériu (Ireland)

Gaul (France)

Kyrnos (Corsica)

Latium (Italy)

Sikelia (Sicily)

Agylla (Caere, Italy)

Ardea (Ardea, Italy)

Ariminum (Rimini, Italy)

Bibracte (Autun, near Burgundy)

Cenabum (Orléans, France)

Clusium (Chiusi, Tuscany, Italy)

Lugudunon (Lyon, France)

Massalia (Marseille, France)

Pyrgi (Borough of Santa Severa, Italy)

Sens (Sens, France)

Sutrium (Sutri, Italy)

Syrako (Syracuse, Sicily)

Veii (Isola Farnese, Italy)

Alpes (Alps)

Appenninus (Apennines, Italy)

Mons Capitolinus (Capitoline Hill, Rome)

Mons Palatinus (Palatine Hill, Rome)

Great Sea (the Mediterranean)

Mare Adriaticus (Adriatic Sea)
Mare Ligusticum (Ligurian Sea)
Lacus Benacus (Lake Garda, Italy)
Ariminus (the Marecchia River, Italy)
Clanis River (the Chiani River, Italy)
Durantia (the Durance River, France)
Eridanus (the Po River, Italy)
Rénos (the Rhine River)
Rodonos (the Rhône River, France)
Souconna (the Saône River, France)
Tiberis (the Tiber, Italy)
Máistir (mistral wind)

ABOUT THE AUTHOR

Born in Belfast, Northern Ireland, David H. Millar is the founder, owner, and author-in-residence of Houston-based 'A Wee Publishing Company'—a business that promotes Celtic literature, authors, and art.

Millar moved from Ireland to Nova Scotia, Canada, in the late 1990s. After ten years of shovelling snow, he decided to relocate to warmer climates and settled in Houston, Texas. Quite a contrast!

An avid reader, armchair sportsman, and Liverpool Football Club fan, Millar lives with his family and Bailey, a Manx cat of questionable disposition known to his friends as "the small angry one"!

Conall V: Retribution is the fifth and final novel in the Conall series. All are available in print and eBook formats from all major online and retail channels and distributors. If any of the books are not on the shelf of your local bookstore, please quote the ISBN number and ask them to order a copy for you.

LET'S CHAT

I would love to hear from any readers of the Conall series. Comments and feedback will be greatly appreciated. You can find me at any of the following:

BLOG
http://www.aweepublishingco.com/blog.html

FACEBOOK
https://www.facebook.com/aweepublishingco/

GOODREADS AUTHOR PAGE
https://www.goodreads.com/DavidHMillar

INSTAGRAM
Author.DavidHMillar

TWITTER
@DavidHMillar

www.ingramcontent.com/pod-product-compliance
Lightning Source LLC
Chambersburg PA
CBHW031932110726
47902CB00001B/139